United!

United!

KARREN BRADY

LITTLE, BROWN AND COMPANY

A *Little, Brown* Book

First published in Great Britain in 1996
by Little, Brown and Company

A CIP catalogue record for this book
is available from the British Library.

ISBN 0 316 87818 9

Typeset by Palimpsest Book Production Limited,
Polmont, Stirlingshire
Printed and bound in Great Britain by
Clays Ltd, St Ives plc.

UK companies, institutions and other organisations wishing to make bulk
purchases of this or any other book published by Little, Brown should contact
their local bookshop or the special sales department at the address below.
Tel 0171 911 8000. Fax 0171 911 8100.

Little, Brown and Company (UK)
Brettenham House
Lancaster Place
London WC2E 7EN

For David Sullivan, without whose constant help, support and friendship over the last nine years this book could not have been written.

And Huw Williams.

ACKNOWLEDGEMENTS

With thanks to the following people for their help in writing this book:

Jason Bennetto, Karen Bowring, Jonathan Doherty, Bob Dynowski, Dominic Green, Sharon Kelly, Dr David MacDougal, Caroline North, Jo O'Neill, Vikki Orvice, Paul O'Shea and Jane Turnbull.

Prologue

London, England, 25 June 1993

Cynthia Hargreaves looked out of her office window and down on to Canary Wharf fifteen floors below her, feeling a twinge of nostalgia for Fleet Street. She'd been reluctant to OK the move to Docklands, but as her rivals decanted, one by one, to vast, anonymous buildings by the river, she'd been forced to admit that the Herald Group could no longer swim against the flow. And so the company had relocated, just before the country went bust, dashing all hopes of a gleaming new city rising in the east. What was left was a windswept wasteland of half-finished buildings, marauding gangs and the persistent feeling that someone had made a huge mistake. What a truly wretched place, she thought, turning to face the small, bespectacled man who was waiting nervously in front of her desk.

'Couldn't this have waited until the reading next week, Gerald?' she asked, sitting down. 'I've had to cancel a number of meetings.'

It was no more than a couple of days since her husband's death, yet Cynthia was her normal intimidating self. If she felt any bereavement it was hard to tell. Her clothes gave nothing away, for with Cynthia, black for business was de rigueur at all times. She was an austere-looking woman with a grey precision-cut bob which emphasised the severity of her skull-like face. Her leathery, lined skin was stretched tight across her cheekbones, pulling her thin-lipped mouth back into a permanent sneer – the result, it was whispered, of one too many visits to the plastic surgeon. Her heavy-lidded eyes, set far back into their sockets, showed little life and Gerald Scott very much doubted that they'd shed many tears over the last few days.

She flicked her bony wrist, indicating for him to sit down. It amazed him how such a wrist could support so much jewellery.

'I take it this *is* about the will,' she said, lighting a cigarette.

He nodded silently. He had been the Hargreaves family solicitor for many years, and yet he'd never been comfortable dealing with Cynthia. Her brusque manner unsettled him, made it hard for him to collect his thoughts. She suffered no fools, and, to Cynthia, everyone was a fool.

'Did Stuart ever talk to you about the provisions he made in his will, Cynthia?' he asked, knowing full well that if Stuart had done so, there was no way she'd be behaving as reasonably as she was now. At her most controlled, Cynthia was not a pleasant woman; angry, she was a demon.

'What was there to talk about?' she said, drawing deeply on her cigarette. They had no family. Who else would be a beneficiary? 'Everything's coming to me, bar anything he left to the party.'

Gerald cleared his throat and chose his words carefully. 'He, er, didn't leave the party anything. He thought they had quite enough money as it was.'

Cynthia's lips tightened at this remark. Stuart had been a senior minister in all the Conservative governments since 1970, but towards the end of his career he had become something of a Wet. She had not approved of what she saw as Stuart's decline into woolly liberalism over the years. 'Well, what's the problem then?'

Gerald knew that her patience was running out, but how could he tell her? 'Obviously, the various properties come to you.'

As part of the business, the Hargreaves owned property across the globe, much of it in South America and south-east Asia. But what Gerald was referring to were the places which the family regarded as home: a house in Kensington, a château with vineyards in Bordeaux and a large, rambling estate in Norfolk.

'I should think so too. Let us not forget, Stuart bought them with my money.'

Cynthia let nobody forget that Stuart, though he had been by no means poor himself, had come into much of his fortune on his marriage to her. She, the daughter of Arthur Carstairs, was one of the richest women in the country. Control of the newspaper empire Carstairs had started from scratch had, on his death, passed to Cynthia and Stuart. Stuart had been happy to be a silent partner, collecting his share dividends and pursuing his career in politics, and leaving the running of the empire to his wife. This she did with a ruthlessness that quickly became legendary in Fleet Street.

Cynthia looked at the framed picture of Stuart on her desk. It had been taken a good few years before his death and he still looked very debonair. The reason why she continually harped on about her money was that she secretly knew she had had very little else to offer him. An illusion of beauty was easy to create with wealth, and when young she had maintained that illusion well. But that was all it had been, a trick of the light, and Stuart had known that. He had hated her lack of compassion but he was a weak man and had allowed himself to be bought. It had been a forty-year marriage of convenience, a trade-off. He gave her glamour, and she gave him luxury.

Irritated that she'd let her mind wander for a moment, taking the pressure off Gerald to explain himself, she quickly returned to the matter in hand. 'Out with it, Gerald. Money to a cats' home, a bequest to the hospital?'

Gerald steeled himself for the eruption. 'It's about his share-holding in the company.'

Surprisingly, Cynthia remained calm. 'According to the figures,' she said, reaching into her desk drawer and retrieving a file, 'at the end of last month he held just over twenty-two per cent.' Her 30 per cent still gave her comfortable control of the business. She knew that over the previous few years Stuart had been selling off some of his shares to 'maintain the vineyards'. When he had sold his first 10,000, she had been very suspicious. She thought perhaps he'd needed to set up another of his little tarts in Chelsea and had told him so to his face. Stuart had just laughed at her. By this stage of their marriage he was the one person in the world who wasn't afraid of her. She had no power over him. If he said it was for the vineyards, she had no choice but to go along with it.

'You know the figures better than I do, Cynthia,' said Gerald, unable to stall any longer. 'But whatever his current holding, Stuart's will instructs that it be sold immediately.'

'What?' screamed Cynthia. She leaped up and lurched across the desk at the timid solicitor. A few inches from his face, close enough for him to smell the smoke on her breath, she bellowed, 'To whom?'

Gerald gripped the arms of his chair, shrinking back into his seat. Beads of sweat were beginning to form on his forehead. He took a deep breath and tried to adopt a consoling tone. He hadn't told her the worst part yet. 'He didn't specify that he wanted the shares to be sold to anybody in particular, just that he wanted his holding to be liquidated.'

'Was the fool in some kind of debt? I'll not let that bastard screw up the business.'

'As far as I know, Cynthia, there was no debt. Stuart specified that the proceeds of the sale be given to a Sara Moore.'

'That *tart*?' exclaimed Cynthia, falling back into her chair, her mouth gaping and what little colour she had in her face draining away completely.

Gerald jumped up. 'Can I get you some water?'

She sat there, still open-mouthed. For the first time in her entire life, Cynthia Hargreaves was speechless.

Gerald took advantage of the silence. 'I need to notify Miss Moore, she needs to be at the reading. And—'

Cynthia found her voice once more. 'Get out. Get out now.'

Gerald didn't wait to be told a third time.

Part I

Chapter One

London, England, July 1986

Sara Moore adjusted the shoulder strap on her gold lamé mini-dress and playfully swiped away the man's hand. 'Behave yourself,' she said through gritted teeth.

He responded by gripping her small waist tighter and pulling her closer to him. Although he was not exactly short, Sara was just under six foot in her bare feet and her stiletto heels added easily another four inches to her height, which allowed him to nuzzle his bald head between her firm breasts as they danced. Running his hand through her near waist-length red hair, which tumbled across her shoulders in a cascade of corkscrewing curls, he looked up and whispered into her ear: 'You've got nice titties.'

A look of barely concealed disgust flashed across her green, almond-shaped eyes. 'And you've got a dirty mouth,' she said, pushing him away.

'Has anyone ever told you you could be a model?' he asked,

running a dirty-nailed finger down the freckled bridge of her nose.

'Yes,' she said, clenching her full lips tightly to stop the probing finger finding her mouth. It was true. People told her that all the time. She'd been stopped on several occasions in the street by scouts from modelling agencies and had taken their cards with bemusement. Being a model played no part in her career plans.

'A real one, I mean,' said the man, placing her hand in his wet palm as if to underline his sincerity. 'Not like the slags round here. Models, my arse. You walk through any door in Soho and see what sort of models are waiting behind them. But you, you're something else.'

Sara had had enough. She'd heard those same lines time and time again, and spoken with much greater sincerity than was being expressed now. She wasn't interested in the way she looked. If she was beautiful, why should that be any credit to her? Her appearance was simply an accident of the genes. And anyway, this man wasn't paying her a compliment for nothing. She sighed. 'Look, can I get you anything else?'

He leered at her and reached out to cup one of her breasts in his hand. 'You know what I want.'

'If you don't take your hands off me this second I'll have you escorted off the premises,' she hissed, picking up a tray of empty glasses.

As she walked away, she felt him grabbing at her behind and she had to quell the urge to bring down the tray on his sweaty bald head. She knew that Brenda, the manager of Mickey's Bar, was watching her in the mirror as she cleaned the optics, a cigarette, as always, dangling from between her mean lips. The manager was a blowsy, middle-aged woman who wore an endless series of unflattering micromesh outfits which did nothing to hide her sagging body. Over a fortnight had passed since Sara had taken the hostess job, but Brenda was still very wary of her and it wouldn't do to be seen hitting one of the punters.

'There you go,' said Sara, fishing a ten-pound note out from her cleavage and throwing it down on the bar.

Brenda put the note in the till and gave Sara a fiver. That was the rule. All tips were split fifty-fifty between house and hostess, and woe betide any girl who was caught keeping anything to herself. Of course, any money made after hours was your own business, and according to one of the hostesses, Elaine, there was plenty of 'overtime' about if you wanted it. The mere thought of it made Sara feel sick to her stomach.

'It's a bit quiet tonight,' said Brenda, lighting a new cigarette with the butt of the old one. 'Do you want to take your break in a minute?'

'I thought Billy would be in this evening,' replied Sara, looking around. It was difficult to make out any of the faces. The black-walled basement bar had no natural light and the handful of bare red bulbs hanging from a dangerous-looking cable cast a sickly hue over the place. Along the back wall, which receded into the darkness, there was a row of red velvet-covered booths. Most of the other hostesses were crammed into one of them, noisily playing cards. No one was paying any attention to the sweaty bald man – he wasn't where the real money was.

'Oh, he'll be here,' said Brenda, suppressing a cough. 'Mickey's back tonight.'

The flesh on Sara's bare arms goose-pimpled. Mickey Nash was coming back tonight! This was the news she'd been waiting for since the day she'd started. 'I might as well take my break now,' she said trying to sound calm. 'Shall I tell Maggie and Kathy?'

Brenda squinted at the group of women playing cards. 'Go on, then. Forty-five minutes. Any more and it comes out of your wages.'

Sara didn't bother to point out that she didn't get any wages. All of their pay came from tips, and on a slow night like tonight it was no wonder that most of the hostesses were supplementing their income through prostitution. Sara knew that Brenda was only too aware of this. She was probably on a cut herself.

'Maggie! Kathy! I'm going across the road. Meet you there,' she called, making her way to the exit, her long legs striding across the floor in double-quick time. She raced up the stairs, eager not to spend a second longer in the bar than was necessary. Outside, beneath the red neon sign that had read 'Mickey's Bar' before the fuse in the

M had gone, she took a deep breath, welcoming the polluted Soho air into her lungs. After the dank smell of the club, a mixture of cigarette smoke, disinfectant, stale beer and staler bodies, even car fumes smelled good. She sniffed a strand of her hair. No matter how much she scrubbed herself clean after a shift, the frowsy odour of the bar still clung to her.

The night was warm and Brewer Street was as crowded as it was during the day. Dodging the pimps and hustlers, punters and tourists who lined the street, Sara strode through the crowds with an erect, almost equine grace, her movements controlled and precise but somehow hinting at a wildness lying just under the surface. A hundred yards along, Sara darted out into the road, crossing in front of a taxi, unselfconsciously oblivious of the jaws that dropped in her wake. It was as if she simply didn't see the turning heads or hear the wolf whistles. Even if dressed in an old T-shirt and jeans she could stop traffic, but she was totally indifferent to the effect she had on men and women alike. Her beauty disinterested her, and this disinterest served only to make her all the more beautiful.

'Good evening, gorgeous,' said Al, the café owner, as she entered and took her usual seat. 'Let me guess. A Greek salad with extra feta?'

Sara smiled and nodded. The other night she asked for extra onions too, as she'd been feeling especially venomous towards one of the gropers in Mickey's Bar. He'd been trying to kiss her all night. Funny how he didn't seem to want to when she'd come back from her break. Al brought over a mineral water and Sara stared out of the window, watching the blinking pink lights of a peepshow screaming SEX! SEX! SEX! across the street. She shuddered and hugged herself, suddenly feeling very exposed.

It was always the same when she got out of the club. While she was on duty she could keep up the act to perfection but safely cocooned in the cosy atmosphere of Al's café, the tart get-up and thick make-up she was forced to wear sat ill at ease with the real person underneath.

Picking at her salad, she pulled a letter out of her bag and read through it, perhaps for the hundredth time, even though she now knew almost every word by heart. A few weeks earlier, just before her final exams, this unsigned letter had been placed in Sara's pigeonhole at the college where she studied journalism. Its author had written in some detail about the prostitution and drug-taking that was happening in a Soho drinking club called Mickey's Bar, suggesting that Sara might wish to check it out and use it as a possible basis for a newspaper article. At first she had thought that it was one of the idiots on the course playing a trick on her for turning down a date with him. But after some cursory fact-checking it appeared that at least the basics of the letter were true. From Westminster Council she found out that the leaseholder of the premises was Mickey Nash, and that the owners were named as Red Admiral Entertainments. She then went to Companies House to check out the relevant fiches, but the firm was based in Guernsey and so no information was given apart from the name of one director, Robin Ripley.

Her friends on the course were sceptical that she'd uncover anything particularly interesting – after all, there weren't too many clubs in Soho where prostitution and drug-taking didn't take place – but after two weeks of working undercover alongside her, Maggie Lawrence and Kathy Clarke were forced to admit they'd been wrong. The drugs and the hookers only scratched the surface of what was going on in Mickey's Bar. For starters, half the men doing the drugs and hiring the girls were Premier League footballers. More importantly, some of those players were possibly being paid to throw matches. Sara was a soccer fan – in fact, football was one of the major passions of her life. She hated seeing the game tainted by so much corruption.

Sara put the letter down, realising that, again for the hundredth time, she was looking for a clue to the sender's identity, and that this was futile. If she thought about it too much it irritated the hell out of her, and she wanted to conserve her mental energy for later. Mickey Nash was obviously no fool, and she would need her wits about her.

An angry shout from outside drew her attention and she looked out to see Maggie in the middle of the road, a motorcyclist hurling abuse at her. Clearly he'd nearly knocked her down. Maggie was giving as good as she got, but Sara knew that it was probably her fault. Her closest friend since their schooldays was incredibly short-sighted and usually wore glasses. Brenda wouldn't let her wear them in the club; in fact, Brenda wasn't keen on having her working there at all.

Maggie was a short, plump girl with watery blue eyes and a mangled bush of tightly permed hair which, against Sara's advice, she'd dyed red too soon after the perm. The colour hadn't taken properly, leaving streaks of marmalade and her natural mouse which, as she'd said herself, made her head look a little radio-active. This, coupled with a taste for clothes two sizes smaller than she was, made Brenda of the opinion that Maggie was more likely to drive the punters away than to bring them in. In private, Sara had told Brenda that they, along with Kathy, were a package. She either took them all on or none at all.

The altercation passed and Maggie flat-footedly carried on across the road, stopping outside the café to search in her bag for her glasses. Putting them on she entered the café and sat down, slipping a hand between her over-ample breasts and producing a five-pound note. 'Brenda can go whistle for that two-fifty,' she said. 'D'you know, some cheap bastard tried to put a pound coin down there earlier?'

'Are you all right?' asked Sara, her nose twitching to deal with the familiar assault of Maggie's ever-present perfume. Her friend had read in a magazine that a woman should have a signature scent. She had chosen patchouli, which she ladled on by the pint.

'What? Oh, out there. I think I made him cry,' replied Maggie, lighting a cigarette.

Sara didn't doubt it for a second. Maggie's tongue was quite capable of making grown men cry. 'Do you have to smoke in here as well?' she pleaded, wafting away the blue cloud. 'Couldn't we just have a little break from it?'

'Will you get off my back? Al, double sausage and chips, please, and a Coke.' Maggie thought she could discern a look of disapproval on Sara's face. 'I'm hungry. Is that OK with you?'

Sara said nothing. Maggie was always putting words into her mouth. Taking a notepad from her bag, she began deciphering her shorthand. Maggie seemed to be having one of her bad days. At the moment most days seemed to be bad days. On form, Maggie was such fun to be with, and she had a wicked sense of humour. Sara tried to remember the last time they'd really laughed together. Just a few years ago, the idea of the two of them ending up working in what was tantamount to a brothel would have been hysterical. But that was before the summer they'd spent in Wales, a summer during which most of the laughter seemed to go out of Maggie's life. Sara shook her head. Why was she suddenly thinking about Wales?

'Brenda put me on table five again,' said Maggie, sipping her Coke.

Sara looked up from her notepad. 'Did you write it all down this time?'

'I think I remember the gist of it.'

'Maggie!'

'I can't do shorthand and it looks very suspicious if I spend too long in the toilet. I told you, I should have had my bra wired for sound.' Maggie pointed to her breasts. 'AM and FM.'

Sara giggled and ripped a clean sheet of paper from her pad. 'Here,' she said, handing it to her friend, 'do it now, before you forget everything.'

Maggie looked out of the window. 'Here she comes. Does she really think any man would want to pay for something that looks like that?'

'You are such a bitch,' said Sara, watching Kathy walking along the street.

Maggie screwed up the piece of paper and threw it back at Sara. 'Thank you,' she said smiling broadly.

'And you've got lipstick on your teeth again.'

Maggie fished her mirror out of her bag, checked her teeth, grimaced at her reflection, then reapplied her pillar-box red lipstick, in a wildly exaggerated Cupid's bow. Sara hated wearing make-up and only did it for the job; Maggie, however, wouldn't even appear at the breakfast table without the full works on. Sara wanted to tell her that under all that foundation and mascara there was a very pretty face struggling to get out, but she guessed now was not the time to say it. Instead, she waved as Kathy slowly pushed open the door of the café, looking as if she had the weight of the whole world on her shoulders. As she flopped leadenly into the seat next to Maggie, Sara gave her an 'I know how you feel' smile.

'I hate that place,' Kathy sighed.

'No tips again?' asked Maggie viciously, then yelped as Sara kicked her shin under the table.

Kathy rested her head in her hands, letting her long, straight black hair fall forward over her face, a protective curtain against Maggie's venom. 'I don't want to go back.'

'It won't be for much longer,' soothed Sara, reaching out and stroking her arm. 'Listen, Brenda said Mickey's coming in tonight. I just need a couple of days to work on him.'

'Sara, there's something I have to tell you—'

'That you mugged an old bag lady to get that outfit?' interrupted Maggie.

'Just eat your chips,' snapped Sara.

Kathy shook her head. 'I know I don't look right.'

It was true that Kathy was no conventional beauty. Her grey eyes were a little too small and too far apart, and gave her an odd, almost alien stare. Her nose was too large and her mouth could only be described as gaping. If Kathy had been the type to read the sort of magazines from which Maggie had learned about signature scents, she would have known that she should have been using a subtle make-up to play down the harsh geometry of her features, but instead she accentuated it with wild stabs of colour above her eyes and across her cheekbones. It was a recipe for disaster, and yet Kathy somehow managed to pull it off. Quite simply, Sara thought Kathy was stunning.

And her clothes! She was wearing a short black dress she'd found in Oxfam, black tights and Dr Marten boots. Over the dress was a filmy white wraparound blouse on to which she'd printed black skull-and-crossbones to echo the motif of her silver earrings. She topped off the outfit with enough junk jewellery rings on her fingers to make Liberace weep. It was a look Kathy had copied from a fashion spread in the *Face*.

'You look amazing,' said Sara honestly. 'What was it you wanted to tell me?'

'*Mariella* have offered me a job. Well, they've asked me to put some clothes together for a shoot and then they'll see how it goes. I haven't said yes to them yet. I can't work nights and days, but I really don't want to let you down.'

Sara shook her. 'That's brilliant!' *Mariella* was the hottest new women's magazine. Half the girls on the journalism course had applied to do their work experience there, and here they were offering Kathy a proper job. 'Congratulations. Of course you've got to say yes. Maggie and I can finish this off.'

Maggie tutted. 'I knew she wouldn't be able to see this through.'

'Would you turn down an offer like that?' asked Sara.

Maggie slurped the last of her Coke. 'Actually I turned down a job on Sunday.'

Sara raised an eyebrow. 'Oh yeah? Sunday, let me think ...' Maggie's idea of looking for a job involved sleeping with as many men working in the media as possible in the hope that one of them would return the favour by giving her a job. Sara had seen a particularly unattractive man creeping out of Maggie's bedroom on Sunday afternoon. 'Local radio or provincial newspaper?'

'It doesn't matter,' mumbled Maggie, pulling a face. In fact he worked for a dairy industry magazine and he hadn't actually offered her a job. However, he had said that he'd like to sleep with her again. If she told Sara that she would just get another lecture on how she didn't need to use her body to get on. Sara was such a hypocrite. How was the way Sara used her body at the club any different? 'I said no. I'm holding out for something London-based.'

Sara knew she'd hurt Maggie's feelings. Her friend could be difficult, to put it mildly, but you had to make allowances for the awful life she'd had, and Sara tried her best not to put Maggie down. 'There's nothing wrong with local radio or provincial newspapers. Nobody's offered me anything yet.'

'Don't patronise me,' said Maggie. 'I've turned it down.' She picked up the menu again and ordered chocolate pudding.

'I just want to say thank you,' said Kathy.

'What for?' asked Sara.

'For pushing me.' Sara had practically forced her to send her CV off to *Mariella* along with some photographs of the clothes she made as an example of her sense of style.

'I knew as soon as they saw you they'd be begging to take you on.' Sara looked at her watch. 'We've got to be back in twenty minutes. Have either of you got anything new?'

'I've been playing cards all night,' replied Kathy, 'but Elaine did tell me something interesting. Well, not interesting, so much as disgusting, really. She went home the other night with a footballer—'

'Who?' asked Sara, sitting upright.

'She wouldn't say. But whoever it was, he told her that it's quite common for four or five players to go out to a club together, pick up the ugliest woman there and gang-bang her.'

'That's revolting,' said Sara. 'I wish she'd said who he was.'

Maggie's face turned scarlet. Two nights earlier, four players from Ashton had made her sit at their table with them. They were trying to talk her into going on with them to another bar. They were chatting her up, but she'd had the feeling they were taking the piss in some way and so she'd declined. Why was she putting herself through this humiliation? Going undercover was all Sara's idea, and as usual Maggie had just been caught up in the whirlwind which followed in her friend's wake. Sara was still controlling her life too much. That summer in Wales should have been a watershed, but Sara's high-minded bossiness was worse than ever.

Sara interrupted her thoughts. 'What were the men on table five talking about?'

Maggie tried to remember the conversation she'd heard earlier. 'I think someone called Steve plays a big part in controlling the gambling syndicate,' she said, flustered. Sara always put her on the spot like this. Any second now she'd ask her what Steve's surname was, and she had no idea. While the men were doing their deals she was busy trying to steal their cigarettes without them noticing. 'They said Steve had put a lot of money up for a match to be thrown last week and somehow the player hadn't been able to pull it off . . .' Her voice trailed away. Not only could she not recall Steve's surname, but the name of the player and the team were a blank too. She'd been stealing their drinks along with their fags and was by now fairly tipsy. There had to be some perks from this stupid job. 'Apparently, this Steve was pretty pissed off.'

'You haven't got any of the names, have you? I told you to make notes as you went along.' Sara was furious. 'You know something really dodgy is going on there.'

'I don't know why we can't just sell the Billy Todd story and leave it at that. Now Kathy's pulled out. The whole thing seems to be falling apart.'

'Sara, if you want me to stay on I will,' said Kathy, looking down at her lap. Maggie was just trying to shift the blame. Maggie was always getting at her, but she never seemed to have the words to hand to defend herself. And if ever she did venture a less than flattering opinion of Maggie, Sara would jump to her friend's defence. It wasn't fair to make Sara piggy in the middle, so for most of the time Kathy kept quiet.

'Billy Todd is only a small part of the story.' Sara had watched Elaine selling cocaine to Todd, the goalkeeper and captain of Brighton's Ashton Athletic, on several occasions. He'd taken a shine to Sara, and for the last few nights he'd requested that she join him at his table. So far she'd not actually seen him take any coke, but he seemed pretty wired all the time. 'OK, so he takes drugs, but he's not the one selling them at Mickey's.'

'Then shop Elaine.' Maggie hated that tart. On their first night there Elaine had remarked that it was good to have a fat girl around the place as some of the punters were really into big women. 'The skinny whore's got it coming to her.'

Sara rolled her eyes in exasperation. 'Mickey Nash is the main man as far as the drugs are concerned. Elaine just carries out his orders.'

'I think we'd better go back,' said Kathy, getting up to pay the bill.

Maggie put her glasses back in her bag. 'I'm just going to the toilet.'

Al, the café owner overheard her and shouted, 'Sorry, love, it's out of order.'

'Shit,' said Maggie, lighting another of her stolen cigarettes.

'Come on,' said Sara taking Maggie's arm. 'We'll run back. You can hold on, can't you?'

The three girls ran back to the club, their stiletto heels clip-clipping across Brewer Street and down the basement stairs. Several

men had come in during their absence, including Billy Todd, and
Brenda quickly assigned the three girls to tables. Kathy was sent
over to a group of Japanese businessmen which meant big tips
for her but nothing as far as their research was concerned. Maggie
was told to go back to table five, and as Sara joined Billy Todd,
she surreptitiously signalled to her friend to take notes before she
remembered that Maggie could see nothing without her glasses.

'Billy. How's it going?' asked Sara, sitting down beside the Ashton
player. 'I hear Mickey's back tonight.'

'So?' Todd stared at her, his pupils twice their normal size. His
unkempt black hair hung in greasy strands and the clothes he was
wearing, the typical off-duty footballer's uniform of V-necked
pastel jumper and casual slacks, clearly hadn't been changed for
days. 'What's it to you?'

Their conversations so far had rarely strayed off the subject
of football, and Sara didn't want to make too much of Todd's
association with the owner. 'I've been working here over two weeks
and I haven't met him, that's all. What's he like?'

'Just a bloke. A bit flash.' Todd looked around the club. 'Is Elaine
around? I need a word with her.'

'What about?' From the glare which met her question, Sara knew
she was pushing it. Spotting Maggie going into the toilets, she saw
her chance to remind her friend to write something down. 'I'll see
if I can find her.'

On her way Sara found Elaine on her knees beneath the table
in the corner booth. Sitting at the table was the bald man who'd
groped Sara earlier, and he had an ecstatic smile on his face. As Sara
looked on in horror, he let out a little grunt. Seconds later, Elaine
reappeared above the table, wiping her mouth.

'What did we say?' asked the man, opening his wallet. 'Fifteen?'

'Twenty,' growled Elaine, snatching a note and standing up. 'Sara,
do you want something?'

Embarrassed to have been caught watching, Sara stuttered, 'Er,
Billy wants a word.'

'Oh for Christ's sake, I told him he'd have to wait until
Mickey got here,' said Elaine, walking off in the direction of
the toilets.

Sara followed Elaine and watched her splash water over her face and rinse her mouth.

'Fifteen quid,' moaned the hostess. 'Cheap bastard, I tell you—' she stopped as the sound of violent retching was heard coming from one of the cubicles. 'Charming!'

Sara banged on the door. 'Are you OK?'

The toilet flushed and Maggie unlocked the door, looking flustered. 'I think it was something I ate.'

'I'm glad I've got a strong stomach,' shrieked Elaine, winking at Sara.

Sara ignored the innuendo. 'You sure you're all right? It's happened quite a lot lately. Perhaps you should see a doctor.'

'I'm not pregnant, if that's what you think.'

'I just worry about you.'

'Why don't you just leave me alone?' shouted Maggie, slamming the door on her way out.

'She's a real charmer, that one,' said Elaine. 'You'd think looking like that she'd at least try to have a nice personality.'

Sara turned on Elaine, ready to jump to Maggie's defence. Who was Elaine to talk? She could have only been in her early twenties, a year or two older than Sara herself, but her rangy body and lined face could easily have belonged to a woman in her late thirties. But Sara stopped herself before any insults tripped off her tongue. She wanted Elaine on her side. 'I think it's just PMT,' she said. 'She's not normally like that. Will you talk to Billy? He seems pretty agitated.'

'Tell him to fuck off. I've had it up to here with this place.'

'It does get you down a bit,' said Sara, leaning against the sink.

'You don't know the half of it.' Elaine had on a dirty yellow wrap, which she untied to reveal that she was wearing only black underwear underneath. 'Look at these,' she said pointing to her chest. 'It does more than get you down.'

Sara looked at Elaine's chest. On her breastbone were several painful-looking sores. 'My God! What are they?'

'Cigarette burns,' said Elaine nonchalantly. 'A present from the boss.'

'Brenda?' said Sara, scandalised.

'Don't be stupid. Mickey.'

'Why—'

'Sara, you're a smart girl. I've clocked you watching me. And even if I'm wrong, I'm sure Billy's told you what's going on.'

Sara nodded, transfixed by the angry welts on Elaine's chest. 'I think I've got the idea.'

'Mickey caught me taking a cut. It was that wanker out there's fault. Billy told Mickey how much I was charging him a gramme. Billy's desperate and he'll pay over the odds for it, so I was making a bit extra.'

'And Mickey did this to you?'

'It was just a warning. He's one evil bastard.' Elaine gingerly touched her chest. 'So I'm not making any money from the coke and now he expects me to flog steroids as well. I've tried telling him that people over here don't want them, but he's convinced that's the way the business is going. Coke's a party drug. Steroids shrink the dick. I'm a fucking prostitute, for Christ's sake, why would I want to sell something like that?'

Sara shrugged her shoulders. 'It looks so painful. I'm really sorry.'

'Not half as sorry as Mickey'll be when I tell Steve how much of a cut he's taking. I'm not the only one with my hand in the till.'

That name again. 'Steve who?' asked Sara, wondering if she would get away with asking such an outright question.

Elaine looked at her and laughed. 'God, what have you and Billy been talking about? He hasn't told you anything, has he? And there's me shooting my mouth off. Sara, if you're going to continue working here, you'd better sort out what's what. Steve is—'

The door to the toilets flew open and Brenda rushed in. 'Elaine, get out there. Mickey's back and he's not in a good mood.'

As the two women returned to the bar, Sara went into a cubicle and locked the door. Lifting up her dress, she took a small pad and pencil from under her suspender belt and quickly recorded the main points of the conversation, unable to get the horrific picture of the burns on Elaine's chest out of her mind. What kind of sadist was this Mickey Nash?

In a million years she would never have guessed him to be the comically short figure she saw standing at the bar as she came out of the toilets. Dressed in a white tuxedo with wildly padded shoulders, Nash was a dark-skinned five-footer with brilliantined hair and built-up shoes. To Sara, he looked like a contestant on *Come Dancing*. She was just on her way over to introduce herself when something caught his eye. He swaggered across the club to where Maggie was sitting on table five.

'What the fuck do you think you're playing at?' he shouted, grabbing Maggie by the arm. 'Brenda! Get over here now!'

'Get your filthy hands off me, you greasy dwarf,' screamed Maggie, pulling her arm away.

Sara ran over to the table, though she didn't know what she was going to do. Kathy was only a few paces behind her.

'Back to work, girls,' ordered Brenda. Kathy picked up a tray of drinks and took them over to the Japanese men, but Sara stayed where she was.

'Brenda, is this some sort of joke? Sadie's on Wardour Street covers the fat-slag market, not us.' Mickey jabbed a finger into Maggie's breast. Sara could see her clenching her fists. 'And if it's not enough that she's some pug-ugly sow, I've just spent the past five minutes watching her steal people's drinks.'

Sara expected Maggie to hit him. Instead she burst into tears and ran to the exit.

'Kathy, come on, we're going,' shouted Sara, drawing Mickey's attention for the first time.

'You don't have to go anywhere, darling,' he said, bowling over to her. 'Sadie's wouldn't know what to do with a stunner like you. Who are you?'

Sara looked down at the top of his head. 'I'm Sara. And that was my best friend you just spoke to like an animal.' She pushed past him and followed Kathy to the door.

'You come back any time you want,' shouted Mickey after her. 'Any time.'

'You wouldn't come back here, would you?' whispered Kathy as they walked up the stairs.

'Of course not,' said Sara, but she knew she would.

Chapter Two

Maggie winced as her head banged against the headboard. She tried easing herself down the bed. It was not an easy task considering the weight pinning her down.

'Are you OK, Maddy?' asked the man on top of her, noticing her discomfort.

'Fine,' she lied. She didn't bother to correct him on her name. She couldn't remember his, either. Another night, another bar, another man. She guessed that he probably had something to do with the media – why would she have invited him back otherwise? – but as to exactly what she didn't know. The way things were going at the moment he was probably assistant props master on *Take the High Road*.

She let him continue pounding away, feeling nothing except a certain obligation to let him do it. That was the trade-off. Her body for whatever glimmer of hope she could get of an opening into some kind of career. But what chance was there really of that? She couldn't even make the grade as a prostitute.

The things Mickey had called her two nights ago were true. She was a fat ugly sow. Her parents would have agreed, if not in so many words – 'useless' was one of their favourites. They made no secret of what a disappointment she was to them. Sylvie and Terry Lawrence had no room in their lives for a child – especially a difficult and unappealing child like Maggie. Sylvie's unplanned pregnancy had come as an unpleasant shock and the relationship went downhill from there. From the proceeds of their East End scrap business Sylvie and Terry sent Maggie to a succession of boarding schools, supposedly for her to 'better herself'. The truth was that they just wanted to be shot of her. Invariably she would be expelled and then they'd all suffer until another school willing to take her on was found. It was at the last of these that she had met Sara, the first person in her life to show her any real kindness. But on that summer holiday before their journalism course had started, her so-called friend had shown her true colours. Sara was just as bad as her parents. Why shouldn't she think the same way? What was there to love about a fat, ugly, useless sow?

The man's breathing grew more laboured. Maggie thought briefly about faking it, then decided there was no need.

'Thank you, thank you,' the man gasped, letting his elbows go limp and bringing his full weight down on top of her.

Oh God, this one actually said thank you, she thought, sliding an arm out from under him and reaching for her cigarettes. 'Don't mention it,' she said.

The man rolled over and let out a satisfied sigh. 'You were fabulous,' he said, slapping his beer belly in contentment.

Maggie sat up and lit a cigarette while she tried to think of a way to get rid of him. It was gone ten and she could hear Sara in the kitchen. She wanted to be able to sneak this one out without having to deal with Sara's disapproving looks. Still, she had to concede that any disapproval about this one would be perfectly justified. She put on her glasses and looked at him. She decided that unless he turned out to be Rupert Murdoch's right-hand man, she'd made a big mistake.

'Er, darling,' she said – and then it came to her – 'Steve. I'm really going to have to be getting on in a minute. Aren't you late for work?'

'No, I've got all the time in the world,' he said, putting his arm round her shoulder and stroking her breast.

Maggie brushed him away. Damn, this one didn't even have a job. God, her standards were slipping. 'That's enough, lover boy. I think it's time you went.'

Steve noticed the threat in her voice and slipped out of bed. Maggie averted her gaze as he bent over to find his underwear among a pile of festering clothes on the floor. 'Nice place you've got here, Maddy.'

'I've thought about sacking the cleaner but she's from the Philippines with seventeen children to support,' she replied, exhaling smoke through her nose. Maggie hadn't cleaned her room in all the time she and Sara had lived at their Archway flat, but she wanted to tell the cheeky sod that her domestic habits were about as good as his lovemaking. She said nothing, not wanting to do anything that would delay his departure. She could hear the bathroom door closing and if she was quick, she could get him out without Sara clapping eyes on him.

'Would you like to meet up again some time?' asked Steve, struggling to do up his flies.

'Oh, what? Sure,' said Maggie, taken by surprise. Not on your life, she thought, pulling the duvet up around her neck, aware that he was looking at her body.

'That job I was talking about,' said Steve. 'I'm serious about it. Of course, if you're interested it would mean relocating.'

'To where?' A job. Maggie couldn't believe she'd heard right.

'Well, Bournemouth, of course. You could hardly work for the *Bournemouth Clarion* from here.'

Maggie's shoulders sank. The trade-off for her second-class body was a second-class newspaper. She ran her hand over her thigh feeling the cellulite, and guessed that that was probably the going exchange rate. 'Of course. How soon would you want me to start?'

'As soon as you like. I've got a nice flat overlooking the front,' said Steve, sitting down on the bed and squeezing on his boots. He went to kiss her, but Maggie pulled away. 'Do you want to show me out?'

Maggie reached over the side of the bed and picked up her dressing gown. Slipping into it under the covers, she got up and took him to the front door. 'By the way, Steve,' she said as he walked out on to the landing, 'the name's Maggie.'

'Who was that?' asked Sara, appearing behind her in a towel.

'He's offered me a job,' started Maggie excitedly. Her sense of exhilaration quickly drained away as she saw the pitying look on Sara's face. 'I don't give a fuck what you think, I'm taking it,' she said, running back into her bedroom and locking the door.

Tripping on the strap of a bra which had become wedged under the leg of the bed, Maggie cursed loudly and opened her knicker drawer. She sorted through her underwear impatiently, then pulled the drawer off its runners and tipped the whole lot on to the floor. A family-sized bar of chocolate fell out too, and Maggie tore off the wrapping. Biting into it she caught sight of herself in the mirror. Behind her glasses every blood vessel in her eyes was etched in stark relief. Her face was round at the best of times, and drinking so much alcohol didn't help. She pinched the loose flesh on her neck and tried to pull it up behind her ears. 'A total pig,' she said, noticing a large purple and yellow love-bite.

Sara banged on the door. 'Maggie, I've got to talk to you.'

'Go away,' shouted Maggie, her mouth full of chocolate.

'Please. I want to go back to the club but I need to know that it's OK with you.'

Maggie was silent. Sara was actually considering going back to that club? How could she do this to her?

Kathy walked into the catering-supplies shop, still not quite able to believe that she was out shopping for a *Mariella* fashion spread. She'd had a phone call from Sara the night before to wish her good luck and her friend had said that Maggie had left London. Sara seemed to think it was all to do with what had happened at the club and had decided to drop the investigation. It had taken Kathy a good half-hour to convince her to continue. She'd even repeated her offer to go back with her. She'd been relieved when Sara had finally decided to do it alone. Kathy would have found herself, as always, being content to take a back seat. Sara's enthusiasm and vitality was infectious, but Kathy didn't want to have to rely on her as the motor driving her own career. She had to do her own thing, and investigative journalism just wasn't it.

'Can I help you?' asked the owner, who, unused to seeing such an exotic apparition in his shop, had been eyeing her quizzically ever since she'd walked through the door.

'I'd like to look at some chef's trousers, please,' said Kathy, scanning the racks. Instinctively, her head tipped forward to allow her fringe to fall across her face. But there wasn't a fringe any more: indeed, there was barely any hair left on her head at all. That morning, emboldened by being given the chance to prove herself on *Mariella*, she had gone wild with the scissors and left herself with little more than a half-inch crop, which she had then peroxided white.

The assistant pointed to a display stand, feeling that it wasn't quite proper for a young lady to be showing off quite so much of her underwear in public. Kathy knew what he was thinking and didn't give two hoots. The red chiffon blouse she was wearing was knotted deliberately to show off her bare midriff and a black lacy bra, and her low-waisted denim shorts were cut as high on her thigh as they could possibly go without falling apart. But she didn't feel in the least bit vulnerable: the knee-length biker's boots with metal shin-plates saw to that.

Kathy had always wanted to be different, to stand out from the crowd. It had a lot to do with the fact that her late father had called her Number Four. He was an overbearing Catholic stockbroker who rarely called any of his seven children by their names. To him they were just numbers. On Kathy's ninth birthday, her mother had taken her to see *The Sound of Music* as a treat. When she arrived home from the cinema, her father asked her about the film and she pointed out the similarity between their family and the Von Trapp children, who were all expected to respond to the sound of a whistle. Eric Clarke, a strict disciplinarian, instructed that Number Four should be given a nail brush with which to clean the parquet flooring laid throughout their six-bedroomed house in Muswell Hill.

Eric saw this as more than a mere punishment. This was proper training for Number Four's future role in life. Whereas the boys in the family were encouraged to go to university and then into banking, the girls' 'careers' would be no more than a stopgap until they fulfilled the proper destinies as wives and mothers; in other words, the same domestic drudgery he'd forced their mother, Gloria, to endure for thirty-five years. Her mother had put up with it, and her sisters looked as if they would do, too. But Kathy was determined that everything about her would be different from the rest of the Clarkes. She would never allow herself to be just a number.

With an unerring eye, she selected two pairs of trousers and took them off their hangers, comparing the cut and feel of each. The *Mariella* feature was to be on workwear, and though she fancied the look of the dog-tooth-check ones, she rejected them in favour of a more traditional white pair, liking the heaviness of the cotton and the wideness of the legs. They'd look great cut just over the ankle. She bought them and left, pleased to find that the price kept her well under budget.

The catering-supplies shop was just off Brick Lane, an area of the East End which was home to a large Bangladeshi community and whose shops and factories were largely devoted to the garment industry. Kathy loved the clothes shops there. She was bowled over by the unrestrained exuberance of Asian fashions and the way the gaudy golds and pinks defied traditional English tastes. Attracted by some fairy lights which twinkled out of season around the window of one sari shop, she stopped and thought about buying herself a *bindi*. She decided that she'd better finish her task before indulging her own whims.

Her next stop was an old and musty shoe shop which she knew sold workboots at workmen's prices. The assistant here was an elderly Jewish man, a representative of the area's chief population a generation earlier. He stared at her for a moment, then grinned. 'I barely recognised you,' he said, giving her outfit the once-over. 'You look lovely. Strange, but lovely. And the boots are holding up well.'

Kathy thanked him and asked him if he had anything new since the last time she'd been in. The man disappeared into the stock room and reappeared with a pair of black slip-on boots.

'They are new in from Australia,' he said.

Kathy took the boots and studied them, liking the triangular insert on the inside and the way that the steel toe-caps left a pleasing ridge at the front. 'They're perfect,' she said, trying one on. 'How much?'

'Forty-five pounds,' said the assistant. 'They're from Australia,' he added apologetically, seeing Kathy's frown.

She took the boot off. They were too much and she still had so many other things to buy. 'I'll have to leave them.'

The assistant produced a piece of chalk from his trouser pocket and marked a cross on the boot. 'They're seconds now,' he said, 'and that makes them ten pounds cheaper.'

'Thank you,' said Kathy, delighted. 'You didn't have to do that.'

'What can I say?' said the old man. 'You look lovely and you wear my shoes. You're a good advert.'

Making her way to a leather wholesalers, Kathy realised that the elation she always felt when she secured a bargain was probably the same sensation Sara had when she got hold of a story. When Sara had prompted her to write off to *Mariella*, Kathy felt as if her bluff had been called. She knew that Sara had no time for people who paid lip service to things they had no intention of doing. The thought of trying to break into fashion magazines frightened Kathy, but the danger of being held in low esteem by her friend scared her even more. Sara gave of herself endlessly, but she expected the returns to be high. For all the support and encouragement Sara had shown her throughout college, Kathy knew that she was now expected to realise her own potential. By leaving the investigation at Mickey's Bar, Kathy was announcing her intention to do just that.

In the leather shop, Kathy bought a wide black belt and a selection of clip-on buckles depicting various American landmarks, all, of course, at wholesale price. Her inventiveness stemmed in part from her parents' parsimony. They were comfortably off, but self-indulgence was frowned upon. Kathy was forced to look further afield than the high street for places to buy her clothes. It came as a great joy to discover that wholesalers would, on occasion, sell to the public if you were prepared to go in and barter. By the end of the morning Kathy had added a white denim jacket to her *Mariella* outfit (she intended to overdye it a bottle green and cut the arms off to turn it into a waistcoat) and a selection of shirts and T-shirts, all at less than cost price. Doing this felt so comfortable, so right. She was so sure in her judgement that it hardly seemed like work at all. *Mariella* had given her a chance, and she was going to take that chance and run with it.

Sara walked through the Soho evening feeling much less certain of herself than she had a few days earlier. Although she had always known she would have to face Mickey alone, having Kathy and Maggie there in the background had been reassuring. Their absence sapped some of her confidence. There was also the lingering doubt that she was betraying Maggie by coming back, despite Kathy's protestations to the contrary.

As she turned on to Brewer Street, she could see Mickey standing outside the bar in his white tuxedo. He noticed her and let out an appreciative wolf whistle.

'I knew you'd be back,' he called out. 'Come and give Mickey a kiss.'

Sara tensed as Mickey reached up and planted a kiss on her neck, leaving a snail trail of pomade where his hair had brushed against her cheek. Again, she saw the burns on Elaine's chest in her mind. 'Busy night?'

'Not bad, not bad. Why don't you go in and see Brenda, and I'll be down later. I've got a bit of business to sort out.'

Sara watched him bowl along the street. He walked as if he were carrying a large suitcase under each arm. As he turned up an alleyway, she took a deep breath and walked into the club, noticing that the 'K' on the sign had now also fused.

Brenda looked surprised to see her. 'I didn't think you'd come back. Mickey said you would. He must see something in you that I can't.'

Sara didn't respond to the jibe. Mickey must have torn a strip off Brenda over Maggie, and now she was taking it out on her. 'Where do you want me tonight? Is Billy in?'

'He's over there.' Brenda pointed to the far booth. 'But I don't think he needs any company tonight. A new shipment's in.'

Sara looked over at the footballer and couldn't quite cover her surprise. He was quite blatantly snorting cocaine through a rolled-up banknote. 'Oh—'

'I don't know what he sees in it, myself,' said Brenda, putting a bottle of Scotch and some glasses on a tray. 'Give me a slimming tablet any day.' She shoved the tray across the bar top to Sara. 'This is for table five. And keep your mouth shut. Frank doesn't want some silly girl rabbiting on when he's doing business.'

Sara picked up the tray with a sigh. Brenda went along with the view held by all the customers that the perfect woman would score a ten for her beauty and roughly the same in an IQ test. She walked over to table five, slid the tray on to the table and sat down. The men sitting with Frank, another regular, barely acknowledged her presence.

'How much do you reckon he'll want for doing it?' asked Frank.

'Fifteen thou, tops,' replied another of the men. 'He's got to make his maintenance payments so he might do it for less.'

'And he's kosher?'

'You saw the match against Ashton. What do you reckon?'

'What about Steve's cut?'

Sara leaned forward in her chair and rested her elbows on the table.

Frank noticed her for the first time. 'You want something, darling?'

Sara stood up. 'I thought you might like some company.'

'You're in there, Frank,' leered one of the men.

Frank reached into his pocket and produced a wad of notes. Peeling off a twenty, he handed it to Sara. 'There you are, darling. To keep you honest. Now piss off.'

Embarrassed, Sara took the money and walked away, hearing Frank laughing with his friends. 'Fuck me, these tarts are as hard as nails,' he said. 'Mind you, I might give that one a go. She's a right looker.'

Brenda looked unimpressed. 'What did you say to them?'

'Nothing,' said Sara, handing over the money.

'Look, if you're going to carry on like that because your fat friend got the elbow, I don't want you here. I told you right at the start she wasn't Mickey's type.'

'And what is my type?' Mickey appeared from behind Sara and looked up at her. 'Baby, it's you. Bren, bring a couple of G and Ts over to my table, will you?' He put his hand on Sara's bottom. 'Come and sit down.'

She slid into a booth next to him. As Brenda brought over the drinks, Sara felt him grasp her knee.

'You're something special, you know that?' he smiled. 'I've just been in New York and the girls there are pretty hot. But you, you're something else.'

Sara thought briefly about removing his hand but decided she'd just have to grin and bear it. 'Cheers,' she said knocking back the drink in one.

'Mickey!' A girl came running over and sat on Mickey's lap. It was Elaine. She began to undo her wrap. Sara flinched, waiting for the awful sight of the burns. To make matters worse, as she pulled the wrap off her shoulders, Sara realised that the hostess was topless. 'It's brilliant stuff. I reckon I can get rid of twenty grammes tonight, no problem.'

'Fuck off, Elaine,' spat Mickey, slapping her breasts. 'Get them disgusting dugs out of my face.'

'Don't be like that, Mickey,' she pleaded, squirming in his lap.

'I won't tell you again. Put your clothes on and leave me alone.'

Sulkily Elaine pulled her wrap over her chest and stood up. 'I think I'll go and ring Steve. Tell him about you.'

Quick as a flash, Mickey jumped out of his seat and pinned her to the wall by her throat. 'Don't you ever threaten me.'

Elaine's eyes seemed to bulge. 'M-Mickey, you're hurting me. It was just a joke. Let me go. Please.'

Mickey released his grip. 'Go away and we'll sort something out later.'

Elaine rubbed her throat and glared at Sara. Obviously she suspected that the new girl was trying to muscle in on her territory.

'She's on her way out, that one,' said Mickey, as she walked away. 'We need a few more like you around the place. Mind you, Elaine did tell me you were asking a lot of questions.'

'I just like to know who I'm dealing with,' she said, keeping her voice neutral, fighting off the panic she felt as she realised that Mickey's hand was trying to part her legs. 'I've been here for nearly two weeks now and every evening I seem to end up with some time-waster. I want to be meeting the right men. Like you.' She pictured herself taking Elaine's place, selling coke and sitting topless on his lap.

'Well, tonight's your lucky night,' grinned Mickey, his fingers brushing against the lace trim of her underwear. He was wearing a ring on every finger and Sara could feel a diamond scratching against the soft skin of her inner thigh. Leaning over, he sank his teeth into her ear.

Sara gasped, feeling her body go rigid. 'Mickey, I—'

'Need a little something? Sure.' Mickey pulled a large bag of cocaine from his pocket and poured a small amount on to the table. Deftly, he chopped up the crystals with a razor blade and scraped them into a line. Then he rolled up a fifty-pound note and handed it to Sara.

Hesitantly, Sara took the rolled-up note. For a moment she just looked at it. She had never, ever taken drugs. As Mickey watched her expectantly, she realised that she'd let her bravado take her too far. Why had she thought that someone as inexperienced as she was would be up to this kind of assignment? 'I don't think—'

'Have some,' said Mickey, a note of menace creeping into his voice.

Sara fixed her eyes on the line on the table, aware that Mickey was staring at her. Then, despite all of her better instincts, she inserted the note into her left nostril and held the right one closed with her finger, the way she'd seen it done in so many films, and inhaled the line in one go, desperate to get it over with. Immediately the powder seared the back of her throat, making her eyes water. 'That's good,' she gasped, the bitterness making her gag.

'Then have another line.' It was an order, not a suggestion.

Sara's nose burned like mad and an acrid slurry slowly dripped down her throat. 'I think one was enough,' she said, wiping her nose. It felt as if it was bleeding.

'Have another line and then we'll go somewhere a bit more private.' Mickey chopped some more coke and handed her back the fifty-pound note.

Sara snorted the second line of coke and then got to her feet, feeling the sensation of a million pins pricking at her brain. Her whole body was shaking as she let Mickey put his hand on her behind and lead the way.

He pulled her into his office and closed the door, turning on the fluorescent light. Sara realised that there was an almost piercing clarity to her vision, but she knew the drug was wresting control away from her. She was frightened. How could she rely on her wits if they were being interfered with?

The office was also used as the store cupboard and Mickey had to clear away a pile of boxes to get to his desk. Sitting down, he held up the bag of cocaine and said, grinning, 'I think I've got a bit of catching up to do.' He opened a drawer and took out a mirror, on to which he poured a mound of the coke. After he'd taken a line himself, he picked up the phone. 'Just a quick call, then you've got me all to yourself.'

Sara was rooted to the spot, a blackness now creeping through every corner of her mind. How could she have been so stupid?

'Is Steve there? Cheers.' Mickey held the phone away from his mouth. 'Get undressed.' He opened a desk drawer and pulled out an address book. 'All right, mate. Just a quick call. Ronnie's moved the business. I thought you'd want the number. Got a pen?' Mickey covered the mouthpiece. 'Did you hear me?'

Sara stood there, immobile. Thankfully, Steve came back on the line. Mickey read out a number and put down the phone. He walked over to Sara and flicked the strap of her dress over her shoulder to reveal her left breast.

'You've been a bad girl, haven't you?' he asked, lighting a cigarette.

'W-what do you mean?' Her head was pounding.

'Don't come the innocent with me. All you bitches are bad. It's the nature of the beast.' Mickey flicked off his ash and held the cigarette millimetres from her nipple. 'It's a good thing there are men like me around to keep you under control.'

Suddenly, the instinct for self-preservation cut through the drug-induced haze and, almost without realising what she was doing, Sara smacked away his hand, knocking Mickey back against the desk. The bag of cocaine fell open and its contents poured on to the floor.

'You crazy bitch!' screamed Mickey, diving to the floor and trying to scoop up the scattered powder.

As he crouched before her, Sara kicked him, digging her heel into his side. No longer in any kind of control, she found herself possessed by a need to hurt this man.

'You fucking whore, I'll kill you,' gasped Mickey. Winded and bloody, he struggled to his feet and swiped her across the face, his rings cutting into her cheek.

'You bastard, you bastard!' Sara clenched her fists and hammered Mickey's face, beginning to cry hysterically. In a frenzy, she knocked him to the floor and began kicking him again. As Mickey rolled up into a ball, somewhere at the back of her mind it occurred to her that if she didn't stop she could quite easily kill him. Then she spotted his address book. Jumping over his prone body, she snatched it, opened the office door and ran as fast as she could back through the club, knowing her life depended on it.

Mickey stumbled through the door. 'Stop her, somebody!'

Frank and Brenda gave chase, but Sara had hurled herself up the stairs and burst out on to Brewer Street. Almost hysterical, she ran along the middle of the road, dodging the traffic. She practically threw herself in front of a vacant black cab that was turning into Wardour Street. As they drove away, Sara looked behind and saw Mickey, Frank and Brenda fading into the distance.

Chapter Three

Sara picked up the phone, hoping it might be Maggie. They hadn't spoken since Maggie had left and the flat seemed awfully quiet without her.

'Can I speak to Sara Moore, please?' It was a man's voice.

'Speaking.'

'Hello, this is Simon Holland, editor of the *Sunday Voice*. I hear you're working on a story we might be interested in.' He rattled out the words as if he were dictating them.

'Sorry?'

'I have got my information correct, haven't I? You've been working undercover in a hostess bar?'

'Who told you that?' asked Sara, immediately thinking of Maggie. Perhaps she had told one of the men she had bedded to help get her a job.

'Come now, Miss Moore, the media world is a small, gossipy and indiscreet place. Anyway, you haven't answered my question.'

'I have, yes.'

'Is there a story?'

Sara had to think fast. Whoever had told Simon Holland, this was her big chance. She couldn't blow it. 'I haven't got to the bottom of what's going on yet, although I know there's a lot of cocaine sold there.'

'That isn't news. Anything else?'

'Steroids.'

'Who's taking them?'

'I'm not quite sure—'

'You can't put "we're not sure" under a headline,' he said gruffly.

She thought briefly of telling him that she *was* sure people were being paid to throw football matches, but she knew he would ridicule her lack of hard facts.

'Sorry, I think we're wasting each other's time,' he declared.

Sara was silent for a second, dazed by the speed with which she'd discovered you could blow your big chance. Then, knowing that she'd hate herself forever for doing it, she said, 'What if one of the men taking cocaine were Billy Todd?'

'Now, that would be interesting,' said Holland, his voice becoming a shade warmer. 'Come to the office tomorrow. Ten a.m., sharp.'

June Moore's hands trembled with excitement as she read the headline in the *Sunday Voice*: 'SILLY BILLY, Drug Shame of Ashton Captain.' Sara's name was underneath, not in quite big enough print for June's liking, but all the same there it was on the front page for all the world to see. Fixing her reading glasses firmly on the bridge of her nose, June read through the piece, savouring each word her daughter had written. At the bottom of the page there was a line saying that the story continued on pages 2 and 3. Proud that her daughter's work was important enough to merit three whole pages of the newspaper, June turned over and was very surprised to see a large picture of Sara occupying most of page 3. She knew that it was very unusual for a reporter's picture to be used, and surmised that the paper must have been very pleased with the job she'd done. Why hadn't Sara wanted her to read the piece? Surely she must have known that June would be aching to show it off to all the neighbours?

She soon discovered the reason. The story on page 3 chilled her. She read and reread the piece, scarcely able to believe what her daughter had put herself through to get this information. The marks on Sara's face were visible in the photograph. What type of man was this Mickey Nash person, that he could do this to her little girl? When June had last spoken to Sara, her daughter had seemed so carefree, and yet this incident must have happened only nights before. Drugs, prostitution, violence – how could Sara have become mixed up in something so dangerous? How had she even known about the club in the first place?

Before June could collect her thoughts the telephone trilled. She rushed along the hallway, hoping it would be Sara, with some explanation.

'June.'

'You!' she said, feeling sick. June wasn't the kind of person who was equipped to deal with any kind of confrontation. She was a small-boned woman, erring towards comfortably plump, with a worried, unassuming face and a taste for dull, sensible clothes which, she told herself, were fitting for a woman approaching sixty. It was much the same thing she'd told herself when she'd been approaching thirty. At pains to keep the world and its woes at a distance, she had designed her whole life to blend into the background. From the immaculate blandness of her bungalow to the prosaic chutneys she made for the WI, everything was engineered to avoid undue scrutiny. And so now, even with so much at stake, any ability to be rude or aggressive, to make her presence felt, totally escaped her.

'Have you read the *Sunday Voice*?'

'Yes, but—'

'I'm so sorry. I realised as soon as I'd sent Sara the letter that I'd made a stupid mistake.'

'What letter? I begged you to have no contact with her.'

'I wrote to her giving her some details about the club. It was brought to my attention that something was afoot there. I had no idea she'd go undercover. And I did—'

'You did what! Are you mad?' June could feel her heart in

her mouth. 'What else did you tell her?' What if she knew everything?

'Nothing. The letter was anonymous. I truly thought the story would be a rather marvellous chance to launch her career.'

'By nearly getting her killed?' Suddenly, the thought of what might have happened to Sara frightened her so much that she was forced to throw off a lifetime's mild-mannered politeness. 'What that . . . that pervert did to my daughter's beautiful face – well, you as good as did it to her yourself. I hope you have that on your conscience. Now, for the last time, I'm warning you, stay away from her.' June reached into her cardigan pocket for a handkerchief to dab her streaming eyes. 'If you have any feelings at all, you'll leave me and my daughter alone.'

'I can't let her go just like that.'

There was a long silence as June struggled to find the right words to express her anguish. Nervously, she picked at the lace doily on the telephone table, wishing that there was some way she could convince the caller that no good could come from continuing this conversation.

'June? Are you still there?'

June looked at the crumpled newspaper in her hand. 'If you have any more contact with her, any letters, anything, then it'll be your face in this newspaper. Because I'll tell them everything. Believe me, if that's the only way to stop you, I'll do it.'

June put the phone down and dropped to her knees on the carpet, knowing she could never carry out her threat. She spread out the creased newspaper and, looking at Sara's photograph again, began to sob.

'Hi, Mum, how are you feeling?' asked Sara gently. The snuffle at the other end told her all she needed to know. 'I wish I could be there with you.'

'I can't believe it's been nine years. Nine years,' repeated June.

Nine years ago, to the day, Sara's father, Harry, had died of a heart attack in the bathroom of their house in Finsbury Park. June had since returned to Backwell, a village just outside Bristol, where she'd buried Harry, having fond memories of the early years they'd spent here.

'I miss him too,' said Sara, remembering, as if it were only yesterday, her father picking her up and swinging her around. Harry would pretend he was going to let go and she would scream with delight, knowing that he never would. Then he would hold her tight in a bear hug, press his ruddy cheek against hers, tickling her with his beard, and she would run her fingers through his red hair and kiss him, knowing that in all the world, there wasn't another man as strong and brave as her daddy.

'Have you been to the cemetery?' asked Sara, trying to stop herself from crying too.

'I went early this morning. Honestly, it took me a good half-hour to clear up all the rubbish around the grave. It's a disgrace.'

Sara smiled, relieved that her mother was sounding a little better. Her battles with the cemetery always brought out June's Dunkirk spirit. 'What have . . .'

'Can you speak up a bit, Mum?' asked Sara, looking around the office at the rows of harassed-looking journalists hammering ferociously on their keyboards. The place was bedlam. Men in rolled-up shirtsleeves bellowed into their phones to make themselves heard as they watched the news on the television screens suspended from the ceiling while faxes and printers spewed out yards of paper, each machine adding its own contribution to the racket. 'It's really noisy in here.'

'What have you been up to? Nothing dangerous, I hope,' shouted June, her voice, with its gentle West Country lilt, sounding shakier than ever.

Ever since the Mickey Nash fiasco, June had called her daughter regularly to make sure she was deskbound. Unfortunately, thought Sara, she always was. It was amazing how quickly her initial feeling of triumph at landing a job at the *Sunday Voice* had worn off.

'I'm perfectly safe. I haven't left the office all week. I've got to go now, Mum,' said Sara, noticing her colleague Dave Teacher motioning to her. 'I'll call this evening.'

'You take care, do you hear?' said June, ringing off.

'Hey, Bruiser, good news,' shouted Dave, shadow-boxing around the desk.

'Would you stop doing that?' It was nearly a month since the Billy Todd story had appeared, but the running joke about Sara beating up Mickey Nash showed no signs of abating. She guessed it was the way the men in the newsroom dealt with the way she'd made such a splash with her first story. She couldn't be just a competent journalist: they had to pretend that she was some screaming virago to keep their own egos intact. The story had been huge, and the fallout was still coming.

'So what's happened?'

'Nash's been arrested.' Dave ducked to miss an imaginary right hook. 'There was a raid on an address in Pimlico this morning.'

'How do you know that?'

'A police source,' he replied, tapping the side of his nose.

At last, thought Sara. When the police had finally raided the club and picked up Billy Todd, Mickey Nash was nowhere to be seen. This had meant that the whole focus of her story had to be Todd. As a result, Ashton had suspended him pending further inquiries and Sara doubted his chances of getting back into the team in the near future. It was a sad, sordid little story, but she was still insistent that it was just a sideline to the real crimes going on in Nash's club. 'That's great news. Did your police source say what they thought the chances of getting a conviction were?'

'Good. He reckons Nash's looking at seven years. But he'll be out in four. You know how soft these judges are on criminals. Anyway, never mind that, Holland says if you've not found another randy vicar by lunchtime, you're fired.'

'I'll get straight on to the Synod,' she said, her shoulders drooping slightly as she considered the truth behind Dave's joke. The *Sunday Voice* did seem to exist on an endless diet of sex-and-scandal stories. Sara prided herself on the fact that all the articles she had written so far maintained some kind of integrity – which was probably why they were often spiked in favour of fluff about the amatory exploits of TV weathergirls, has-been pop stars and of course, the ubiquitous randy vicars. Plus the odd story about drug-taking football players, she thought, still suffused with guilt about what she'd done.

It didn't look as if she was going to ever get to the bottom of the Nash story. She wanted to pursue the names and numbers in Mickey's address book, but as not one of them belonged to a celebrity, Simon Holland wasn't interested. There was no further clue to Steve's identity, either. It bugged her that the match-throwing would continue unabated. Even worse, another journalist could uncover the whole story first. If only she knew who had sent her that letter.

The college's grand hall was packed to the rafters for the graduation ceremony. Sara looked from side to side as she walked down the aisles, desperately searching for her mother's face in the audience, berating herself for her lateness. She'd only just finished moving all her stuff into the new flat she was sharing with Kathy. Her friend couldn't come to the ceremony as *Mariella* had sent her to Glasgow on a shoot. Maggie wasn't there, either, having failed the course.

'Sara, Sara over here!'

'Hi, Mum. Sorry I'm late. Let's get you sat down,' said Sara, guiding June towards the back of the hall, where she'd seen a few spare seats.

'That's a lovely dress you're wearing,' said June.

Sara scrunched up her face in mock disdain. For the ceremony, she had forgone her normal uniform of jeans and T-shirt and was wearing a jade linen shift which sparked off the virescence of her eyes. She'd made an attempt to tame her hair with a green velvet bow but in the rush to get to the hall, strands had escaped and auburn curls fell over her shoulders, enhancing the milkiness of her bare arms. 'It's just something cheap from a market,' she said, dismissively. Then, pleased that her mother was pleased, she allowed her full, generous lips to spread into an expansive smile. 'I'm glad you like it.'

'Have you read the programme? I forgot to bring my reading glasses,' said June, searching through her handbag. 'When are you on?'

'First there's a few speeches. Then they give out the certificates, and finally it's the special awards, which are being presented by the Right Honourable Stuart Hargreaves.'

Just then, an announcer called everyone to take their seats, the lights went down and Sara missed the look of panic on June's face as she registered the name.

The ceremony passed by in a blur. June was barely able to look when her daughter took the stage and received a rapturous round of applause as she received her award for the Billy Todd story from the minister. As they stood for the National Anthem, June was desperately trying to think of a good excuse for getting herself and her daughter immediately out of harm's way.

'What did you think then, Mum?'

June jumped, lost in her thoughts of escape. 'Oh, my love, I'm so proud of you.'

'You've every reason to be. Your daughter is a very remarkable girl. And may I add, a very beautiful one at that.'

The comment came from the man walking towards them in an immaculate grey pinstriped suit. Sara had seen his face many times in the papers, but today was the first time she'd seen him in the flesh. When he'd presented her with her award she'd been struck by the fact that even though he had to be the same age as her mother, Stuart Hargreaves was still a fine-looking man. There was an unforced, natural youthfulness to him: only the first flecks of grey and white were appearing above his sideburns and the lines on his face were restricted to a few delicate traces around his slightly sad-looking brown eyes. When he'd shaken her hand he'd given her a huge smile, and Sara had instantly warmed to him.

'Thank you, Mr Hargreaves,' said Sara, amazed that such an important man had made a special point of coming over to talk to her. The minister stood next to her mother, head erect and back ramrod straight, as if he were on parade, his breeding evident in the way he carried himself. 'My mother should take most of the credit for who I am.'

Stuart held out his hand but June completely ignored him. 'I've been talking to your lecturers. They've got great hopes for you, young lady,' he said, trying to carry on as if nothing had happened.

'I've got to go to the ladies',' said June, turning away.

Sara, astounded by her mother's rudeness, which was completely out of character, blushed with embarrassment. 'I'm very sorry about that,' she apologised, as she watched her mother scurry away.

'Another dissatisfied voter, I feel.' Stuart forced a laugh but it was clear that June's abruptness had unsettled him. 'Anyway, congratulations on your award.'

Sara noticed the way he was intently studying her face, not dropping his gaze even for a second. She knew from the gossip columns that he was reputed to be a bit of a ladies' man, but she dismissed the idea that he was trying to pick her up as laughable. 'I don't feel that proud really. I feel sorry for Billy, he's not the real culprit.'

'You're right there. It's the people who push drugs who sicken me. I've tried to put through a private members' bill to toughen up the sentencing, but to no avail. They really are the lowest of the low. I quite understand your feelings, but I think you tried your best. Even so, you shouldn't have put yourself in danger like that.'

'Well, it was all for nothing. The *Sunday Voice* has no interest in pursuing the matter. All they want are soap stories and sex scandals. It's so frustrating,' she exclaimed.

He thought for a while before replying. 'I don't know whether anything will come of it, but why don't I give your number to a television director for whom I did an interview recently? His name's Joseph McCabe, and his company is making a programme about drug abuse in sport. Maybe the two of you could work something out.'

'That would be fantastic. Thank you ever so much,' said Sara, hastily scribbling down her number.

'Think nothing of it,' he said, slipping the piece of paper into his jacket pocket. 'I gather you're a big football fan.'

'How do you know that?'

'Oh, just from the tone of your Billy Todd story.'

'It's one of the biggest loves of my life,' said Sara. 'It's something that I inherited from my father. He never missed a Saturday at Highbury.'

'Really? I'm something of a fan myself. Maybe we could go to a match together some time. I follow Camden.'

Sara reassessed her opinion of him. Was he trying to chat her up? The remark about her being beautiful was a bit forward, which was probably why June had taken umbrage. 'Oh, here's Mum,' said Sara, spotting her mother's slightly stooped body emerging from the crowd.

'It's time I was leaving,' said Stuart, handing her his House of Commons card. 'Remember, if you'd like to go to a match some time, get in touch with me.'

Chapter Four

It was Saturday morning. Sara woke up feeling on top of the world. Not only was there the meeting with Joseph McCabe to look forward to in the evening, there was also the match. In the summer, with the exams and the rush to launch her career, she'd missed most of the World Cup, but now she was going to be able to enjoy one of the best things about living in Highbury: being only a stone's throw from her beloved Arsenal. She couldn't believe that anyone could fail to be seduced by the game if they were to see it live. Sara got out of bed and decided that she would try to persuade Kathy to come with her.

Kathy was in the kitchen, drinking coffee and flicking through an interior-decorating magazine. She smiled at Sara and said, 'Thank God it's Saturday.'

'I know. And what better way to spend a Saturday afternoon than going to the football? You can wear my bobble hat.'

'I take it you're joking,' said Kathy. 'I've had such a hellish week. I haven't told you about Fran Best, have I? Our fashion editor?'

Sara buttered a croissant and sat down at the table. 'I take it she's giving you a hard time.'

'The cow is on my back continuously. She's so critical. She sent me out to buy accessories for the "Details" section and I thought I'd go for an anglicised B-Boy style.'

'Sorry?'

'You know, how American rappers look. Big chains and VW pendants, that kind of thing. I thought I did a really good job. But when I showed the stuff to Fran she took one look at it and said, "Fabulous, darling. We'll use it when we do that feature on what one should wear to a three-piece-suite-warming party in Golders Green."'

Sara choked back a laugh. 'That's terrible.'

'Everyone else at the magazine thought what I'd done was really good, but she junked the whole lot.'

'It sounds as if she's jealous.'

Kathy was in full flight. 'A foul-mouthed Armani-plated bitch is what she is. She's just like Maggie.' She stopped, realising that she was getting carried away, and laughed, 'If Maggie ever did her ironing, that is.'

'It sounds as if you need to come with me to the match. It's only down the road. You'll love it. The atmosphere's fantastic and it'll be a good game. We're playing QPR.'

Kathy looked at her as if she had gone mad. 'How would I know good football from bad? What about all the violence? You don't really expect me to spend two hours standing on a windy terrace being jostled by a bunch of hooligans, do you?'

'Jostle them back and pretend they're Fran. Go on, I'll teach you all about the offside rule.'

'How about if we stay here and I'll teach you how to ragroll a living room?' Kathy could see that Sara wasn't about to give in. 'OK, just this once. But the bobble hat stays at home.'

Later, as Kathy and Sara left the safety of their front garden, they were immediately swallowed up by the crowd of chanting men marching down the hill to the stadium, swept along on a tide of testosterone. The whole area had become a sea of red and white, and despite the best efforts of the many policemen on horseback, traffic had ground to a halt. The chanting was good-natured but deafening, and Kathy was terrified. She wondered why they had moved to an area which would be regularly overrun by football supporters, police horses and numerous hawkers selling Arsenal paraphernalia.

Sara grabbed Kathy's hand as they neared the Highbury Hill gate so that they wouldn't lose each other in the surging crowds. As they reached their seats in the Upper West Stand, a voice came over the tannoy: 'Ladies and gentlemen, boys and girls, please welcome Arsenal.' As the Arsenal players ran on to the pitch, Sara underwent a metamorphosis, lifting the red and white scarf of her youth and taking up the chant of the crowd.

'Come on you Reds!' she sang.

Kathy just stood there wishing that the ground would open up and swallow her. 'I can't believe you're singing along. It's so embarrassing.'

'You've just got to get into it,' said Sara, booing and pointing as Queen's Park Rangers appeared from the tunnel.

Kathy booed half-heartedly, then looked around to see if anybody was watching her.

A roar went up around the stadium as the match started. Kathy didn't have the foggiest idea what was going on. Sara was singing at the top of her voice, completely immersed in what was to Kathy a totally pointless game where twenty-two grown men made fools of themselves by running about on a cold winter's day in little more than their underwear.

'Yes, yes, yes!' screamed Sara, grabbing Kathy's arm. 'The one there with the ball, that's David O'Leary.' The player ran with the ball up the pitch and Sara chanted, 'There's only one David O'Leary'.

Kathy knew that the name should mean something to her, but it didn't. She consoled herself with the fact that Sara probably didn't have a clue who Issey Miyake was and stamped her feet, trying to get some feeling back into them.

As the footballer cut through the Rangers' defence and screwed up a shot at goal the impatience that Sara held at bay in the rest of her life erupted, 'Come on, come on!' she yelled. 'Oh, what an idiot. It was an open goal!'

Kathy tried to concentrate on what was happening but all she was really aware of was the fact that by now her feet were completely numb. She thought that men were welcome to their little hobbies, it just showed what an alien lot they were. But it didn't explain why Sara was jumping up and down with the best of them.

'If you think I'm bad,' said Sara, reading her mind, 'you should have seen my dad. He was like a big kid. When we came here together it was as if we were the same age. That's partly why I still love it, it's where I'm closest to him.'

Kathy tried to picture her own father in the Upper West Stand at Highbury. She doubted whether he'd ever been anywhere near a football pitch in his life. To feel his presence she would have to go and sit in the local rotary club.

'Yes!' screamed Sara as Martin Hayes put the ball in the back of net.

At last it was half-time and Kathy insisted that they went and got some coffee. Four cups later, she still hadn't thawed. Sara pointed across to the press box. 'It's about time there were some women sitting there,' she said wistfully.

'I take it the second half's as long as the first,' said Kathy.

'Don't you find it exciting?' asked Sara, disappointed that Kathy seemed so unaffected by the magic of the game.

'Do I look like I find it exciting? Why have they all got terrible haircuts?'

Sara didn't bother to try to answer the unanswerable. Anyway, the second half was about to begin. The home-team supporters were in high spirits, taunting the Rangers fans at the Clock End. Kathy watched the ball as it went up and down the pitch; as players were sent off while others lay on the floor rolling about as if they were dying. Every few minutes she looked at her watch. Arsenal scored again. Kathy was confused. She thought they had kicked the ball into their own net until Sara explained about changing ends.

Suddenly the North Stand exploded as a player eased through the Rangers defence. 'Look at Champagne Charlie go!' yelled Sara as Charlie Nicholas set up another goal for Hayes.

Sara's cheers quickly turned to hisses when QPR's Gary Bannister put one in for the away team five minutes from the end.

'Yes!' cheered Kathy when the final whistle blew.

Still on a high after the match, Sara ran a bath and selected an outfit for her meeting with Joseph McCabe. Despite the cold, she decided to wear her one and only little black number. Mr McCabe had arranged for them to eat at Café de Flore in Covent Garden. She hadn't heard of the place, but Kathy had told her that Fran Best had a regular table there, so she guessed it was probably pretty smart. Sara found it difficult dealing with people for whom image was important and hoped Mr McCabe's choice of restaurant wasn't a bad omen.

Having battled with her curls, which had decided to mutiny after her hour in a steamy, indulgent bath, Sara slipped into the dress and hurriedly put on a little make-up, mascara, a hint of green eyeshadow and a rich, caramel lipstick. She grimaced at herself in the mirror, deciding that she would have to pile her hair on top of her head as it was definitely out of control. She pinned it up quickly and left the house.

Typically, she arrived at the restaurant a little too early. A bored-looking waiter grumbled under his breath to let her know how inconvenient it was for him to have to show her to her table. Ordering an orange juice, she cast a surreptitious eye around the restaurant, which had been decorated along the lines of a French bistro, right down to the manufactured nicotine-coloured walls, and noticed that the other diners, to a woman, were also dressed in black. It's like a wake, she thought, glancing at the menu, which was in French, with no translation and nothing so vulgar as a price list.

'You must be Sara, right?' said a disembodied voice.

Sara looked up, 'Joseph?'

'Yes, hi. Pleased to meet you. I recognised you from your hair, it's amazing.'

Sara looked perplexed.

'Stuart Hargreaves mentioned it.'

'Oh, thanks.' Sara accepted the compliment, relieved that at least Joseph sounded human but unnerved by Stuart Hargreaves' personal comments about her.

'Sorry for dragging you here,' he said, sitting down and picking up the menu. 'It's just that I'm really bad about remembering the names of places. When I spoke to you yesterday I saw a box of matches from here that someone had left on my desk.'

Sara warmed to him immediately. She didn't believe him for a second, but it was nice that he recognised her discomfort and didn't brag on about the Café de Flore being *the* place to eat in London. She watched him as he ordered the meal and could see that Joseph McCabe lived on nervous energy. He constantly used his long, slender hands to emphasise his words, and she could feel him kicking the table leg as he spoke. She tried to guess his age but it was impossible to tell from the contradictions in his features. His boyishly cut blond hair gave him a youthful air, but the deep-cut lines around his grey-blue eyes suggested a man much older. He was wearing a black double-breasted suit over a black turtle-neck jumper. Kathy would have been able to spot the designer immediately, and even Sara could tell from the cut that it was very expensive. Joseph wore his clothes with ease, unlike some of the stiff-necked fashion victims Sara could see sitting at the other tables.

'Down to business,' said Joseph, coughing, as if uncertain about his role in the conversation. 'Let me tell you a bit about the programme. Drug abuse in sport is a hot new area. Take Billy Todd, for example.'

Sara winced, but the subject was inevitable. 'I hear he's just checked into a rehab clinic. I wouldn't have thought that Channel Four were prepared to finance a documentary on the strength of that story.' She regretted what she had said instantly. Pooh-poohing Joseph's idea was not the way to conduct a job interview.

'They're not,' replied the director. 'I was just using him as an example of the pervasiveness of drugs in the sporting world with which you'd be familiar. No, what the documentary is going to focus on, in the main, is performance-enhancing drugs.'

'Such as anabolic steroids?'

'Exactly. The authorities here really don't want to know about it. They think we're just talking about a few female shot-putters from East Germany.' His arms rose up into the air in indignation. 'But the problem's serious, and it's here in Britain now. I'm sure steroids are being abused all the way through the system from the amateur bodybuilder right up to the professional athlete. Only nobody's talking about it.'

Sara immediately thought about Elaine. 'One of the prostitutes at Mickey's was complaining about selling steroids. She didn't believe there was a market for them.'

'Do you know where they came from?'

Sara leaned down and opened her bag. 'When I had the fight with Mickey—'

'What you did was pretty amazing,' interjected Joseph. 'I don't know whether I would have been able to keep my nerve.'

'To be honest, I'm more uncomfortable here,' said Sara, as the surly waiter reappeared and, without breaking off from the conversation he was having with friends at another table, casually plonked her starter in front of her. 'Is this a salad or a bouquet?' she asked, to puncture the waiter's smugness. The salad had been liberally scattered with flowers.

'They're nasturtiums,' hissed the waiter, walking away.

'I knew that,' said Sara laughing when he'd gone. 'My flat-mate works for *Mariella* and she tells me that edible flowers are very now.'

Joseph raised an eyebrow and said, mockingly, 'Nobody who's anybody eats radicchio any more. Personally, I don't understand what's wrong with a good iceberg lettuce. Anyway, you were saying . . .'

'I managed to grab this.' She handed over the black leather address book.

Joseph flicked through the pages. 'And?'

'I haven't managed to get very far. Most of the numbers I've rung are unobtainable or ostensibly legitimate. The last number I called was a flower shop. How many grammes of coke would you like with your tulips, sir?' She smiled. 'However, there is one interesting thing in the back.' She leaned over the table and pointed to a page. 'These are New York numbers next to someone or some place called Firetto, and look at these old dates with initials, "H.", "G." and "D." next to them.'

Joseph looked puzzled.

'I think,' said Sara, hoping she didn't sound completely off the wall, 'that they stand for Heathrow, Gatwick and Dover. They're drop-off dates.'

'Right. I get the picture,' said Joseph, excitement mounting in his voice.

'Before you get too carried away, that's as far as I've got. All the numbers are dead lines and I've rung the airports on the chance that someone called Firetto came in on those days.'

'No go?'

'Nope. And no one at all had been stopped at customs, either. I really don't know what to do next.'

'Work for me on this programme.'

'Are you serious?'

'You've done half the work already. I can tell you're bright and committed, and that's exactly what I need my researcher to be. Of course, I'd need you to go to New York. A contact of mine there, a reporter called Patrick Byrne, suggests that seventy per cent of the American black market is controlled by one drug cartel. Perhaps these people are the ones supplying your friends at Mickey's. But, let me warn you . . .' he paused. 'The waiters there are even more hostile.'

Sara laughed. 'I think I can handle it.'

'What about the *Voice*? You're only just getting started there.'

'What has been the biggest tabloid headline this year? "FREDDIE STARR ATE MY HAMSTER". Holland wants me to chase after headlines like that. I didn't get into journalism to do rodent stories.'

'Wait until they tell you what they do with gerbils in New York.'

Sara felt exhilarated by the chance to continue with the Nash story, but one question occurred to her. 'If Patrick Byrne is a reporter, why isn't he working on this story himself?'

'He's tried, but his paper's not interested. He wrote a couple of pieces on the subject, but apparently they weren't considered patriotic enough. It's too close to the Seoul Olympics to question the training of American athletes.'

'I can't believe that.'

'Sara, I'm serious. Your association with this programme is going to make you a lot of enemies.'

The impassioned look on Joseph's face convinced Sara that he was telling the truth.

Chapter Five

The early November snowfall had come unexpectedly. Maggie edged her way on to the ice, fuming. She'd arrived at work that morning only to find that her mission for the day was to go to the local children's zoo to meet a king penguin called Fluff. Steve, her news editor and boyfriend, had barely been able to control his laughter as he gave her the details of the story: apparently, the penguin had become anorexic. When she arrived at the zoo, Maggie discovered that Fluff had merely been off his food since the birth of his son, but was well on his way to recovery. Nevertheless, the news editor wanted a hundred words and a photograph, preferably of Maggie actually trying to feed the starving penguin.

'Careful, he's a bit skittish,' said the keeper, as Maggie stepped gingerly on to the frozen pond. She could hear the photographer, Liam, sniggering behind her as she made a grab for the bird. The penguin scurried further out on to the pond. Maggie gave chase, determined that, even if it was a crummy story for a crummy newspaper, she would be a total pro.

'Go on, girl,' yelled Liam as she flew across the ice.

She was just a couple of feet away from the bird when she heard the ice crack. She lunged at the penguin and caught hold of it, and promptly sank to her knees in the icy water. She stood there, holding on to Fluff, blinking back the tears as Liam, howling with laughter, took picture after picture.

'I think the wrong bird's on a diet,' she shouted, forcing a laugh.

Back at the office, Liam quickly developed the pictures and pinned one of them on the noticeboard. Maggie saw that someone had scrawled underneath it, 'Guess which one's anorexic?' Something had to be done. She'd had it with writing about ailing animals, glamorous grannies and talented tots. This was not what she had dreamed of on the journalism course. On Monday she would buy the *Guardian* and start applying for a decent job. In the meantime, she would get rid of Steve.

'Fantastic pictures,' said Steve. 'Don't forget I've booked a restaurant this evening.'

By way of response, she glared at him. He was repulsive. Steve had the ability to sweat even in sub-zero temperatures. He was only twenty-nine, but already his lank hair was wispy around the forehead and for every hair he lost, she suspected he gained another centimetre round the waist. Maggie had hoped that his position on the newspaper would do her some good. She hadn't reckoned with the fact that Steve was a total wimp who let the other journalists walk all over him. As the news editor's girlfriend, Maggie was treated with contempt by the others, who made sure that she was always bottom of the pecking order when it came to stories. Hence the penguin piece. Yes, Steve had become a liability. He would have to go. She didn't even want to think about how awful he was in bed. The man was a useless lump.

As the word lump sprang to mind, Maggie looked down at herself. She knew winter was her worst time in the figure department. She seemed to retain more weight when it was cold and the extra layers of clothing needed to keep warm didn't help her appearance. She hated everything about her life, but her body was the worst thing of all. Every pound she put on made her feel that little bit more worthless, that little bit more out of control. The laxatives that she was getting through by the boxful weren't working. She need to do something else. Opening the Yellow Pages on her desk, she found the number of a gym, called it and booked herself a training session. She felt thinner already.

The model who was covered in gold body paint to resemble Shirley Eaton in *Goldfinger* was complaining bitterly about the heat of the arc lights and was refusing to let the make-up artist retouch her face. They had the studio for only one more hour and Kathy was beginning to wish she'd done the Yves St Laurent piece as Fran had suggested instead of insisting on being left to do her own thing. She looked at her Swatch and realised that Fran and the editor, Nula Cardinal, would be arriving any second. If they saw the current chaos they wouldn't even trust her with the freebies page in future.

'Mimi, get back in front of that bloody camera,' Kathy screamed as the model made a break for the door. 'Or I'll see to it that you won't even get work on knitting patterns.' The normally impeccably placid Kathy hated sounding like Fran. She had a strong desire to prove that you didn't need to exhibit a monstrous ego to get on in fashion journalism, but she'd already had a Pussy Galore look-alike exit in tears after breaking her nails applying a karate chop to Oddjob. Things were getting out of hand.

The model reluctantly slunk back, protesting as the make-up artist reapplied the gold paint to her cheekbones. Noticing that the photographer had now walked off for a quick cigarette, Kathy used the moment to escape the studio for a breather. Standing on the fire escape above the street, she opened a can of diet cola and tried not to think about the shoot. Instead she made a note of all things she needed to buy for the flat. Sara was totally immersed in her new job and rarely came home from the office before midnight, so buying builder's whitener for the living room wasn't on her list of priorities. Kathy didn't mind. They were both very busy at the moment and had divided up the chores according to each other's strengths. If it needed to be paid, it was Sara's department; if it needed to be painted it was Kathy's.

Just as she was about to go back into the studio, Kathy spotted a cab depositing Nula and Fran on the pavement below. The two women, both dressed from head to toe in black, waved up at her. Kathy, thinking that they looked like a couple of crows, waved back and raced into the studio to find Shirley Eaton trying to wrestle a light meter out of the photographer's hand.

'Don't tell me there's not enough light. I'm fucking frying up there!' she screeched.

'Stop it!' bellowed Kathy, but the pandemonium continued until the squeal of the goods-lift gate announced the arrival of Nula and Fran. Suddenly there was quiet. The two women seemed to glide across the studio floor. If she hadn't seen it for herself, Kathy could have sworn that they'd just stepped out of a coffin instead of a cab.

Fran was the first to break the silence. 'Kathy, what's going on here?'

'It's been a difficult shoot. Mimi's been a real trouper, but she's getting a bit uncomfortable under all that gold.' Kathy could see from the carmine smirk on Fran's lips that she was taking great delight in making her squirm in front of Nula.

'No, I mean what is this shoot all about?' Fran picked up the top of a white seventies-style bikini and held it at arm's length, the smirk curling dramatically into a disgusted moue.

'Babes and bullets,' said Kathy, sheepishly. 'I'm playing around with the idea of power-dressing. When I think of strong women I think of Bond girls. I'm fed up with the idea that women are empowered by wearing shoulder pads. Uzis seem much more efficient.'

'This is straight off the top shelf,' said Fran, throwing the bikini top to the floor, 'and it has no place in our magazine.' Then she put the boot in. 'This is *Mariella*, love, not *Mayfair*.'

'I'm sorry,' said Kathy, bending down to pick up the swimsuit. She'd made a mistake. She'd let herself believe that her individuality was a good thing, but even nominally cutting-edge-type magazines like *Mariella* really wanted conformists like Fran Best.

Nula let out a peal of laughter. 'I rather like it.'

Fran rounded on her. 'Nula, you're not serious!'

'I am. Kathy's right, and I think our readers are intelligent enough to interpret this with the right degree of irony.'

Fran looked as if she was about to implode. 'And you're saying

I'm not? I've given over four pages to the puffball skirt in March. This is just tacky. Nula, it's wrong for *Mariella*, and you know it.'

Nula made for the fire exit. 'A quiet word, Fran.'

Fran scurried off after the editor and Kathy put her head in her hands. Mimi came over and tried to put her arm around her without smudging the body paint. 'I thought it was a really good idea,' she said comfortingly.

Kathy forced a smile but she sensed that it was all over. She'd dared to be different, and now she was going to get the knock-back she deserved. Fran would stand her ground and Nula would eventually give in, she'd seen her do it before. Kathy knew that Fran would make things impossible for her at the magazine from now on. The job was going to go as quickly as it had come. 'Good, but tacky,' she replied.

'I saw her in the Café de Flore last week groping a waiter,' whispered Mimi. 'Fran Best could write the book on tacky.'

Nula appeared again through the fire-escape doors and marched over to Kathy, obviously in something of a temper. 'Kathy, Fran has just resigned. If you want the job of fashion editor, it's yours.'

Sara uncorked a bottle of wine and poured two glasses. 'What are you cooking?'

'It's spinach and nori rolls. I didn't think a prawn cocktail would be good enough for Joseph.'

Sara choked on a mouthful of wine. 'What does that mean?'

Kathy picked up a handful of the spinach cooling in a colander and rolled it into a tube. 'Well, I think you want to make an impression on Mr McCabe.'

'I do not. Joseph suggested going out for a goodbye drink, so I thought, why not invite him to dinner here? Besides, it's a chance for you to meet him at last.'

'You're just as busy as I am,' said Kathy apologetically as she wrapped the seaweed around the spinach and began slicing it up. Sara had tried to arrange several nights out before but their diaries never seemed to coincide.

'I know, I know.' Sara watched as Kathy prepared the food, amazed at the care she took in arranging the chopped-up rolls on the serving dish. 'That looks lovely. Honestly, I haven't got a thing about Joseph.'

'I believe you. Hand me that tamari,' said Kathy.

'I rang Maggie today,' said Sara, changing the subject. 'We hardly spoke. She said she couldn't talk because of deadlines, but I know she's still hurting.'

Before Kathy could give her opinion the doorbell rang. 'Go on, let him in,' she said.

Sara ran to the door and showed Joseph into the living room.

'You've got a fantastic place here,' he said, looking around and sitting down on a wooden church pew Kathy had bought from an architectural salvage warehouse. Somehow Kathy had managed to find the time despite becoming an overnight success to decorate the living room in what she called a 'Gothic-organic' style. Around the room were several wrought-iron candlesticks, tortured into surreal curlicues, which threw a flickering light on to broken pieces of plaster figures, some abstract, some representational, which Kathy had mounted on the high walls. 'It's amazing.'

'Thanks. But you'll have to tell Kathy that – it's all her work. She's in the kitchen at the moment, doing something unusual with spinach. She'll be out in a minute. So. My bags are packed and I'm all ready for New York. Although I had a scare when I couldn't find my birth certificate for my passport.'

'But you have got it, and the visa?'

Sara laughed. 'You're as bad as my mother. It was her fault in the first place. She had the certificate stored among her *very* important papers, you know, like her authenticity certificates for her Capo di Monte collection. I think she thinks I'm a real klutz incapable of doing the simplest thing. She insisted on going to Newport and getting the passport for me.'

'Oh, I nearly forgot,' he said, reaching into his black leather rucksack and producing a copy of the *Rough Guide to New York*. 'A small token to wish you on your way. I'm sure you'll have a few spare moments to go sightseeing.'

'What, with you as my boss? I don't think so, but thanks anyway.'

Joseph smiled. 'Are you scared?'

'A little apprehensive, but excited mostly.'

'Just be careful.' Joseph looked as if he meant it. 'Drugs, and sport, too, for that matter, are big business over there, and certain people will go a long way to protect their interests.'

'You've been watching too many B movies, Joseph,' said Sara, not wanting to believe him.

'I'm serious. Don't think you have to be heroic. You were very lucky with Mickey Nash. You're going to need more than luck with this Firetto person – if he is a dealer. Sorry, this was meant to be a pep talk. I know you can pull it off. I'm more worried about them having to deal with a tiger like you.'

'The cheek of it!' laughed Sara, secretly pleased with the description.

'You know, this place is completely amazing,' said Joseph, admiring the yards of muslin artfully swagged above the windows.

'Thank you,' said Kathy coming out of the kitchen. She took one look at Joseph and couldn't understand why Sara wasn't totally in love with her boss. The man was absolutely gorgeous. 'That's a lovely jumper you're wearing. It's Missoni isn't it?'

'And you're wearing Comme des Garçons,' he replied, looking ever so slightly bashful.

Sara looked down at her jeans. Everything decent had been packed. 'And these are Levi's.'

Over dinner, once all the New York plans had been discussed in detail, the conversation turned to fashion and design. Sara struggled to keep up, aware that throughout the meal Kathy and Joseph hadn't taken their eyes off each other for a second. Just before eleven she yawned and said, 'Well, I've got a plane to catch.'

Joseph stood up. 'I suppose I'd better get going, too.'

'I didn't realise it was so late,' said Kathy.

'I'm sure Joseph would like another coffee,' said Sara, winking furiously.

'Only if you're making one . . .'

Kathy blushed. 'Sure.'

Sara said her goodbyes and went to bed, certain she was witnessing the start of something big.

Chapter Six

Sara stood on the prow of the ferry as it made its way back across the bay to Manhattan. Following the guidebook's advice, she didn't get off at Staten Island, and instead used the round trip purely for its wonderful views of the city. Out in the bay, the wind picked up and she turned up the collar of her coat, her red hair, flying across her face, obscured her view of the Statue of Liberty as it passed by on her left. The twin peaks of the World Trade Center loomed closer, glinting in the cold March sunshine and dwarfing every other building on the Manhattan skyline. Sara felt a rush of pure unadulterated pleasure. She'd been in the city for less than forty-eight hours and, though it could have been the jet-lag talking, she had already promised herself that, one way or another, she wasn't going home.

When the ferry docked, she strolled along to Battery Park, dodging the trains of joggers puffing along the track by the water's edge. The sparse greenery of the park was a little disappointing compared with the verdant expanse of Central Park, which she'd visited the day before, and she hailed a cab, still not quite able to shake off the feeling that she'd walked on to a set, so familiar were the buildings and street names from the countless New York movies and cop series she'd seen over the years. She instructed the driver to take her to Herald Square via Broadway, which provoked her first confrontation with one of the locals. The driver insisted that it was easier to go via Seventh Avenue. Sara wasn't to be moved: Seventh Avenue didn't sound as exciting as Broadway, and this was sightseeing time. As soon as she started work she would have to get from once place to another as quickly as possible, so she wasn't going to miss out on the luxury of dawdling in this frantic city.

As they passed rows of anonymous-looking shops instead of the expected theatres, Sara looked at her map and realised that the driver had probably been right to suggest Seventh. Times Square was on Forty-second Street, and the theatres were clustered around that area. She thought about how snooty Londoners were with American tourists who asked the way to Leicester Square and pronounced it Lysester Square, or those who inquired, in all innocence, if Liverpool Street was the home of the Beatles. When the cab reached Thirty-fourth Street, she got out, tipped the scowling driver a dollar and vowed to get to know the place as well as any native.

Tourists in New York are the ones who look up, Sara told herself, but approaching the Empire State Building it was impossible not to. Taking the elevator to the eighty-sixth floor, she emerged on the observation deck and gasped, as much at the slap of cold wind as at the view laid out before her. She circled the deck, mentally ticking off the names of each building she recognised. Downtown, that building shaped like a thin wedge of cheese was the Flat Iron; uptown to her right, the gleaming art-deco spire of the Chrysler, and on her left, though she wouldn't have known it had its name not been painted in huge black letters on the side, was Macy's. Kathy would have loved it.

But Kathy at that moment was probably very happily wrapped up in bed with Joseph. Sara was still trying to sort out her feelings about what had happened before she left. When she had woken up on the morning of the flight, she'd found Kathy in the kitchen making coffee, wearing only Joseph's jumper. She and Joseph hadn't been to bed, at least to sleep, for the whole night. Kathy seemed racked with guilt about the whole thing, and Sara had to spend a good fifteen minutes assuring her that it was OK when deep down she wasn't so sure that it was. Her friend had offered to accompany her to the airport but Sara had detected a certain amount of relief when she'd insisted she'd be all right.

Much to her irritation, she had to admit to herself that she was feeling slightly jealous of Kathy. Joseph had never been in the least bit flirtatious with her, but from the second he clapped eyes on Kathy, he changed. And Kathy, who had, only months before, been a shy, awkward girl who needed to be pushed into absolutely everything, had responded like the confident, accomplished woman she had so evidently become. Sara didn't feel like a woman, mostly because she didn't allow men to treat her like one.

Doing another lap of the deck, she realised that maybe Kathy and Joseph were the reason she was having rash thoughts about staying on here. The couple were such a perfect match, she just knew that they'd be in it for the long term. The endless parade of men who had fallen drunkenly through Maggie's bedroom door when they were students hadn't bothered Sara in the slightest. None of those relationships had lasted. Maggie was just as screwed up about men as she was. Her experience of boys at school and college had led her to distrust them. She couldn't get over the feeling that they were only after one thing. Nobody ever seemed to look beyond her so-called beauty. But if Kathy were to fall in love, being around her would be a constant reminder of something that she believed she could never feel.

Sara looked down across the city and thought about work. Somewhere out there a man called Firetto was waiting for her.

Making good her promise, by the start of her second week in Manhattan, Sara had the lay-out of the city pretty much in her grasp. Her body clock was still having difficulties adjusting, and every morning she found herself waking up just after 5 a.m. Any attempt at getting back to sleep was futile, for by six o'clock the whole city seemed to be wide awake. Sara doubted that anyone could sleep through the cacophony of car horns and streams of invective that announced the start of the Manhattan rush hour.

This morning she lay in bed toying with the idea of ordering breakfast in her room, but then decided that room service was a luxury the programme budget couldn't afford and reluctantly got up. In the bathroom, any remaining notion of trying to sleep through until a more reasonable hour was quickly pummelled out of her by the force of the power-shower, which, like everything else in New York, was designed to assault the senses. She dried herself, revelling in the luxury of having fresh towels brought to her room every day and dressed in her 'work uniform', a white shirt with a fawn gabardine blazer and matching Oxford bags and a pair of brown penny loafers. Pulling back her still-damp hair with a chocolate-coloured bow, she picked up her natural leather satchel, thought briefly about putting on some make-up, rejected the idea and left, steeling herself for the speed with which the lift descended from the eighteenth floor of the hotel.

As usual, Sara breakfasted at the diner across the street. The hotel's own restaurant was fantastic, but eating there Sara felt a little sealed off from the real New York. She preferred the brashness of the diner with its fast-moving waitresses screaming orders in impenetrable code across the steamy room. She'd quickly found out that ordering a fried breakfast would result in being presented with a plate piled high with meat smothered in maple syrup, not something she could countenance at such an early hour, and so, taking a window seat so as not to miss a second of the life going on outside, she ordered a cinnamon bagel and the first of the day's many coffees.

Waiting for her order to arrive, Sara read through her research notes. She'd been working in earnest for a couple of days now and had talked to several doctors and officials in the sporting field who, when pressed, had admitted that drugs had invaded every level of sport in America. The problem was huge, far too much to tackle in a single programme, and she needed to find some individual stories which could properly represent the situation. She'd spoken several times to Patrick Byrne at the *Post*, but so far he had drawn a blank on the name Firetto. Nevertheless she had arranged to meet him later in the day in the hope that he could provide her with some new leads.

Taking out her diary, she sipped at her coffee, checking the day's appointments. She had secured a meeting with a senator's aide at ten, though she doubted whether she'd get much hard information from such a senior official. After that she'd arranged an interview with a policeman on the drugs squad. She had also written a note to remind herself to ring her mother, just to let her know that so far she hadn't been mugged or shot down by a crazed sniper in McDonald's.

Now mentally prepared for the day ahead, Sara paid her bill and left the diner, still mesmerised by the Manhattan streets. Steam really did swirl up through the roads from the subway air vents – it wasn't just something dreamed up by an art director to make adverts look more atmospheric. Taking her life into her hands, she stepped out into the road to try to force a cab to stop for her.

By the time she arrived at Kelly's Irish Bar on the East Side later that evening, Sara was just about ready to quit. The senator's aide had kept her waiting for over an hour, so she had had to contact the policeman to shunt their meeting back, thinking that she wouldn't be able to make it in time. When the aide finally did show up, he granted her a terse five-minute interview, which he told her was strictly off the record, even though he said nothing at all which deviated from standard political propaganda about 'mobilising all available resources to combat this serious problem'. Sara knew that Joseph didn't want a programme filled with empty rhetoric; he wanted hard facts. She had higher hopes for the policeman, but he turned out to be a macho braggart more interested in trying to secure a date with her than in talking about the failure of the police to control the spread of narcotics in sport.

There was a Gaelic football match being shown on a cable TV station in the bar and the place was packed with noisy supporters. One of them, a man in a crumpled suit nursing a pint of Guinness, turned out to be Patrick. He spotted her first from the brief description she had given him and called her over to his table, ordering her a pint of the black ale.

'You look like you've had a day of it,' said Patrick, his second-generation accent, a kind of mid-Atlantic brogue, emitting a great deal of warmth.

Sara told him about the difficulties she was having pinning people down. 'Everybody here seems so clued up on how to deal with the media. People talk a hell of a lot without saying anything. I've done hour-long interviews with a person and then looked over my notes and what I've basically got is a "no comment".'

Patrick nodded and laughed. 'But if they said, "no comment," they'd be missing up on a chance to be on TV. No right-minded American wants to do that.'

Sara sighed. 'I really need this programme to be a success.'

'Well, I've got some good news for you,' said Patrick, looking over her shoulder. 'The man who's just walked in got very excited when I mentioned the name Firetto to him.' He called out, 'Hey Louie, over here!'

Sara looked round and her mouth dropped open in amazement. The man coming towards them had to be at least six foot seven tall.

'Need I add,' said the journalist, 'that Louie Stevenson is a basketball player.'

Louie had crossed the bar in a couple of long strides, and Patrick introduced them. Aware that Louie had noticed her staring at him, Sara stuttered an apology. 'S-sorry to be so rude, but I don't think I've ever met anyone as tall as you before.'

'No problem, ma'am,' he said, extending a massive hand which completely enveloped her own. His fingers had a powerful grip. He turned to Patrick and gave him a high-five. 'How are you, my man?'

'All the better for seeing you. And for having a drink, of course. What can I get you?'

'Diet Coke. I'm training later.'

Sara pushed a stool towards Louie. She was beginning to get a crick in her neck looking up at him.

'So you're the little lady asking about that sonofabitch Ronnie Firetto,' he said. As he sat down, his knees appeared above the table top.

'I take it he's not a friend of yours.'

Louie glared at her, making her feel stupid for having asked. She tried again. 'Am I right in guessing that Ronnie Firetto is a dealer?'

Louie nodded gravely. 'That mother's screwed up so many lives.'

Sara wanted to ask if Louie had had any personal involvement with Firetto but she didn't want him to take it the wrong way. 'Where does Firetto operate from? I had a couple of numbers which I thought might be his, but they were both disconnected.'

'He moves around. The mother knows he wouldn't be safe to stay in one place too long, you know what I'm saying? If I get hold of him after what he did to Vince . . .'

'Who's Vince?'

'My homie. Vince used to be an athlete, making good money, too. But you know the pressure. His manager told him it was the steroids or else, and Vince had his lady and two kids to support, so he took them. Now the poor sonofabitch is wasted. Kidney cancer, and his liver's not much better. Barely a tooth left in his head. The man's a wreck. His old lady took the kids and split. Now Vince is washed up in the Bronx with his Medicare running out fast.'

'Would Vince talk to me?'

'Lady, I don't want no camera poking in his face. I've seen those programmes. "And now we have the dumb black man who's taken too many drugs." Vince has been exploited enough.'

Sara blushed. She had already been imagining how the interview could look on camera. 'It's OK, I understand,' she said. 'But if I could just talk to him, off camera, whatever he wants. I've had a run-in with a Ronnie Firetto type myself.' She explained what had happened in Mickey Nash's club and how she had come by Firetto's name.

Louis looked impressed but he was still guarded. 'I'll talk to Vince, but I'm not promising anything.' He rose from the stool which had barely supported him. 'Apologies, but I've got to get to the court.'

Sara walked along Third Avenue, caught up in the army of people marching to work. Over a week had passed since she'd met Louie and she'd decided that Vince didn't want to talk. But late the night before Louie had called her and given her an address in the South Bronx where he would meet her this morning. Being a little early, she decided to walk part of the way along the avenue before catching a cab, still fascinated by the way New Yorkers went about their business with such grim determination. She noticed that a lot of the executive-type women really did wear ankle socks and trainers as they strode along in their power suits. She knew that they replaced them with more flattering heels when they got to the office, but she couldn't imagine women walking along Bishopsgate doing the same. It seemed too showy, but there again, New Yorkers were big on making statements. The buzz was that time was money, and there wasn't a second to waste. But the panhandlers on every corner, holding out plastic cups in desperation, told her that was only half the story.

It took her a while to persuade a cab to take her to the South Bronx and when she finally succeeded, the Hispanic driver told her, in broken English, a stream of horror stories about the place, interspersed with racist observations about black people. She started to challenge him but then thought better of it. If she annoyed him, he could just dump her in the middle of nowhere, and she had to admit that some of his stories had got to her. So she glowered in silence, looking out of the window as they crossed the Harlem River on the Third Avenue Bridge, the architecture soon changing from the slick steel and glass of Manhattan Island to the desolate, decrepit, rubble-strewn wasteland of the Bronx. By the time the cab pulled up outside a decaying tenement block, Sara was keyed up and ready for the worst.

As she stepped out of the cab, the driver looked at her as if she was mad. Louie was nowhere to be seen. 'Would you mind waiting a while?' she asked. 'My friend isn't here yet.'

'Sorry, lady,' he replied, slamming his doors and pulling away, driving straight through a group of boys who were throwing a ball around in the middle of the road.

Sara stood on the kerb not knowing what to do, cursing the driver for filling her head full of rubbish and trying to ignore the inescapable fact that the boys had stopped their game and were watching her suspiciously. She reminded herself of the many times she'd walked through groups of kids playing football in the street on Highbury Hill. This was no different, she told herself, but the thumping of her heart said otherwise.

'Yo!' called one of the boys, and suddenly the group ran towards her. She stood rooted to the spot. The boys surrounded her and she shut her eyes, waiting for the first blow.

'Yo, Louie! This your new girlfriend?'

'Hey, Louie! You cheating on Jeanie with a white girl?'

Sara opened her eyes and immediately felt very stupid once again. Louie was coming up behind her and the boys darted off to swarm around him. The basketball player was obviously something of a local hero. He stood chatting to the boys for a while before leading Sara into the tenement block, stepping over an old woman who was sitting at the entrance drinking from a bottle wrapped in the obligatory brown-paper bag.

Louie called the lift, and when it finally came Sara wished they'd walked. It smelled of urine, was covered in illegible graffiti and had been scorched by some arson attack. As the lift groaned slowly upwards, Sara tried to block out the vision of being trapped and suffocating in such a place.

'Out there on the street,' said Louie, 'I saw the look on your face.'

'I'm sorry,' said Sara, looking at her feet. 'The cab driver on the way here told me a lot of awful stories. He shook me up a bit.'

The lift came to a halt, stopping the conversation, and Sara followed Louie out on to the equally dank-smelling and heavily littered fourteenth-floor landing. She wondered how anybody ever managed to escape such a place. Louie banged on the grille which covered the door to Vince's apartment and Sara steeled herself for what lay inside.

'Hey man, this is the lady I was telling you about.'

The door opened and Sara put her hand out to Vince, a prematurely wizened man who she guessed must have been at one time extremely handsome. 'Thanks for agreeing to see me.'

He nodded and, clearly in a great deal of pain, hobbled back into a very small but spotless living room. Sara had expected the apartment to resemble its exterior, but, though poorly furnished, it was impeccably neat, which served only to heighten the tragedy of a man trying to keep himself together in the most appalling conditions.

'Sit down,' said Vince, wincing as he eased himself on to a bashed-up sofa.

'Vince, you don't have to say nothing you don't wanna,' said Louie, pulling up a kitchen chair and sitting on it back to front.

Sara sat next to Vince. 'Louie's right,' she said softly. 'If you want to talk, fine, but any time you feel I'm stepping over the line, just say.'

Vince coughed violently and put his hand on Sara's arm, shuddering as he tried to catch his breath. 'I don't really know what I can tell you,' he gasped. 'I was stupid. Guess I got what was coming to me.'

'That's shit, Vince,' said Louie, smashing his enormous fist down on the back of the chair. 'You didn't have any choice.'

'We all got choices,' said Vince, steadying his breathing. 'I made the wrong ones.'

'But Ronnie Firetto helped you make yours, didn't he?' probed Sara.

'At first it was just a few pills. Made me feel real good.' Vince had his eyes closed and was slowly shaking his head. 'Then my coach, Spike Samuels, he says it's better if I start shooting them up. I said, I don't do that shit, but he says, go on try it, if you're gonna be a winner you gotta take steroids. So I did.'

'How did it make you feel?'

'Hard. More aggressive. I could train for longer, I was faster. I am . . . I mean, I was a sprinter. I took over quarter of a second off my best time. Won every cup in the state.'

With some effort, Vince pointed over to a cabinet filled with trophies. Sara noted that they had been recently polished. The image of Vince still lovingly tending to them despite the damage they represented to his life, broke her heart. 'You must have been very good,' she said.

'The best,' snapped Louie.

Vince began to cough again. 'Can I get you something?' asked Sara. 'Some water?'

Vince nodded and Sara went into the kitchen. There was little light in the room as the window was broken and had been boarded over. On the drainer was a Mickey Mouse beaker, the kind given away free in burger bars. Sara filled it to the brim. On the wall was a picture of a runner breaking through the tape at the end of a race. It took her a couple of seconds to realise that the healthy, muscular athlete in the picture was Vince. Feeling incredibly sad, she took the water back into the living room. 'There you go,' she said.

Vince put the beaker to his lips, fighting hard to control his shaking hands. When he was done he wiped the spilled water from his chin and continued. 'I was taking way over the proper dose. I started stacking.'

'What does that mean?'

'I'd use a mixture of steroids, trying to get the balance that suited me.' He laughed. 'As if there's a right balance. Then things started really getting out of control.'

'How?'

'Vince, you don't have to go through all this again,' said Louie. 'Lady, you're pushing the man.'

'It's OK, Louie,' said Vince. 'I want people to know that what I did was wrong. This lady's coming in my house thinking I'm some kind of hero.' Vince pointed to the trophies again. 'Ask Loretta what kind of hero I am.'

'Is she your wife?'

'Not any more,' said Vince, his bulging eyes filling with tears. 'What I done to that woman . . .'

He was openly crying now. Sara took his gnarled hand and squeezed it tight. 'Do you want to stop?'

'I beat her so bad. Like I said, I was filled with so much aggression from the drugs. Roid rage, they call it. She only had to cook something I didn't like and I'd break her ribs. All the time I was still taking that shit. Used to strut around the big I am. So big I put my wife in the hospital for Thanksgiving with concussion. I knew it was out of control then, but Samuels said, fuck your wife, I'm gonna get you to the Olympics. That Thanksgiving was the last time I hit her, but only 'cause she didn't wait around to take no more. Took the kids and went.'

There was silence for a moment. Louie shifted uncomfortably in his seat. 'Do you mind if I make some coffee?' he asked.

'You know where it is,' said Vince. Louie left the room. 'He's a good man.'

'Why did you agree to talk to me?' asked Sara. 'Surely you could be in a lot of danger.'

'Didn't Louie tell you? I've got kidney cancer. Ronnie Firetto can't touch me now. I'm gonna die soon enough anyway. But I talk to the kids in the gyms. Each one dreaming about being a hotshot, getting out of here. I know that bastard is pushing stuff on them. Ain't there enough drugs out on the street? These kids are trying to do something and he's fucking with them.'

'Have you been to the police about this?'

Vince sneered at her. 'And tell them what? Black kids be taking drugs? Hey, hold the front page.'

'There must be something someone can do . . .'

'I'm trying to set up an anti-drugs group. Which is why I talked to you. Maybe you can publicise it.' Resting his hand on Sara's shoulder, Vince stood up and shuffled over to the trophy cabinet. From a drawer at the bottom he produced a sheaf of papers. 'I took these from Ronnie's office,' he said. 'I'm not sure whether he knows it was me. Either way, I don't care.'

Sara took the papers from him and helped him to sit down again. The papers were order forms and delivery notes for something called Brasquanil. 'What's Brasquanil?'

'It's a vitamin pill. Only it ain't. It's steroids.'

'So where's this Brasquanil coming from?'

Vince shrugged his shoulders. 'I'm not quite sure. I think somewhere in South America.'

'Is Firetto still at this address?'

'No.'

'Do you know where he is?'

Vince looked her in the eye. 'If I tell you, you gotta promise me that you won't say nothing to Louie. He'll kill Firetto if he finds him. That ain't no bad thing, but I don't want Louie to ruin his career on account of me. I'd shoot the mother myself if I had the strength.' Vince coughed and Sara saw a small fleck of blood appear on his lips. 'Promise me.'

'I promise.'

Vince hastily scrawled the address on a scrap of paper.

'Thank you,' said Sara, slipping the address and the papers into her bag.

'Do you have any idea who's supplying him?'

'I don't . . . hang on – I overheard a mention once of someone called Pinte, Pinto, that's it, but I heard nothing more. They clammed up when they saw me in the room.'

'Vince, is there anything else that could help us nail Firetto?'

He shook his head. 'I only wish there was.'

Sara took a deep breath. 'I know this is a lot to ask, but would you be prepared to say some of this on camera?'

'We'll see,' said Vince as Louie returned.

'You're all out of coffee,' said the basketball player. 'Do you want me to get you some?'

'No thanks. Can't drink it anyway.' Vince laughed bitterly. 'Hurts my kidneys.'

'Sara, I think we better be going. Vince needs his rest.'

Sara stood up, unable to find the right words to conclude this meeting. Whatever words of consolation she offered to Vince would sound hollow and inadequate. 'Is there anything that you need?'

Vince shook his head but the look on his face suggested the answer was everything. 'I really gotta lie down,' he said, insisting on showing them to the front door first.

Sara walked out on to the balcony. As she turned to say goodbye, she saw Louie slipping some money into Vince's pocket. 'I'll call over the weekend,' he said. When the door closed he turned to her and said angrily, 'Seen enough?'

Sara said nothing and, unable to face the lift again, began to walk down the foul, badly lit stairway. She kicked something on the stairs and shuddered when she realised that it was a used syringe. Somewhere above her she could hear a woman screaming and glass breaking. It was all too much for her. She burst into tears.

'Hey, hey,' said Louie, encircling her with his massive arms.

'It's so sad,' she sobbed, burying her face in his chest. 'That poor man.'

When the tears finally subsided, she pulled away and ran out of the building, gratefully gulping in the fresh air.

Louie followed on behind. 'Are you OK?' His voice was more gentle now, less confrontational.

'I just couldn't stop myself,' apologised Sara.

'You know, when I met you the other night in the bar, I had you pegged as some hard-bitten newshound. Seems I was wrong. Sorry if I've been a bit rough on you.'

Sara smiled to show that she hadn't taken offence and Louie waved at the boys playing ball in the road. Sara looked at them. They were just children. She had to stop that bastard Ronnie Firetto.

Two days later Sara stood outside Firetto's 'office' on the Lower East Side. She had kept her word about saying nothing to Louie; in fact, nobody knew she was there. Her plan was to use Mickey Nash's name. She was hoping that a phone call to England to check her story might be too much hassle. To calm her nerves she kept reminding herself of Vince polishing his trophies in that awful tenement block. Gritting her teeth, she knocked on the door.

'Waddaya want?'

'I need to speak to Ronnie.'

'Yeah,' said the dark-haired, stocky Italianate man who opened the door.

'Hi. I think we have a friend in common.'

'Waddaya talking about?' he said, squaring up to her and looking her straight in the eye.

'Mickey . . . Mickey Nash – told me to contact you. I was a hostess in his club in London. He said you might have some work for me.'

Firetto said nothing.

'Maybe I could be a mule or something,' she said, making up her story as she went along. 'Mr Firetto, I need some money badly.'

Firetto thought for a moment. 'I think you'd better come in,' he said.

It was only then that Sara noticed the baseball bat he was carrying.

'Actually, now's not a good time,' she said, backing away. She was frightened and angry with herself for being so naïve. Joseph was right. This wasn't England. In all likelihood, Firetto had a gun inside as well. 'I need to settle in first. Could I get back to you on this?'

'I know who you are, you fuckin' bitch,' he said, making a grab for her. 'Mickey's real pissed at you, and you know what? He says if I should happen on you, I gotta give you a little present from him.'

Sara turned on her heels and ran. The terrifying sound of Firetto's baseball bat being dragged menacingly along the railings as he chased after her rang in her ears. 'Help me!' she screamed. People had stopped to watch what was happening, but nobody came to her aid.

'You're gonna die, whore.'

Sara put her head down and raced along the block, aiming for the subway entrance she could see in the distance.

'Hey, Sara, I'm gonna cut you up in little pieces.'

The shock of hearing her name momentarily pierced her concentration and she tripped over a paving stone and fell to the ground. Instinctively, she clasped her hands at the back of her head to protect herself, feeling her fingers crunch as Ronnie Firetto's bat found its target.

Chapter Seven

Kathy spread the contact sheets of the footwear shoot out in front of her. The shoes had been photographed in exaggerated close-up, the camera paying almost fetishistic attention to details such as buckles and stitching. The pictures had then been solarised to create a silvery, blurred, almost abstract quality. Kathy was pleased with the images – they accurately represented her own dreamy obsession with footwear – but she was a little unsure about whether she'd strayed too far from fashion reportage.

'What do you think of these?' she asked, calling across the office to her assistant, Carly, who was staring vacantly out of the window. She didn't answer. Then someone pushed a clothes rail in front of her. 'What about these dresses? One's had a slight accident,' said the delivery man, pointing to a tear.

'Who's the designer?' whispered Kathy, horrified.

The man just stared at her uncomprehendingly, as if she had spoken in Urdu.

'Just leave them there,' she sighed. She popped her head through the clothes on the rail. 'Sue, can you come and sort out these dresses?'

Sue appeared and removed the offending rail. For a moment Kathy sat back in her chair with her eyes closed, breathing deeply, trying to dissipate the stress. She'd spent the morning at Battersea Power Station overseeing, of all things, an underwear shoot. Most of her time had been taken up trying to get rid of some builders who kept walking into shot trying to ogle the scantily dressed models. She couldn't think for the life of her why she'd chosen the power station. The ring of a telephone disturbed her thoughts. She opened her eyes again and laughed. God, she loved this job.

'Kathy?'

'Hi, darling. I'm so glad you called. What a day I've been having.'

'I've been trying to reach you for an hour.'

Kathy registered the panic in Joseph's voice. 'What's the matter?'

'It's Sara. She's been attacked,' said Joseph. 'I'm leaving for the airport now.'

Kathy looked at her watch. 'I'll meet you there in an hour. I'm coming with you.'

Twelve hours later Patrick Byrne picked up Kathy and Joseph from La Guardia Airport. 'Where are your bags?' he asked.

Kathy held up the carrier bag containing the two dresses she'd swiped off the rail at *Mariella*. 'This is everything,' she said getting into the back seat. Joseph slid in beside her and tried to take her hand. 'Don't,' she snapped. She had spent the entire flight in a state of high anxiety, barely able to bring herself to speak to him. 'This is all your fault.'

'Kathy, how was I to know?'

'You know what she's like, that's why you took her on. To do all the things you were too scared to do yourself.'

'I was planning to go straight to the hospital,' interrupted Patrick. 'But we can stop off at a hotel first, if you'd rather.'

Joseph looked at Kathy to check that he was saying the right thing. 'To the hospital.'

The three drove on in silence. Kathy was far too het up to

appreciate her first sighting of New York. It took them nearly an hour to reach the hospital, a huge rambling building with several annexes in the surrounding streets, and when they finally arrived, Patrick told Joseph and Kathy to wait in the car while he checked with the main reception to see which one Sara had been taken to.

Five minutes later, the Irishman reappeared, out of breath. 'She checked out hours ago. She's gone back to her hotel.'

Sara sat up in bed, keeping her bandaged fingers under the covers in an attempt to play down the severity of the attack. 'It's only concussion,' she said. 'Louie, you didn't have to come over. But thanks, it's really nice of you.'

Sara felt the bed dip as Louie sat down on the edge. 'Why didn't you tell me you were going to see him?'

'I promised Vince. He didn't want you to get into trouble.'

'He's going to be broken up when I tell him about this.'

'Please don't say anything,' said Sara, reaching out to touch Louie's arm.

'Sara, my God, girl, look at your hands!'

'There's a couple of broken bones, but it's mostly just bruising. The doctor said it looks a lot worse than it actually is.'

At that moment, the door opened and Patrick, Kathy and Joseph burst into the room.

'Kathy, Joseph, I don't believe it!' she said jumping out of bed too quickly and feeling the room begin to sway.

Kathy dropped her carrier bag and rushed to support Sara, leading her back to bed. 'How could you have been so stupid?'

Sara knew that Kathy was frightened rather than angry and she felt guilty about the panic she had caused. 'I'm really sorry. But didn't the doctors tell you that I was OK?'

'When we left all we knew was that you were unconscious in hospital,' said Joseph. 'Why did you discharge yourself?'

Sara tried to lighten the atmosphere. 'Have you seen how much a bed costs? I thought you'd be pleased that I was keeping the programme on budget.'

'As for going to see Firetto on your own—'

'I knew you'd try to stop me if I said anything.' Sara's guilt was quickly turning into indignation. 'Look, the police have got him now, and there were a lot of witnesses. Isn't that what you wanted?'

'What I want,' snapped Joseph, 'is a researcher with some notion of professionalism.'

Kathy rounded on him. 'She was just doing your dirty work.'

'OK, OK,' said Louie, standing up and using his imposing body to quell the room into quiet. 'I think everybody needs to calm down a little. What say we all go down to the bar and leave Sara to get some rest?'

'Good idea,' said Patrick, making for the door.

'Kathy, would you stay a while?' asked Sara as the others left. Her friend closed the door and began to laugh. 'What's so funny?'

Kathy opened her carrier bag and pulled out two filmy dresses. 'I'm going to have to do some shopping,' she said. 'I didn't have time to go home and pack. On the plane all I could think of was that I'd be sitting at your hospital bedside dressed in a stolen two-thousand-pound cocktail dress. Very Florence Nightingale.'

'I am sorry,' said Sara. 'Joseph's really upset with me, isn't he?' His remark had cut her to the quick.

'He's just transferring his guilt. I've been bitching at him ever since we left. Is there anything to drink?' Kathy looked around and found the minibar. 'Well, here's to New York,' she said, opening two whisky miniatures.

Sara wasn't sure that mixing drink with the painkillers was all that bright an idea, but now everything had calmed down the seriousness of the situation was beginning to dawn on her. She could easily have been killed. Downing the whisky in one, she said, 'I was so scared.'

Kathy kicked off her shoes and sat next to Sara on the bed, registering the matted blood as she gingerly stroked her friend's hair. 'We were all scared. But, Joseph was out of line speaking to you like that. I'll talk to him about it. But, Sara, you've got to calm down a bit. Stop thinking you're so invincible. Look, the reporter's flying over in a couple of days with the film crew. There isn't much more for you to do. Take some time off for a while.'

'Maybe,' said Sara, slightly uncomfortable with the obvious

intimacy between her boss and her best friend. 'I take it that you and Joseph are an item?'

'I don't want to sound too gushy, but I think – I think I'm in love. And I know Joseph is, because he keeps telling me so.'

Over the next week, Sara showed Kathy around Manhattan. Kathy's infectious excitement made her feel as if she were seeing all the now familiar sights for the first time. Although things were quickly sorted out between Sara and Joseph, the director insisted that he didn't actually need her on the shoot. Vince had agreed to be interviewed, and the Firetto side of the story was to be dramatised. Sara had tried to get Joseph interested in finding out who was supplying Firetto, but he was adamant that they had enough material for the programme. Pinto, he argued, was probably just another dealer and not worth a probable wild-goose chase. In the end, she was forced to concede defeat. During the day, while Joseph was busy filming, Sara took the opportunity to spend some time with Kathy, knowing that the couple wanted to spend their evenings alone together.

Since leaving college she and Kathy had become enmeshed in their working lives, and it felt good to let it all go for a while. But the gnawing feeling that they had to attend to their careers was never far from the surface.

One afternoon, as they lunched in a little trattoria near Washington Square, Kathy announced that she'd been talking to Nula the night before. 'She wanted to know when I'd be back. I did sort of leave everything up in the air.'

'What did you tell her?' asked Sara, wondering what she herself had to go back to. Simon Holland had said that she could pick up where she left off at the *Voice* if she wanted to, but it seemed like a step backwards now.

'One of the joys of being a fashion editor is suggesting faraway locations for shoots. So I put it to Nula that Coney Island might just make a wonderful backdrop for the August swimwear spread.'

'And she bought that?'

'Carly's packing her bucket and spade right this very minute. It would be nice if you could stay on and watch. When do you think you'll be going home?'

Sara stopped eating and thought for a moment. 'Kathy, I know this sounds completely ridiculous and typical of me, rushing into things without thinking them through, but I don't want to go back.'

'I knew it,' said Kathy, slapping the table. 'I've been watching you, listening to the way you talk about being here. I *knew* this was what was going on in your head.'

'I've finished my work on the programme, and I don't want to go back to the *Voice*. What's London or England got to offer me?'

'Aside from your friends, family and home?'

'So you think I'm being stupid?'

'Yep. But I think you've already made up your mind, and I know you well enough to know that nothing I say will change it. Just one problem – you've only got a temporary visa.'

'I'm going to apply for a green card.' Sara knew that this did sound stupid: there was no way she would get a green card. How many fledgling journalists were there in America already – and with just as much talent as she had – looking for a chance to make it into the big time? Why would the USA want to start importing more from Europe?

'You'll never get one as a journalist,' said Kathy, reading Sara's thoughts. 'But if you're serious about this, I know how you can. What bra size are you?'

Despite its glamorous past, present-day Coney Island had about as much allure as Southend-on-Sea. The famous fairground had gone to ruin and all along the boardwalk tatty little bargain shops announced closing-down sales. In the daytime, elderly people dotted the dirty beach, vainly trying to remember the way it was in their youth; at night muggers and drug-pushers made the place a virtual no-go area.

'I'm really not sure about this,' said Sara.

At the edge of the beach, Kathy and Carly held up a sheet to shield her from prying eyes as she took off her jeans and T-shirt and changed into a rather discreet pastel-yellow fifties-style swimsuit, the price of which would have paid a month's rent on the Highbury flat.

'Think of the Stars and Stripes,' said Kathy, dropping the sheet to a round of applause from the photographer. 'You look wonderful.'

Kathy watched as Sara sat in a canvas fold-away chair while the stylist, Marlon, savagely back-combed her hair and pulled it up into a pleat. Her answer to the green-card problem was, of course, that Sara should become a model. Kathy would use her for the swimwear shoot, and those pictures could be the basis for a portfolio. In the six months Kathy had spent at *Mariella*, she had made quite a few contacts at the modelling agencies in New York. Not that Sara would need her to pull any strings: her friend's beauty spoke for itself. A few appearances in American magazines, a couple of catwalk shows and the green card would be a cinch. No one looked quite like Sara, so she couldn't be accused of taking anyone's job.

'Ow,' screamed Sara, shooting the hairstylist a filthy look. 'It may interest you to know that I was hit over the head with a baseball bat not too long ago.'

'Why am I not surprised?' he replied, through a mouthful of kirby grips. 'Oh girlfriend, look at your hands! Honey, you just gotta change that detergent.'

Sara held up her hands and stretched out her long fingers. The knuckles were still mottled with purplish-blue bruises. 'Does it really matter?' she asked impatiently.

The stylist called over to the make-up artist. 'Wanda, could you do something with Freddy Kreuger here, I'm just about through.'

Wanda, a large, slightly sweaty blonde, waddled over, dropped a heavy black make-up box in the sand beside Sara and silently inspected her hands. Finally she made her pronouncement. 'Yeah, I can fix it. But she'll never do wedding-ring work.'

Marlon began packing up his equipment. 'Well, if you can't, I suppose she could always wear a muff. Call it Christmas in July.'

Wanda set to work covering Sara's fingers with a heavy body make-up. When she'd finished Sara thought the result looked like she was wearing tights on her fingers, but she said nothing. She just wanted the whole humiliating experience over and done with.

'Lift,' said Wanda, putting her hand under Sara's chin and forcing her face up into the light. She studied it for a while. 'Well, I don't think there's that much I can do for the rest of you,' she announced finally.

Sara scowled. 'You people are so rude.'

'Relax,' drawled Wanda, unscrewing a pot of foundation. 'Jesus, it was a compliment. I meant this isn't going to take me that long. Your face doesn't need much, just a little foundation, maybe.'

Wanda proceeded to spend the best part of an hour applying Sara's make-up, drawing a small crowd of onlookers in the process. Despite her sloppy appearance, her deft fingers worked delicately, blending the foundation into Sara's skin and covering the small patch of freckles which had broken out on her nose. Then, taking a ridiculously large brush, she applied a matt powder, stopping every now and then to stand back and check the effect.

'You've got the most fabulous lips,' said Wanda, searching in her bag and producing a violently vermilion lipstick.

'Thanks,' said Sara, embarrassed at having snapped at the make-up artist earlier.

'Pucker up.' Sara complied obediently as Wanda smeared the creamy lipstick across her lips. 'You know, you've got Kim Basinger's mouth.'

At the mention of the actress's name Sara suddenly thought of Maggie and that ridiculously over-emphasised Cupid's bow she had plastered over her mouth for that 'Basinger effect'. She hoped Maggie was happy, wherever she was. Sara had tried to contact her the week before to tell her of her plans. The receptionist at the *Bournemouth Clarion* had informed Sara, in terse tones, that Ms Lawrence had quit her job and hadn't left a forwarding address.

'Let me see, eye shadow,' said Wanda, laying out her pencils. 'I know it's a cliché, but it's gotta be green. Are you wearing coloured contacts?'

Sara just couldn't get used to the presumption of this woman, all these personal comments. And it was so boring having to continually talk about her appearance. It was the last straw when Wanda, finishing her eyes, asked her if she'd had a nose job. 'I could have sworn you'd had a shave.' Seeing the look on Sara's face she added, 'You know, a piece of the bone shaved off the bridge of your nose. It's pretty flawless. Listen to me, two compliments in one day

– I gotta stop sniffing the polish remover.' With a quick dusting of blusher to accentuate Sara's high cheekbones, Wanda announced that she was finished.

'Thank God,' said Sara walking across the sand to where Kathy was waiting for her with a pair of white mules and matching winged sunglasses.

'Sunglasses?' said Sara. 'Wanda Woman over there has just spent twenty minutes slapping a whole pot of April Verge on to these babies.' She fluttered her eyelashes at Kathy and mimicked Wanda's voice. 'You know, you got Isabella Rossellini's eyes. 'Course, hers go in the same direction all the time.'

'You don't have to wear the sunglasses, just suck on the arm of them pensively like all the other models do. Have you ever looked at a women's magazine?'

Sara laughed, glad to see that Kathy wasn't taking it all too seriously, and took her place in front of the camera, next to an old couple who had been coerced by the photographer into sitting in shot to give the picture some atmosphere. It was acutely uncomfortable to feel so many pairs of eyes boring into her as the photographer shouted instructions. Sara had never been forced to pay so much attention to her body before and she didn't like having to play up to the camera.

Gradually, though, she got the hang of it. She felt her body relax and take the poses more naturally, and she began to forget about all the eyes on her. Not that her enjoyment increased, however: the only interesting aspect of the whole thing was seeing the way Kathy worked. As soon as the shoot started, she stopped smiling and became incredibly professional. She seemed so confident doing this, so able to juggle all the elements of the shoot – marshalling the troops, making endless suggestions on how to improve the shots, and dealing diplomatically with the egos involved without ever for a second leaving anyone in any doubt that she was the person in charge. She was so different from the bag of nerves Sara had had to force through the door of Mickey Nash's club.

After a quick costume change into a prim high-waisted black and white bikini, the shoot moved to a rusty beach shower, where Sara had to pose under a feeble trickle of water and look relaxed while at the same time keeping her head out of the spray. She was aware as soon as the water hit her that her costume was becoming translucent and her nipples were now fairly visible. It was awful feeling this exposed. She tried hunching her shoulders, awkwardly holding her arms in front of her to cover herself up, but the photographer shouted at her to straighten up.

'That's it, smile!' he said. 'Good, good. Gorgeous. Move your head a little to the left. You're so beautiful. Let the water caress your body. You're so hot.'

Sara knew that this endless barrage of suggestive compliments was merely intended to coax her to enter into a love affair with the camera, but all the same she found it excruciating. She was glad when a bank of clouds ruined the light and forced a break. Wrapping herself in a towel, she brushed the sand off her legs and sat down in the canvas chair. The high-heeled mules were uncomfortable so she kicked them off, not really caring where they landed.

Wanda hovered over her, touching up her nose and cheeks. 'You got the same problem as me. I sweat like a pig.'

One of Wanda's eyebrow pencils had fallen out of the box. Sara vengefully buried it in the sand with her heel before the make-up woman noticed it.

Marlon reappeared with his teasing comb. 'You're looking a bit nappy-headed,' he said, attacking her hair with gusto. 'Oh, Wanda, hold the rouge. You're not at the funeral parlour now, girlfriend.'

I'm going to kill them both, thought Sara. She was just about to call over to Kathy to ask how much longer she would have to endure this torture when she saw her friend run across the beach. In the distance she saw Joseph approaching along the boardwalk. Spotting Kathy, he broke into a trot and soon the two of them were locked in a passionate clinch. When they separated they walked hand in hand over to Sara.

'I can't believe it,' said Joseph. 'You look stunning.'

'That's it, Topsy and Tim, I've had enough,' barked Sara, waving away Wanda and Marlon as if they were irritating flies. 'Hi, Joseph. How did it go today?'

'Fine. It was just some bits and pieces – a few establishing shots, that kind of thing. The filming's pretty much finished.' As he spoke he slipped his arm around Kathy's waist and pulled her closer. 'Sara, I've got some great news for you.'

'Isabella Rossellini's cross-eyed too?'

'What? No, some friends of mine need someone to house-sit their loft in Greenwich Village for a year. They're artists and they're off to an ashram. I said you'd be interested.'

'Definitely,' said Sara. She hadn't even begun to think about her housing problem yet. Louie had said that Sara was welcome to move in with him and his wife, Jeanie, until she got herself sorted out, but a loft in the Village sounded just right for an up-and-coming journalist-cum-model.

'That isn't the best part,' continued Joseph, ruffling Kathy's cropped blonde hair. 'I've just sold the programme to PBS.'

'Fantastic!' said Sara, clapping her hands together. Her mind began to race: she would suffer the modelling until the programme was shown in the States, and then use that as her calling card. 'Joseph, you're a genius.'

'OK, you two,' said Kathy. 'Cut the chit-chat. You're on my time now. Sara, would you mind too much if we did another outfit now? It'll be the last for the day. We're losing the light.'

Reluctantly, Sara went to change. She put on another one-piece, this one ivory-coloured with a peplum waist. As she pulled it on Kathy said carefully: 'I was talking to Joseph – he says the tenancy of his flat is up for renewal soon but he doesn't like the place. Would you mind very much if he moved in with me?' She looked flustered. 'Of course,' she added hastily, 'if you wanted to come back, at any time, he'd have to leave.'

'Don't you think this is all a bit sudden?' asked Sara, before she could stop herself.

'You of all people shouldn't lecture anyone about rashness,' retorted Kathy, slighted.

Sara knew that Kathy wanted her approval and she felt churlish for not having given it immediately. 'Don't take any notice of me,

Kathy. I think Marlon's been hitting me on the head too hard. I think moving in together could be really good for both of you.'

As Sara walked across the beach she watched Kathy whispering into Joseph's ear. A smile spread across his face. Feeling, unaccountably, a little bit sad, she slipped on those ridiculous mules.

Chapter Eight

The heat was stifling. New York was no place to be in August, especially in a grotty Village apartment where the air-conditioning consisted of an encyclopaedia jamming the window open. Dressed only in a man's white vest and a pair of boxer shorts, Sara lay down on the bed and fanned herself, wondering, not for the first time, about the direction of her life. She should have been ecstatically happy: the modelling jobs were coming thick and fast, several magazines were only too happy to sponsor her for immigration, and it looked as if her green card would be processed in the very near future. And yet she was thoroughly miserable. She hated modelling with a passion. It was so vacuous. In all the time she had been doing it she hadn't made a single friend and she missed Kathy desperately. The only friends she had in the whole city were Louie and Jeanie. The other models she met thought she was a stuck-up bitch, but there was only so much she could say about the latest waterproof mascara. Correction – there was nothing she could say about the latest waterproof mascara.

But it wasn't just the boredom of modelling that was getting to her. She was scared as well. Patrick Byrne had rung her the day before with the disquieting news that Ronnie Firetto had jumped bail and disappeared. The police had been quite nonchalant about the whole affair. They just told her not to worry, Firetto wouldn't be bothering her again, but she couldn't believe that. Her one run-in with Firetto was enough to convince her that he wasn't a man who'd forgive and forget.

Getting off the bed, she went to the fridge and took out a Coke, rolling the cold can up and down her neck before opening it. The thought of Firetto led her back to Mickey's. She had hundreds of questions and not one single answer. She still didn't have a clue who'd sent her that note in the first place. She finished the Coke, scrunched up the empty can and threw it at the wall in frustration.

In an attempt to think about something more pleasant she picked up the copy of *Mariella* which had arrived that morning and looked again at the results of her first shoot. She had to hand it to Kathy: as much as she hated seeing herself looking so gormless and stiff, the pictures were quite something. The special developing process had resulted in a nostalgic pastel tone that captured the wistfulness of Coney Island. The pictures harked back to a simpler age while at the same time reminding you that that had been then and this was now. It was a neat trick, and well executed. That Kathy Clarke certainly knew her stuff.

Sara looked at the clock and tried to remember what time it was in England. She thought about phoning her mother, then changed her mind. Every time she spoke to June the conversation would follow the same pattern. At first June would be totally freaked out that she'd rung at all – to her, a transatlantic phone call could only mean that Sara was in desperate trouble. She'd successfully concealed the Ronnie Firetto incident – the brawl with Mickey Nash had been quite enough for June to take – but her mother was convinced that New York was the most dangerous city on earth and that it was only a matter of time before Sara was fatally wounded. She'd tried to tell her that the worst thing that was likely to happen to her was falling over in those stupid shoes she had to wear on the catwalk, but June would have none of it. Next would come the bit where June would say how much she missed her and how she wished she'd come back, and Sara would be filled with a homesickness that would take days to shrug off. She missed having her mother only a train ride away almost as much as she missed having Kathy in the next room.

Another shower would cool her down and improve her mood. She pulled back the curtain to the bathroom and turned on the light, screaming as loud as she could. This was an established ritual which gave the cockroaches the chance to get out of the way. At first Sara had been horrified to find the apartment, on top of all its other faults, so heavily infested, but she'd come to accept the little brown beetles as a fact of life in New York. Everybody had them, and after spending the first few nights keeping watch, armed with a rolled-up newspaper and a can of Raid, she developed an uneasy truce with them. As long as they stayed out of her way she left them alone.

Sara sat under the sluggish spurt of water in her clothes. How New Yorkers could complain about British sanitary standards while a feeble excuse for a shower like this existed in Manhattan, she didn't know. The water ran down her in warm rivulets, neither refreshing her nor enabling her to face the thought of braving the heat to go shopping for food. It looked as if it would be another Dial-a-Pizza night.

The phone rang. She ignored it for a while – it was probably just another job. She'd earned enough to pay the rent this month and she hated the work so much that it seemed pointless to force herself to take on any more than was absolutely necessary. The shrill ringing persisted, so she sighed, struggled to her feet and dripped across the studio floor to answer the phone.

It was Louie. 'Hi Sara, I knew you were there. Hot enough for you?'

'Louie, it's good to hear from you.'

'I got some real bad news. Vince died this morning.'

Vince had been in the public hospital for weeks but this still came as a shock. 'I'm so sorry. I didn't realise the cancer was that far advanced.'

'It was his heart in the end,' said Louie. 'Just couldn't take no more drugs being pumped into him, I guess.'

'What about his funeral? Who'll arrange it?'

'Jeanie and me will take care of everything.'

'I'd like to do something.'

'What did you have in mind?'

'I don't know. Maybe I could talk my agency into organising a benefit for his drug project.'

'That'd be real nice of you.'

'It's the least I can do.' She thought it sounded a pretty insincere gesture. She'd taken part in quite a few benefits of this type – drugs, AIDS, the homeless – and though they undoubtedly raised money, she felt they were probably organised more to salve the consciences of the over-privileged people who bought the tickets than anything else.

Louie said goodbye and promised to meet up with her soon. She could hear his deep, sonorous voice beginning to crack up and she pictured Jeanie standing there next to him, massaging the small of his back, trying to soothe away some of his sadness. She hung up and went back into the shower, her tears falling as slowly as the water from the faucet.

The November fashion shows were Sara's cut-off point. At the end of the month PBS were due to air *Sporting Highs*, so she flatly refused to take any more bookings after that point. At the last of the shows, after a week of hectic activity, she decided that, as her modelling career was over, speaking her mind could no longer jeopardise it. She walked up to the show's designer, wearing only her knickers, and told him in no uncertain terms what he could do with the dress which, artfully, wittily and chicly, had been designed to fully expose the left breast.

'There is no way in the world a woman would have designed this piece of misogynist shit,' she said, throwing the outfit on the floor at the outraged man's feet. 'When was the last time you wore a pair of trousers with a hole in the crotch to let your left ball hang out?'

The designer lifted his silver-skull-topped black lacquered cane and pointed it at her. 'Now listen, you uppity bitch. There isn't one fucker out there who wants to see those miserable tits of yours, anyway. Now get your fat British ass into a dress – any dress, I don't care – and schlep on to that catwalk.' He clicked his fingers and a nervous dresser came running. 'Find something for Princess Anne that doesn't show too much cleavage. Something from the *fatwa* range.'

The other models stood in a group and tittered. Sara flicked a V-sign at them and, feeling immeasurably better, allowed the dresser to pin her into an over-fussy chartreuse shot-silk evening dress.

'Go!' screamed the designer, pushing her through the curtains as ear-splitting heavy-rock music burst from the sound system. Sara made her way down the catwalk, a plastic grin fixed on her face, and received a smattering of polite applause. The designer was on his way into obscurity and the assembled hacks were strictly second division. She reached the end of the catwalk and turned, noticing a chic, skinny blonde standing up and cheering. Silly cow, thought Sara, this dress is hideous. She twirled once again then strode back up to the curtain, a little quicker than the choreographer would perhaps have liked.

'Well, thank you Flo-Jo,' seethed the designer.

Seconds later she was out again, this time in a little rhumba number. '*Arriba!*' trilled the music, and Sara ruffled her ridiculous skirts and cha-cha-chaed as rehearsed. The applause was even more scant this time, except from the skinny blonde, who was cheering even louder. Good grief, thought Sara, she must be the buyer from Piggly Wiggly. She tried to see who the woman was, but the glare from the spotlights defeated her. On the way back she passed the model who'd lucked out with the exposed-breast dress. She looked ludicrous, and Sara was glad she'd stuck to her guns.

Many changes of costume later, each of which was met by a cheer from the blonde and zilch from everybody else, Sara was dressed for the finale. As was traditional, the show ended with the bridal outfit.

The designer screwed up his mouth. 'God knows why I picked you. Could you please, just for this one outfit, manage a little fucking dignity out there?'

Sara looked down at her outfit, a lace and tulle wedding mini-dress with a neckline that plunged to her navel. 'How could I look anything but dignified in this?' she said sarcastically.

'Cherish it, witch,' said the designer, thrusting a bouquet at her. 'It's the closest you'll ever get to a wedding.'

To the strains of 'Carmina Burana', Sara made her entrance and was greeted by a chorus of perfunctory 'oohs' and 'aahs'. As had been arranged, she reached the end of the catwalk and waited for the designer to join her and take his bow. Out of a sense of duty rather than appreciation, Sara felt, the audience gave him a standing ovation. These were her last few seconds of being a model. By now the very word made her feel sick. She knew that the rest of the models defined it as 'a paragon', but she preferred the alternative meaning – 'a facsimile'. Nothing like the real thing at all.

As the applause subsided, one woman continued to clap. The skinny blonde. Sara shielded her eyes and tried to make out the figure beyond the lights. As recognition dawned at last, she let out a yelp of delight and threw her bouquet out into the darkness. 'Maggie, catch!'

At four in the morning, Sara kicked open the door of her apartment and staggered in. She turned on the light, screamed and watched the cockroaches scurry for cover. Seconds later Maggie crawled in on all fours, still clutching the bedraggled bouquet.

'Is there any alcohol in this dump?' she asked, struggling to her feet. 'Oh, my head!'

'There's some beer in the fridge, but you'd be better off having some coffee.'

'Whatever,' said Maggie, lurching across the room and throwing herself on to the bed.

Sara made coffee and sat on the floor next to the bed. Maggie rolled over and looked at her, her make-up smeared across her face. Sara was instantly reminded of the many mornings she'd seen Maggie in a similar condition back in Archway. But this was different. Maggie had to have lost at least three stone. The mangled hair had been replaced by a sleek blonde bob; the glasses had been discarded in favour of contact lenses. Even the suit she was wearing, which was pretty creased after their night out, was a million miles away from the 'fuck-me' clothes she had worn in those days. Maggie looked terrific – or at least, she had done before they'd started drinking all that champagne.

'I still can't believe you managed to find me,' said Sara, blowing on her coffee.

'You really are a model, aren't you? You want to watch yourself, or the next thing you know you'll be appearing at trade fairs pointing at cars. Finding you was the easiest thing in the world. I was coming over for the shows anyway. I just called the agency and asked where you'd be. Of course, I didn't know you were a model till I saw your wet swimsuit pictures in *Mariella*. You could see your nipples, you know.'

'They were very artistic,' said Sara, realising that she was sounding more like a model by the minute.

'It's bloody freezing in here.'

'It isn't that cold,' lied Sara, getting up and banging the radiator. 'At least, not cold enough to kill off the cockroaches.'

'I'm trying not to think about that,' said Maggie, crawling under the covers. 'I watched *Sporting Highs*. Did I tell you that?'

'At least fifty times.'

'The *Guardian* said that it was "a well thought-out piece which showed great journalistic tenacity".'

'You said that, too.'

'It was marvellous, simply marvellous,' Maggie went on, waving her arms expansively.

'Maggie, why did you never get in touch with me? What did I do?'

Maggie sat up in bed. 'Make me another cup of coffee. I think we need to talk.'

Once the coffee had percolated, the two women sat at the kitchen table, Maggie with the duvet wrapped round her, Sara pulling on a hand-knitted jumper which a designer had given her as a thank-you present.

'Do you want something to eat?' asked Sara. 'I think there's a couple of cinnamon bagels in the bread bin.'

'I'm really not hungry,' said Maggie. The coffee was sobering her up. 'Sara, when you got the job on the *Voice* and I went off to bloody Bournemouth, I felt like such a failure.'

'You got a good job, which was more than most people on the course did.'

Maggie banged down her mug. 'You're doing it again, and you don't even realise it. Part of the reason I felt like a failure was because you made me feel like that. You can be so patronising. I know what you thought about the *Clarion*. It was a "crappy provincial newspaper", somewhere you swore you'd never end up.'

Sara stared into her coffee. She hadn't realised Maggie felt like that, and she couldn't think of anything to say in her own defence.

'Anyway, you were right,' Maggie continued, 'it was a crappy provincial newspaper. But I'm out of there now. And I like the job I'm doing.'

'I'm really pleased for you.' Maggie was now the beauty editor on a downmarket high-circulation women's magazine called *Chloe*. Sara's mother bought it sometimes.

'But even as I say that to you, I feel embarrassed about working on *Chloe*. I know you still think it's trivial and below you.'

'How could I think that? Look at the kind of stuff I was writing on the *Voice*.'

Sara's head was starting to ache. She found some painkillers. 'Want some?'

Maggie took two tablets. 'You're patronising me again. Everything you do has this great high ideal behind it. If you do tacky kiss-and-tell stories, it's part of the sacrifice you have to make to be a serious reporter. You show your tits in a magazine and it's about making it in America.'

'Do you really think I wanted to be a model?'

'Do you really think I wanted to sleep with all those dogs? Like you, I did what I had to do.'

Sara grabbed hold of Maggie's hand. 'But you were better than that.'

'Who are you to sit in judgement?' Maggie pulled her hand away and walked over to the window. The first shards of light were beginning to crack through the spaces between the sky-scrapers. 'Yes, you have done things just as tacky as I have. You use your body when it suits you. You give everybody all that crap about looks meaning nothing, but they've come in very handy for you, haven't they? It doesn't hurt being beautiful, does it?'

'You're drunk, Maggie, and you're overstepping the mark.'

'You decide the mark, Sara, you always have done. You're the one who decides the difference between making a noble sacrifice for your career and being a tacky slut.'

'I've never, ever said anything like that about you,' blazed Sara. 'I think this conversation has come to an end.'

'No, it fucking well hasn't,' yelled Maggie. 'Just you sit there and listen to me. Not only did you go back to Mickey's after what that bastard said about me, but you didn't even bother to give me a credit for the Billy Todd story.'

'I'm sorry about going back. I had to. But I did try to get you a by-line. I can't believe that that is what all this is about.'

Maggie snorted derisively. 'You think your shit doesn't stink, don't you? You can be the tackiest slut on the block and you still come up smelling of roses. But no matter how hard I try, I can't live up to the standards you expect of me. I'm not smart enough, talented enough, beautiful enough.'

'Is that comment directed at me or at your parents?'

'That's so New York.'

'Maybe, but it sounds to me like you're angry with them.'

'Oh for God's sake I'm angry with you. I'm angry with the way you've tried to control every aspect of my life since I met you. Maggie do this, Maggie do that.'

'Where is this going?'

'You still don't know, do you? Do I have to spell it out for you? Wales, Sara. The fucking abortion you made me have.'

Sara took a deep breath and tried to keep her emotions under control. If she didn't, she was going to say something she would bitterly regret. 'That's a disgusting thing to say,' she replied quietly. 'I tried to help you. It would have ruined your life, Maggie. College, everything. It would all have gone out of the window.'

'College? Everything? What are you talking about? I didn't want to go to college. *You* did. I had to do everything you wanted to do. This was your life – you had it mapped out and I had to follow along in your wake. People get caught up with you and they have to do what you want them to do. Look at Kathy. You dragged that silly cow into a job in a whorehouse. She had to be an investigative journalist because you wanted to be one. But I give her this much: she's managed to throw it all back in your face, hasn't she? She's gone off and done exactly as she pleased. And she's made a bloody success of it.'

The notes of truth in Maggie's invective pierced Sara. She was finding it hard to control her own tears. 'Wales . . . I was trying to *help* you.'

'You took away the one thing that was mine, the one thing I'd managed to create on my own. What was so wrong with me having a baby?'

Sara was sobbing now, rocking herself backwards and forwards as each sob jolted her body. 'I had to be strong for you, Maggie. I had to look after you. Your parents didn't give a fuck. And *he* certainly didn't care.'

'Look after me? By making me kill my baby?'

Sara leaped up from the table. 'Maggie, stop it! It was your decision.'

Maggie began to sob too. 'It was the wrong one,' she said.

Chapter Nine

The temperature had fallen another degree to −5 centigrade and Sara shivered as she climbed out of the limousine behind Louie and Jeanie. They were attending a New Year's Eve party on the wealthy Upper East Side. As they entered the apartment block, Sara was a little bemused by the overripe opulence of the marble-clad hallway.

'I feel as if I should leave my shoes at the door,' she said. 'Do you think we should go round to the tradesmen's entrance?'

'Wait till you see inside,' laughed Jeanie, pressing the elevator button. 'These people are seriously rich.'

And this from a woman whose husband had just recently signed a multi-million dollar deal to play for the Knickerbockers. Sara was glad that she'd chosen to wear her strappy black Lycra dress, one of the very few designer outfits she'd acquired during her modelling days. She looked at her reflection in the lift mirror and remembered Kathy's oft-stated belief that if you armed a woman with enough LBDs, she could bring down an empire. Sara wasn't so sure. She'd tied her hair back in a black velvet bow which, she decided now, had been a mistake. The dress showed too much of her shoulders, and if she'd worn her hair loose it would have covered them a little. As it was, she felt half naked. She also felt she was wearing far too much make-up.

Jeanie noticed her frowning. 'Honey, you look fabulous,' she said, putting her arm around Sara's waist. Jeanie, who was a singer, was a tiny woman, totally dwarfed by her two companions, but her huge personality more than compensated for her lack of stature. When they'd first met Sara had been a little put off by the sharpness of her tongue, but her targets were always well chosen and, unlike Maggie, Jeanie exuded a genuine warmth which made up for the occasional barb.

On the fifth floor they were greeted at the door by a silver-haired man with soap-opera-type good looks. 'Come in, come in,' he said, handing them a glass of champagne each. 'Good to see you, Louie, glad you and Jeanie could make it. And this must be the Revlon girl you were telling us about.'

'See?' whispered Jeanie.

'No, she couldn't make it tonight – she's in Aruba,' laughed Louie.

'But you must be a model, too,' said the man.

Sara shot Louie a look. She didn't want to be introduced to anyone as a model. She had given it up when her green card had been processed but now the status she had done so much to earn seemed to mock her.

'This is Sara Moore,' said Louie on cue. 'She worked on *Sporting Highs*, that documentary on PBS. Sara, this is Ed Teller.'

Sara shook his hand, immediately wondering if this could be her lucky break. 'I hope you don't mind me gate-crashing.'

'Not with an accent like that. Do you specialise in sport?'

'No, general reporting.'

'You're not looking for a job, are you?'

'Doing what?'

He took her to one side and whispered conspiratorially: 'I've got a little pilot we're working on for a new quiz show and I could do with a real cute hostess.'

Before Sara could tell Ed Teller politely what he could do with his job he was distracted by the arrival of his next guest, a woman with peroxide blonde hair whipped up a foot high and a cleavage affectionately known to television viewers across the States as the 'Grand Canyon'. Sara recognised her from the pictures she'd seen of her in the *Enquirer*. This woman earned more in a month than Sara's father had in a lifetime – and all for standing there vacantly pointing at a scoreboard.

'Come on, honey,' said Jeanie, leading Sara away. 'Let me tell you something. That girl worked real hard to get where she is today.'

'Really?' said Sara sarcastically.

'She sure did,' laughed Jeanie. 'Been laid more times than my Grandmammy's tablecloth.'

They grabbed themselves another drink and circulated for a while in the wood-panelled interior of the apartment, which was in marked contrast to the trash-palazzo style of the entrance hall. Sara knew that the block couldn't have been more than five years old and yet the apartment looked like a turn-of-the century literary salon – or at least, it would have done if it hadn't been peopled by blonde fluffheads with a gross annual income higher than Scotland's. Jeanie introduced Sara to several of the other guests, and as soon as they were out of earshot she would wickedly reveal exactly what plastic surgery they'd undergone in the previous year. Jeanie was still struggling to make it in her own career, and Sara could tell that she felt just as out of place among these people as she did herself. Both women were totally bewildered by the lengths some people would go to in pursuit of the dollar.

Realising that nobody wanted to talk about anything other than their salaries, they sought out Louie and found him standing by an enormous Christmas tree, deep in conversation with a big, friendly-looking man.

'Sara, there you are. I'd like to introduce you to William Newman, Bill to his friends.'

'Nice to meet you,' said Sara, taking his hand. 'Please tell me you don't have anything to do with quiz shows.'

'I've been spinning the wheel on *The Money Game* for nigh on fifteen years,' he said soberly.

'Oh, I'm sorry,' apologised Sara.

'Don't listen to him,' laughed Louie. 'Bill's a sports commentator for NBC. The best.'

Bill raised his eyebrows, 'Just because I once said that he slam-dunked like the Archangel Gabriel. The man's a sucker for cheap praise.'

Sara immediately warmed to his low, booming laugh. She stared at his handsome and kind, if weather-beaten, face. From the pepper-and-salt colour of his hair, she guessed he was in his early forties, and in spite of his expensive tuxedo, which was inappropriate to the image, he reminded her of a grizzly bear right down to his big, paw-like hands. Like Louie and Jeanie, he appeared completely out of place in the phoney atmosphere.

'Anyway, enough of the old pals routine,' he said. 'What are you doing here, Sara?'

'I'm not quite sure—'

She was interrupted by a man pushing past her. 'There you are, Louie. Have you thought any more about the cereal endorsement? Kellogg's needs an answer soon.' Putting one arm around Louie and the other around Jeanie, the man said, 'Can we go somewhere more private?'

'You were saying?' said Bill, as Sara distractedly watched the man lead Louis and Jeanie away. 'Sara?'

'Oh . . . what? Sorry. Some people are pig ignorant.'

Bill laughed again. 'You're exactly like Louie said you were.'

'Oh . . . and how was that?' She began to blush, uncomfortable to find that she had been discussed.

'Smart, a little hot-headed and very, very beautiful,' said Bill, his eyes boring into hers.

Sara averted her gaze, uncertain of how to respond. Normally when a man threw her a line – and this was most definitely a line – she'd immediately put him in his place to show him that she was out of bounds. But there was something in Bill's voice, a bass note she could almost feel in her stomach, which made her feel slightly dizzy. Maybe it was just the drink. 'Thank you,' she whispered.

'Louie also mentioned that you were having trouble finding a job,' he said, changing the subject as if he sensed her unease.

'If nothing happens in the next month or so, I'll have to go back to London.'

'That'd be an awful shame,' said Bill with a sincerity which made Sara's heart pound. 'You know, maybe I could help you. I've got some good contacts on the *New York Globe*.'

'Oh – I really wasn't hinting . . .' Everybody at the party seemed to be networking like mad, and Sara probably needed a job more than any of them, but she wasn't looking at Bill Newman as a stepping-stone. What was happening to her?

'I know you weren't,' he said, catching her gaze again. 'You've got the most stunning green eyes.'

Sara half closed her eyes and put her fingers to her lips, unable to speak. Her chest felt tight, as if she were being crushed. She wanted to respond, but for so long she had protected herself against men by burying the woman in her too deep for any man to find. She wanted to run away, to stop the conversation. Just then the clock struck twelve, and Bill took her hand and dragged her into a circle of people drunkenly singing 'Auld Lang Syne'. Close up against him, she could smell his scent, a fresh, soapy smell, as if he had just stepped out of the shower.

They broke away from the circle and Bill put his arms on her shoulders, shouting above the din, 'Happy New Year, Sara. I can tell you now that 1988 is going to be the perfect year.' He bent his head slightly to kiss her but she turned her head so that his lips brushed against her ear.

'Happy New Year, Bill,' she said, trying to extricate herself from his embrace. 'Let's hope you're right.'

He loosened his grip and Sara felt the hard skin of his hands as they ran down her arms. He took one of her hands and began to gently rub her fingers between his, seemingly content for this one small gesture to speak for the whole of his body. At first Sara tensed every muscle in her hand; then she allowed a tentative finger to tap lightly against his hot palm.

'Happy New Year, guys,' shouted Jeanie and Louie from the other side of the room, breaking the spell.

Sara snatched her hand away. 'We should go over and talk to them.'

'Later,' said Bill, sliding his arm around her waist, palming the small of her back. 'Would you like to dance?'

'Wouldn't you rather have a drink?' she countered, trembling as her hips grazed against his.

'Can't,' said Bill, pulling her tighter against him. 'I'm driving.'

Unable to escape, not wanting to escape, she let one hand rest on his shoulder while the other explored the back of his neck. She felt his cheek touch hers. The tiny movement of his eyelash against her temple sent a tremor through her whole body.

'You're shaking,' said Bill, responding by increasing the firmness of his hold.

'Tighter,' said Sara, breathlessly. She could hardly hear the music, hardly see the other guests. Only she and Bill seemed to exist in the room. He kissed her cheek and she closed her eyes, turning her head until her mouth met his. Their lips only touched for a second before Sara jerked away. 'I'm sorry, but I can't do this.'

'Sara, what's wrong?'

'Bill, would you say goodbye to everyone for me? I've got to go.' The impulse to take flight had grown too strong to resist. She pulled away from him and made for the door.

Bill shouted after her. 'Sara, wait!'

To her own utter astonishment, she did. Against all her better instincts, she turned and waited for him to catch up with her.

'If you're leaving, I'm coming too,' he said, picking up his overcoat and wrapping it around her shoulders.

'What about Louie and Jeanie?'

'They'll understand,' he said, opening the door.

Outside the building, the cold air winded her and she pressed up close against Bill. 'I'm sorry for running away from you in there. I don't know, I just panicked.'

Bill smiled. 'Am I that awful?'

Sara shook her head. 'I think it was the drink. What do we do now?'

'I'm driving up to my house in New Hampshire. And I'd. . .I'd love you to come with me.'

Sara was silent. She had never imagined a time when she would want to go home with a man, and she didn't know the protocol. Bill misinterpreted her reaction. 'Hey I'm sorry, I'm going way too fast, aren't I?'

'Bill, it's not that it's just—'

'You don't have to explain. Let me drive you home.'

'I want to explain. Look, I've never done anything like this before and . . .' she paused, feeling that she was pulling down the shutters again. What was there waiting for her back at her apartment? She took a deep breath. 'I'd love to go to New Hampshire.'

Chapter Ten

The headlamps of the red Chevy lit up no more than the flurry of snow in their beam. The blizzard had picked up. Bill pulled over into the car park of a roadside diner.

'Sara?' he said, touching her gently on the arm.

Sara was half asleep, lulled by the warmth of the car and the mellow jazz coming from the radio. 'Are we there?' she yawned.

'I think we should stop for a while. The snow's getting real heavy.'

'Where are we?' she asked, shifting in the warm leather seat. She'd slept off most of the effects of the alcohol and was beginning to question the wisdom of travelling across the state with a virtual stranger.

'It's a diner. Where is anybody's guess. I think I came off the main road a while back. Come on, let's get inside.'

The place was empty apart from a middle-aged waitress who was wiping down the tables and singing along to a country-and-western radio station.

'I'm starving,' said Bill, brushing the snow from his shoulders. 'How about you?'

'Just a coffee,' said Sara, wanting to gather her wits about her again. What on earth was she *doing*?

Bill ordered two coffees and a steak plate. 'You should eat something. We've still got a long way to go.'

'I'm not hungry.' She spoke a little too sharply and noticed the waitress flashing a sympathetic smile at Bill.

'OK,' he said, shrugging his shoulders. 'I guess you think I'm mad driving hundreds of miles on a night like this, but I just have to get out of the city. Of course, a few days in the country and I'm hankering after Manhattan again. I can't stand being in one place too long. It's a big fault of mine.'

Sara's reply surprised her almost as much as it did Bill. 'Are you married?'

His laugh boomed out, ricocheting around the diner and drawing an amused look from the waitress. 'Good God, Sara, what do you take me for?'

Embarrassed, Sara looked away, tracing circles in the steam on the window with her fingers. 'Well, you wouldn't be the first married man ever to try it on.'

'Look, I used to be married, but Jess and I split up five years ago. Before you ask, I have no children, but I'm certainly getting broody in my old age. Which is, by the way, forty-two. I saw you studying my lines. And,' he said, putting up his hand to prevent any interruptions, 'I'm not in the habit of picking up young women. There was simply something special about you and you'll just have to believe that.'

His easy-going sincerity chastened her. 'God, and I talk about other people being rude. I'm sorry.'

'What for? If I were in your shoes, I'd be asking exactly the same questions. And then some. You've got every right to be wary of me.' The food arrived and Bill noticed Sara eyeing his plate. 'Waitress, the same again please,' he said, pushing his meal over to Sara.

'I get like it too,' she said, picking up a fork. It had been hours since she'd last eaten.

'Like what?'

'Being in one place too long. I hate it. I like to be moving on all the time.'

He smiled. As the snow formed a blanket on the Chevy outside, Sara felt herself beginning to thaw.

The house in the distance looked as if it could have been made of gingerbread. Surrounded by snow-covered pines, it stood at the end of a driveway on the shore of a mist-shrouded lake.

'Have you really got a yacht down there?' asked Sara.

'See that jetty over there? Third along from the shore?'

'Bill, I can't see anything.'

'Trust me,' he said, glancing at her mischievously.

Since leaving the diner they'd talked non-stop. About friends and family; about football, both English and American; about films they loved, countries they wanted to visit; their hopes, fears and dreams – everything. Sara was amazed by the speed with which she had come to feel totally at ease in Bill's company. She still wasn't sure he was telling the truth about the yacht, though. 'I don't believe you,' she said. 'And, I don't believe this is your house. It's so beautiful.'

When the car pulled to a halt, as if on cue, a golden retriever bounded up to the driver's door and barked delightedly.

'OK boy, calm down,' said Bill, getting out of the car and ruffling the dog's fur. The dog became even more hysterical, jumping up at Bill's face and knocking him back against the car. Sara climbed out and the dog ran round towards her.

A woman called from the doorway of the house. 'Max! Come here!'

'Who's that?' whispered Sara.

'Mary. She's the housekeeper, but she thinks she's my mother.'

'Is that you, William? Why didn't you tell me you were coming up? The house isn't warmed.'

As they got closer, Sara could see Mary standing on the porch. The sharp voice was matched by her appearance. Her face was hidden under a mass of frizzy grey hair and her body skulked behind a mummifying candlewick dressing gown.

Bill laughed at Mary's annoyance. 'Mary, this is Sara, an English friend who's staying in New York. I want you to use all those extraneous maternal energies on her.'

Mary seemed only too pleased to comply. In gentler tones, she ushered Sara into the house and out of the cold. 'It's typical of William not to forewarn me. I'll get some logs and get a fire going.'

'Please don't put yourself out,' urged Sara.

'Hush child, it's no bother.'

Bill and Mary disappeared and Sara investigated the house. She found the living room, where three comfortably worn tartan-covered sofas were arranged around a large stone fireplace. The wooden walls were stained a pale green and covered with shelves full of books on sport and various awards Bill had obviously won for his work, lovingly polished, she guessed, by Mary. Even without the fire, the room glowed. It seemed so natural compared with the fussiness of her old flat back in London.

Just as she was beginning to wonder where Bill had disappeared to, he came into the living room with two glasses. 'Some mulled wine to warm you up. Sit down.'

Mary brought the logs through, and argued with Bill over who should set the fire. 'Go back to bed,' he said gently, 'I know you think I'm completely hopeless, but I can just about manage a fire.'

Mary finally gave in. 'I'll just sort out Sara's room,' she said as she left.

Bill nodded his head. Sara was confused. In one way she was relieved that Mary was in the house and that she had her own room; at the same time, she was disappointed that Bill seemed perfectly happy with that.

Bill tried to light the fire, laughing at the time it was taking him and conceding that maybe Mary did have a point after all. Once he'd got it going, he came and sat down next to her, wrapping one of his large arms around her shoulders, pulling her towards him. This time, when her mouth found his, Sara didn't want to run away. At first, she was uncertain, her mouth stiff; then, gradually, she began to respond to the urgency of his kisses, her lips parting, allowing their probing tongues to meet. As Bill kissed her, Sara experienced a warm sensation which trickled down her body from her head, through her stomach, around her thighs and down her legs.

As Bill kissed her neck, Sara arched her back, her breath coming in small, excited pants. Tentatively, he placed a hand on the strap of her dress. He looked up at her, waiting for her to give her assent before he continued. She kissed his forehead to let him know that it was OK. He slipped his thumb under the strap, pulling it down over her shoulder. As he began to kiss the top of her breast, she drew his face up to meet hers, wanting to slow the pace for a moment.

'Slower,' she whispered.

Bill ran his fingers through her hair. 'Sure,' he said, kissing her eyelids.

She traced the line of his chin, feeling the faint beginning of stubble. Bill's hand moved to her shoulder, and she shifted, allowing him to pull down the other strap and free her soft, white breasts. She let her hair fall over her face, embarrassed that she was allowing Bill to undress her, but he smoothed back the curls and put his hand under her chin, forcing her to look at him.

'Is this OK, Sara? Please tell me if it's not. It won't matter.'

Crossing her arms in front of her chest, she said, 'It's just . . . I've never done this before.'

The shock registered on Bill's face and he sat back, slightly dazed. 'Jeez, Sara, I didn't realise.'

It was an awkward moment, but Sara, wanting him to touch her again, reached out, took his hand and placed it on her breast. 'I want you to teach me. Show me.'

Bill cupped her breasts and kissed them, taking each nipple in turn into his mouth. Sara finally knew that this was what it was meant to feel like. 'I want to undress you,' he said, nuzzling her breasts.

Shyly, Sara let him pull her to her feet and turn her round. He continued to kiss the back of her neck as his fingers found the zip. The dress fell to the floor and Bill slipped his hands beneath the waistband of her white cotton knickers.

'Are you OK?' he said.

'Don't stop.'

Still behind her, he slid his hands over her hips, pulling the soft cotton down around her thighs. Sara stepped out of her knickers and turned to face him, to show him the body she had never revealed to any man before. Standing before him, naked in the flickering light of the fire, she was surprised to discover that she felt no embarrassment. She touched herself, her shoulders, her breasts, her thighs, as if this undressing was as much of a revelation to her as it was to Bill.

Bill was entranced by Sara's self-discovery. 'You're so beautiful,' he whispered, undoing the buttons of his shirt.

Quickly he took off all his clothes. Sara watched, fascinated, as each part of him was revealed. Bill's body, slightly tanned, was broad and muscular. His chest, covered in a fine mat of brown hair, engulfed Sara as, naked now, he hugged her. She felt as if she were drowning in his body. Taking a deep breath she savoured, once again, his clean, scrubbed smell.

She let him guide her down on to the rug in front of the now-blazing fire.

'You're so beautiful,' he said again, repeating the phrase like a litany. For the very first time, Sara was appreciating her own body and the pleasure it was capable of giving her.

She lay back on the rug and groaned as Bill's mouth travelled all over her body. Each touch of his lips was electric, and as he began to kiss a trail along her thighs, a primal instinct overtook her. She parted her legs, knowing that she wanted to feel his mouth at the very core of her. Pushing her hips upwards, she let out a startled gasp, hardly able to believe the sensations she was experiencing. Hot tears began to run down the side of her face as she realised at last how long she had wanted to savour such intimacy.

Hearing her muffled sobs, Bill stopped and cradled her in his arms, gently rocking her. 'Am I going too fast?'

Finally managing to calm her breathing, she answered him. 'No. It just feels so right. Make love to me now, please.' As Bill showered her with kisses, she felt his hand between her thighs. 'Oh, that's so good,' she murmured, pressing down on to his hand.

Sensing that she was ready, Bill placed a hand on each of her knees and manoeuvred himself in between them. Gently, he entered her. Sara let out a long, low moan. At first she felt a sharp pain, but as Bill thrust into her, she picked up his rhythm, their bodies moving together in perfect synchronisation. As she opened up to him she was overwhelmed by a feeling more sensuous, more complete than any she had ever known; a feeling of total connection to another human being.

Afterwards, they lay there in each other's arms for what seemed like hours, watching the fire slowly die down, every now and again touching and kissing each other as if neither of them was quite convinced that the other was real.

Suddenly, there was a noise overhead.

'Shit, it's Mary getting up,' said Bill, looking at his watch. 'Quick, up the stairs.'

Sara made a dash for the door.

'With your clothes,' said Bill, starting to laugh. Sara giggled too as she ran around the room looking for her underwear.

'That's your room,' whispered Bill, at the top of the stairs. 'See you in five.'

Sara smiled, pleased that they were to be parted only for a short time. They had just managed to close their respective doors when Mary opened hers. Five minutes later, Bill crept into her room and jumped on to her bed on all fours pretending to be Max. She grabbed him by the neck and hugged him until he begged for mercy.

Bill began to move down her body again, running his hands across her flat stomach, admiring the softness of her skin and the firmness of her breasts. The first time, so totally overwhelmed by the newness of the experience, Sara hadn't climaxed, but now she ached for that ultimate sensation. As Bill kissed the most intimate part of her, she felt herself losing control. His fingers explored her, delving deep into her secret recesses, skilfully taking her to the brink, then pulling back, allowing the sensation to subside before starting again, this time drawing her nearer until her nails dug into his shoulders and her whole body went into a joyous spasm.

'Oh my God,' she gasped as pleasure tore through her body.

Five hours later they finally crawled out of bed, neither of them having slept for a second. Mary was in the kitchen. She shot Sara a huffy look, noting that she was wearing one of Bill's check shirts and a pair of his jogging pants. 'I was just about to throw your lunch away,' she said to Bill.

Until Sara smelled the bacon she hadn't realised how famished she was. 'Thank you, Mary,' she said, as she hurriedly tucked in. Mary merely nodded. Clearly the housekeeper didn't approve of what had happened.

'Ignore her,' whispered Bill. 'She's not as shocked as she pretends to be.'

'She's seen all this before, then?' said Sara, once Mary was out of earshot.

'Oh, many, many times,' joked Bill. 'Oh, I almost forgot,' he said jumping up. He went into the living room and returned eventually with a scrap of paper. 'I keep promising to buy myself a Rolodex,' he said apologetically. 'This is Jacob's number. He was the friend on the *Globe* I was telling you about. I'll call him now.'

'You don't have to do that,' said Sara, keen to make it clear that she didn't consider his help to be part of the deal.

But Bill ignored her and called the *Globe* anyway. When he put the phone down, he said, 'He can see you Monday. How does that suit you?'

Sara whooped with delight.

'Can you stay here until then?' Bill asked.

'What about clothes?'

'I don't think you're going to need them for what I have in mind.'

Three days later they drove back to New York. There was an atmosphere of impending doom as they approached the city. Sara was worried that leaving New Hampshire would mark the end of the affair. Bill had said nothing to indicate this, but then again, he hadn't said anything to the contrary, either. Everything had been so perfect but now she felt a sense of rising panic at finding herself in a situation she couldn't completely control.

As the journey neared its end, Sara decided that she had to say something to pre-empt the inevitable rejection. 'I've really enjoyed myself. Thanks for everything,' she offered, trying to sound as businesslike and formal as she possibly could. 'Perhaps we could meet up again some time.'

'Wait a minute,' said Bill. 'Am I getting the brush-off here?'

'I just didn't want you to think that I was expecting anything more,' she lied.

Bill's knuckles whitened as his fingers gripped the steering wheel, 'Is that because you've already got everything you want from me?'

'No, not at all. I just don't want you to feel under any obligation,' she said, gazing out of the passenger window, unable to look at the hurt that was spreading across his face. This was all going terribly wrong. She was trying to give him an easy get-out but all she'd succeeded in doing was making herself look like a woman on the make.

'Where did you say your apartment was?' asked Bill, his voice completely devoid of any emotion.

'Bill, I'm scared,' she blurted out, her heart in her mouth. This was it. This was where she would make an even bigger fool of herself than she had done already, but she couldn't bear to let him walk away thinking she'd used him. 'I'm scared because I think I could quite easily fall in love with you.'

The silence seemed to last forever. Again Sara felt an uncontrollable urge to run away. As Bill stopped the car, she actually had her hand on the door handle ready to bolt, but he reached over and gently took hold of it. He kissed her fingertips, stroking them against his face and said softly, 'Well, I know I could fall in love with you, and it doesn't scare me one bit.'

There was no need for anything more to be said. Bill came back with her to the apartment which, after the house in Lake Winnipesaukee, was more unappealing than ever. She noticed that ice had formed on the window sills and, embarrassed by this, she tried kicking the radiator again, to no avail. It was a truly awful place. Bill rolled up a magazine and gamely took on the cockroaches, which had multiplied in her absence, while Sara took a shower and got ready for her interview. She had hardly turned on the tap before the shower curtain flew back and Bill stepped in beside her, pressing her face up against the tiled wall.

There was no preamble. His need to possess her was overwhelming, and matched perfectly by her need to be possessed. He parted her legs with his knee, his hands clasping her breasts. Sara, desperate to feel him inside her, stood on tiptoe and pushed herself on to him to meet his thrusts.

'Harder,' she implored as the water ran between their bodies.

The sex was swift, almost brutal, but Sara had never felt safer and very quickly their mutual need to say with their bodies what they felt in their hearts was satiated as they climaxed together.

'I'm going to be late,' said Sara freeing herself from Bill's embrace.

Bill followed her out of the shower. 'This place is pretty disgusting.'

Sara threw a towel at him. 'After this meeting, we can go out and choose wallpaper.'

'I've got a better idea,' he said, drying Sara's back. 'How about, after that meeting, you pack up all your belongings and move in with me?'

'What, in New Hampshire?' said Sara, shocked at the speed of events.

'Don't be silly. I have a very cosy loft in SoHo.'

Sara went quiet. This was too much, too soon. 'Don't you think we should slow down a bit?'

Bill looked crestfallen. Sara immediately wanted to take back her words. 'I just don't want it all to go wrong,' she said.

'It will if you keep on worrying about it. The weather forecast alone should make you think about it.'

Sara looked as if she was considering this aspect seriously. 'Do you think the temperature's going to drop any more?'

'Right, you will suffer for that,' said Bill, giving her a playful punch on the shoulder.

Sara battled with herself. She had known this man for only a few days and yet there was already an obvious bond between them. She remembered how she had questioned Kathy's decision to let Joseph move in with her – and they'd been seeing each other for months. Impulsiveness had got the better of her before. She looked at Bill and felt swamped by her feelings for him. He winked back at her and the warmth he created in her told her that impulsiveness was about to get the better of her again.

'OK, I'll do it.'

Bill kissed her. 'You won't regret it.'

She wanted to savour the moment but a glance at the clock on the wall put paid to that. 'God, look at the time,' she said running to her underwear drawer. 'Which department did you say Jacob worked in?'

'He doesn't work in any department, he's the editor.'

Sara's eyes widened. 'So Jacob is Jacob *Weinberg*? Why didn't you tell me ?'

'I thought you'd realised.'

'I don't believe this. I feel sick.'

Bill walked over and took her in his arms. 'The woman who's tussled with a drug-dealer or two feels sick about taking on a pussycat like Jacob Weinberg? Baby, you'll eat him alive.'

Chapter Eleven

The cheerleaders for the New York Giants cartwheeled on to the Shea Stadium pitch, a blur of pom-poms and ra-ra skirts, and the home team supporters leaped from their seats and roared.

'Way to go, girls,' laughed Jay Buckley, noisily draining his Coke through a straw. Then he belched theatrically, lifted his back-to-front baseball cap and scratched his ginger hair. 'Would you look at the pom-poms on the blonde.'

Sara knocked his Reeboked feet out of her seat and sat down next to him in the commentators' box. 'Here,' she said, handing him a hot dog, ketchup dripping down her arm. 'I can't believe you're actually going to eat that.'

Jay put the whole hot dog into his mouth in one go and smiled at her. 'Make it a chilli dog next time,' he said, swallowing and belching again.

Sara looked at him in disgust, shaking her head. She'd met Jay on her first day at the *Globe* when Jacob Weinberg had asked him to show her the ropes. Despite his appearance, he was the paper's hottest reporter and, secure in his position, he was only too willing to take Sara under his wing. The buzz had gone around the paper that she had got the job on her connections rather than merit, and already the knives were drawn. In truth her interview with Weinberg had probably been the most stressful hour of her working life to date. In spite of Bill's reassurances, the editor could certainly not have been described as a pussycat, and the fact that she was Bill's lover made it doubly difficult for her to convince him that she was right for the paper.

'So how does this compare with, what d'you call it, the Arsenal?' said Jay, affecting a Cockney accent.

'Listen to Mr Noo Joisey taking the mickey out of accents,' responded Sara. 'But if Dick Van Dyke seriously wants to know what I think about the NFL, then I'd say it's bigger, brasher, brighter but not necessarily better.' As she spoke the cheerleaders contorted themselves so that they spelled out G-I-A-N-T-S. 'It's too showbizzy. And to be honest, I don't understand the rules.'

'It isn't that different from your rugby,' said Bill appearing behind her and kissing her on the back of the head.

'Hi,' said Sara, reaching up and stroking his face. 'I didn't realise you were there. Where have you been?'

Bill took a seat and adjusted his microphone. 'A couple of pre-match interviews. Look, it's simple. The idea is to reach the end zone with the ball. That's called a touchdown.'

'Only the ball doesn't actually have to touch the ground like it does in rugby,' said Jay, crushing a paper cup on his head.

'The action is organised into a series of plays, and each time the player with the ball is tackled to the ground, that play is concluded.' Bill pressed his hand to his earphone. 'What was that? Sure. Sara, the producer wants a word. Ask Jay to explain.'

Bill left the box and Jay said, 'OK, the blonde with the pom-poms is being porked by the receiver—'

'It's all right, Jay, I'll figure it out for myself,' laughed Sara. Jay's lecherous slob bit was just an act he put on to counteract what he considered to be her English refinement.

'I read your piece on the subway shootings,' said Jay. 'Good stuff.'

'Thanks, but I didn't really have anything to do with it. I'm not used to the way American papers work. On the *Voice* I did much more of my own research. The kind of stuff I'm doing here – well, most of it would probably be done by the subs back home.'

'Do I sense a hint of frustration from our English correspondent?'

'A bit. I didn't expect working at the *Globe* to be so much of a desk job.'

'Give it time. Jacob likes you, you'll get there. Christ, Sara, how old are you? Twenty-one? I didn't get my big break until I was at least, oh, twenty-two.'

Sara realised that impatience was one of her faults. She'd only been doing the job for three months, after all. Why did she always want everything to happen so fast? 'Do you want to go with me to that junket?' Out of the blue, Sara had received an invitation to an informal afternoon cocktail party for the Anglo-American Safety in Sports Committee, to be held at the British embassy. 'I'm sure it's going to be very boring.'

'I don't think they'd be too pleased if I turned up instead of Bill.'

'Do you think that's why I was invited?' asked Sara, her heart sinking a little. 'I thought someone out there had actually watched *Sporting Highs*.'

Bill slipped back into his seat. 'Jay, you're a real – what is that expression of yours, Sara? – you're a real wind-up merchant. I'm sure they invited you on your own merit, Sara. The party was organised by the Brits, and they don't know jack shit about American sport, as you've amply demonstrated. Wow, Jay was right about those pom-poms.'

Jay lifted his hand and slapped the commentator's palm. 'Put it there, my man.'

Bill pulled Sara on to his lap. She pretended to struggle to free herself, loving the way it only made him hold her tighter. 'You're a couple of misogynist Anglophobes,' she said, digging her fingers into Bill's thigh and feeling the hardness of his muscles.

Jay jumped up. 'You two lovebirds will just have to make out without me for a moment. I've got to have a Jimmy Riddle.'

'Dick, what's a "loveboid"?' Sara shouted after him as he left.

Bill laughed and playfully bit her ear. 'You're beautiful. Did I ever tell you that?'

'Millions of times,' she said, feeling his hot breath on her neck.

'Well, here's something I know I've never told you. I love you.'

Sara turned so that they were face to face. 'What did you just say?'

'I love you.'

Since that first night in front of the fire in New Hampshire, she had been waiting for him to say those words. She kissed him long and hard and then said, 'I love you, too. You make me so happy.' Revelling in the moment she kissed him again and was surprised, to say the least, when he burst out laughing. 'What's so funny?'

Bill fingered his earpiece. 'My producer is telling me that he's very happy for the both of us but could I now get the fuck on with the commentary. I guess I should have turned the microphone off.'

'I'm so embarrassed,' Sara whispered.

'About the producer? Well, that makes me real glad I didn't do what I originally intended to do.'

'And what was that?'

'Have "Bill loves Sara" flash up on the scoreboard at half-time.'

'Bill, I would've died.'

'You English are too uptight. You shouldn't be afraid of the big gesture.'

Sara grabbed hold of the microphone and yelled, 'I'm sitting on Bill's lap and I know that he's telling the truth. I can *feel* that he loves me.'

Bill snatched the microphone away laughing uproariously. 'What a classy dame,' he said. Seconds later, he had nudged Sara off his lap, taken a deep breath and said into the mike: 'This is Bill Newman for *Sport in View* coming to you live from Shea Stadium.'

Sara took her seat next to Jay, who, now that the game had started, was taking it every bit as seriously as Bill. The continuous stop-start of the play seemed meaningless and Sara could now understand how Kathy must have felt when she'd taken her to see Arsenal. Bill's commentary scarcely enlightened matters.

'And it's second down and ten. There goes Buck Davies, and I believe he's a religious boy. He had to be to say, "God bless!" when Troy Gates, the Giants' larger-than-life quarterback, just questioned him about his family heritage. And now – oh no, there's a major dog fight.'

On the pitch the referee seemed to be sorting out a contretemps between two players. He was decked out in earphones and holding a mike. It all seemed a bit excessive compared with a red card and a whistle, but even so, he still seemed ill equipped to deal with a grudge match between two extremely large men in crash helmets with panda eyes and shoulder pads that Maggie would have killed for.

'And here's a rocking fifty-four-yard goal attempt.'

She looked at Bill, scarcely able to believe that this wonderful man was in love with her. She knew that every day brought them closer together.

'First and twenty on the ten-yard line and just under two minutes to go until the end quarter.'

'I love you, Bill Newman,' she mouthed to him.

The drinks waiter passed Sara over in favour of a senator's wife standing under the portrait of the Queen. Sara had had enough of being ignored by all and sundry. She marched over to him and took a glass of champagne from his tray with a curt, 'Thank you.' Despite Bill's assurances to the contrary, she had the feeling that she had indeed only been invited because of him. As soon as they had arrived at the embassy, Bill had been whisked off by the American head of the committee, leaving Sara to fend for herself with a lot of fussy Republican wives. To a woman, the politicians' wives wore subdued twinsets and pearls. Sara felt desperately out of place in her rust-coloured pioneer skirt and clumpy hiking boots.

She wandered into another room and was amused to see that the poor souls who usually worked in here had to do so under the beady-eyed stare of a bouffanted Mrs Thatcher, whose chocolate-boxy portrait was the only adornment of an otherwise featureless space.

'Her eyes seem to follow you wherever you go, don't they?' laughed an English voice behind her.

Sara turned to see another familiar face. 'Mr Hargreaves! What an unexpected surprise.'

'It's lovely to see you, Sara.' The politician's voice registered less amazement than Sara's, as if it was perfectly natural that they should bump into each other halfway round the world.

'I didn't know you'd be here.'

'You haven't been doing your homework, have you?' he reprimanded her gently. 'I'm on the committee.'

Sara blushed. 'I'm not really on business today. To tell the truth, I think the only reason I was invited was because our hosts knew I'd bring Bill.'

'Can we sit down for a moment?' asked the politician. 'The flight's really taken it out of me, I'm afraid.' Sara followed him into an interconnecting side room where they sat down on a blue velvet banquette. 'Where were we? Ah yes, we were talking about Bill. Who's he?'

'Bill Newman, a sports commentator for NBC. He's a . . . a very good friend of mine.' Sara still wasn't sure what she should call Bill. Boyfriend sounded a bit inappropriate for a man in his forties; partner was too businesslike and lover a bit in-your-face. And no matter how long she stayed in America, significant other would never sound right.

Stuart leaned over conspiratorially. 'Well, as we're being honest with each other, I have something to admit, too. You were invited for yourself, not for Bill. I should know. It was me who sent you the invitation.'

'But how did you know I was in New York?'

'I contacted Joseph McCabe and asked of your whereabouts,' he said, as if it went without saying that he should want to know where she was. 'He told me about the attack. Absolutely dreadful. You're all right now, I hope?'

'Right as rain.'

He smiled. 'After the programme – which was very good, by the way, and ruffled more than a few feathers – I thought I'd be seeing a lot more of you.'

'I thought the same,' Sara sighed.

'Really? You know I was very much looking forward to going to a match with you.'

There was such an eagerness on Stuart's face that Sara didn't have the heart to tell him she was referring to the job opportunities she'd thought the programme would bring. 'It's not quite the same, but maybe we could go with Bill to an American football match. Come on, I'll introduce you to him.'

'You don't have to,' said Stuart. 'It's lovely just catching up with you.'

'I insist,' replied Sara. 'You'll like him.'

In the main function room, Bill was signing his autograph for a hatchet-faced senator's wife. 'And what is your grandson's name?'

The woman cleared her throat and Sara could have sworn she heard her pearls rattle. 'Dolores.'

Bill laughed and signed his name. 'Here you go, Dolores. It was good talking with you, ma'am.'

Introducing Stuart, Sara put her arm round Bill's waist. A shadow of concern crossed the politician's face as he registered the intimacy between them. Sara could tell that he'd only just realised that they were a couple. 'Bill, this is Stuart Hargreaves, our sports minister. He's a friend of mine.' This last remark made Stuart smile broadly and reassured Sara that she hadn't been too presumptuous.

'Really?' said Bill as if this news were the most wonderful thing in the world. He was a staunch Democrat with little time for right-wing politics – not that anyone would have known it from the politeness with which he addressed Stuart. 'Pleased to meet you, sir. Sara, you didn't tell me you moved in such high circles.'

'Mr Hargreaves was the person who put me on to Ronnie Firetto,' she said laughing.

The politician blanched. 'What do you—'

'I'm only joking, Mr Hargreaves. But you did make it possible for me to work with Joseph. I'm still not quite sure why.' She looked at him quizzically.

'Your, er, girlfriend,' said Stuart to Bill, 'left quite an impression on me.'

'Isn't she something?' said Bill proudly. Sara shot him a look to warn him not to be too patronising.

'Quite,' said Stuart. 'Anyway, Sara, you simply must tell me everything you've been up to since you left England.' From the less than approving way he looked at Bill, it was clear that he meant everything bar their relationship. She couldn't understand why the politician seemed to be so uncomfortable with him. Bill was so easy-going that it was very rare for anyone not to take to him instantly.

'Bill, Ida wants one too!' It was Dolores, approaching with a matching friend.

'Would you excuse me for a second?' asked Bill, raising his eyebrows.

Stuart whispered, 'Sara, could we go somewhere quiet? Ida is Senator Harrelson's wife, and if she spots me we're done for. The senator organised this trip and I've been a bit remiss about thanking him for my invitation. But if I have to speak to him now, I won't get another chance to talk to you.'

Before Sara could protest about waiting for Bill, Stuart had taken her arm and led her back to the room where they'd been sitting earlier. Sara was pretty sure that the politician harboured no unseemly desires for her, but it seemed that the old rake still liked to monopolise the attention of a young woman. What else would explain his coolness towards Bill?

'Has America turned out to be the land of opportunity?' asked Stuart.

Sara thought about the question. 'Not quite. I suppose I shouldn't complain. I have a job at the *Globe*, but I don't feel I've made my mark yet. It's all a matter of luck. I just need to make a splash, but there are plenty of other people on the paper in front of me in the pecking order for the really big stories.'

'So might you go back home to England?'

'No,' said Sara firmly. 'I did think about it for a while just before Christmas, but then I met Bill. The one unequivocally good thing about America is being with him.'

Stuart was pensive. 'That's a shame,' he said finally. 'Oh I don't mean about Bill, I'm very pleased about that. I mean it's a pity that you're not coming back to England.'

Sara wasn't sure that was what he meant at all. 'I'm doing the right thing, I'm sure,' she said, deliberately vague. He could interpret her remark as he wished. Stuart was silent, and the atmosphere seemed heavy, as if there were something he wanted to say to her but couldn't. She decided to make herself clearer. 'He's one of the nicest men I've ever met.'

'Are you sure that he isn't a little too, er, old for you?'

Sara was shocked by his frankness. 'Mr Hargreaves, I don't think that's any of your business. Now if you'll excuse me—'

She made to leave but Stuart took her hand. 'Sara, that was terribly rude of me. You're right. Of course it's none of my business. Please, I didn't mean to offend you. Please stay.'

Stuart's expression was so embarrassed, imploring, that Sara sat down again. She smiled at him, which served only to increase his embarrassment. She tried to lighten the tone of the conversation. 'I don't know much about art, but that's a vile portrait,' she said, looking at the painting of the prime minister on the wall.

'It's a very good likeness,' said Stuart, poker-faced.

She laughed, glad that the unpleasant moment seemed to have passed. 'That's the kind of remark which could get you the sack.'

'She wouldn't dare,' he said, smiling at the very idea that there was anything that the PM wouldn't dare to do. 'So tell me everything about your life in America. Right from the beginning.'

Sara told him all about her abortive modelling career, which made him hoot with laughter.

'I don't think I was cut out for the catwalk.'

'Absolutely not,' said Stuart. 'A complete waste of time for a girl with your talents.'

Sara wondered about the model types she had seen photographed with him over the years. 'Maybe. But if I do possess certain talents, I feel they're being sadly under-used at the moment. And I still feel that I should have got much further into Nash and Firetto. Not getting the full story has dented my confidence. Perhaps I'm not as good as I think I am.'

Stuart looked agitated. 'Isn't that all best forgotten? You did as much as you could.'

'I'm surprised you think that. After all, I've seen the interview you did for Joseph on drugs. Your fervour was pretty inspiring.'

'It's all very well to be an armchair campaigner, but you went out into the battlefield. You could have been killed.'

Sara was touched by the concern in his voice. 'I know. But it's still galling. I know Nash and Firetto are just the tip of the iceberg, and Billy Todd is even more so. I still feel guilty about what I did to him. I suppose I feel if I could get to the bottom of all this it would somehow justify what I did to Todd.'

Stuart appeared lost in his own thoughts, finally murmuring, 'It's always the innocents who really suffer. Those responsible are never brought to book.'

'Sorry?'

'Oh nothing, I was just thinking about someone I used to know who became a victim, rather like Mr Todd.'

'And I still wonder who was supplying Firetto. You know, Mr Big. I've tried to interest the *Globe* in doing something, but the news editor laughs and tells me to come back when I have a story.' She paused. 'What about your contacts over here? Perhaps you know someone who might be able to help me. I've got a name, I just need to see if it's worth following up.'

'What name?'

'Pinto,' replied Sara, rather taken aback by the sharp tone of the politician's voice.

'I don't know, Sara. You seem to have this knack of going right into the middle of the storm. These people are dangerous.'

'I know. Even I wouldn't be silly enough to confront a drug-dealer again. Give me some credit.'

'Well . . .'

Sara sensed that he was struggling with himself. 'Please.'

'I do have one name, a senator who might be able to help you. He has close contacts in the FBI and CIA. If anyone knows anything, he will.'

'Who is it?' asked Sara excitedly.

'Clay Tucker. But, Sara, if he says leave it alone, please take his advice.'

'Mr Hargreaves—'

'Isn't it about time you called me Stuart?'

'Thank you, Stuart. That's twice you've helped me now. I owe you.'

'Don't be silly. It's just that I see something in you, a rare fire. So many people are content to be mediocre. You'll never be like that.

From the moment I first clapped eyes on you at your graduation, I knew you had the potential for great things. Believe me, Sara, being in politics I'm very used to mediocrity, and when somebody like you comes along it's like a breath of fresh air. So if I can help you in any way to achieve that potential, then I will.' Stuart laughed wistfully. 'Maybe it's just the whim of a very silly old man. I never had children of my own . . .' His voice trailed off.

Sara took hold of his hand. 'Thank you, again.'

'Right,' said the politician briskly, 'now that we've dealt with business, what about pleasure? This is just a flying visit, but would it be too much for me to suggest that we meet up again the next time I'm in New York? I'm due back in the summer some time, and it would be lovely to see you. And Bill, of course.'

Sara was immensely touched that he had spoken about her in such glowing terms and she wanted to show him how much she appreciated it. 'I think we can go one better than that. Bill and I are planning to spend part of the summer up in New Hampshire. Why don't you come up and visit?'

'That would be . . . wonderful,' said Stuart. 'Simply wonderful.'

Sara thought she detected an odd hint of uneasiness in his acceptance.

Sara whistled as she put down the phone. At last she was getting somewhere. After several calls which required all her powers of persuasion, she had finally managed to get Senator Clay Tucker to speak to her, albeit briefly. As she read back through her notes, she wondered whether Stuart had used his influence in some way. She remembered the politician's advice that if Tucker told her to lay off, she should. He had, and she wouldn't. As the senator had said, it was a war out there, and as far as Sara could see, the good guys were losing.

Now all she had to do was to persuade Jacob Weinberg to let her investigate her new lead. She walked purposefully across the crowded, bustling room to the editor's office. The door was open, but Jacob didn't notice her standing there until she coughed.

'Hi, Sara. What can I do for you?'

'I've just got off the phone from a contact who's given me some really interesting information on Pinto.'

'Pinto?'

'You know, the person I believe to be connected with Firetto.'

Jacob pulled a face.

'I know what you're thinking – not this again – but just listen.'

'OK. Shoot.'

'From FBI investigations, it's known a third of all illegal steroids imported into this country are from Brazil. It is believed that Pinto, Leonel Pinto, is the mastermind behind it all. He's based in Rio and has never entered the USA – at least, not in any guise the authorities would know about. So far they haven't been able to nail him.'

'Is that all?'

'My contact says—'

'Who's the contact?'

'A senator who wishes to remain nameless.'

Jacob nodded. 'Go on.'

'Some of the steroids come in as Brasquanil, as we know, but they've also stopped several shipments from Brazil and found the drug hidden in plastic fruit or real fruit, hollowed out. The customs don't stop fruit because it's perishable.' Sara was speaking rapidly in an attempt to keep Jacob's attention. 'They believe the money is laundered through a property company, and—'

'And what can we do? I don't want to sound defeatist, Sara, but if the FBI can't nail this guy, what hope do you have?'

'I just . . . I know it sounds stupid, but I know I'm on to something here. Look, it's all very well us going for the Firettos of this world – they're the easy targets – but no one ever does anything about the big operators. When I think of Vince and all the young kids that—'

'OK, OK,' said Jacob, holding up his hands in surrender. 'I'll give you a week, but Jay can dig around Rio.'

'But—'

'That's my final offer. Take it or leave it.'

Sara sat at her desk cursing Jacob Weinberg. Leonel Pinto was her story, and here she was, deskbound, while Jay got to do all the interesting work. Since he'd left for Rio, her investigations had come to zilch. She'd rung every port in the country and none of them took kindly to her suggestion that massive shipments of drugs were getting through in fruit containers. All had pointed out in the tersest of tones that with thousands of fruit shipments coming in every day there wasn't much they could do. 'What do you suggest? We starve New York?' asked the man from the New Jersey Port Authority. He, like everybody else, had refused to meet her. So far, the total sum of her knowledge was that Firetto was still underground and a couple more dealers had been arrested in connection with selling steroids. Big deal, she thought, throwing her pencil on to her desk. The telephone rang.

'Hi, Sara, it's me,' said Jay.

'You must be telepathic. I was just thinking about you having all the fun.'

'I'm not having that much fun, honestly. Look, I can't talk for long, so take this down. Pinto not only exports steroids but he's running a multi-million-dollar cocaine trade in the slums here. Christ, they're totally above the law. They've even got private armies.'

'That's brilliant,' shouted Sara over the crackly line. 'Any proof of the laundering?'

'Proof might not be the right word. I've looked at a number of property companies. It could be one of three or four, or all of them. There's Almeida, maybe Borboleta, but so far I've got nothing we can print. Not that I think Pinto'd sue,' he laughed.

Sara laughed back, trying to disguise her disappointment. Jay picked up on it anyway.

'Hey, I have got something for you, and I can tell you it cost me – or leastways, Jacob – an arm and a leg.'

'What?' she asked excitedly.

'After paying a considerable bribe to a customs official here I've discovered that Pinto is smuggling cocaine as well. You gotta give it to them, they're ingenious. One shipment had it mixed with plaster of Paris and moulded into bathroom fittings. The latest is coke mixed with fibreglass and made into dog kennels.'

'Have you seen them?'

'Hell, no. They've been sent. I'm sure Pinto pays out a lot more in bribes than I've just paid, but the really interesting thing . . .' he paused for dramatic effect.

'Go on,' said Sara, impatiently.

'. . . is that the kennels have been sent to your old friend Ronnie Firetto, and I think I've found where he's gone to ground. My customs man showed me an address where they believe the last shipment was sent.'

Sara looked around for her pencil. 'Give me the address.'

'I'm getting the next flight back, we'll talk about it then.'

'Jay!'

'Sara, I know you, you'll be off to confront the bastard, and I'm not going to be responsible for your death. Bill would never forgive me.'

'OK,' she conceded finally. 'I'll talk to you later.'

Bill was on the veranda having breakfast, dressed only in his white boxer shorts. He didn't notice her immediately, so she stood for a moment, watching him from the doorway, loving the way the muscles on his chest flexed under his skin. They'd made love for most of the night but Sara wanted him again.

'Good morning,' she said, sitting on his lap.

'Morning, sleepyhead,' he said, ruffling her tangled hair. 'Sleep well?'

'For about five minutes,' yawned Sara, pouring herself a glass of orange juice. 'Mmm. It's so quiet here.'

'You've missed the best part of the day. Give it another hour or so and the lake will be crawling with day-trippers. You won't be able to hear yourself think for the noise of power boats. I guess it's the price we pay for living in a beauty spot.'

Sara looked across the lake and the marina to the hills covered in pine trees. 'I guess so,' she said, putting her hands behind her and grabbing hold of the small amount of spare flesh on Bill's waist. 'You're getting love handles.'

'And so are you,' he said, slipping his hand under her dressing gown but finding only the tautness of her stomach. 'Damn! There's nothing there.'

'Keep looking,' she said, as his hand moved up on to her breast. 'Mmm, that feels good. Wouldn't you rather have breakfast in bed?'

'What a wonderful idea,' he whispered into her ear. 'I could get Mary to serve.'

'As long as she's blindfolded,' replied Sara, standing up. 'Oh, sod it. I forgot. Stuart Hargreaves is on his way here. There goes breakfast in bed.'

'Oh, Sara, did you have to invite him? It's so rare for us to have any time on our own. You work all the hours God sends. If I didn't know that your taste was impeccable, I'd have a sneaking suspicion that you were having an affair with Jay.'

Sara laughed. 'Ah, but I am. It gives me something to do in all those lonely evenings when you're at a game. I'm not the only workaholic in the family.'

'OK, so we're two very sad people whose lives are defined by our work. So can you blame me if, on the rare occasion we do get together, I'd rather not share you with some Limey politico?'

'We're not on our own. Poor Mary stays awake half the night waiting for every creak of the bedsprings. She watches me like a hawk. She thinks I'm a gold-digger.'

'That's not true at all. She's told me she's very fond of you.'

'Well, I wish she'd say it to me. You know, I'm quite frightened of her.'

Bill laughed. 'Same here. That's part of her charm. I've just had an idea. If we've got to have Mr Hargreaves here, perhaps we could fix him up with Mary. They're about the same age.'

Mary briefly stuck her head around the door. 'Sara, there's a call for you,' she said sharply.

'Do you think she heard me?' whispered Sara, getting up.

'Yes,' said Bill, gravely.

'I'll have to say something to her.'

'Or there'll be no apple cobbler for you tonight,' he laughed.

He was winding her up. Sara pulled hard on his nipple. 'I'll get you back for that.' She ran into the house and picked up the phone.

'I've just had a lovely chat with Mary.'

Oh dear, thought Sara, recognising her mother's voice. June's opinion of her relationship with Bill was not dissimilar to the housekeeper's, but she was a little more vocal about it. 'Mum, how lovely to hear from you.'

'Well, I know you're far too busy with that man of yours to think of calling me.'

'His name's Bill,' said Sara. It was awful that, for the first time ever, she and her mother were at loggerheads. 'And if you accepted his invitation to come over and stay with us, you'd see how lucky I am to have somebody as nice as he is.'

'You know I won't fly,' said June stubbornly. 'You could have any man you wanted. Why did you choose somebody old enough to be your father?'

Sara was unwilling to go into this with June, but her mother had touched a nerve. Bill was very paternalistic, and she knew herself well enough to know that this was a big part of the attraction. She desperately missed having an older male figure in her life. Bill made her feel very safe. Apart from that, he was incredibly hot in the bedroom, but that was another thing she didn't feel she could discuss with June. 'Let's not go over that again. Oh, Stuart Hargreaves is coming to visit today. Remember I told you that I met him at the embassy? Aren't you impressed?'

'I don't understand why you want to see him,' said June, sounding unusually harsh. 'Honestly, Sara. Since you've been in America, I think you've started mixing with the wrong people.'

A cabinet minister and America's top-rated sports commentator were the wrong people? Sara seriously wondered if her mother was starting to lose it a little. 'Mum, I love Bill and I wish you would make more of an effort with him. It's so unlike you to be like this.'

'It's having you so far away. How can I know that you're all right?'

'I thought you'd got used to me being in America.'

'I miss you. Isn't that what mums are meant to do?'

'Then come over. Look, I'm going to put Bill on the line to try to persuade you.'

'Sara, don't you dare.'

'Too late,' said Sara. She rushed back out on to the veranda.

'Bill, my mother wants a word with the cradle-snatcher who stole her baby.'

Bill stood up. 'You certainly got me back.'

She sat down and buttered some toast, looking down on the jetty, where a group of men were unfurling the sail of a twelve-man yacht. A gopher ran across the yard. She craned her neck to follow its progress. Just then a car appeared at the bottom of the driveway and she jumped up, wondering if she had enough time to go and get dressed. Deciding she didn't, she ran down the drive to meet her guest.

'Stuart! We weren't expecting you so early,' she said, noticing that there were more flecks of grey in his hair than there had been when she'd last seen him.

'Oh, I'm sorry. Is this an inconvenient time? I passed a restaurant up the road. I could go and have breakfast there.'

'Don't be silly,' said Sara taking his hand and leading him up to the house. 'Come in. Bill was really pleased when I told him you'd be coming up. Did you do the drive all in one go?'

Stuart shook his head. 'I started out last night and stopped off at a motel. Dreadful place. It actually *boasted* that the rooms had vibrating beds,' he said, scandalised.

'Did you try yours out?'

'What kind of a man do you think I am?' he asked, sitting down on the veranda. 'Of course I did. My teeth rattled shockingly.'

Sara laughed, trying to picture someone as refined as Stuart on a vibrating bed, and poured him some orange juice. 'I expect Mary's putting the coffee on now. Bill will be out in a minute. He's on the phone to my mother – they're having a slight disagreement.'

'Is everything all right?'

'She thinks Bill is too old—' She stopped herself, remembering what Stuart had said to her at the embassy.

'Your mother is a formidable woman.'

'How do you . . . oh, of course, you met her at the graduation ceremony. She isn't normally like that, though.'

'I'm sure she'll come round eventually, just like I have.'

By now Sara was getting used to Stuart's proprietorial manner.

'I hope so,' she said, wondering how he would react if she were to tell him that June was gunning for him just as much as for Bill.

'She's an impossible woman,' said Bill coming out of the house. Sara was glad to see that he had pulled on a T-shirt. 'Good to see you, sir.'

Stuart shook his hand. 'This place is wonderful, Bill. Such a view.'

'We planned to take the boat out today. Do you sail?'

'A little. I do try to put in an appearance at Cowes every year.'

'I thought we'd fish. How does that sound?'

'It sounds perfect. As long as it isn't putting you to any trouble. I wouldn't want to interrupt your routine.'

Bill looked at his watch. 'We'll leave in an hour or so. Sara, your mother cut me off.'

'I'll call her later. Would you show Stuart where to put his things? I have to get ready.'

An hour later, the three of them walked along the pier and climbed aboard Bill's yacht, the *Mary II*.

'What happened to the *Mary I*?' asked Stuart.

'She packed the lunch,' laughed Bill.

Sara sat on the starboard side, a little hot in her white cotton crew-necked sweater. It would be quite breezy once they were out on the lake. She had plaited her hair and was wearing one of Bill's many commemorative baseball caps. It was obvious from the moment Stuart stepped on board that his claim that he sailed a little was a major understatement. She left the two men to get on with it, glad to see them getting on well.

'Watch yourself!' shouted Stuart as the boom swung out over the water. The sail billowed as it caught the wind and the boat lurched away from the jetty.

When they were out on the open water, Stuart came and sat down beside her. 'I saw your piece on Leonel Pinto and Firetto. Your name seemed to appear in every paper. Excellent. So what's the state of play at the moment?'

'Ronnie Firetto has been arrested. This time no bail,' she said with relief. 'And there's a warrant out for Pinto – not that it'll ever be enforced. But we never got enough proof about the money-laundering.'

'Were there any Britons involved?'

'Why do you ask that?'

'No reason, really. I just thought that, as Nash was connected . . .'

'Nothing showed up in our investigations, but that doesn't mean anything. I think I'll just have to accept that I'll never get the full story on Nash, though it's clear that ultimately his drugs were coming from Pinto.' Sara took Stuart's hand. 'Thank you for putting me in touch with Senator Tucker.'

'I'm glad I could help,' he said, patting her knee. 'Now, I think I'd better go and help that fellow of yours.'

Sara opened a book but barely had she read a page before, lulled by the gentle rocking of the boat, she drifted off to sleep.

When she awoke, she found that a blanket had been placed over her. The sail was down and they were now bobbing around in the middle of the lake. She could hear what was unmistakably an intense argument coming from the other side of the yacht.

'Capitalism doesn't work. End of story.'

'Forgive me for saying so, Bill, but for a man like yourself, earning hundreds of thousands of dollars a year, capitalism seems to be working rather well.'

Sara climbed over the boat, anxious to break up the row.

'Hi. Would you tell your friend here that he's talking out of his ass?' said Bill, looking up.

'Bill! Don't be so rude.'

'He doesn't care. He just called me a deluded commie.'

'Who talks out of his arse,' chipped in Stuart.

She looked at them both and realised that they were enjoying it. Each had a beer in his hand and the several empty bottles lined up on the deck showed that it wasn't their first. She pulled up a chair next to them and opened a beer, noticing that the fishing gear lay untouched.

'We've argued about sport and now we're working through politics,' laughed Stuart.

Bill took a bite out of one of Mary's meatball subs. 'Next, we're gonna see who can pee the furthest. Honey, you want to make sure your legs don't get burned.'

'It's OK, I've put some cream on,' said Sara. Reassured that the argument was good-natured, she sat back in her chair content to say nothing and just enjoy the moment. The banter between the two men was very comforting, the clash of the two accents a reminder of her old and new lives. She felt blissfully happy.

'I want to make a toast,' said Stuart, standing up a little unsteadily. 'To Sara.' As he raised his bottle, a gust of wind blew his panama hat over the side. 'Oh dear. I was quite attached to that.'

Without any fuss, Bill calmly peeled off his T-shirt, dived into the water and retrieved the hat. 'Now you're trying to drown me,' he said to Stuart, shivering as he climbed back on to the boat.

'I'll get you a towel,' said Sara going below deck. A second later Bill followed her down and crept up behind her. 'Ugh. Get off me, you're all wet.' She found a towel and began patting him dry. She pointed to his soaking chinos. 'You'll have to take those off.'

'He's a good man, Stuart. I really like him.' Bill's underwear soon joined his trousers on the floor. 'Come here.'

'Bill, we can't. Stuart can see us.'

'Look at him. He's out for the count.'

Sara looked through the cabin window and saw Stuart slumped in his chair, asleep, his sodden panama once again atop his head.

'I love you,' said Bill and Sara kissed him as she slipped out of her shorts.

June knelt on the kneepad and began weeding the rosebed in her front garden. It was hard work, especially with the heat of the sun on her back, and for the millionth time she thought about how much easier life would be if her husband were still alive to help her. Wiping the sweat from her brow, she sat back and thought about admitting defeat. Perhaps it was time to get a gardener in to do it for her. It was hard to know which was worse: seeing her precious garden go slowly to ruin, or watching a stranger taking care of it.

Her neighbour, Mrs Samuels, popped her head over the fence. 'Lovely weather for it,' she said.

June nodded. 'A beautiful day. Mind you, the weeds love it as much as the roses.'

'They're beggars, aren't they?' said Mrs Samuels. 'Still, if we don't see to them, no one else will. Why don't you pop over when you're finished? I'm thinking of repainting my kitchen and we could go through the colours together.'

'I'll bring some teacakes,' offered June, smiling. Mrs Samuels was a widow, too, a good few years older than June, and what she'd said was right. It was up to them to take care of things. Their husbands wouldn't have wanted to see them become so helpless. If Mrs Samuels wasn't about to let life get on top of her, then neither would June. She set to work on the weeds again with renewed vigour, stopping only when she heard the phone ringing inside.

'Bother,' she said getting up and wiping her hands on her apron.

A rickety old fan whirred on the dining table, making the lounge feel lovely and cool. Just as she got to the phone, it stopped ringing.

'Bother,' she said again, more loudly. She had a feeling that it might have been Sara. June still felt extremely guilty about the way she'd spoken to her daughter the day before. This Bill business was silly, and she wished she hadn't put the phone down on him. She just couldn't help it. The man seemed a little too sure of himself. Those Americans are all the same, she thought, and then laughed at her own ignorance – the sum total of her knowledge of Americans came mostly from musicals, plus the odd GI she'd met in the war.

She was just about to go back outside when the phone rang again. Her heart quickened. If it was Sara she would have the chance to put things right. Her daughter knew what she was doing, and if she was happy, then June would have to learn to accept Bill. Eventually.

'Hello?' The static on the line promised good things.

'June, I hope I'm not interrupting you.'

Why did he have to ring? 'What do you want?'

'I know you don't approve of me seeing Sara, but yesterday we spent the most wonderful day together. I wanted to tell you how happy she is and to try to reassure you that I would never do or say anything that would affect that happiness.'

'When she told me that she'd met you in New York . . .' Words failed her. She just couldn't express how angry and powerless she had felt.

'I just can't let her go from my life, June.'

'You are a truly despicable man.'

'Perhaps so, but I love Sara. I thought you'd understand.'

'Never, never, never,' bawled June, losing the transatlantic rhythm and shouting over him.

'June, calm down. I don't need it, but as you're her mother I'd like your blessing. I give you my word that I'll never tell her anything.'

'Your word means nothing, Mr Hargreaves,' said June, pointedly. She put down the phone and pulled the lead out of the socket. She couldn't deal with two confrontations in one week.

Chapter Twelve

Bill slid back under the candy-striped sheets, balancing a tray. Sara kept her eyes closed just a little bit longer, relishing the luxury of having breakfast brought to her in bed at midday. She'd heard Bill sneaking out of the bedroom earlier and she didn't want to spoil his surprise. Bill rubbed her in the small of her back and kissed her on the cheek. She smiled, realising that he'd already had a shave. No doubt when she opened her eyes she would find him looking scrubbed and immaculate.

'Happy anniversary, darling,' he said, placing a single rose on her pillow.

She sat up just as Bill popped the cork on the champagne. 'You've cheated,' she said, stroking his smooth chin. 'I bet you've even brushed your teeth.'

Bill looked all wide-eyed and innocent. 'Me? Never.' He filled a glass with champagne and then in one swift move, whipped back the sheets and poured it over Sara's bare stomach. She gasped as the cold liquid splashed against her skin and then ran in icy rivulets over her smooth thighs. She responded by grabbing Bill's head and forcing it down over her stomach. The coldness disappeared in a welter of kisses as Bill lapped at her navel. She lay still as Bill's mouth kissed a path down over her hips and came to rest between her thighs. Familiar with every nook of her body, he soon brought her to a tremulous peak. Before the sensation had subsided Sara pushed Bill back on the bed and straddled his hips. He gasped as she bore down and enveloped him. She made love to him until he could control himself no longer and as he climaxed she was overcome by a second, even deeper orgasm.

As they lay naked in each other's arms, warmed by the bright winter sun streaming in through the skylight, Sara smiled, remembering her reservations about moving in with Bill. His SoHo home couldn't have been more different from the miserable Greenwich Village apartment. Like the Village place, it was open plan, but there the similarities ended. The spacious loft was clearly demarcated into different sections, whereas in the other apartment she could practically have cooked breakfast while sitting on her bed. While the New Hampshire retreat was decorated totally in keeping with its rustic surroundings, the white-walled loft paid homage to the modern metropolitan single man. Sparse and functionally, if expensively, appointed, its pared-down style suited Sara perfectly.

Not that she would have cared if she were still battling against the cockroaches and the central-heating system in Greenwich Village, as long as she'd had Bill there to share it with her. Every day she seemed to grow more in love with him, and she had even managed to convince him that the age difference between them was a positive factor. He was fiercely protective of her and very nurturing, but never, ever condescending, despite the wisdom his years had given him. When it came to her career he was endlessly encouraging, calming her down on the many occasions when she came home from the *Globe* on the verge of quitting.

'So what would you like to do now?' asked Bill, aware that he had drifted off.

'First I'd like some champagne,' said Sara. She noticed a wicked leer on Bill's face and added, 'Just leave it in the glass, thank you.'

'No stamina, you young girls. Oh, by the way, these came for you.' He handed her two envelopes.

They were both from England. She could tell from the handwriting that the first one was from Stuart. She opened it to find a Christmas card, wishing her and Bill all the best and, in a hastily scribbled note at the bottom, announcing that he was standing down as a cabinet minister but staying on as an MP. 'I hope he's OK,' she said, half to herself.

'What's that?' asked Bill.

'It's a card from Stuart, saying he's standing down as a minister. I hope everything is all right.'

'Of course it is,' said Bill. 'Everyone deserves a rest some time. Who's the other one from?'

The address on the other envelope had been printed but there was a *Chloe* franking-machine stamp on it. 'It's Maggie!'

Sara had written to Maggie several times care of the magazine, but up until now there had been no response. She was upset that they'd parted on such bad terms. For all the trouble Maggie had caused, she wasn't somebody Sara wanted to lose from her life for good. They went back too far for that. She tore open the envelope to find what was obviously the official *Chloe* Christmas card. It depicted a downmarket version of an upmarket Christmas, right down to the After Eight mints and colour co-ordinated tree, all lovingly captured by starburst photography. Inside there was a hastily scrawled note from Maggie. It read:

Hiya Sara,
   Happy Christmas!
   Glad to hear everything's going well for you. Everything's fabulous here. Job's great – more free lippy than you can shake a stick at. Flat's fantastic – it's near the British Museum, very good for waylaying nice Greek boys looking for the Elgin Marbles. Not that I need to much now – I've pulled a right cracker, called Huw. He owns the Totem Club in Piccadilly (remember when we went there and that bloke put his hand

up my skirt?) so he's loaded. Anyway must dash, Huw's taking me to Marbella for Christmas and I haven't packed the condoms yet!!!

Keep in touch,

Love, Maggie xxx

It was typically Maggie. It was as if their argument had never happened: no apology, no soul-searching, nothing.

'Good news?' asked Bill, reading over her shoulder.

'Kind of. She sounds like she's trying a little too hard to impress, but that's Maggie all over. Still, it's great to hear from her. When people walk out of your life you lose part of your past, don't you think?'

Bill grabbed hold of her, tickling her. 'Hey, let's not get too serious. It's party time.'

'So, didn't I order a drink?' she replied, laughing.

'Sorry, ma'am,' said Bill, reaching for the bottle. 'So what are we doing today? Do you want to go to Ed Teller's party tonight?' Sara mimicked a game-show hostess pointing vacantly at an imaginary scoreboard and Bill laughed. 'I'll take that as a no.'

Sara sipped her drink. 'Jeanie's singing at the Blue Horizon. I kind of said we'd be there. Do you mind?'

Bill thought for a moment. 'No, that'd be perfect. It's just right.'

'Right for what?'

'Um, nothing. That still leaves us the rest of the day.'

'Well, there's still half a bottle of champagne left,' said Sara, pouring the remains of her glass over Bill's chest. 'I think we need some more practice for making babies.'

Bill winced at the coldness of the drink. 'Now remember I want about ten.'

'You'd better be quick. Jeanie's on at eleven o'clock.'

The phone rang and Bill held up his hands, unwilling to move with the champagne running down him. 'Don't answer it.'

'I'd better, it might be work.' Sara leaned over him and picked up the phone.

'Happy New Year, Sara!' shouted June.

Sara put her hand over the mouthpiece and mouthed, 'It's my mother.'

Bill groaned. 'Tell her if she wants grandchildren, she'd better get off the line quick.'

'Shhh,' said Sara nudging him. 'Hi, Mum. You're a little bit early, but Happy New Year anyway.'

'I just wanted to catch you in. It's just a quick call. Is that lovely man there with you?'

'Yes, he's here.' Sara looked at Bill who was signalling that he didn't want to speak to her. 'Yes, I'll put him on.' She handed the phone over and lay back in bed, amazed at the miracle which Bill had worked on her mother over the last few months. From 'that man' to 'that lovely man' in five easy phone calls.

Bill spoke to her for several minutes. 'OK, June, you take care of yourself now.' He put down the phone. 'She wants to know when I'm going to make an honest woman of you.'

'What did you tell her?'

'Straight after I've made a dishonest one of you.'

The Blue Horizon was a jazz club in Harlem. For years it had been a run-down dive but of late the cognoscenti had rediscovered it and it was *the* place to go slumming. Part of its charm, if it had any – and Sara wasn't sure that it did – was that even though it had undergone something of a rebirth, the decor remained unchanged from the days when the place had been occupied by a few heroin addicts, slumped on the broken wooden chairs and nodding along to some third-rate blues singer. To Sara, the fact that now there were men in Armani suits slumped across the broken wooden chairs listening to first-rate singers like Jeanie, didn't make the place any less of a dive. She knew that by next month the in crowd would have moved on to somewhere else and that irked her. Even though she was now moving in that circle, she still had a healthy distrust of pretension.

As she entered the club on Bill's arm several people turned around and waved. Something she hadn't bargained for when she and Bill had first got together was the celebrity which surrounded him. It took her a while to adjust to the fact that he was well known across America. When they were out together, the paparazzi and the autograph hounds were never far behind, and Sara was impressed by the casual way in which Bill dealt with his fame. Because of their work commitments, their time together was precious, but if a fan came up to their table in a restaurant, wanting to shake Bill's hand and for him to pose for a snapshot, he was always obliging and courteous. She respected him for that, knowing that what was a minor inconvenience for Bill would probably be the highlight of the fan's evening. Still, sometimes she did wish she could have him all to herself.

Sara forced a wave back, whispering to Bill, 'You're going to have to go over there and speak to them. What's-her-name's over there, the banker's wife. She said she'd be here.'

'Kitty Shelby? What's wrong with her?'

'She's so rude. Do you know, she even turned my collar over the last time I saw her to see what label I was wearing?' Bill laughed uproariously, squeezing her tight, trying to dispel her indignation. 'It's not funny,' said Sara laughing despite herself. 'I was going to buy a jacket from K-Mart for tonight just to see her face. The shock would have probably killed her.'

In fact, Sara was wearing a creamy brown body under a matching skirt and was looking ravishing. Bill's love had given her extra confidence about herself and her body which hadn't gone unnoticed by the paparazzi and now, in the stories on Bill, the photographs of her were getting bigger and bigger, especially since the Leonel Pinto story. Her own fame amused Bill no end, but the fact that she was almost always described as a former model irritated the hell out of her. Couldn't she just be a beautiful journalist?

'I'll tell you what,' said Bill. 'I'll fend off the old harpy while you go and find Jeanie. She's probably backstage.'

Sara was grateful for the chance to escape. 'Backstage' was rather a grandiose name for the converted toilet where she found Jeanie, putting the finishing touches to her make-up. Jeanie planted a big kiss on Sara's cheek, leaving a smudge of brown lipstick. 'Hiya, girl, glad you could make it. Oops, let me wipe that off,' said Jeanie, looking around for a cloth. 'Is that big hunk of a boyfriend of yours out there?'

'He's talking to my good friend, Kitty Shelby,' said Sara, raising her eyebrows.

Jeanie clapped her hands delightedly. 'Straight here from the plastic surgeon. Have you seen her eyes? She went in Mrs Wasp and came out Madame Butterfly.'

Sara knew that she could always get through these celebrity functions as long as she had people like Jeanie around to deflate a few egos. 'You're terrible. Speaking of hunks, where's yours tonight?'

'Ed Teller's. He couldn't get out of it. But I've warned him. Miss Grand Canyon will be there but he'd better not go looking for gold in them there hills.' In unison, the two women pointed vacantly, screaming with laughter as they parodied the hostess. 'Listen, honey,' said Jeanie, 'I'm on in five minutes. I'll see you afterwards.'

Back in the club, Bill had secured them a table, thankfully well away from Kitty Shelby. The lights went down and Jeanie appeared in a single spotlight, the sequins on her dress flashing furiously in the glare. As soon as she opened her mouth there was complete silence. The whole audience was in total rapture. When she finished her first song everyone leaped to their feet and the roar of applause was unbelievable.

'Thank you, you're so kind,' said Jeanie when they'd quietened down. 'This next song is for my two dear friends over there, Sara and Bill.' Once again the audience erupted. There was no need for surnames – everybody in the club knew who they were. 'It's an old standard, but hell, I'm in a schmaltzy kind of mood tonight.'

Jeanie launched into 'That Old Black Magic,' and Bill embraced Sara, kissing her passionately, oblivious to the fact that most of the audience was watching them. 'I love you.'

Towards midnight, Jeanie took a break for the countdown to the New Year to begin. Bill stood up taking Sara's hand. 'Come outside, I need to talk to you.'

'But we'll miss the countdown.'

'There'll be another one next year. This is important.' Bill led her outside and they stood, freezing, in a garbage-filled alleyway. 'I needed to be alone with you.' There was such a serious tone in Bill's voice that Sara half knew what he was about to say. She rubbed her bare arms to keep warm but she wasn't sure if it was the cold or her nerves which was making her shiver.

'Sara, you know that I love you. And I'm pretty sure that you still feel the same way about me . . .' He was struggling to find the right words. 'I can't believe how difficult this is.'

Her heart was in her mouth. She knew Bill wanted her to say something to make it easier, but she couldn't speak.

He reached into his pocket and produced a gold ring set with a single emerald. 'Sara, will you marry me?'

It was several seconds before she could compose herself enough to answer. Fighting back tears of joy, she whispered, 'Yes.'

At that moment, a cheer went up inside the club, the noise rebounding around the alleyway, as 1989 began.

Chapter Thirteen

For Sara, mid-March was about the best time to be in New York: after the harsh winter winds had stopped blowing along the avenues and before the unbearable heat of the summer incited people to riot. This morning she had an extra reason to be happy. Any minute now Kathy would be arriving with Joseph. Sara hadn't seen her in over a year, and the previous weekend she had been delighted when Kathy had called to say that she was coming over with Joseph for a shoot. With her wedding planned for July, Sara had thought that she would have to wait until then to see her best friend.

Bill had wanted to get married sooner than July, but the network wouldn't give him a month off until the summer. They thought it would be good publicity if Bill and Sara arranged a big, splashy affair, but Sara was adamant that she wanted close friends and family only. Bill was happy to agree – he didn't even intend to invite his real family. Bill had two older sisters of whom he seldom spoke, saying only that there was bad blood between them. As far as he was concerned, he said, Mary was his only family.

Sara looked at her watch. The plane had landed hours ago. She'd offered to meet them at the airport but Kathy had said not to bother as she didn't want their first hour of their reunion to be held in a traffic jam. It was typical of Kathy to want the mood to be just right.

Going from room to room, Sara made sure that everything was just so, something she had already done at least twenty times. In the bathroom, she checked herself in the mirror. She was wearing a coffee skinny-rib T-shirt and a short brown tartan skirt over oatmeal leggings. Her hair was down, the blunt tips falling to the small of her back evidence of a recent expensive cut, and her make-up was of her favoured 'barely there' variety. She looked at her reflection, trying to decide if she needed to put on something more dressy, but just then the entryphone sounded. She ran to answer it.

'Send them up,' said Sara, strangely nervous. A year was a long time. Whenever they spoke on the phone, Sara had a snapshot of Kathy in her head looking the way she had the last time they'd met, but people changed – and Kathy changed from week to week. But appearance was neither here nor there. What if they had nothing in common any more? She undid the impressive array of locks on her front door (an absolute necessity living in New York, and such a contrast to the one rusty latch which sufficed most of the time in Lake Winnipesaukee) and looked out into the corridor expectantly as the elevator door opened.

'Sara!' screamed a woman in sunglasses, a red headscarf and enormous hoop earrings, running down the corridor as fast as her red platform shoes would allow, a short cherry fun fur falling off her shoulders to reveal a Stars-and-Stripes mini-dress.

'Kathy?' said Sara, unable to conceal her amazement.

'I told her it was too much,' shouted Joseph, far more recognisable in a black suit. He had let his blond hair grow and was wearing it swept back, but otherwise he looked just the same. He struggled along the corridor with the suitcases as Kathy ran into Sara's arms and kissed her.

'It's so wonderful to see you.' Kathy took off her sunglasses. 'It's my "Pepper Anderson salutes America" look. Customs loved it. What do you think?'

Sara studied her friend. Even with her sunglasses off she was barely recognisable under her thick seventies-style pearly make-up. 'Who's Pepper Anderson?'

'Angie Dickinson in *Police Woman*. Do you know nothing about the culture of your adopted homeland?'

Sara kissed Joseph and began to laugh. 'I'm so glad you two are here.' She showed them into the apartment and once bags and coats had been sorted out, they sat around the kitchen table while Sara brewed some coffee.

'You're still looking at me strangely,' said Kathy. 'Oh – it's the coloured contact lenses.'

'That's it!' exclaimed Sara. 'You've got blue eyes.'

'I never know who I'm living with,' said Joseph, gulping down his coffee. 'Sara, I know this is going to seem incredibly rude, but I've got to shoot off. I've got a meeting with some possible backers.'

'You don't have to go this minute,' said Kathy. 'They just said to call them when you were in town.'

'I need to see them as soon as possible. You know how it is.'

Sara sensed the tension between the couple. 'Kathy, it's fine. Bill won't finish work until late this evening and I thought we'd all go out for a meal.'

Joseph was halfway to the door. 'I've got your number. I'll call to let you know where I'm going to be.'

After he'd gone, Kathy said apologetically, 'He's had this idea for a documentary on Cuba that he's been trying to get off the ground for ages. Channel Four isn't commissioning as much as it was and he hasn't had a programme for a while. This trip just about cleaned him out so he needs to make it work for him.'

'Forget it, it gives us a chance to talk.'

'Not for all that long, actually. The reason I wanted Joseph to stay here is that I've got to go off soon. There was a baggage mix-up and half the clothes for the shoot are on their way to Mexico. I called the photographer to let him know that we might have to delay things for a couple of days and he threw a fit. He was expecting to start this morning. It's the same old story. I'm going to have to go over and massage his ego a bit.'

'You need to slow down,' said Sara, noticing that Kathy's face under all the make-up was looking tired and pinched.

Kathy reached into her handbag and produced a packet of cigarettes. 'Tell me about it,' she said, lighting up.

'What are you doing?'

'This?' Kathy waved her cigarette. 'I know it's disgusting. Everybody in my business smokes. You're around it all the time and gradually you find yourself buying them. I sound like a pathetic thirteen-year-old, don't I? "All my friends are doing it."'

'I think you need a proper break, to get yourself together a bit.'

'You know, we take on these high-powered jobs and they're meant to facilitate these wonderful lifestyles. But I don't have a lifestyle because I'm never away from my high-powered job.' Kathy's voice had an unfamiliar querulous tone. 'I wasn't going to do this shoot – I was going to let Carly organise it – but Joseph insisted we came. And of course, what Joseph wants, Joseph gets.' She stopped talking, noticing the look of concern on Sara's face. 'It's probably just the jet-lag talking. I'll be fine once I've had a shower and I've sorted the photographer out. Honest.'

Sara said nothing.

Kathy walked into Sheldon Stone's studio knowing that there was going to be trouble. Deciding that the Pepper Anderson outfit lacked authority, she'd changed into a tailored black suit, her tomato-coloured hair gelled into rigid waves.

'I never work with people I don't know, especially some snotty British bitch,' screamed the man on the phone, unaware of Kathy's presence.

'Is that me you're talking about?' said Kathy icily. This could only be Sheldon Stone himself.

'Oh, you're here, then.' There was no hint of an apology. Sheldon flicked his long mauve hair back from his face to reveal a scowl. 'Now that you are we might as well see the models. They're waiting downstairs.'

Kathy detected a gleeful note in his voice. She understood why as soon as she walked into the room. 'Sasha, what the hell have you done to your hair?' she asked, trying to keep the fury out of her voice.

Sasha, the main model for the shoot, had had long brown hair when Kathy had chosen her. In front of the fashion editor now sat a cropped blonde, grinning as she sucked on a boiled sweet – her lunch. 'It was for another job.'

'And you couldn't be bothered to get on the phone and tell me? Thanks.'

Sasha looked at the floor.

'Aw, leave her alone,' said Sheldon. 'It won't make any difference.'

Kathy contemplated sacking them both on the spot but the thought of finding replacements was too much to bear. She'd just have to hope for inspiration. 'OK, let's sort out the timetable. Have you thought about what we're going to do, Sheldon?'

Sheldon looked disdainful. 'I'm inspired by the moment. I don't *think* about anything.'

One, two, three, counted Kathy, summoning up all the cool she could muster. 'Well, that's transparently obvious, Sheldon, but on my time and money it would be very helpful if you at least tried exercising whatever it is you have under those beautiful magenta locks of yours, if only for a moment.'

Sheldon glowered and pulled out some Polaroids he'd taken of Sasha earlier. Kathy had to admit they were fantastic.

By the end of the afternoon some of her anxiety had lifted. The clothes had been located and were on their way back to New York; Sasha wasn't that bad and even Sheldon had started to loosen up a bit – though she did find it disconcerting that when she took him out for tea he insisted on walking through the streets in his bare feet. 'It's a bit cold for that, isn't it?' she asked.

'Style hurts,' declared Sheldon.

'I thought we had reservations for Tony's,' said Bill as the cab pulled up outside Biology.

'We did, but Joseph phoned and said that he wanted to see this,' said Sara.

They got out of the cab and Bill eyed the queue. 'It's all kids. What are we doing here?'

'Apparently, it received the honour of a two-page spread in *Interview* this month. Joseph and Kathy are style freaks.'

The doorman recognised Bill immediately. 'Good to have you here, Mr Newman,' he said letting them jump the queue and making Sara feel a little conspicuous.

Sara immediately spotted Kathy at the bar. 'There she is,' she said, waving.

'I've been standing here trying to get served for ages,' fumed Kathy. 'Why we couldn't have gone out for a meal, I don't know.'

'Kathy, this is Bill,' said Sara with difficulty as she was jostled by the crush at the bar.

'Good to meet you at last.' Bill shook her hand. 'Would you like me to try my luck?'

'Thanks,' said Kathy as he pushed his way to the front. 'Let's just have one here and go somewhere else. It's horrible.'

Sara looked round. The bar's designer had taken a chainsaw to several classic American cars and had bolted the pieces to the raw concrete walls. 'I thought you'd like it here. It drips—'

'Condensation,' supplied Kathy. 'And in about half an hour some awful thrash band is going to come on.'

'Where's Joseph?'

'Over there with Sheldon.'

Sara looked over and saw Joseph deep in conversation with a strikingly odd-looking man with purple hair and bare feet. 'Who's his friend? He doesn't look like a financier.'

'Oh that's the great Sheldon Stone,' said Kathy, 'the photographer. He's brilliant, but you'll absolutely hate him. I wasn't going to bring him along but Joseph wanted to meet him.'

Bill reappeared clutching a bottle of champagne and four glasses. 'There goes your honeymoon,' he said. 'You'd think with the prices they charge they could at least plaster the walls.'

They joined Joseph and Sheldon and while the photographer took a quick breath in between monologues Sara made the introductions.

'I was just talking about *The Colour of Pomegranates*,' said Sheldon.

'Red and yellow, the last time I looked,' said Bill, uncorking the champagne.

'It's a film, you dumb jock,' sneered Sheldon.

Bill looked at him impassively. 'By Sergo Paradjanov, tracing the life of the eighteenth-century Armenian poet, Sayat Nova. Mr Stone, you don't appear to have a glass.'

Sheldon produced a bottle of bourbon from his pocket and took a swig. 'I don't need one.'

'So tell me all about the wedding,' interjected Kathy quickly.

Sara was cringing. It was going to take a superhuman effort to make this evening work. 'Well, I'm a bit worried about the dress. Our housekeeper begged me to let her make it.'

'She used to be a seamstress,' said Bill. 'It'll be fine.'

'Do you know what style you're going for?' asked Kathy.

'I'm not sure,' said Sara, 'but if it's left up to Mary it'll be turn of the century farm-hand.' Bill laughed and she was glad to see that Sheldon's remark had left him unruffled. 'Maybe while you're here you could come up with some designs.'

'Something Empire line would look beautiful on you,' said Kathy, having to raise her voice as Sheldon was banging his fists on the table. 'Has your mother agreed to fly over?'

'She's started taking the Valium already,' said Bill. 'Hey, Joseph, do you think you'll be able to make it?'

'Definitely,' replied Joseph. 'Maybe I could film it for you. I bought a Hi–8 this afternoon. They're so cheap here compared with England.'

Kathy put down her drink. 'Would you excuse me?'

'Are you OK?' asked Sara, but Kathy was already on her way to the toilet. 'I'd better go after her.'

In the toilet, Kathy was smoking furiously. 'I'll be out in a minute. And then I'll tell that Sheldon to piss off. This was such a mistake.'

Sara put her arm around her friend. 'You deal with people like that all the time. That's not what's bothering you, is it?'

'I can't believe Joseph bought that bloody camera. We talked about it on the way over and I told him it wasn't a good idea.'

'You know what boys and their toys are like. With Bill it's

pre-1960 World Series baseball cards. He spends a fortune on them.'

'Well, I'm sure it's his own money. I paid for that sodding camera. I told you he hasn't worked for months. Did I also tell you we're exchanging contracts soon on a house in Chelsea? It's used up all the money my dad left me. But Joseph thought it would be nice to live there. He needs the right environment to house all those Paul Smith suits.'

Sara could feel Kathy shaking. 'This doesn't sound like the Joseph I know at all.'

'How well did you ever know him? He was all over you because he knew he was on to a good thing. He never stopped you doing any of that research. He knew damned well how dangerous it was.'

'That's a bit unfair. I chose to do it.'

'Yes, and I thought I'd chosen that house. It's amazing the way Joseph gets you to do all these things for him and then manages to convince you that it was your own idea. Tomorrow he'll have me believing that it was my idea to buy that camera.'

'Then you're going to have to sort this out with him. Lay a few ground rules.'

'I know, I know. But when I try to talk about it, he turns on the charm and I always end up feeling like a complete bitch. Sara, I feel so worn out.' Kathy took a deep breath. Now she had the chance she wanted to tell her friend everything. 'And his schmoozing all the time for money drives me mad. There's no discernment – that's why he's all over Sheldon. Worse, in London he's taken to wining and dining Fran Best.'

'Fran Best?'

'You know, the bitch who used to make my life hell at *Mariella*. Now she's a commissioning editor at Channel X. God knows how she did it – on her back probably,' said Kathy bitterly. 'Anyway, he says I've got to make an effort to get on with her or it'll be my fault if his next project doesn't get off the ground.' Tears were beginning to form in her eyes. 'And you know what's the worst thing about it all? I still really love him.'

Chapter Fourteen

In June, Sara and Bill spent a weekend at Lake Winnipesaukee so that Mary could make the final alterations to Sara's wedding dress. Working from the sketches Kathy had made while she was in New York, Mary had delicately stitched the entire ivory silk dress by hand, confounding all Sara's misgivings. The result was stunning.

'You'll look like a princess,' said the housekeeper, carefully folding the dress in layers of tissue paper and putting it into a box.

So long as the dress still fits on the day, Sara thought, keeping her misgivings to herself. She had missed her last period and was finding it difficult to face food without being overcome by nausea. Hopefully, her doctor in New York would confirm her suspicions when she visited him tomorrow. She was dying to tell Bill, but she wanted to be certain before she did so.

'Come on,' shouted Bill from outside. 'I want to beat the traffic.'

'I wish you would have the wedding here,' said Mary, carrying the box downstairs. 'It's so much nicer than the city.'

'I know,' said Sara. 'But it's too difficult to organise. There are people flying in from all over the place. How would we get them up here?'

'I suppose you're right.' They walked out on to the veranda. 'Bill, would you keep the noise down? Decent people are still trying to sleep.'

'Sorry,' said Bill in a stage whisper.

The housekeeper put the precious dress into the back of the car. 'Don't you go peeking now, Bill.' She took hold of Max, who desperately wanted to get in the car with his master.

'Bye, Mary, and thank you again. It's beautiful,' said Sara.

Mary took the dog into the house and Sara started up the car. 'Bill,' she said as they drove away, 'I got a letter from Kathy asking if it was OK to come over for two weeks.'

'Sure, if she cheers up a bit,' said Bill looking up from his notes. He often used the journey back to New York to go through his broadcasting schedules so that they could have their weekends off all to themselves. 'I didn't see her smile once that week.'

'Don't be so horrible. You know she was having a really bad time with Joseph. Things have calmed down a lot since then. He's got the money for Cuba now. We're lucky we don't have those kind of financial problems.'

Bill reached over and massaged her neck. 'We're lucky for so many reasons. Not just money.'

Sara smiled at him. 'I love you so much.'

'It couldn't possibly be as much as I love you.'

Sara slipped a classical tape into the deck and drove on in silence, letting the music soothe her while Bill scribbled away on his schedule. This was one of their perfect moments together. Being with each other but needing to say nothing, feeling everything. Her life was wonderful – her man, her job, her apartment. And, hopefully, soon a child to make her happiness complete. Everything was just perfect. Who said that you couldn't have it all?

It was her last thought before the truck appeared, bearing down on them from the other side of the road. She twisted the wheel wildly, trying to escape from its path, but whichever way the car turned the lorry seemed to turn as well, until it was all but on top of them. Suddenly, all she was aware of was the car spinning and spinning. Then darkness.

'It's a car crash. We think she has a fractured pelvis and there's also a nasty gash to the back of the skull. We've put her on a drip but her blood pressure's dropping fast.'

'Name?'

'Driving licence says Sara Moore.'

'Doctor, her pulse is increasing rapidly.'

'Right. We have severe internal bleeding here. Have we got a match on her blood type yet?'

'A positive.'

'Set up a transfusion.'

'Blood pressure still dropping.'

'We're going to have to do a scan. Come on, people, let's move it. Sara, can you hear me?'

'Bill?'

'Sara, you're in hospital, do you understand?'

'Yes, Bill.' Sara had the sensation of floating. She tried to work out why Bill was shouting at her. Why was she so groggy?

As the doctor looked at the picture on the screen he shook his head. 'She's pregnant – or rather, she was. Her uterus is bleeding. I'll give her another hour. If the internal bleeding doesn't stop we'll have to open her up. How old is she?'

'Twenty-two.'

'Let's try to save her uterus. Is that understood?'

Sara floated in and out of consciousness, dimly aware of the ghostly voices and the glare from the overhead lights.

'The transfusion's not working. Get her ready for surgery.'

Sara felt a pinprick in the back of her hand.

'Come on, people, we're going to have to move quickly.'

'Sara, can you hear me?'

Sara shook her head, trying to shake off the fog. Her head throbbed and every joint ached. Her mouth felt parched, her lips swollen. She lifted her hand to her mouth and discovered that it wasn't the shape it used to be.

'What's happened? I want Bill,' she pleaded to the shadowy figure swimming in front of her. She could barely form her words.

'Sara, there's been an accident. You're in hospital.'

Sara was vaguely aware of tears falling down her puffy face and a sense of panic rising through her bruised body. 'Bill, please get Bill.'

'You should get some rest.'

'I want Bill.' Sara had intended to shout but her voice sounded like a young boy's breaking.

'Please rest for now.'

Sara tried to lift her head. A hand was firmly placed on her shoulder and a voice came from above her. 'He's not here, Sara.'

'Where is he? He wouldn't leave me like this.' She could hear her own voice quivering.

She heard a sigh and then another voice answering the one above her. She couldn't quite make out what they were saying.

'Tell me what's happened,' she screamed, using up the little strength she had left.

Someone nervously cleared their throat. 'We did everything we could to save him. I'm sorry.'

'What do you mean? I don't understand.'

The hand on her shoulder pressed a little harder. 'Bill's dead,' came the voice.

Sara opened her mouth to scream but nothing came out. Again the blackness swallowed her up.

'Keep her under sedation.'

For three more days Sara drifted in and out of consciousness. When she finally came round, there was a doctor waiting at her bedside.

'Sara, can you hear me?'

She looked at the man dressed in green, her eyes not quite focusing. 'I had a terrible dream. Bill. He's not dead, is he? It was a dream?'

There was a deathly silence but it said everything Sara didn't want to hear. As she tried to get out of bed a searing pain ripped through her abdomen.

'Please stay still. You've had an operation.'

'An operation. What for? I'm fine.' She paused, dimly remembering voices discussing a pregnancy. 'My baby? What's happened to my baby?'

'There's no easy way to say this.' The man stopped speaking and took a deep breath. 'I'm afraid the baby died as a result of the accident. You were haemorrhaging and we had to carry out an emergency hysterectomy. You would have bled to death otherwise. I'm terribly sorry.'

'Bill wanted five boys and five girls,' Sara said blankly.

Sara was not able to attend the funeral and only after several weeks of convalescing was she finally allowed to go home. Her face was still ink-blue, the internal bruising still scorched her insides and one side of her beautiful hair had been shorn clean away. Mary came to collect her and the old woman looked on the verge of collapse. From the redness around her eyes it looked as if she hadn't stopped sobbing from the moment she'd heard of Bill's death.

'My poor, sweet William. Why did it have to happen to him? The house is so empty and Max is pining away.' Mary saw Sara starting to shake. 'I'm sorry,' she said, realising that she was only making things harder for Sara. 'How are you, child? You look so thin. Are you sure you're ready to come home?' she said, hugging Sara close to her.

'I can't feel anything,' said Sara. 'There's nothing.'

When they arrived back at the house Sara followed the housekeeper into the living room. It was so strange not having Bill there to greet her and in that moment it hit her that she would never see him again. Still she fought off the tears until she spotted Bill's baseball glove on his writing desk and for the first time she allowed herself to cry.

For days she wandered from room to room, consumed with grief. At times she forgot she would never see Bill again and would call out his name. She knew that along with the baby and her womb, she had lost her heart and she doubted it could ever be found again. That hurt was much worse than the physical pain of the operation.

Mary looked after her as if she were her own child and the two women locked themselves into their grief, minimising their contact with the outside world. Until, about three weeks after Bill's death, Sara received a letter asking her to vacate the house as Bill's sisters intended to sell it. He never did get around to making a will, Sara thought numbly.

Along with the letter came a number of newspaper cuttings. Sara picked up the first one. There was a big picture of Bill and a smaller one of her. For a while she just stared at Bill, tracing the outline of his face with her finger, biting her lip to stop herself crying. When her eyes stopped blurring, she read the cutting and soon got the gist of the story. The implication was that she was a young, silly English girl unused to driving on the right and that her inexperience had led to the accident. This was only a mild accusation: other newspapers which had once covered her relationship with Bill in glowing terms were even less kind. Some even suggested that she and Bill had been arguing when the accident happened. The truck driver, who had escaped completely unscathed, was reported as saying that Sara had, at great speed, driven into his path.

'It's not true,' she shouted as she threw the papers down. Not for the first time she wished she had died with Bill. She replayed that car crash in her head for the thousandth time. Surely she was right in remembering that the lorry had come towards her. But perhaps she was just trying to find excuses; what the papers said must be right. All that she was imagining now was an excuse not to deal with her guilt. She had probably been driving too fast.

She went into the kitchen and showed Mary the letter and the cuttings. 'I'll pack my things now.'

'Please don't listen to them, child. I know you did your best,' said Mary, helping her up the stairs.

Sara said nothing, finding no comfort in Mary's words. Within twenty-four hours, she was on a plane bound for England.

Chapter Fifteen

England, January 1990

June looked at the tray outside Sara's bedroom door and saw that she hadn't eaten a thing. 'Sara, love,' she said trying the handle and finding it locked, 'are you sure that you don't want any of this? You should eat something.' There was no answer. Wearily, June picked up the tray and took it into the kitchen to throw the food away. Her daughter had barely left her room in the past week. It had been an awful Christmas, and as for New Year's Eve – the anniversary of the night on which Bill had proposed to Sara – her daughter had calmly told her that she wanted to die.

Six months had now passed since Bill's death but instead of gradually coming to accept it, Sara was sinking ever further into depression. June was worried that she might never get over it. Why should she, when June herself had never fully recovered from losing her own husband? June had resigned herself to spending the rest of her days on her own but she couldn't let that happen to her daughter. A tear trickled down June's cheek as she thought about the grandchildren she would never have.

Over the previous few months the neighbours had been wonderful, especially Mrs Samuels, running errands or coming to sit with Sara whenever June had to leave the house. Of course they knew all about grieving, but they had memories of long and happy lives with their husbands to sustain them. What could a bunch of old women say that would bring comfort to a younger one whose happiness had been so cruelly cut off before it had really begun? June had tried to persuade her daughter to go up and see Maggie. If anyone could shake away the blues, June thought, it was Maggie, but Sara wouldn't even speak to her on the phone. She sensed that there had been some sort of disagreement, but she was sure it was nothing that the two of them couldn't sort out. Kathy had come to stay with them the first couple of weeks, which had helped enormously, but now she was back in London and planning a trip to Japan. It was something to do with a new magazine launch. Sara was pretty vague about the details. Sara was pretty vague about everything now.

Sara needed to find some sort of purpose to her life again. June knew how important work had been to her daughter in the past but whenever she brought up the subject, Sara would say that she didn't care if she never worked again. All she wanted to do was lie in her bedroom with the blinds drawn, twenty-four hours a day. Often June was woken in the night by the sound of her daughter crying. It couldn't go on like this. She couldn't have her brave, beautiful daughter ending up like her, living on memories and scared of the world. It would be too tragic a waste.

Something had to be done, but she'd tried everything she could think of. Only one last resort remained. June did something that she vowed she would never do. She picked up the phone and rang Stuart Hargreaves.

'June, what's happened? Is she OK?'

'Of course she's not OK.'

'Let me come down there. I could make it in three hours—'

'How many times do I have to tell you? I don't want you here.' Having Sara living with her, June was at least able to prevent Stuart from getting anywhere near her daughter. 'But I do need your help.

I don't know what I can do for her any more. She needs to start rebuilding her life.'

Stuart was silent for a moment. Then he said: 'Leave everything to me. I know that asking for my help must have been very difficult for you. Thank you for doing it.'

Sara stood in the front porch watching the rain, a blanket wrapped around her shoulders. All she wanted to do was sleep but her mother had tried to persuade her to go for a walk, saying that she would feel better for the fresh air. Letting the blanket fall to the ground, she stepped out into the garden and just stood there, motionless, oblivious to the weather. Soon the rain had slicked down her short, shapeless hair and soaked through the fleecy cotton of the shirt she was wearing. It was Bill's shirt, one of the only things of his which she had brought home with her. She began to shiver, the tremors of her shoulders the only sign that she was able to feel anything at all.

She heard the phone ringing but made no move to answer it. Instead, she surreptitiously took a bottle of sleeping pills from her pocket and undid the cap to see how many she had left. She slipped two of them into her mouth, wondering if she had the energy to go to the doctor's to renew the prescription. She couldn't bear the thought of not being able to sleep. Only when she slept could she escape the living nightmare of all those empty years which lay in front of her.

'Sara, my love,' called her mother, 'you're wanted on the phone.'

'I don't want to speak to anyone,' she said, walking back into the house.

'It's Kathy,' lied June, knowing that she was the only person Sara would talk to.

Sara stopped at her bedroom door, wondering whether she could face talking to her friend. She knew that Kathy would feel that she had to cover up her excitement about being in Japan out of consideration for Sara. 'Tell her I'll speak to her next week.'

June held up the phone expectantly, desperation evident in her voice. 'It must be costing her ever so much money.'

'All right, I'm coming.' Sara walked into the living room and took the phone from June's hand. 'Hello, Kathy?'

'Hi, Sara, it's Simon Holland.'

'What can I do for you, Mr Holland?' asked Sara, scowling at her mother.

'I just wanted to say I was sorry. About what happened.'

The sleeping tablets were taking effect and Sara couldn't even begin to work out how Simon had heard about the crash. She didn't respond to his condolences. When people offered her their sympathy, Sara always felt as if she were expected to say something that would somehow smooth over the awkwardness of the moment. People wanted to hear that everyday things were getting a little easier, but she couldn't tell them that. It simply wasn't true.

'Sara, are you there?'

'What? Oh thank you for calling, it was very . . . thoughtful of you.' This was as much as she could manage. 'I've got to hang up now.'

'Hold on, that's not all I wanted to say. I want you back on the *Voice*.'

Her mind getting foggier by the minute, Sara was half aware that her mother must be behind this call in some way. 'Thanks, but I don't need your sympathy.'

Holland laughed. 'It isn't that often I get accused of being sympathetic. Look, there's a freelance job here if you want it. Have a think about it.'

Wordlessly, Sara handed the phone back to her mother, walked into her bedroom and locked the door.

Perched awkwardly on a squeaky red leather sofa, Sara looked around Maggie's living room with dismay. For days, her mother had pestered her about taking the job and finally she gave in, lacking the energy to fight. It didn't make any difference to her anyway. She didn't care what she did. She had made no comment when June had arranged for her to stay with Maggie while she looked for somewhere to live, but the second she walked through the door of the Bloomsbury flat, she knew that she had made a big mistake.

The living room was cramped and airless. The sofa was pushed tight into the corner to make space for Maggie's multi-gym. Scattered around the floor among the piles of old newspapers and overflowing ashtrays were several tinfoil trays, each containing the remnants of a take-away meal. Chinese, Indian, Italian – a gastronomic United Nations lay on the dirty carpet, the conflicting stale aromas mixing with Maggie's ever-present patchouli to form a noxious scent which hung over the room like a mushroom cloud. Back to square one, thought Sara, staring at the dirty cream woodchip-covered walls.

Maggie brought their drinks in. 'To a new start,' she said, as she clinked her glass against Sara's. 'I love this flat. You can practically spit on Oxford Street from here.'

Sara smiled weakly, trying to take in the changes that had been wrought in Maggie in the two years since their last meeting. Her over-peroxided hair had gone past white into near green, and her angry red scalp showed clearly through the gelled strands. But that was nothing compared to the weight loss. There didn't seem to be a spare ounce of flesh anywhere on Maggie's body and her skin had taken on an unhealthy translucence. She was wearing a low-cut top which revealed deep indentations in her breastbone and her hip bones protruded, almost painfully, beneath her tightly belted jeans.

'My office is just around the back of John Lewis, so it's perfect.'

'What's it like being a hotshot features editor?' Sara asked.

'It's OK,' replied Maggie, not sure whether Sara was being facetious. '*Chloe*'s doing well, selling over two hundred thousand a week. I enjoy telling people what to write about, but I'd like to move on and work for one of the dailies. Women's magazines seem the soft option, more for the Kathies of this world.'

It's not only her skin that's transparent, thought Sara, but she let the remark ride. Instead she pointed at the home gym. 'So what's this?'

'Isn't it fantastic?' answered Maggie, a smile breaking across her face. 'I use it in the morning before I go to work and sometimes in the evening if I miss my class.'

'Don't you think you're overdoing it a bit?'

'No, I don't.' A scowl replaced the smile. 'I suppose you'd like it better if I still looked like I did at school.'

Sara left a fraction of a second's silence before answering to leave Maggie in no doubt that, if she had to choose between the two extremes, she did think her friend had looked better in the old days. 'Of course not.'

'To be honest, Sara, a few hours on that thing wouldn't do you any harm. And a couple of tanning sessions wouldn't go amiss.'

'Touché,' said Sara, acknowledging the truth of this remark. 'So when will I get to meet Huw?'

'Tomorrow morning. He doesn't get in until late from the club.'

'He lives here, then?'

'Most of the time. His fat pig of a wife got to keep the house. Didn't I mention it?'

Sara shook her head, more in despair than in answer to the question.

Hearing Maggie leave the flat, Sara got out of bed. She'd run out of sleeping tablets and had been awake for hours but she had stayed in her small room, not wanting to see Maggie punishing herself on the home gym. Slipping on an old pair of shorts and a T-shirt, she decided that if she was going to stay in the flat, even for just a week, she would have to clean it from top to bottom.

The living room smelled no better than it had done the night before. She tried opening the windows but they'd been painted shut. She went into the kitchen to find a knife to jemmy them open and cringed at the sight of the sink, overflowing with pots and pans. She could feel her feet sticking to the lino and, as she gingerly fingered something unidentifiable but definitely green in a frying pan, she wondered why she hadn't vetoed her mother's suggestion. For someone who barely ate, Maggie certainly managed to make enough of a mess. Sara decided that the washing up was in greater need of attention than the windows, but as she bent to look under the sink for some washing-up liquid somebody came up behind her and grabbed her hips.

'I can tell from that great ass that it's definitely not Maggie down there. Hi, Sara.'

Slapping the hands off her, Sara stood and turned round, blazing with anger. The man standing in front of her wearing a floral silk dressing gown and an inane grin was obviously Huw. 'Do you mind?'

'Not at all,' he said, in an accent that floundered somewhere between a Los Angeles film set and a Hemel Hempstead public school. He was chewing gum over-dramatically like an extra in an amateur production of *West Side Story*, and every so often his tongue escaped between his over-full lips and lolled suggestively. 'How about making Huwie baby a nice cup of coffee? I'm absolutely zonked. And if you throw in some breakfast I might even let you rub my feet.'

Sara gripped the handle of the frying pan and fought the urge to smash it in his greasy face. She looked at him in disgust. Huw got the picture, and, with a suit-yourself shrug, he reached over her and flicked the switch on the kettle. As he did so, the cord on his dressing gown came undone. 'Whoops,' he said, making no attempt to cover himself up.

'Oh, please!' said Sara. 'Put it away.'

Huw put his hands on his hips and let out a juvenile snigger. 'See anything you like?'

'Grow up,' snapped Sara, wishing that she hadn't held back with the frying pan. How old was this man, anyway? From his shoulder-length streaked blond hair and perma-tan skin she couldn't tell whether he was a haggard thirty-five or a deluded fifty. Either way, it was clear that mentally he was firmly stuck in adolescence. Where did Maggie find them? 'It's a bit too early in the morning for all this,' she said, edging past him.

'It's never too early,' Huw shouted after her as she slammed her bedroom door.

'It couldn't have been as bad as this,' said Kathy, looking around the squalid bedsit. 'Sara, you can't live here. Come on, get your things, you're coming home with me.'

'It's fine here,' said Sara, lying on the single bed, staring at the patch on the ceiling where the plaster was missing.

'I'm sorry, Sara, but it's not. It's disgusting.'

Sara watched as Kathy tried to light the gas on the two-ring stove squashed up by the sink. 'You'll have to put something in the meter to get it to work. I don't use it much. There's a bottle of gin in the cupboard above you if you want something to drink.'

Kathy opened the cupboard and found the gin and two mugs. She'd arrived back from Japan only a few hours ago and in an uncomfortable telephone conversation with Maggie, she'd discovered that Sara had moved out after only a fortnight. When her cab had pulled up outside the rundown block of flats in King's Cross, she had thought Maggie was winding her up and had given her the wrong address. She'd been amazed when her friend had answered the door.

Handing Sara a mug she said, 'Please, come home with me. Joseph would hate it if he thought I'd let you stay here.' She placed a hand on her friend's shoulder. 'You'd save on rent. It would help you pay off your medical bills from the States.'

'How are things between the two of you?' asked Sara, changing the subject.

'Good,' said Kathy guiltily, feeling that it was probably not what Sara wanted to hear. 'Joseph's got some work, which always helps. Anyway, we'll talk about that some other time. When you've moved in.'

Sara gulped down the neat gin as if it were water. 'I can't. Look, Maggie's flat was pretty disgusting, but that wasn't the only reason I moved out. She didn't tell me she had her sleazy boyfriend living there. It's just too difficult to be around other couples at the moment. It makes me feel bitter and jealous.' She started to cry. 'It's pathetic, isn't it? I never thought I'd get to a point in my life where I'd be jealous of Maggie.'

Kathy sat down on the bed and cuddled Sara, not knowing what she could say to make her feel any better. 'You've just got to give it time.'

Sara pulled away. 'I know,' she said, wiping her eyes. 'Kathy, would you mind going now? I need to be on my own.'

'I don't want to leave you here,' said Kathy, on the verge of tears herself.

'Please,' implored Sara.

Kathy stood up. 'OK. What's the phone number here?'

'There isn't one,' said Sara. 'You'll have to call me at work.'

'I'll call you tomorrow,' said Kathy, opening the front door.

Sara shrugged her shoulders, staring at the ceiling again.

When Kathy called the *Voice* the next day, Sara told Dave Teacher to say that she wasn't there. She did the same thing the following day. And the day after that. It wasn't just Kathy – she avoided her mother and Maggie too. Occasionally, to prevent them making a fuss and turning up on her doorstep, she had to speak to them. She'd make vague promises to see them soon, assuring them that everything was all right and that life was getting back to normal. She didn't want anybody to see that her life was far from normal. She kept up the pretence at work, but when she got home in the evening she would climb straight into bed, put the light out and wish the world away.

She felt that her will to succeed, even to carry on at all, had died with Bill. She knew he would have hated to see her so self-pitying and lethargic. Sometimes it took all of her strength just to get out of bed again in the morning. Those were the times when she'd dreamed that Bill was still alive. She would wake up hopeful and happy and then the realisation that he was gone forever would come crashing down on her again more heavily than ever.

'There you go, Sara,' said Dave Teacher, putting a cup of coffee down in front of her. His nickname for her, Bruiser, had been quietly dropped out of respect. 'You seemed miles away.'

Sara looked up from her computer. 'Thanks, Dave. It's just this article. It's driving me mad.'

Dave read over her shoulder. '"Breast Op Changed My Life." Do you want me to have a look at it for you? You're wanted on the phone.'

'Would you tell them I'm busy? Who is it, anyway?'

'It's Stuart Hargreaves, and I've already told him that but he said he'd wait on the line until you weren't. Come on, Sara, he's clogging up my phone.'

Sara hit the save button and sighed. She picked up Dave's phone and replaced the handset on its cradle, then sat down and continued her article.

> Before her new boobs, she never had the confidence to wear a halter neck. Says Sally: 'Paul loves my new slinky look. He can't keep his hands off me!'

For several minutes she just stared blankly at the screen as if the words she had written were some unintelligible hieroglyphics. Then she closed the file in total despair. Remembering the news coverage of the accident, she had to ask herself whether she was any better than those journalists who had mercilessly ripped into her. She couldn't honestly say that she was. She needed to write about something that was completely detached from people's sordid confessions and petty obsessions.

Dave's phone rang again. He answered it, then put his hand over the mouthpiece. 'Stuart Hargreaves again. Sara, will you sort this out? I can't play these silly games all day.'

Sara shook her head. 'I don't want to speak to anyone.'

'Oh, for God's sake.' Dave removed his hand. 'I'm sorry, she's in a meeting. OK, just let me get a pen. Right. Right. Eight o'clock? Sure. I'll tell her. Bye.' He handed Sara an address. 'Mr Hargreaves is expecting you for dinner at eight.'

The Italian restaurant off Charlotte Street was authentic without being a caricature of all things Italian. Not that Sara gave a damn. She was angry that her hand had been forced. She'd tried to ring Stuart back but it had been his turn to be 'unavailable'. For the rest of the afternoon she toyed with the idea of standing him up; finally, she decided that she would go, but only to let him know that she wasn't staying and that he needn't waste his evening.

Stuart was there waiting for her, having already ordered a bottle of wine. 'Sara, how lovely to see you. Thank you for coming.'

'I'm not staying,' she snapped. 'And you shouldn't have presumed that I'd come at all.'

Stuart looked taken aback. 'I'm sorry.'

She turned to leave and then hesitated. Why was she running away from him? Why was she trying to shut out all the people who wanted to help her? Most of her life was destroyed in that accident and now she was doing her best to ruin the little that was left. 'Stuart, it's me who should be saying sorry,' she said, taking a seat.

The politician took her hand. 'It does get easier, believe me.'

However good their intentions, she was so tired of people telling her that. 'How do you know? Your wife is still alive.'

'Cynthia?' snorted Stuart. 'The woman could walk under a bus tomorrow and I wouldn't lose a second's sleep over. . . That was in very poor taste. Forgive me.'

Stuart rarely mentioned his wife and Sara was surprised at the vehemence with which he did so now. 'It's OK. I can't expect people to walk on eggshells with me for the rest of my life.'

'No, you can't. Sara, despite what you think, I do understand what you're going through. Once, a long time ago, there was somebody I loved very much. I was already married to Cynthia, but I would have given up everything for this woman. One day she just walked out of my life. Just upped and went, and I never saw her again. She didn't die, but she might as well have done. I had to go through exactly the same grieving process. That feeling of loss never goes away. Even now I can still feel it, but, bit by bit, it becomes a manageable pain.' He smiled. 'One morning you'll wake up and Bill won't be the first thing you think about.'

His last sentence touched her very deeply and she knew then that he did understand. 'I just can't imagine that morning ever coming.'

'But it will,' insisted Stuart. 'I know it makes you feel guilty to think that. But the memory of the love you shared with him won't fade away when it stops hurting. It will become a strong, positive part of your life. It's a subtle change. You stop dwelling on the loss and start being glad that that person was part of your life for whatever short space of time. So many people go through their lives without ever experiencing what you and Bill had together. I know it doesn't seem so now, but you were lucky.'

Sara could feel the tears welling up.

'Something has to change, Sara,' continued Stuart, his voice gentle and pleading. 'You can't go on with what is to all intents and purposes a living death. Bill gave you so much. You owe it to him not to waste your life. Celebrate what you had with Bill, but don't let it affect your chances of ever experiencing that happiness again. As I said, take it from one who knows what he's talking about.'

'Did you let it affect your happiness?' asked Sara knowing the answer already.

Stuart nodded sadly. 'But I'm an old man, and it's too late now to have any regrets.'

Even though he spoke eloquently about grief, she got the feeling that his own sadness was insurmountable.

'You're young, you have the whole of your life ahead of you. There'll be new loves, maybe one day a family.'

Sara winced and looked away. Stuart didn't know about the hysterectomy or the baby. 'Maybe,' she said, not wanting to dwell on the subject. 'I'm feeling really hungry. Do you think we could order?'

'Of course. I do go on rather, don't I?' He called the waiter over and ordered for both of them. When the waiter had gone he said, 'You know, your friends are very important at times like this. And I'd like to think that we are good friends now.'

'Yes, I think we are.'

'So what about taking me up on that previous invite to see Camden play?' he said smiling. 'My friend is one of the owners and there's a testimonial in a couple of weeks.'

'I'm not sure I'm up to it.'

'Please.'

'I'll think about it. Anyway, who's the friend, Stephen Powell?'

Stuart blanched. 'Oh, good God, no! It's Peter Barratt.'

'You never hear much about him. He's a rather silent partner, isn't he?'

'When you meet Stephen Powell, you'll realise that's sometimes the best way to be.'

Chapter Sixteen

One Wednesday evening in May Sara found herself pushing through autograph-hunters and devoted fans to get to the entrance of Camden United's boardroom. Once inside she looked around for Stuart. As if to place football on an unfamiliar intellectual plane, the room had been decorated in mock mahogany, like a library. Black and white photographs of all the teams since the creation of the club in 1920 adorned the walls, while a glass cabinet groaned under the weight of all the cups they had won.

'Glad you could make it,' said Stuart, coming over to her. 'Let me introduce you to Peter.'

Peter Barratt was an art dealer by profession and looked more like a cricket fan than a typical football-club owner. There was a gentleness about him that would have been more appropriate to the slowness of a summer's day on a village green than to ninety minutes of frenzied action on the football pitch. 'Very pleased to meet you,' he said, in a quiet voice that matched his appearance.

Before Sara could reply, a coarse, Mancunian voice broke through the group. 'Still can't keep your hands off the young girls then, Hargreaves?'

Sara knew the voice belonged to Stephen Powell, chairman of Camden United who, unlike Stuart, looked vastly better in his publicity shots than he did in real life. Although he was slightly taller than Stuart, the middle-aged Powell was losing the battle of the bulge in a big way. His face reminded Sara of a pug and from the sneer he was wearing, Stuart was the bone he was intending to worry.

'This is Sara Moore. She works for the *Sunday Voice*,' said Stuart coldly.

'Don't let the wife find out you're sleeping with the opposition.' He looked Sara up and down. 'I see you're still going for the same type.'

Sara was unnerved as Powell studied her intently.

'Yep. Still going for the same type,' he repeated.

Stuart squared up the chairman. 'One day, Powell, events are going to force that smirk clean off your face.'

Sara was shocked at the animosity between the two men. Stuart's gentlemanly façade had completely fallen away and she was sure that, had he been twenty years younger, he and Stephen Powell would have been brawling on the floor by now. Stuart excused himself and, still trembling, walked off towards the toilets.

Sara turned to Peter Barratt. 'What on earth has happened between those two?'

Peter shrugged. 'I have no idea. Forget about it and let me get you a drink.'

When Stuart returned, the angry red glow had almost disappeared from his face. 'Sara, I'd like to offer you my most sincere apologies for that little scene. Powell is what we, in my day, would have called a cad,' he said, trying to make light of the situation. 'I'm sorry if he offended you.'

'Not at all,' she replied. 'But let's hope the game is a little more friendly.'

Both Peter and Stuart laughed as they escorted her to the directors' box.

'How much do you reckon the match will raise for Ian?' she asked Peter as they took their seats.

'Looking at the crowd, I'd say about two hundred thousand.'

'That'll help his retirement.'

'I don't think he'll be retiring for a while. Unfortunately, Ian will be lucky to see any of the money after he's paid off his gambling debts. It's not a lot to show for ten years.' Peter stopped. 'This is all off the record, Sara. I'm telling you this as a friend of Stuart's, not as a journalist.'

'Pity,' she said, and then she smiled to allay Peter's fears. 'I understand.'

As the match began Sara saw Stuart shed another piece of his stiff-upper-lip image. He had a boyish enthusiasm for the game not, Sara noted a little sadly, too dissimilar from her father's. He relished every tackle, every save with a positive zeal. Sara was reluctant to use the word undignified, but such ebullience seemed slightly unbecoming in a former cabinet minister. However, she found it very endearing and it reaffirmed just another one of the many things that she loved about the game: football was a great equaliser.

Stuart jumped out of his seat. 'Run faster, man!' he shouted. His command degenerated into a splutter as he clutched his chest and began to cough violently.

Sara leaped up and put her hand on his elbow. 'Sit down, Stuart,' she said softly.

'Don't worry,' he said, catching his breath.

'Stuart, sit down for a while. Please.'

He acquiesced. 'I'll be fine in a minute.'

'Are you OK?'

'Another late night in the House. Just ignore me.'

Sara found that hard to do. Suddenly Stuart seemed very old. Since she'd got to know Stuart better, she'd become very fond of him. She was aware of a certain vulnerability about him which made her want to look after him. She felt drawn to him, as if he needed her to care for him.

Half-time came and Stuart was looking composed once more. 'I think a brandy would warm us up, don't you?'

There were very few women in the boardroom and those who

were present were mostly wives there on sufferance. Once again she reflected on the 'boys' club' mentality surrounding the game. It seemed that the only places open to women in football were the terraces and the tearooms. She couldn't imagine the ruckus it would cause if women ever had the temerity to want to *play* alongside men.

A noisy argument interrupted her reverie. She looked across the boardroom to see where the commotion was coming from.

'I'll bloody well have another drink if I want to,' slurred a female voice. 'A double whisky, if you'd be so kind.'

As people moved discreetly away from the altercating couple, Sara saw that the woman was arguing with Stephen Powell. She guessed that the woman in black ski pants and a leopardskin Lycra top was in her mid-fifties and having a problem accepting it. Her bloated face seemed to have remnants of an earlier beauty but it was hard to tell under the layers of blusher and mascara. Her brittle red hair, backcombed from its black roots to breaking point, teetered perilously atop her head.

'If you don't want a scene, get me the bloody drink,' she said once more to Stephen, through gritted teeth.

'Can't you keep it down for once?' hissed Stephen. 'You're a sodding embarrassment.'

'That's right, blame me. You always do.' Whether from the drink or the admonition, the woman then burst into tears and ran from the room.

'Who was she?' asked Sara.

'That's Stephen's poor unfortunate wife, Jackie,' replied Stuart. 'You're obviously much too young to remember, but back in the sixties, Jackie was quite a famous model. However, time – and, more significantly, Stephen – have been rather unkind to her, hence the drink problem. It's hard to believe, but at one point she was right up there with Jean Shrimpton, Twiggy and the Butterfly . . .'

'Stuart?' Sara touched his hand. 'You seemed miles away.'

'Sorry. An old man daydreaming. Now, where was I? He bullies Jackie relentlessly. No wonder the poor woman drinks.'

'Are there any more characters here I should know about?' asked Sara, feeling for Jackie.

'Not for the present. Let's get back out to the game.'

The second half started. Ian Sumner ran on to the pitch and the cheers from the crowd rose to a crescendo.

'Is he staying on?' Stuart asked Peter.

'I think he wants to stay as long as possible. What's waiting for him after football? A career in insurance at best. I think there's still a year to run on his contract. He's not a bad player and he's young enough for us to renew it.'

'He's playing better today than he has for—' Before Stuart could finish, Ian had scored. The home crowd rose in appreciation and roared. 'Perhaps there's life in the old dog yet.'

'I expect that's what he's hoping we'll think.'

The final whistle went and as they turned to leave Sara noticed Jackie Powell slumped in her seat, asleep. Gently shaking the woman's shoulder, she asked, 'Are you all right?'

'What? Who are you?' Jackie quickly wiped the dribble from the side of her mouth.

'Sara Moore. I'm with Peter and Stuart. Are you all right?'

'As right as I'll ever be married to a bastard like that.' Noticing Sara's surprise at her frankness, she reassured her: 'Don't worry, love, everyone knows about him and me. You're just new around here.' She held out her hand for Sara's help. 'Did we win?' she asked, laughing.

Sara nodded her head.

'At least he won't be in a completely foul mood, then. What did you say your name was again?'

'Sara.'

'Thanks, pet, for waking me up. Stephen would've left me there all night.' The slur was still there but Jackie was doing a good job of sobering up.

Stuart came up behind Sara. 'Do you mind if we get out of here?' he said, seeing Stephen walking towards them.

'I don't blame you, Stuart,' laughed Jackie. 'Go on, get going. I'll distract his attention.'

As they left, Sara turned to see Stephen berating Jackie and shaking a finger at them. Stuart's car was waiting outside.

'Can I give you a lift?' asked Stuart. 'Or have you brought your own car?'

Sara hadn't driven since the accident. She wasn't ready to face getting behind the wheel again. 'That would be great.'

Relaxing in the back seat of the Daimler, Stuart said, 'I'm sorry about that episode with Stephen Powell. I did warn you!'

'What was it all about?'

Stuart pointedly ignored her question. 'So how's the job?'

'Awful. I hate it.'

'I must admit, with the exception of you, tabloid reporters aren't my favourite group of people.'

'I'm no better off now than I was the day I left college. Worse, in fact. At least I was inspired then. I hate writing about scandals.'

'Then write about something you do like.'

'Such as?'

'Surely the answer should be staring you in the face. Why not write about football?'

Chapter Seventeen

Sara stood on the half-empty terrace, trying to ignore John Rudman, a cocky young reporter who was trying to needle her, but it was hard to lose herself in the dismal football being played by Boreham Rovers. At least there was somebody there to talk to, whatever the quality of the conversation. The week before, at a Brunswick game, she'd been the only reporter in the press box – the club had even welcomed her over the tannoy.

Over a year had passed now since Bill's death and Stuart's prediction was beginning to come true. She still thought about Bill a lot, but he was no longer the first thing on her mind when she woke up in the morning. Nowadays it was her career. Her relaunch as a football writer had been less than spectacular. Simon Holland wasn't prepared to let her cover more than the odd match, and only then when no male alternative could be found. She was one of his favourite freelancers and he constantly pleaded with her to go back to the sex stories. But Sara was adamant: she would be a sportswriter or nothing. As a result, her workload was dwindling and she had still hardly made a dent in those American medical bills.

Stupidly she had imagined that she would be covering the big games; the reality was that, more often than not, on the rare occasions when she did get work, she ended up at Third Division matches, and unless a centre forward took out an Uzi and gunned down the opposition, she'd be lucky to get more than a couple of lines into the paper. But if the matches themselves were way down the League, the insults she had to endure from the other, male, writers were in the First Division.

'I'm not being sexist,' said Rudman, who was obviously going to be, 'but you have to admit that women are not built for football.'

Sara looked him up and down slowly. Rudman was a pie-faced, chain-smoking seventeen-stoner. 'And you are?'

The other men laughed. 'She's got a point there, John,' shouted one.

'Yeah, but at least I've played in my time. She hasn't.'

'So what you're saying, John, is that only doctors should write medical pieces and lawyers the legal articles?' Sara tried to hide her anger: it didn't do any good. But she'd just about had enough of this little boys' club which so desperately wanted to keep her out, worried that if women came into the sport all of its blokeish mystique would disappear. As if on cue, the men closed ranks.

'You watch out, John,' one of them roared. 'You know what they say about redheads.'

Saved by the half-time whistle, Sara followed the others to phone in her first-half match report. The play was as grey as the weather and the boring 0–0 score was unlikely to change. It looked as if, apart from the introduction, she would be adding nothing to her story after the final whistle.

She had just put the phone down when Stan, one of the old boys who looked after the press bar, came and stood next to her.

'Do you think we've done enough sandwiches, Sara?'

Sara looked at him incredulously. 'Well, they'll do for John. But I don't know what the rest of us will eat.'

The dingy press bar of Boreham Rovers did nothing to improve her spirits. The first time she had been there Stan had asked her if she was there to make tea. Predictably, the others thought this was hysterical and Stan had played up to them ever since. As she ate one of his curling ham sandwiches the thought of articles headed MAN MARRIES MOTHER-IN-LAW didn't seem so bad after all.

'I've got to get a permanent job. I can't stand this hand-to-mouth existence much longer,' moaned Sara, ensconced in the warm kitchen of Kathy's Chelsea home.

Taking some jacket potatoes out of the Aga, Kathy nodded. 'Well, you know the offer still stands. If you want to move in here you—' A firework exploded outside, making her jump and drop the potatoes. 'Those bloody kids. They've been letting off those things for weeks.' She bent down to pick up the potatoes, wondering how she could best break her news to Sara. 'You don't mind them with a bit of fluff on them, do you?'

Sara shook her head. Clearly it was more than fireworks that was making Kathy so jumpy. 'They'll be fine. Kathy, is everything all right between you and Joseph?'

'Actually, I've got something to tell you,' replied Kathy, sure that she was blushing. She lit another cigarette, despite having just stubbed one out. Ever since Joseph had asked her, she'd been worried about how Sara would take the news. 'We're getting married.'

'Are you sure you know what you're doing?' blurted out Sara without stopping to think. It was an awful thing to say, but she couldn't take back the words now. She just stared at her friend in silence.

Kathy sat down at the table. 'If anybody else but you said that, I'd be furious.'

Sara bowed her head, unable to look Kathy in the eye. 'I just meant, you know, you've had your rough patches . . .' She started to cry. 'I'm just a horrible, jealous bitch.'

Kathy jumped up and tore off a strip of kitchen roll. 'I'm sorry. I'm so insensitive.'

Sara took the kitchen roll and blew her nose. 'What have you got to apologise for? I can't believe I was trying to justify what I said.'

'Shh, don't worry about it.'

'You know when you told me just now, all I could think of was why should Kathy be happy?'

'You don't have to explain yourself. I know why you feel the way you do. If someone had been watching us that night in New York, they'd never have predicted that this would be the way it turned out. Remember how I was crying in the toilet? I felt exactly the same as you do now. I looked at you and Bill, and I thought, why can't I have that?'

'But you kept it to yourself. It was a despicable thing I just did.'

Kathy put her arm round Sara's shoulder. 'Who said our emotions had to be pleasant all the time? I'm amazed at the way you've pulled yourself back from the brink. When I came back from Japan and saw you in that bedsit . . . But let's not talk about this.'

'No, go on.'

Kathy's eyes misted up. 'I really thought that you might kill yourself. Remember when you first went back to the *Voice* and you wouldn't answer my phone calls? Well, I still rang every morning anyway. I spoke to Dave Teacher, just to make sure that you'd made it in. But look at you now – you got through it and you're making a new life for yourself.'

'What life? It's awful. Look at my job, where I live – it's all awful.'

'That's because you deliberately make things difficult for yourself. And I admire you so much for it. You could have just moved in here and stuck to writing about boob jobs and things would have ticked over nicely. But it wouldn't have given you what you wanted. You started from scratch again, like you did in America. And just like America, you'll make a success of your life again.'

'When's the wedding?' Kathy had been so understanding, but saying congratulations now would have seemed insincere, however much she meant it.

'When we both find a window in our schedules,' laughed Kathy. 'Next year some time. I know you didn't mean what you said, but I would understand someone having doubts about me marrying him. We have had our ups and downs, but I think I'm just as much to blame as he is. We both let our jobs rule our lives too much and we don't give each other enough time. I think it's the same for all professional couples . . .' She was aware that she sounded as if she was making excuses for herself.

The second time the waiter brought the menu over to Maggie, she snapped. 'No, I don't want the bloody menu yet,' she shouted, throwing it back at him. This was typical of Sara, she thought. Maggie had wanted to meet in a wine bar, but, no, Sara insisted on going to a restaurant. Maggie was sure that she just wanted to check that she was eating properly. Every time she spoke to her it was the first thing that she asked. Maggie looked at her watch, fuming. She'd cancelled gym to make this date, and now Sara was late. She was just about to leave when Sara raced into the restaurant.

'I'm sorry. I just lost all track of time,' she said, sitting down. 'Have you ordered yet?'

There, barely ten seconds here and already she's starting, thought Maggie. 'I was waiting for you.'

'I'm starving,' said Sara ignoring Maggie's exasperation. 'Have you been here before? The tuna steak's delicious.' She was trying too hard: she changed the subject. 'How's work?'

'It's going well,' replied Maggie, relieved. 'I've just started a new section called "Showy Chloe". You know, cheap chic and all that. I just look at *Mariella* and rip off their ideas. I know our readership is twenty years older than theirs, but who cares? Personally, I think a grandmother should feel comfortable going round Sainsbury's in a conical bra.'

The waiter returned, eyeing Maggie warily. 'Ready to order?'

'The tuna steak, please,' said Maggie, determined to prove a point.

'The same for me,' said Sara, pleased. 'And I'll have the mushroom tagliatelle to start.'

The waiter looked at Maggie. 'Whatever,' she said.

They ordered a bottle of white wine, and as they waited for the starter, Sara filled Maggie in on her attempt to break into football writing.

'It's not very glamorous, is it?' declared Maggie.

Sara looked at her, wondering about Maggie's skewed notion of glamour. If it were possible, she was even thinner than the last time Sara had seen her. The tramlines on each side of her mouth were etched deeper and her cheekbones looked as if they could burst through her skin at any moment. Her make-up was thicker than ever, painted on in broad brushstrokes. Sara was reminded of a skull daubed for a Mexican Day of the Dead celebration.

The food arrived and they ate in silence, the atmosphere tense. Sara desperately wanted to establish a normal relationship with Maggie again. She didn't want to lose any more people from her life. She had even hoped that she could now tell Maggie about her baby and that perhaps, through both their losses, they could heal the old wounds. But looking at the ghastly vision in front of her, Sara wondered if a normal relationship with Maggie was possible.

Sara had lost count of the number of times she had tried to tackle the subject of Maggie's eating disorder but her sympathy always met with instant rage and denial. Now, as much as she knew it was wrong, she felt angry at Maggie's inability to acknowledge how much the illness had changed her.

Maggie, meanwhile, was conscious that Sara was watching every mouthful she ate. She had to clear her plate, but every bite made her feel a little bit more out of control. The feeling of food in her stomach made her panic.

'What are you wearing to Kathy's wedding?' asked Sara, desperately.

Maggie grimaced. 'I know she only invited me because of you and there's no mention of Huw on her tasteful invitation.'

'How is Huw?' asked Sara, not wanting to argue over Kathy.

'We had a bit of a fight last weekend. He accused me of chatting up some bloke in his club.'

'Were you?'

'Of course. You have to keep them on their toes. Huw asked me to invite you along to Totem. He really likes you.'

'Does he?' asked Sara, surreptitiously checking Maggie's plate.

Maggie could hear the contempt in Sara's voice. Why, after all that had been said in New York, did she still have to behave as if nothing Maggie did was good enough? 'I've got to go to the toilet.'

'I'll come with you,' said Sara, standing up.

She's incredible, thought Maggie. 'Could you order a dessert first?'

'Sure. What about Mississippi mud pie?'

'Sounds great.'

Maggie went into the toilet and locked the door. Dropping to her knees, she clutched the toilet bowl and stuck a finger down her throat, welcoming the familiar spasm of her diaphragm which signalled the onset of vomiting. Nothing I ever do is good, she thought as she heaved. Stupid. Fat. Ugly.

Once her stomach was empty, she wiped her mouth, feeling slightly more in control again. Flushing the toilet, she unlocked the door and reapplied her lipstick. The other toilets were empty. Good, no one had heard her.

When she returned to their table she found Sara paying the bill. 'I didn't order dessert,' she said, looking Maggie straight in the eye. 'There didn't seem to be any point.'

The February snow was starting to melt and the referee had declared the ground to be playable. Sitting between Stuart and Stephen Powell in the Camden directors' box, Sara could feel the hostility which bristled between them. She'd seen more bonhomie at an Arsenal–Tottenham match. Going to football with Stuart conjured up memories of being at Highbury with her father, and while she enjoyed that feeling, she couldn't understand why he didn't support a club where he'd get a friendlier reception. It wasn't as if Camden were playing that well. They were languishing at the bottom of the division, and today's Cup tie against Ashton was something of a foregone conclusion. Despite the rumour that Billy Todd, the Ashton goalkeeper, was back on cocaine, the team were playing some amazing football.

Stuart leaned over to her. 'Enjoying the match?'

'Wouldn't you rather be at Arsenal?'

'Never!' he laughed.

Suddenly his attention returned to the match. 'I don't believe it!' he screamed, pointing at the pitch. 'Did you see that?'

On the pitch, Camden midfielder Ian Sumner had set up a break down the left wing. As Ashton's Richie Davies got on his case,

Sumner executed a perfect cross to striker Benny Wright, who brought the ball down with his chest. Just as he was lining himself up for a shot at goal, the Ashton full-back, Sam Margetts, knocked him to the ground with a crunching tackle, taking the heel of his boot to the striker's shin as he fell.

'Send him off!' Stuart was almost apoplectic. 'That man has no business playing football!'

Wright lay on the ground in the slush, clutching his shin as the referee ran over to the jeers of the Ashton supporters. As the centre forward was helped to his feet, blood gushed from his leg. After some deliberation, the referee held up the red card. Margetts walked off the pitch and Camden were awarded a penalty.

Sara looked at Stephen Powell to see what he had made of the disgraceful exhibition, but his face was impassive, betraying nothing. In all the time she'd been coming to Camden, she'd never seen him get excited one way or another about football. Everything else – Stuart, his wife Jackie, having to wait at the bar – could throw him into an instant rage. But when it came to the game, which was, after all, the whole reason why they were there, nothing. Even when Ian Sumner took the penalty and scored the first goal of the match, the chairman remained completely detached.

'I'm really surprised at that,' said Sara. 'Sam Margetts is an old-school type. I didn't think that was his style.'

'We've got them on the run now,' said Stuart delightedly.

It wasn't true. For the rest of the first half and for most of the second, Camden played a defensive game, the ball very rarely making it to the Ashton end. Camden were sluggish, and it was left to some gravity-defying work from their goalkeeper, Ross Heywood, to compensate for the rest of the team's inadequacies. Then, five minutes before the end, Camden attacker Les Sutton showed a rare moment of inspiration and took the ball from the halfway line into the Ashton penalty area unchallenged. Billy Todd came out to meet him. Sara was sure that the man wasn't even aware of the ball flying over his head and into the net.

When the final whistle blew, Sara saw that, for the first time, Stephen had permitted himself a small smile. She nudged Stuart and said, 'He looks happy.'

'So he should. No one thought Camden stood a chance today. Especially the bookies.'

The game over, they filed out. Sara declined Stuart's suggestion to hang around for a drink. Even though Camden had won, she felt slightly depressed. Seeing Billy Todd still brought a twinge of guilt. Although he was back in the team, she had taken two years out of his professional life with her exposé. And for what? She was still at the *Voice* writing rubbish. Her mood was exacerbated by the fact that she had just spotted John Rudman going into the press bar. She was not working today – watching Camden was strictly recreational – but it rankled her that talentless slobs like Rudman were doing better than she was purely by dint of what hung between their legs. She'd had to go back on her word and write ordinary articles again to make ends meet. Simon Holland had given her an ultimatum: give up the football or get out. She'd been in no financial position to argue.

'I'll give you a lift,' said Stuart, taking her arm.

As they walked across the snow-covered car park to the Daimler, Sara became aware that, from the pressure he was putting on her arm, Stuart was actually leaning on her for support.

'Stuart, are you all right? You seem to be struggling a bit.' She looked at him carefully. Over the last month or so he seemed to have aged considerably.

'This weather's playing merry hell with my rheumatism,' he replied, his laboured breathing creating a constant flow of steam in the cold air. 'I shouldn't have come today, but I do so look forward to our afternoons together.'

'So do I,' said Sara, opening the car door for him. 'But it would be nice to be here sometimes as part of the press.'

With great effort, Stuart slid across the back seat of the car and Sara climbed in beside him. 'Did you know that the *Herald* was looking for a football writer?' he said, taking a hip flask from his pocket and handing it to Sara.

She took a swig and felt the gratifying burn of the neat whisky on the back of her throat.

'I haven't seen a job advertised.'

'That's not the way the paper works. You'll never have seen a job there advertised. Cynthia likes to keep it all word-of-mouth. The way she sees it, if you're clever enough to find out that there's a vacancy, you're halfway to being the kind of person the *Herald* wants for the job. Why don't you give the sports editor a ring?'

'It's Dean Gavin, isn't it? I will do, first thing Monday morning. Can I—'

'Sara, you can't say I told you about it.' Stuart looked very alarmed. 'Cynthia would have you blacklisted immediately. God knows how she hasn't found out about us already.'

'I was about to say could I have another sip of the whisky. I still feel quite cold. Stuart, you know I'd never presume on our friendship. What is there for Cynthia to find out, anyway?'

'Nothing. But she wouldn't see it like that. Here,' he said, handing her the hip flask. 'Keep it.'

'Do you know if it's a staff job?'

Stuart nodded. 'I don't know any of the details, though. I try not to get involved in Cynthia's business in the vain hope that one day she'll return the favour.'

'It would be brilliant. A proper salary would really help with the hospital bills. As part of the electorate, can I just plead with you to leave the NHS alone? Speaking as someone who'll be in debt to an American insurance company for the rest of her life—'

'You never told me about this.'

'Owing fifty thousand pounds or thereabouts is hardly something to shout about.'

'Fifty thousand! You poor girl.'

'Tell me about it. So leave the NHS alone, or you'll have me to answer to.'

'Pop star Matt Frenton today admitted in an exclusive interview with the *Sunday Voice* that he is checking into a £500-a-night clinic to help combat his addiction to sex.' Sara stopped typing, wondering if she should add that throughout the interview in which the star made this heartrending admission he was trying to put his hand on her leg. 'This is crap,' she said, deleting everything she'd written.

'You can't do that,' laughed Dave Teacher. 'The poor schmuck's tormented. All those birds – it must have been hell for him.'

'And you don't think it has anything to do with the fact that he's got a new album coming out and the last one bombed?'

'It's a story,' shrugged Dave.

'That's so typical of this place,' fumed Sara. She was about to launch into a familiar diatribe against the *Voice* when her phone rang. She didn't answer it immediately as she wanted to compose herself. The reason she was so worked up was that she was expecting a call from the *Herald*. She'd had an interview there earlier in the week and Dean Gavin had said he'd call to let her know.

'Sara Moore, *Sunday Voice*.'

'Hello, Sara. You sound ever so professional.'

Sara's shoulders sank. 'Hello, Mum.'

'It's just a quick call, my love.' June sounded nervous. 'Mrs Samuels has just put the kettle on, but I thought I should ring you to tell you that I'm transferring some money into your bank account.'

'Why?'

'It's to help you pay off some of your bills.'

Sara was touched. Her mother was always phoning to ask if Sara had enough money to pay for her heating. 'You don't have to, Mum. I've done a couple of extra articles this week.'

'I'm sure it won't be enough to pay off all those medical bills. Another of your dad's insurance policies has matured. Harry was always so good with his money . . .' June's voice trailed off.

'Mum, have you any idea how much money I owe?'

'Fifty thousand pounds or so. I'm transferring fifty-five thousand into your account, just to make sure.'

Sara was speechless. Fifty-five thousand pounds? Her father could never have dreamed of realising so much money in his lifetime. 'Mum, you can't.'

June seemed in a hurry to get off the phone. 'I don't want any arguments about it. You'll take the money and that's all there is to it. It's what your dad would have wanted.'

'I don't know what to say . . .'

'Just say that you'll come down and see me soon. That's Mrs Samuels knocking, I'll have to go.'

Sara put the phone down in a daze. Her debts had just been wiped out in one fell swoop. She would argue with her mother, of course, but she knew that June wouldn't change her mind.

'You look pleased with yourself,' said Dave. 'Here's something to put an even bigger smile on your face. You just had a call from a Mr Gavin. And here's the good bit. I told him I'd put him through to someone in your department to take a message.'

Sara froze. 'Who did you put him on to?'

'Holland, of course. You know the miserable bastard goes mental about taking our messages.'

Sara had said nothing to anybody about the interview. 'Do you know what you've done, you bloody idiot?' She looked across the newsroom to Holland's office. He was still on the phone and not looking at all happy. There was nothing else for it, she would have to go in there and take the call in his office. If she had got the job, Gavin wouldn't be too pleased at having some fool playing silly beggars with him. And if she hadn't, and Holland twigged why Gavin was calling her, he wasn't going to take too kindly to having his nose rubbed in it.

Holland saw her through the glass partition and beckoned her to come in. 'This is for you,' he said, handing her the phone.

Sara's stomach was doing somersaults. After Gavin told her the job was hers, she barely registered anything else he said. She put the phone down and looked at Holland.

'You're taking the piss out of me,' said the editor. 'It would have been nice if you had told me you were looking around. I put myself out for you, taking you back after you shot off to America.'

Sara was about to apologise, but then thought, why the hell should I? 'How many times did I ask you to let me write about football? You knew I could do it. I could write about anything if I set my mind to it. If I can inject some sort of sincerity into the crap you force me to churn out, then writing about sport should have been a doddle. But you wouldn't let me because I am a woman. You never did me any favours, Simon.'

Holland glowered for a moment and then began to laugh. 'No. I suppose I never did.'

'Now, if you'll excuse me, I've got the Matt Frenton exclusive to write.' She opened the door to leave.

'Sara?'

She turned to face the editor. 'What?'

'Good luck.' Holland winked at her. 'Oh, and one more thing – send Teacher in to see me.'

Sara closed his office door and let out a scream which brought momentary silence to the newsroom. At last, at last!

Chapter Eighteen

With her first month's salary at the *Herald*, Sara put down the deposit on a one-bedroomed flat in Highgate and moved in at the beginning of May. On the morning of Kathy's wedding, she still hadn't finished unpacking. Nor had she had the time to go shopping for a new outfit. The money she'd earned at the *Voice* hadn't stretched to buying clothes. In a panic she rummaged through the bags of clothes looking for something suitable. In a suitcase which had been packed by Mary and never opened since, she found a simple taupe linen suit which she'd bought in Bloomingdale's in New York. Sara felt a wave of sadness wash over her as the memory of when she'd last worn it, for the Emmy Awards with Bill, flooded back. He'd been presenting one of the awards and had made a short speech which had had the audience falling about in the aisles. Sara remembered watching him up there on the stage, feeling that she was the luckiest woman in the world. She thought about putting the suit away again. She was being stupid: today was going to be difficult enough as it was without her getting all sentimental and tearful before she'd even left the house.

Dressing in a hurry, she took a cab to the King's Road, where she found the bride in a similar state about her own outfit.

'After all the time it took you two to finally name the day, we're still going to be late. You look beautiful, now come on,' urged Sara, convinced that she was more nervous than the bride.

'Do you think Chanel was the right choice? The weather isn't normally this hot in May. I feel like I'm suffocating in this wool. I should have worn white. You know, all my life I wanted to get married in Chanel in Chelsea, but now I feel like a complete frump.'

'Honestly, you look fantastic. Come on, the car's waiting.' Sara tapped her watch for emphasis.

'We've got ages yet. And to keep with tradition, I'm meant to be late.'

Sara sighed, looking out of the kitchen window. 'The garden looks lovely. I don't know why you didn't have the reception here.'

'I wanted to, but Joseph had other ideas. I thought the point of a register office wedding was that it was simple and quiet. The only place that's going to be quiet today is Soho. The whole of Wardour Street's coming. God knows how much all this is going to cost us. It looks as if I'll have to take that job after all.'

'What job?'

'Editor of *Mariella*. Would you open that champagne?'

'Congratulations. You never said anything.'

'That's because I wasn't sure if I was going to take it.'

Sara popped the champagne cork and poured two large glasses. 'Whyever not?'

'It's so much more work. I'm getting married – something's got to give if this is going to be a success.'

Why has it got to be you and not Joseph? thought Sara but she didn't voice her opinion, determined to say nothing which could mar the bride's day.

Kathy sipped the champagne, shivering as the bubbles hit the back of her throat. 'Anyway, I suppose what we're spending on the reception we're saving on the honeymoon.'

'I thought you were having July off to go somewhere?'

'Joseph's away that month, working in New York. I might pop over for a couple of days.'

Sara had to bite her tongue. Why was Kathy talking about forgoing the editor's job to make time for Joseph if he couldn't even fit in their honeymoon? Looking at Kathy, drink in hand, it occurred to Sara that something was missing. 'I thought you'd be smoking, today of all days.'

'Mmm. I've managed to give up.'

'Good for you. Look, we really should go now,' said Sara, realising the time. 'Joseph'll think he's been jilted.'

'Hold on a second,' shouted Kathy, putting her hand over her mouth. 'I think I'm going to be sick.' She raced into the bathroom, only just making it in time. She emerged a few minutes later, breathing deeply. 'I'm sorry about that.'

'Last minute nerves?'

'I think so,' said Kathy, though she knew that her nausea was caused by something else entirely. Perhaps Sara would put two and two together, but she couldn't tell her, not yet. She had to find the right time.

'Are you ready to go, then?'

Kathy took a large swig of champagne, threw on her pearls, picked up her Chanel handbag and said, 'As ready as I'll ever be.'

A white Rolls–Royce was parked outside waiting for them. Sara took Kathy's hand and climbed in. 'I just wanted to say thanks for inviting Maggie.'

Once again, Sara hoped that seeing Maggie would help them mend their friendship. As she gradually began to emerge, step by step, from her own depression she was becoming more acutely aware that Maggie was retreating into a never-ending cycle of dieting and exercise, crowned by an incomprehensible infatuation with the ghastly Huw.

As the Rolls pulled up outside Chelsea Register Office, Kathy giggled nervously. 'I feel like the Queen Mum. It's mortifying having all these people staring at you.'

'Give them a royal wave, then.'

Kathy waved. 'I can't believe that in twenty minutes' time I'll be Mrs Kathy McCabe.'

'I didn't know you were changing your name.'

Kathy registered her disappointment. 'I wasn't going to, but Joseph thought it would be easier – you know, when we had. . . Do you think it's wrong?'

'No, not at all,' Sara lied. She would never give up her own name. She wouldn't even have done it for Bill.

Joseph trotted towards the car, wearing an unstructured grey silk suit which Kathy had commissioned from a Japanese designer. As he approached, Kathy could see the tears in his eyes. 'Oh no, I'm going to start crying,' she said. 'Is my mascara all right?'

Sara wiped at the corner of her eye. 'Let's go before we all start.'

Kathy took her friend's hand. She knew how difficult this was for Sara, and her heart went out to her. Sara, too, should have been as happy as she felt at this moment. As Kathy stepped out of the car she turned to her and said: 'Whatever happens, no matter who comes along, you'll always be one of the most important people in my life.'

'Ditto.' Despite her misgivings, Sara just prayed that Kathy had found the happiness that had eluded her. Spotting Maggie, standing out from the chic crowd in a vile tangerine moiré taffeta dress, Sara joined her and allowed Joseph to take Kathy's arm as they entered the register office.

The guests packed into the ceremony room and soon all were sporting a sheen of sweat as the temperature soared into the nineties. The registrar appeared and the marriage service began.

The heat was truly unbearable and Sara's crisp linen suit was now crumpled and damp. She heard the distant sound of the registrar's voice, posing questions that would now never be asked of her.

'Katherine Juliet Clarke, do you . . .'

Sara looked down in her lap nervously rubbing her hands together, trying to shut out the registrar's voice.

'Will the witness please . . .'

'Psst, Sara!' Kathy tapped her on the knee.

Sara looked up. 'Sorry,' she said, her eyes filling with tears as she moved forward to sign her name.

Outside, a photographer friend of Kathy's took the customary photographs which seemed to go on forever as he snapped from every possible angle. Sara insisted on having a photograph of just Maggie, herself and the bride, but as they huddled together for the shot, it was only too clear that the big smiles on their faces were less than sincere.

'It's a wrap,' said Kathy, recoiling from Maggie. 'Let's go and celebrate.'

The reception was held at the Huntingdon Club, a few doors along from the register office. It was a replica of a traditional gentlemen's club, right down to the leather chesterfields and the old master paintings, but aimed at the young Turks of Chelsea. As a concession to the wedding, the place had been filled with hundreds of long-stemmed white lilies, and in every room an oil burner emitted a thick, musky, dreamy scent. The champagne appeared to be on tap and a team of model-like waitresses in short black dresses flitted between the guests carrying trays filled with hors d'oeuvres.

Balancing a plate and a glass Sara nudged her way through the guests to find Maggie slumped in an ungainly heap on a sofa, fingering a bowl of lilies.

'It looks like a funeral parlour in here,' said Maggie, emptying her champagne flute and belching noisily.

'You're drunk. Have some food,' said Sara, offering her a stuffed quail's egg.

'I ate before I came,' she slurred. Maggie put her foot out to stop a passing waitress. 'Oi, do you mind filling this up again?' she said, waving her glass. Maggie was quite well aware that she was drunk, but it was the only way she could get through the afternoon. She knew that her presence wasn't wanted.

Joseph appeared at Sara's side as Maggie put out her cigarette in the vase of lilies. 'I think there's too much alcohol in the trifle, don't you?' he whispered in Sara's ear, nodding at Maggie.

'She's fine,' said Sara, feeling very protective. People were looking at Maggie. With her emaciated body and that tacky dress, she cut a pathetic figure.

'I wanted to thank you,' said Joseph, planting a kiss on Sara's cheek. 'After all, it was you who introduced me to Kathy, and now, with the baby on the way, I can honestly say that I've never been happier.'

'The baby?' said Sara, feeling the room was rushing away from her.

'Oh, God. I thought Kathy had told you,' he said, holding Sara by the arm and guiding her to a seat.

Kathy was having a baby. The news came to Sara like a punch in the stomach. She thought of the dead baby and all the children she and Bill had planned to have together and felt totally bereft. Now there would never be any children with anyone. Never.

'I'm sorry. It was just such a shock,' she managed eventually.

Guessing what had happened, Kathy rushed over. 'Oh, Sara, I'm so sorry. I was going to tell you but it wasn't the right time.'

'How pregnant are you?' Ten children, five boys and five girls. But now she'd never experience the joy of carrying even one child inside her.

'Seven weeks.'

'So it was a shotgun wedding, then,' said Sara, trying to lighten the mood.

Kathy sat down and cuddled her. 'Something like that. Look, we've discussed it already and we want you to be a friend-parent, you know, like a godmother, but without all the religious rigmarole.'

Maggie appeared, swaying slightly, with a maniacal smile on her face. 'Can anyone join in this conversation?'

Kathy looked desperately at Sara and Joseph.

'Kathy's got some brilliant news. She's expecting,' said Sara, gallantly.

'Well, that's a turn-up—'

'Come on, Maggie,' said Sara, pulling her away from the scene before she wrought havoc.

As the word spread that Kathy was pregnant, the happy couple were dragged off by well-wishers, leaving Maggie and Sara alone. They sat side by side, each lost in her own misery.

'My baby would have been five years old now,' said Maggie, blankly.

And mine a year, thought Sara. But she said nothing.

Chapter Nineteen

'Come on, Tone, for Christ's sake pass the ball!'

'That bloody linesman's blind! He's a fucking moron!'

The air was blue with the running commentary from the punters sitting behind the Ashton press box. Sara was tempted to ask them to finish her report for her as she was sure they would have some strong words on the subject of Ashton's play. It was the team's first match since relegation. After their blistering start to the previous season things had gone rapidly downhill. The Camden fixture back in February had marked a turning point, and Ashton had never recovered their form.

John Rudman shouted something across to her but it was impossible to hear what he was saying. On either side of her, two radio reporters with identical voices spoke nineteen to the dozen into their microphones. Only the occasional word, such as 'volley', 'header' and 'substitute' was distinguishable in their hysterical commentary.

Rudman squeezed in next to her. 'I said, do you reckon Billy Todd's on something?'

'No, he's too sharp,' Sara replied. 'He's playing better than he did all last season.'

'That's what I mean. I reckon he's had a little toot to throw us off the scent.'

The press box was humming with the rumour that Todd was being paid to throw games. Sara was sure that the goalkeeper must be aware of the speculation surrounding him. Maybe Rudman was right. Todd seemed to be running himself ragged, taking on the whole might of Birmingham City single-handedly. For all the good they were doing, the other ten Ashton players might as well have stayed in the changing rooms. Only an amazing performance by Todd had prevented a total hammering. Perhaps he *was* artificially enhancing his performance in some way.

Sara was dreading full-time. Dean Gavin had told her in no uncertain terms not to bother coming back to the office without first interviewing the Ashton goalkeeper. She had been hoping that Todd would pre-empt the situation by calling a press conference, but no such luck. Now she had two problems. First, every other sports editor had told his reporters exactly the same thing, so there was going to be a long queue to get to Billy. Secondly, even if she happened to be at the front of the queue, Billy Todd would, of course, take one look at her and tell her exactly where to get off. There was no way in the world he could have forgotten who she was and what she had done to him.

The final whistle blew on a no-score draw. As Tina Turner's 'Simply the Best' blasted out around the stadium, Sara's colleagues pushed past her in the rush to get to Billy Todd. By the time she reached the players' tunnel, there was a scrum of journalists jostling with each other for space. Flashbulbs were going off everywhere and the glare made it hard for Sara to see exactly where the object of their attention was.

Suddenly, the captain appeared and a shout went up.

'Billy, over here!'

'This way, Billy!'

'Have you got anything to say about the allegations that you've been deliberately throwing matches?'

'Who's paying you?'

'Billy, would you still class yourself as an addict?'

Todd brushed aside the questions, knocking away the hands tugging at his shirt. 'No comment.'

The questions echoed around the tunnel as the goalkeeper pushed his way through the crowd. Sara slipped in behind him, but just as she went to put a hand on his shoulder, Ashton's manager, Tom Banks, stepped in front of her. 'Sorry, miss. If you want an autograph, you can write in for it.'

'I'm the *Herald*'s football correspondent,' she said, more to herself than to the manager, who had by now slipped into the changing room behind his player and locked the door. Her face was burning. Banks' remark had been heard by every other journalist there. John Rudman had a huge grin on his face. She turned and walked back through the tunnel.

Out in the car park she found her car, resigned to the fact that she wasn't going to get an interview. Todd was obviously going to remain tight-lipped, anyway, so she wouldn't be missing out on anything if she didn't wait around the players' entrance with the others. The car, a Ford Fiesta, was a new acquisition. Although driving again made her extremely anxious, it seemed ridiculous to spend half her salary on cab fares, and besides, the practicalities of her job would have been difficult without her own transport. Nevertheless, the days when putting her foot down on the accelerator would have given her any pleasure were long gone.

For a while she sat behind the wheel, wondering what she was going to say to Dean Gavin and watching the crowd of journalists growing around the players' entrance. Suddenly there was a lot of pushing and shoving as a scuffle broke out. Billy Todd had to be somewhere in the middle. With no particular plan in mind, she started the car and drove straight at them, opening the passenger door. 'Billy, get in!' she shouted.

A look of vague recognition crossed the player's face. Looking around, he saw that his options were limited and he jumped in. As a couple of the journalists went for the door handles she quickly closed them with the central locking and sped out of the car park, relishing the look of pure astonishment on John Rudman's face as she passed him.

'Thanks,' said Billy. 'They would have eaten me alive.' He looked at her. 'Don't I know you?'

Sara considered lying, but any second now he was bound to realise who she was. 'I'm Sara Moore, I work for the *Herald*, but you probably remember me from Mickey's.'

'Stop the fucking car,' said Billy, grabbing the steering wheel.

Sara pulled the steering wheel back towards her only for Billy to wrest control of it again. The car began to skid. 'No! No!' she screamed, letting go of the wheel and covering her face with her hands.

'Christ!' shouted Billy. 'Steer the bloody car! Get your foot on the brake!'

Billy's words broke through the fog of fear that had enveloped her. Her hands back on the wheel, she pumped the brake until the car slowed down and came to a shuddering halt. Only then did she notice that they were on the other side of the road facing the wrong way.

'You took two years of my life away from me,' said Billy, quietly.

'I'm really sorry,' she sobbed. 'I've always regretted it. You weren't the story I was after.'

'So why did you do me over?' he spat.

'It was . . . ambition, my big break. I'm not proud of myself.'

The player rested his head against his hands on the dashboard. 'Just one mistake and I'm never going to be allowed to forget it.'

'Was it just one mistake?'

He turned his head to face her, looking totally defeated. 'No, but I don't expect you to believe me.' He turned to open the door.

'Let me make it up to you. *Please*.'

'And how do you propose to do that?'

'If you're innocent, I'll prove it.'

'You're shaking,' he said, looking at her hands.

She had been unaware that her whole body was trembling. 'I was in a bad accident,' she explained quietly. 'I was driving, and my . . . my fiancé was killed.'

'I'm sorry,' said Billy. It was an automatic response, but he spoke gently. 'Let's get out of here.'

Sara started the car, turned it round and drove sedately through the north London traffic. 'Would you like to go somewhere for a drink to talk about this?'

'I don't drink. I haven't touched a drop since – well, you know when. But I wouldn't mind going somewhere quiet.'

'Is there anywhere in particular that you'd like to go?'

He shrugged his shoulders.

'How about Highgate?' There was a pub called the Roebuck opposite her flat. She'd walked past it several times and it always seemed pretty dead.

'Whatever.'

As she'd hoped, the only customers in the pub were a couple of old men sitting at the bar staring into their beer.

'What would you like?' asked Sara, looking at Billy properly for the first time since he'd jumped into her car. He was wearing a suit that was slightly too small for him and, like many footballers, he looked uncomfortable dressed in anything other than a football strip. She knew he was in his early thirties but his chequered past had added ten years to his appearance, which wasn't helped by his long, tightly permed black hair.

'Just an orange juice,' he said, fiddling with the thick gold chain around his neck. 'I meant what I said about giving up the booze.'

Billy sat down in a quiet corner away from the door and Sara brought over their drinks. 'You played amazingly today.'

'Maybe I had something to prove. You said it wasn't me you were after at Mickey's. So who was it?'

'Apart from the drugs, I wanted to find out what was happening at table five. You remember, with Frank and his mates?'

'Yeah?'

'Do they tie in with what's going on now?'

Billy looked at her intently. 'If I tell you, it's off the record. If you stitch me up again . . .'

'I won't,' promised Sara.

'OK. At first they asked me to make predictions on certain matches – you know, assessing form and that.'

'Did they pay you?'

'A few grand.'

'That's a lot of money for a few tips.'

'It was a consultation fee.'

'Fair enough.'

'Actually, it was a softener. We'd been doing business for a while before they asked me to throw a game. I thought they were yanking my chain, but they were deadly serious. Anyway, it was just about the time my wife left me and I was out of it. Completely wasted. I couldn't throw a shadow, let alone a game.'

'So you never took money to throw a match?'

'Never,' said Billy emphatically. 'The game is my life. The only time I feel like I'm worth anything is when I'm in that goal.'

'So why is this rumour persisting?'

'The rumour's right. You've just got the wrong person. At the beginning of this year I was approached by two blokes. One I sort of knew from Mickey's, a mate of Frank's. The other was a foreigner – Argentinian, I think.'

'Why do you think he was Argentinian?'

'Well, he was definitely South American. He could have been Brazilian. Yeah, thinking about it, he was from Brazil—'

'You knew the drugs came from Brazil,' interrupted Sara.

'No, I didn't,' he said sharply. 'Anyway, they put fifteen K under my nose – my payment to influence the Camden United fixture.'

'I was at that match. You lost two-nil.' Sara remembered what an easy goal the second had been. Todd had made no attempt to reach for the ball as it went sailing over his head. His denial was looking less than credible.

'That's how much we were supposed to lose by.'

'But, Billy, one of those goals was totally your fault. How can you say that you're not involved?'

'Look,' he said, angrily, 'I made a complete prat of myself that afternoon. I was having a bad day. Benny Wright was needling me like he always does. I tell you, when Sam took him down I was well pleased. But by then he'd affected my concentration. I was off form, simple as that.'

'Why didn't you take the money?'

'I was tempted. They told me that I was just unlucky to get caught about the coke stuff, but I reckon you make your own luck. I know

I'm no angel, but I knew if I took that money there'd be no looking back. In a funny way you did me a favour with that story, though excuse me if I don't thank you for it. I got my act together after that. I went along to an NA meeting, admitted I had a problem and they've been helping me put my life back together ever since. I've had counselling, constant random drugs tests and regular medical and fitness checks. I've always come up clean as a whistle. What would be the point of going through all that if I was throwing games?'

'OK, I believe you. So the result of the Camden match was just a happy coincidence?'

'I didn't say that. They left me alone after that – though not without first giving me the usual threats about what would happen to me if I said anything. But since then I've seen several blokes turning up in the players' lounge and I'm pretty sure they're all part of the same syndicate. You see guys like that attaching themselves to clubs all the time. This thing is huge. There's a lot of overseas money behind it.'

'Going back to Mickey's for a moment, both Mickey and Frank talked about someone called Steve.'

'Steve? Oh yeah, I heard of him but I never met him. I don't know who he is.'

'What's Frank's background?' asked Sara, hiding her disappointment about Steve. 'Can I get hold of him somewhere?'

'Don't be stupid. They come to you, you don't go to them. They cover their tracks. It's all done on a first-name basis. You go looking for them and they'll disappear into thin air.'

'OK. So if you didn't throw the Camden game, it must have been Sam Margetts,' she said, remembering the foul perpetrated by the Ashton full-back.

'I'm saying nothing.'

'I know your loyalties are torn, but surely you're not prepared to take the rap for all this?'

'I've said as much as I'm going to say. Of course I want to get myself off the hook, but just you remember when you're going after a story there's a person behind that headline. Someone who's probably got the same problems as you and me. We all have to get by the best we can. Just think about that before you go ruining somebody else's life for the sake of your career.'

Chapter Twenty

Kathy winced as the baby kicked inside her. She rubbed her stomach and tried to think positive thoughts, having read somewhere that the unborn child responds to the emotional state of the mother. But looking at Joseph, she found it hard to maintain her equilibrium. He was wearing a grey cashmere pullover which she was sure she hadn't seen before.

'Is that a new jumper?'

Joseph looked up from his laptop computer, another recent acquisition. 'Yeah. Do you like it? I bought it in—'

'I'm the doyenne of British fashion,' she said sarcastically. 'I know where you bought it and I know how much it cost.' Doyenne of British fashion? That was a joke. In its time, *Mariella* had carried several articles on what the well-dressed mother-to-be should be wearing. There was no need to wear floral tent dresses, they lectured their readers, not when Harvey Nichols carried so many beautiful designer maternity outfits. But what was the point of spending thousands of pounds on maternity clothes when there was no way in the world she would ever let herself get pregnant again? She couldn't rememember the last time she'd worn anything that wasn't made from sweatshirting. Thank God she couldn't see her feet any more, because she'd always vowed that she'd go to her grave without ever having worn a pair of trainers. But the Nikes were so easy on her swollen ankles.

Listening to the tap-tap-tapping of Joseph's keyboard, Kathy felt her jaw clench. That was obviously the end of the conversation. They rarely spoke to each other these days. Or did rowing count as conversation? She had imagined that there would be so much to talk about, so many plans to be made for the future, but they hadn't even discussed a name for this child growing inside her. She looked aound her immaculate living room. To an outsider this would have seemed the perfect domestic scene. She wanted to scream.

Kathy heaved herself up off the settee, exhausted and desperate for a cigarette. She could hardly sleep at night with the baby kicking so wildly at her insides. Despite its obvious presence, she had to remind herself continually that she was actually having a baby. The pregnancy had taken its toll on her blood pressure, and her temper, but it still seemed so unreal. 'Well, I suppose I'd better go to work. Somebody has to pay for the cashmere sweaters.' Joseph didn't answer her. 'Can't you leave that bloody thing alone for a minute?' she asked the top of his head.

Joseph snapped shut the lid of his computer. 'I'm trying to finish this proposal. So that I can get a job to pay the credit-card company that bought this sweater. And, if you don't mind me saying so, it wouldn't go amiss if you bought yourself something decent to wear once in a while.'

'You bastard,' she cried. 'Do you think I want to look like this?'

Joseph shrugged his shoulders.

Kathy wanted to hurt him as much as he was hurting her, but she was late for an editorial meeting. Chairing a cat fight between a bunch of egotistical fashion victims was the last thing she wanted to do at that moment, but without work she'd have nothing to do other than sit at home and stare at her ever-growing stomach. She was beginning to hate *Mariella*. The stress of the editorship combined with a difficult pregnancy was just too much – and she dreaded to think what life would be like after the birth. 'I'll see you, then,' she said, picking up her Kelly bag, the one last remnant of her former fashionable self.

Joseph slid a disk into the computer. 'Have a nice day.'

The inanity of the comment was the final straw. 'You were the one who wanted this baby, and now you treat it as if it were the bloody immaculate conception. All the problems are mine, aren't they? My pregnancy, my problems.'

'Not now, eh, Kathy? I've really got to finish this.'

The calm, reasonable tone in his voice inflamed her even more. 'Why is your job so much more important than mine? This pregnancy has completely disrupted my working life, but that doesn't matter, does it? That's what's meant to happen. God forbid that you should have to tear yourself away from your career for a second to deal with the thing that's destroying my life.'

'That's a bit over-dramatic. I know you're having a hard time of it, Kathy, but it really isn't that bad. Look at my sister – she had to lie in bed for the last six months of her pregnancy.'

'Well, fucking lucky for her. Don't you think I'd like to do that? I feel so weak sometimes when I get up in the morning, but the mortgage has to be paid, I have to buy things for the baby—'

'You're being a martyr. A second ago you said that I didn't take your job seriously. Now you're saying you only do it for the money. Kathy, what is all this about?'

'Where were you last night?'

'I told you, I was working.'

'You could have phoned. What if I had gone into labour?' Kathy bit her lip as she felt the tears well up. This time she wouldn't cry.

Joseph let out an exaggerated sigh. 'Don't be silly, you've got ages yet. Look, I was working late. I know you're under a lot of strain, that's why this job is important. To take some of the pressure off you and provide for our baby.'

'Oh please, don't give me that crap about wanting to be the breadwinner. Joseph, I've never needed a penny from you.'

'This is your hormones speaking. I can't deal with you at the moment.' He walked out of the room. 'Is it any wonder I stay out?'

Despite her best efforts, Kathy couldn't stop the tears. 'I wish I'd never got pregnant,' she screamed up the stairs after him. 'It was the worst decision of my life. I thought it was something you wanted.' She sat down on the stairs, feeling the baby's foot pushing against her stomach. 'I'm sorry,' she whispered, speaking to the baby. 'It's not you.' She put her hand under her sweatshirt and felt her distended belly. The baby's foot pressed out as if it was trying to make contact with her.

Joseph came back downstairs and put his hand on her shoulder but Kathy shrugged it off. 'I was thinking,' she said quietly, 'you're just like my father. He just saw my mother as a baby machine. But you're not even as good as him. You expect me to be a baby machine *and* a meal ticket.'

'I'm sorry,' said Joseph, 'I really am. I get worried about work and I just shut off from things. But I do care for you, and I want this baby more than anything.'

'We've had this conversation before and nothing ever seems to change.'

'I'll really try this time,' he said, wiping the tears from her face.

Kathy felt too defeated to argue any further. 'I'd better get going. I'm late already.'

'Did you manage to get hold of Margetts?' asked Dean Gavin as Sara walked into his office.

'He threw me out of his house. I'm not going to get an interview with him.'

'It doesn't matter at the moment,' said the editor. 'You've done a brilliant job.'

The *Herald* had already run the first story on the Ashton scandal. True to her word, Sara had mentioned no names, but the implication was clear. In doing her best to show that Billy Todd was in the clear she had left the finger dangling over Sam Margetts. Sara had traced his form through the previous season's match reports and it had been very erratic. Margetts was a workmanlike player, steady, not flashy, but during the year he had become something of a wild card. He'd been booked several times for fouls which inevitably resulted in penalties, and at one point he had even scored an own goal. The odds against Camden winning against Ashton in the February Cup tie had been 20–1 against. Whoever had paid Sam £15,000 to throw the match must have made a packet.

'We'll lead with the suspension story on the back page,' said the editor. Ashton had suspended Margetts pending a full inquiry. 'And I want you to do a full analysis of his career.'

'Right. Did I tell you that the police have been in touch with me?'

'Really? Have they said anything about who they think is behind this?'

'Well, they've looked through Margetts' bank statements, and it seems payments have been made from a bank in Guernsey.'

'Keep me posted.'

'I can't believe I was so close to them. I sat at their table, for God's sake, and I didn't get the story.'

'Don't knock yourself, you've done really well.'

Sara didn't share the sports editor's opinion. Yet again, she'd only got half the story and added just a couple more pieces to a 1,000-piece jigsaw. Steve was the link, but he might just as well have been the invisible man. And where did a Brazilian fit into the equation? Were the people involved in the match-fixing the same as those supplying the drugs?

'Sara, there's a call for you,' said Dean Gavin's secretary, interrupting her thoughts. 'Maggie Lawrence at *Chloe*. She says it's vitally important that she speaks to you now.'

'Dean, I'll get working on that piece. I've plotted out most of his track record already.' She raced back to her phone, annoyed that Maggie was being so dramatic. She knew exactly what the call would be about.

'Maggie, for the last time I don't want to go out tonight.'

'Go on, please. It's been ages since I saw you. Please. It's always so heavy when we meet up. I just want us to go out and have some fun again. Like we did in the old days.'

'You know what I'm working on now. This is important.'

'I thought our friendship was important,' said Maggie sullenly.

'It is but . . . oh, go on then, I'll meet you at ten.'

'Make it eleven. I'd need longer to pretty up than you do.'

*　　*　　*

It was raining as the cab pulled up outside Totem.

'You did what?' said Sara.

'I organised a blind date for you,' declared Maggie with a wicked laugh. She jumped out of the cab and swanned past the shivering queue, leaving an embarrassed Sara no choice but to follow in her wake.

'Excuse me,' said Maggie, as she pushed past a man struggling with his umbrella in the doorway. Then, under her breath, 'Pleb.'

Sara smiled apologetically and stepped in behind her.

'How's it going tonight, Charlie?' said Maggie to the doorman. 'Anyone in?'

'Two from *EastEnders* and half of Man United,' replied Charlie. As long as there were soap stars and footballers, and those who wanted to pay to stand next to them, Totem would always be a roaring success.

As they crossed the main dancefloor Sara cringed at the way Maggie kissed air with every minor celebrity in the room. Maggie misread her disgust and shouted over the music, 'Look, trust me, Gerry's great. Would I fix you up with a dog?' Maggie glanced at her friend. 'You could have at least put on some make-up.'

Sara, her hair pulled back loosely, had dressed with little care in an old pair of jeans and black T-shirt. Despite this, as they made their way through the crowd, nearly every man turned to look at her.

'Bill's been dead a long time. You've got to get out and get a life.' Sara didn't reply. 'At least I care about you,' Maggie bristled. 'Unless you've got a speculum in your hand, Kathy doesn't seem to want to know.'

'Oh, for once would you just shut up about Kathy,' said Sara, completely exasperated. 'You know she's having a really difficult pregnancy. You don't know how serious high blood pressure can be.'

'It must be from all that worry about how to decorate the baby's bedroom,' sneered Maggie, not prepared to relent for even a second. 'Come on, Huw said they'd meet us in the star bar.'

Sara dragged her feet, trying to delay her fate. She hadn't been in this club since their college days but nothing had changed. It was still as glitzy and garish and firmly stuck in the seventies as ever. It was only 11.30 but already the place was heaving with wannabes, has-beens and never-will-bes. Sara was amused to see quite a few of the footballers she had written about. She just hoped they didn't notice her. The Sam Margetts story was not exactly adding to her popularity in footballing circles.

'Yoo-hoo, Huw, Gerry, over here!' shrieked Maggie, her arms flailing above her head.

Sara looked over Maggie's shoulder at her date and was tempted to flee. How could Maggie have done this to her? Did she have such a singular lack of taste that she could consider for one moment that Sara would be interested in this creep? His gait dictated by his tight, ball-scrunching jeans and Cuban-heeled cowboy boots, Gerry swaggered towards them, a low-rent John Wayne with a curly perm. Sara groaned, remembering her mother's sage advice – 'Never trust a man whose eyes are too close together.' Gerry was practically a Cyclops.

'Here are the two babes, Gerry boy,' said Huw. 'And this one's for you.'

'I'm not a blow-up doll, Huw,' snapped Sara, wondering how quickly she could make her excuses and go.

'You're not gonna be a real drag and go all feminist on us, are you?' drawled Huw. 'Gerry only got out yesterday. The poor sucker hasn't seen a woman in ten years.' He sniggered and punched Gerry in the stomach. 'No, seriously, you two ladies treat Gerry right. There's a new babe working the main bar tonight and I've got to go and sort her out for a minute.'

Maggie smiled. 'Don't be long, now,' she said, blowing him a kiss.

'Maggie, you're much too good for that man,' said Sara, too frankly.

Maggie stared at her, uncomprehending. 'I don't know what you mean. If I were you I'd worry about my own life.'

Sara reassessed Gerry. He looked no better closer up but at least he'd finally got around to attending to his runny nose, even if it was with the back of his hand. He sniffed loudly and cleared his throat. Sara thought that she'd better make an effort. 'Have you got a cold?' she asked, as he cuffed his nose again.

'What? Uh-huh, I guess so.'

Brains as well as looks, thought Sara, ordering a double whisky.

The three of them stood at the bar without speaking. Maggie broke the silence. 'Huw's been gone a long time,' she said, peering at her watch, 'I'm going to look for him.'

Sara was left alone with Gerry, who was flicking olives across the bar. He cleared his throat again. Sara couldn't leave. Maggie would be furious with her if she left without saying anything.

'What a shot!' shouted Gerry as an olive pinged off an optic. 'Want a drink?'

Unsmiling, Sara indicated that she had a full one in her hand. She wanted to give Gerry no encouragement.

'Huh,' he said, fishing another olive out of the bowl.

Sara wondered whether Gerry's nasal problems were attributable to cocaine. But coke would have made him a bit more upbeat. Perhaps he was shovelling tranquillisers up his nose instead. 'I think I'll go and look for Maggie.'

Gerry offered no reply. He just stared into space, reinforcing the tranquilliser theory.

Maggie was nowhere to be found in the club so Sara tried the offices off the star bar. She poked her head around the doorway and shouted down an empty corridor, 'Maggie, are you there?'

'Are you looking for me, babe?' said Huw, appearing from the cashier's office.

'Is Maggie with you?'

'No, you're in luck,' he said, walking towards her.

'Very funny. Maggie came looking for you ages ago.'

'Well, she couldn't have looked that hard. She's probably chatting up Chris Quentin.' Huw was so close she could feel his breath on her face. 'Come on, I know it's me you're really looking for,' he leered, pinning her against the wall. 'You've been after me since the beginning.' He pushed himself against her. 'You know you want it.'

She struggled to push Huw away from her, smelling the alcohol fumes on his breath.

'Come on, don't play hard to get. I know you've had the hots for me for ages.' He licked the side of her face.

'Stop it! Think of Maggie.'

'I'm just a trophy to that cold bitch. I'm looking for *real* love,' he laughed. 'And, of course, you're a much better-looking chick.'

His fingers dug into the back of her neck as he forced her towards him. '*Please!*'

Huw silenced her by forcing his tongue into her mouth. Then, just as she had finally managed to push him away Maggie came running down the corridor. 'What the fuck are you playing at?' she screamed.

Sara wiped her hand frantically across her mouth. 'Oh, Maggie, I'm so glad you're here.'

Sara was unprepared for the force with which Maggie slapped her. She felt her head slam against the wall. 'I'm sure you are, you ungrateful bitch. Did you time it so I'd see what you were up to? After all I've done for you. I turn my back for a second and you're straight into his trousers. Is that why you told me I was too good for him? Because you wanted him?'

'Maggie, believe me it wasn't like that, he—'

'You two-faced tart. I've seen the way you flaunt your body. You killed your own man and now you want mine.'

The remark hit Sara harder than the slap.

'I tried telling her, Mags,' interjected Huw. 'But she just wouldn't take no for an answer.'

'You could have controlled yourself, you bastard. Right, I want you to get all of your tacky clothes out of my flat and get the fuck out of my life. And you,' she said, poking Sara in the chest, 'you're going to wish you'd stayed under that lorry with Bill.'

Sara watched in disbelief as Maggie turned and stormed off back down the corridor. Huw shrugged, apparently unconcerned. 'Win some, lose some,' he said, walking back into the cashier's office, from where Sara could hear the unmistakable sound of a woman giggling.

Blindly, she hurried back through the club, pushing her way through the writhing bodies on the dancefloor. Everyone seemed to be laughing at her.

*   *   *

The following morning Maggie looked at herself in the mirror in the gym, dressed from head to toe in black Lycra. She berated herself for being so overweight. Bubbles of perspiration glistened just above her top lip and rivulets of sweat ran over her chest and down between her breasts. But Maggie hadn't finished her penance yet. She was just a fat, useless, lazy lump, and until she rid herself of all this excess flesh nothing in her life was going to improve. Grunting, she used all her strength to pull the bars forward, her pectoral muscles screaming for mercy. Ignoring the pain she promised herself an extra half-hour in the gym every night.

She knew that if she hadn't let things slide at the gym, Sara wouldn't have stood a chance with Huw. But it was Huw who hadn't really stood a chance. Having lost Bill, Sara was like a cat on heat. Maggie tormented herself, thinking about how Sara and Kathy would be laughing at her, at the way she couldn't even keep her own man. Kathy would sit there being supercilious, saying that if she only lost a little weight, she could be such a pretty girl. Soon tears mingled with the sweat as she ran to nowhere on the treadmill, stepping up the speed the more she thought about Sara's betrayal. She would make that bitch pay, and the day would come when Sara Moore would be sorry that she had ever got on the wrong side of Maggie Lawrence.

Chapter Twenty-One

The party at the Regent Hotel in Knightsbridge had been arranged to announce the launch of Alive TV, the Herald Group's new venture into satellite television. A subdued Sara found herself standing against the wall, nursing a white wine spritzer, wondering why it was she was suddenly thinking about the night at Totem. Huw's assault – and she most definitely did class it as an assault, not just a fumbled pass – had been frightening but nowhere near as shocking as the vehemence with which Maggie had attacked her. She still couldn't believe what Maggie had said about Bill's death. But, thinking about it, it was such a typically Maggie thing to do. Homing in on a weak spot and wrapping a vicious lie around a grain of truth. Maggie knew how to hit well below the belt. Sara did feel responsible for Bill's death. It was something she would have to live with for the rest of her life.

How could Maggie have been so cruel? With some regret, Sara thought that perhaps she had been trying to resuscitate something long dead. It was desperately sad that neither of them had been able to right what had gone wrong in Wales, but that night in Totem was unforgivable. Sara sighed. Another person was gone from her life, despite her best efforts.

It suddenly occurred to her why Maggie had popped up in her mind. That was who Cynthia Hargreaves reminded her of. She could see the proprietor standing on the other side of the function room and realised with a shudder that she was looking at Maggie in thirty years' time. Both women shared a gaunt, brittle, ungiving air. She'd heard the gossip at the *Herald* about Cynthia's ruthlessness and she guessed that, given half a chance, Maggie would be right up there with her, matching Cynthia sneer for sneer.

Sara hadn't wanted to come to the launch, not with Kathy so close to giving birth, but all staff were on a three-line whip for this one. Alive TV, with its commitment to downmarket, low-budget programming, mostly bought in from America, had met with much ridicule when Cynthia had first floated the idea, but her will to succeed, coupled with the backing of the banks, had brought it to fruition. Cynthia's reputation, along with a large chunk of her fortune, was riding on the success of the venture and all Herald Group newspapers had been briefed to extol the virtues of Alive TV at every available opportunity. This was easier for those working on the *Comet*, the *Herald*'s tabloid sister, but there had been a furore when Cynthia had ordered the broadsheet *Herald* to run competitions with satellite dishes as prizes. It'll be bingo next, the *Herald*'s editor had said bitterly – but only once the proprietor was safely out of earshot.

'Penny for them?'

Sara looked up. 'Stuart! How lovely to see you. I was hoping you'd be here to make the evening bearable.' He seemed to get thinner each time she saw him. 'I hope you don't mind me asking, but have you lost weight?'

'Not that I'm aware of,' replied Stuart, denying the evidence in front of her. Since their last meeting, just before Christmas, he had definitely shed several pounds. The weight loss had had an unsettling effect. Whereas in the past he had always looked as neat as a pin, his grey flannel Savile Row suit now seemed to be wearing him rather than the other way around. The collar on his shirt seemed a little loose, too, giving him a somewhat frail appearance.

'Stuart—'

'"Alive – for all the family,"' laughed Stuart, quoting the station's publicity handout and cutting her short. 'That's why I'm here, by the way. Cynthia thought we should put on a show of unity, but she hasn't noticed me yet. That odious snob Christopher Heard is paying her court at the moment.'

Heard was the *Herald*'s suave diarist. Sara was on nodding terms with him at the office.

'What have you been up to? I haven't seen you in ages,' said Stuart.

'I'm sorry, I haven't been to Camden recently. You know how it is – Saturday's my busiest day.'

'Surely we don't have to restrict our meetings to the matches? I spend most of the week at my Commons apartment. You're more than welcome to call any time. Or why not pop into the House? I'd love to show you around.'

'I'll take you up on that.'

'Oh dear. Here comes Cynthia.'

Cynthia was coming towards them, the sharp bangs of her iron-grey bob seeming to slice a swathe through the crowd. 'There you are, Stuart. You're late.'

Sara watched Stuart's face, interested to see how he reacted to his wife. The whole of Fleet Street was petrified of Cynthia, but her husband merely glared at her with a weary belligerence. 'I'm your husband, woman, not an employee,' he said. It gave Sara a thrill to see someone so openly defy her boss's power.

'That's a debatable point,' replied the proprietor. She unfurled a spindly finger and pointed it at Sara. 'And who is this? Your latest "research assistant"?'

There was no way in the world that Cynthia was unaware of who she was. From editors to janitors, Cynthia knew everyone whose salaries she paid.

'Mrs Hargreaves, I'm Sara Moore, the *Herald*'s football writer,' she said anyway, holding out her hand.

Cynthia ignored her gesture. 'I suppose my husband's boring you with one of his ridiculously long-winded football anecdotes. Stuart, please tell me it wasn't the one about the 1966 World Cup. The poor girl probably wasn't even born when that took place.'

'I was merely telling Sara here how much I enjoy her writing,' responded Stuart smoothly. 'She's an excellent journalist – the *Herald* is lucky to have her. Cynthia, shouldn't you be getting back to Mr Heard? He's such a terrible gossip. Aren't you worried about what he's saying about you behind your back?'

Cynthia's chest heaved and she gritted her teeth as she geared herself up to tear a strip off her husband. But just then one of the bankers backing the TV station appeared and Cynthia whisked him away to talk business.

'You mustn't be frightened of her,' said Stuart to Sara. 'Cynthia's power is fuelled by the fear she induces. Take her on on an equal footing and her strength disappears, just like that.' He snapped his fingers.

'That's easy for you to say. As you said, you're not on the payroll.' Sara could see that there would be some comeback to this episode.

'Oh, but I am. What do you think I married her for?'

Sara was shocked by this frank admission. 'Stuart, that's terrible.'

'I know, but it's the truth. Her name, and her money, I am ashamed to say, helped my political career.' He was too anxious to let Sara know that he had not married this cold woman for any other reason to worry that she might think ill of him for this. 'I hate myself for it now, but it seemed far too late to get out of our pact a long time ago. I can only hope that one day there will be some recompense.' Sara was slightly puzzled by his last remark. But Stuart put his hand on hers and said, 'I'm afraid much of my life has been a disaster.'

She was at a loss as to how she could even begin to dispel his evident sorrow. 'But you've had such a successful career.'

Stuart look impassioned now. The frailty Sara had noted earlier had disappeared. 'I know how important your job is to you. I've encouraged you in your career all the way, but never for one second be fooled that it's enough. You got it right once, so don't make the same mistake as me in the future. A long time ago I renounced

love for my career, and without love a life can never be judged a
success.'

Worn out from a whole evening at her Apple Mac, charting Arsenal's
fortunes over the past twenty years for a special feature she was
doing for the *Herald*'s Saturday magazine supplement, Sara ran a
bath, once again mulling over the warning Stuart had given her a
few weeks earlier. She had found love with Bill, but it had been
so short-lived; finished before it had even really begun. She would
never have that with anyone else – she didn't even want it with
anyone else. Bill would be her first and last love. Tears began to
well up. Stop being maudlin, she berated herself, pulling off her
T-shirt.

The phone rang.

'Hello? Sara? You've got to meet me at the hospital – now. I'm
in labour.'

'Oh, my God. Kathy, where's Joseph? Is he with you? Has he
called an ambulance?'

Her questions were met with no more than an occasional grunt
over the line as Kathy struggled to cope with the pain of a
contraction. There was a sharp intake of breath. 'No, he's not
here. He went out. I've called an ambulance.'

Sara looked at her watch. It was 12.30. But now was not the time to
ask what the hell he was doing out at this late hour when his wife was
due to give birth any minute, and after such a difficult pregnancy.
She had given up asking what was really going on between Kathy
and Joseph. Whenever she tried to broach the subject Kathy always
shrugged off her concerns, saying that the pregnancy had turned
her into a screaming harridan and that Joseph was probably better
off out of it. Sara didn't believe her story for a minute.

'Aaargh!' gasped Kathy.

'Kathy! Kathy! Are you OK?' She had to keep the panic out of
her voice. 'Try to relax, and remember to breathe deeply.' Thank
God for the example of hospital dramas, she thought as she tried
to reassure her friend. 'The ambulance will be with you at any
moment.'

'Go straight – aaargh, oh my God, it's unbearable,' she paused and Sara could hear her sobbing. 'Go straight to the delivery suite . . .'

Sara threw her T-shirt back over her head, pulling it down and grabbing a coat as she ran out to the car. Her mind seemed to go into autopilot as she drove through the semi-empty streets of north London towards Queen Mary's Hospital in Paddington, trying not to think about how she was going to make it through the night without her heart breaking.

Sara rushed through the corridors of the hospital until she found the delivery suite. 'Is Kathy McCabe here?' she asked breathlessly the first person she spotted in a uniform .

'She's in room number four. Just there,' replied the nurse, pointing to a door opposite.

Sara knocked and entered the room. Her friend, dressed in a hospital nightgown, was crouching on the floor. 'Kathy, it's me. How are you bearing up?' she asked, throwing her coat and bag on the floor.

Kathy seized Sara's hand in a vice-like grip in answer. Finally she managed to gasp, 'I'm so glad you're here. Thanks for – oh, God.'

'Come on, Kathy, breathe all the way out,' said Sara. 'That's it, breathe the pain out. It'll be all right.'.

'Are you the birthing partner? I thought it was Kathy's husband.'

Sara looked up, surprised. She hadn't noticed that there was anyone else in the room. 'No – er – yes. Yes, I am if he isn't here yet.'

'I'm Lucy – the midwife.' The woman smiled.

'Please give me some gas and air,' pleaded Kathy.

'All right, dear,' replied the midwife, passing Kathy the nozzle. 'Now, breathe like you have been doing. Deep breaths. I need to examine you to see how far the cervix has dilated. Please try to keep still.'

Kathy jumped as the midwife's hand entered her. 'I can't,' she screamed.

'Breathe some more gas, and let me try again.'

Sara brushed Kathy's damp hair back from her forehead. 'It's all going to be OK,' she murmured.

'Well, Kathy, you're nine centimetres dilated, so there's not much longer to go. You're doing really well,' encouraged Lucy.

Kathy held out her hand to Sara again as she sucked deeply on the gas. 'It's not working. I can't take any more,' she shrieked. 'Where's my bloody husband?'

'It'll be all right, nearly there,' soothed Sara. She felt utterly useless. It was frightening to see someone she loved in so much pain. But somewhere in the recesses of her mind she knew that she'd go through a hundred times this agony for a baby of her own.

'Oh, bloody hell, I've got to push.'

'That's good, we're nearly there. Stop using the gas now.'

Kathy reluctantly handed the gas back to Sara. She roared at the top of her lungs as she pushed.

'You need to bear down more,' said Lucy. 'Push your leg against me and your bottom down on to the bed.'

Kathy did as she was told. Sara smiled encouragingly as she lifted a glass of water to Kathy's parched lips. They were both sweating profusely in the hot, stuffy room.

'It's probably going to feel quite scary as the head comes out, but don't worry, everything's fine.'

'Uh, uh,' Kathy grunted in response as the baby's head moved down a little further. 'I think I'm giving birth to a football,' she screamed. 'With a Bunsen burner attached to it!'

Sara laughed. 'That's the spirit. You're doing really well. You're so strong.'

'I can see the head now, one more push,' said Lucy.

Sara could see the bluish, reddish top of the baby's head. A lump formed in her throat as she watched it turning to start the next stage of its journey into the world. It was a miracle. But she was just a bystander, and her barren insides ached with thwarted dreams.

'Stop pushing,' instructed the midwife. 'Just pant while I check the cord's OK. All right, one more push.'

Suddenly there was a cry as the baby slid out and sucked in its first breath. In one swift movement the midwife brought the baby up on to Kathy's stomach.

'What is it?' asked Kathy, tears streaming down her face.

'A little girl, a beautiful little girl,' cried Sara.

Kathy pulled her daughter to her breast and, through her tears, she whispered, 'Welcome to the world, Bette Sara McCabe.'

The room was silent as mother and baby clung to each other. Lifting her head, Kathy asked Sara, 'Would you like to hold her?'

Sara felt the tears begin to fall as she took the little bundle. She was so tiny, so perfect. For a split-second she imagined that it was her baby, hers and Bill's. A sob caught in her throat.

'I'd better check the baby,' said Lucy, gently taking the child away from her.

Kathy took Sara's hand and squeezed it. There was no need for words.

Lucy returned Bette to Kathy. 'She's perfect, and weighs in at seven pounds two ounces.'

'Did Joseph come?'

Sara shook her head.

'How could he have missed this moment?' she asked plaintively.

Sara didn't leave until Joseph finally arrived. Kathy had wanted her to stay, but Sara knew that there was no place for her in the little family circle. She got into her car and sat there, staring at the window. She was happy for Kathy, but her own pain had become physical. She rested her head on the steering wheel and, in a rare moment of complete self-pity, she sobbed until there were no tears left.

Eventually, she started the car and drove out of the car park. And she just kept on driving, circling around London, driving without concentration with no conception of time. It must have been several hours later that she found herself not far from Stuart's Commons apartment. The thought of Stuart was comforting. She wanted to see him.

'Sara, what on earth's wrong?' he asked as he let her in. 'It's not even six o'clock.'

'Oh, Stuart, I didn't realise,' she said, turning in a daze back towards the front door.

'Don't be silly, I've been up for an hour. It's not only our former PM who can get by on four hours' sleep a night. I'm just concerned about you.'

'Oh, it's nothing to worry about. It's strange, really. I've been at the hospital all night – Kathy's had her baby, a little girl. I needed someone to talk to. You seemed the right person.'

'You don't know how much it pleases me that you've come to me. Now, sit down, and I'll put the kettle on, and you can tell me what's bothering you.'

She sat in silence as he made the tea. When he handed her the cup she took it gratefully.

'Now, tell me what's upsetting you so.'

'Stuart, there's something about the crash I've never told you. It's been too painful up until now . . .' For several seconds she choked back her tears. 'I was carrying Bill's child,' she blurted, her tears running freely now. 'I lost our baby, and I'll never be able to have another one.'

'Whyever not? You're young, you'll find someone else to make you happy, and—'

'No, you don't understand. They had to remove my . . . my womb. I *can't* have children.'

'Oh, my dear child, I'm so sorry. Let it all come out,' he said, hugging her close to him and gently stroking her hair. 'No one deserves as much pain as you've endured. But this is the end of it, Sara. I'm making a promise to you. There'll be no more hurting.'

'I want to believe you, but I can't. I just can't see that my life is ever going to get any better. What have I got to look forward to? A life of loneliness. It just feels as though I'm always taking one step forward and two steps back.'

'You're surrounded by people who love you. And you never go back. Everything you feel takes you forward. You never know what's coming next: that's what's so beautiful about life. How could I have ever predicted that I would meet you, or the happiness that has brought me? Never write off life, Sara. It has the most wonderful way of surprising you.'

'But it hurts so much at times.'

Stuart held her tightly as if he were physically trying to relieve her of the burden of her pain by making it his. 'That's to remind you that you're alive.'

*   *   *

After their early-morning conversation the relationship between Stuart and Sara took on a new depth and she felt closer to him than she had to any person since Bill. As Bette brought a new rapprochement between Kathy and Joseph, Sara felt something of an interloper there and she found herself spending more and more of her time with the politician. They indulged their mutual love of music and art at concerts and exhibitions, took in a few plays and kept up their outings to Camden's matches whenever their schedules allowed.

Hurrying to Stuart's office one evening, the sound of her heels echoing through the hallowed halls of Westminster, it occurred to her that what Stuart had said on the night of Bette's birth was true. Life did have a way of surprising you. Who could have seen on the afternoon of the graduation ceremony all those years ago that Stuart would have become such an important part of her life? Her father could never be replaced, of course, but she'd never dreamed that another man would come along to take a paternal role in her life in a different way.

Stuart was waiting for her at the door of his office. 'Come in, come in.'

'Hi, sorry I'm late, I had a deadline.'

'That's perfectly all right. Well, here you are in the centre of the universe, where all the machinations of power are played out. Supposedly,' he said, with a disarming smile.

Sara looked around the room. 'You've made it very cosy.'

'That's all down to Doreen, my secretary. She's been with me since I was first elected an MP. Don't ask me how many years ago that was, I dread to think. To be honest, both Doreen and I are long overdue for retirement. Along with the whole damned government. Don't you agree?'

'I'm sure there's plenty left for you to do, if not your party.'

'The problem is that John doesn't want another by-election at the moment, and my seat's a bit precarious. Without wanting to blow my own trumpet, I think the general feeling is that in the past I've been elected *despite* being a Conservative.'

Sara smiled indulgently. She knew he had no intention of giving up the ghost, even though he had a workload that would give problems to a man half his age. She wished she could persuade him to give it all up. He was looking frailer and paler than ever, but she knew her plea would fall on deaf ears.

'Why are you looking so pleased with yourself?'

'I've just been given every little boy's dream.'

Stuart raised his eyebrows quizzically.

'Next year I get to vote for the Footballer of the Year. I've been accepted into the Football Writers' Association, one of the last bastions of male supremacy.'

'Congratulations! I'm impressed. It's no more than you deserve, of course. I'm glad those old curmudgeons have seen sense at last.'

'I think they still don't want to believe that a member of the second sex can write about the offside trap or whether the multi-million-pound man can play the sweeper system.'

'I believe this calls for champagne.'

Sara laughed. 'Stuart, you think any occasion calls for champagne, but I'd love a glass anyway.'

He pressed a button on his intercom. 'Doreen, could you bring us through a bottle of bubbly?'

'Yes, Mr Hargreaves.' She answered him with an indulgence usually reserved for young children.

Doreen brought in a bottle and two glasses. 'Sara, this is my long suffering secretary, Doreen. Doreen, this is Sara, a very dear friend.'

The women smiled at each other.

'Don't have too much, Mr Hargreaves,' warned the secretary.

Stuart looked properly contrite. 'I won't.' When Doreen had left the office, Stuart raised his glass and said, 'Here's to women taking over.'

'I'll drink to that,' replied Sara.

'Oh, by the way, my doctor thinks I could do with a few days away, so I thought I'd come to Stockholm with you.' Sara was covering the England–Sweden match. 'You'll have time between games for a few meals, won't you?'

'Why are you seeing a doctor? What's wrong?'

'Nothing to be alarmed about. I'm just a bit under the weather. I need something to blow away the cobwebs.'

'Won't Cynthia mind?'

'Of course she'll mind. That's half the fun of doing it.'

Sara laughed. 'You're very cavalier about my career.'

'Not at all,' said Stuart very seriously. 'I've told you. You have to approach Cynthia on her level. And believe me, that will happen.'

As was sometimes the case, Stuart's comment seemed to have a cryptic undertone, but Sara was getting used to this and paid little attention to it. 'I'd love you to come,' she said.

'Glad to hear it. I will make one concession, though. I plan to stay in a different hotel. I'd hate to see what the press could make of us dining out together and then returning to the same place. I intend to keep a very low profile.'

A roar of disapproval arose from the small crowd of English fans at one end of the Ullevi Stadium.

'My God, the man's a fool. I can't believe he's sent Lineker off! It's a national disgrace. You idiot!' shouted Sid Kelly of the *Comet* to the back of Graham Taylor's head.

Sara saw that Gary Lineker shared Sid's feelings as he tossed away his captain's armband. Trying to ignore the uproar Taylor's decision had caused, she quickly wrote the intro to her report:

'It was Gary Lineker's 80th game on the international stage but when he was taken off the pitch by manager Graham Taylor, he was still two goals short of overhauling Bobby Charlton's England record of 49 goals.'

'We're in a right bloody pickle now,' commented Sid. 'That man has tried more patterns than a wallpaper manufacturer. Taylor should be sacked.'

Sara agreed and neither was surprised that when the final whistle blew England were 2–1 down to Sweden.

All the journalists rushed off to interview Lineker. As always it was impossible to tell what 'Mr Nice Guy' was really thinking and feeling. If he was angry he wasn't saying.

Calmly he told the reporters, 'There's no chance at all of me reconsidering my decision to retire from international football. It's not the way I wanted it to finish. I would have preferred a successful ending. But football is full of ups and downs.'

Stuart was also in a stew over the decision when Sara caught up with him in the VIP box. 'I think you're going to have to become as philosophical as Lineker,' she told him.

'Never.'

As they left the stadium it was clear that Stuart, along with most of the English supporters, was in a despondent mood. Sara tried cheering him up. 'Tell me, Mr Hargreaves,' she asked, 'as England manager, what are your future tactical plans?'

It was hard to hear his reply over the angry chants of the crowds milling in the street. 'Well, Miss Moore, I think . . .'

Suddenly Stuart fell to his knees and disappeared in a forest of legs. The events of the next few moments seemed to take place in slow motion. Sara felt herself flying to the ground to protect Stuart, and it was only when she felt the first kick in the ribs that she realised they were in the middle of a riot.

Stuart lay on the pavement, glassy-eyed and breathing heavily. Sara bent over him to shield him from the blows. She had to get him to safety. 'Come on, Stuart, get up! We've got to get away from here!'

Still winded, Stuart struggled to his feet. 'My God, what the Devil is going on?'

Sara turned to see hundreds of English fans, their faces contorted with anger and lust for revenge. 'I don't think they like losing. Quick!'

Armed riot police appeared from nowhere, their mood no better than that of the fans, and for a while Sara and Stuart cowered in a doorway while a pitched battle took place. The marauding England supporters threw anything they could get their hands on – paving slabs, rocks, beer bottles, the missiles flew through the air. Sara looked on, horrified, as over fifteen England fans kicked a Swedish skinhead unconscious. Blow after blow rained down on his head as he rolled into a ball to protect himself.

'I've got to stop them,' said Stuart, moving out of the doorway.

'Oh no you don't, they'll kill you.' Sara pulled him back towards her but once again his knees buckled and he collapsed. 'Stuart, what's wrong?'

'I need to rest for a while. I'll be fine.'

Sara sat down with her arm around him and watched as the riot receded into the surrounding streets. After a while an eerie calm began to settle.

'Come on,' said Sara. 'We've got to get you back to your hotel.' She helped him stand up, hearing the rattling of his chest as he struggled to regulate his breathing.

Arm in arm, they walked through the now-deserted streets of Stockholm. With a terrible sense of foreboding, Sara knew that she had to ask Stuart an important question. 'Why did your doctor tell you to go away? What is wrong with you? And please don't tell me it's nothing, I won't believe you.'

His answer was brisk and matter-of-fact. 'I have cancer.'

Chapter Twenty-Two

Cynthia looked through the window of her office over to the sports department. She tensed as she spotted Sara, sitting on the edge of a desk, swinging her long legs. Cynthia knew herself too well to deny that the sight of Sara Moore didn't create a gnawing jealousy that tore at her insides. It wasn't so much Stuart's doting admiration that upset her, although she could remember him being this smitten only once before, with the same type of woman. That had been nearly thirty years ago. Cynthia had watched impotently as the relationship developed and for the only time in their marriage she had feared she would lose him. And then the little tart disappeared right off the face of the earth. Perhaps this one would vanish too. What was it with her ridiculous husband and his passion for redheads?

She studied the football writer carefully. The similarity was frightening: the same almond-shaped green eyes, the high cheekbones – even the walk was similar. What really hurt was that, for all the plastic surgeons in Harley Street, Cynthia could never have bought the beauty that Sara Moore had naturally. When she looked at her austere face in the mirror, it made her want to weep with frustration.

She rang Stuart to vent her anger. 'Doreen, no excuses, just put my husband on.'

Over the years Doreen had tried valiantly to protect Stuart from his wife but she very rarely succeeded; she was no match for Cynthia.

'What is it, Cynthia? I'm on my way to an important vote.'

'I've had enough. I'm firing your tart. You've made a real fool of me, fawning over her, just like that two-bit model you used to chase. Don't think I don't know what you were up to in Stockholm.'

'Cynthia, you do one thing to harm Sara Moore and I'll give the story of my life to the *Daily Mail*. It should make interesting reading. There are certain things that even you don't know.'

'You wouldn't dare,' she seethed, her voice consumed with hatred.

'Why not? I haven't anything to lose any more, have I? I'm telling you for the last time, woman, just leave Sara alone or else. There is nothing improper going on between us.'

'If you expect me to believe that, you must be suffering from Alzheimer's as well as cancer.'

'Cynthia, you are as ugly on the inside as you are on the surface. One more word from you and I'll bring everything crashing down around your ears.'

'Tick-tock, Stuart. That's the seconds ticking away, and it's the sound of your cells dying one by one. Can you feel it eating through your body? It hurts even to eat or drink, doesn't it, Stuart? Can you smell it yet? They say you can. How ugly are you inside?'

'When you welcome in death, Cynthia, be careful what else comes through the door.'

The proprietor slammed down the phone and kicked her waste-paper basket across the room. He would go to the *Mail*, she had no doubt about it. The old bastard had her over a barrel, but not for long. Nothing would save Sara Moore when he was gone. He might have been a great political fixer in his time but there was nothing that even he could do from the grave.

Thinking about Stuart's illness calmed her slightly and she

reflected on how odd it was that after forty years she still felt the need to control him. Even though the only feelings she had for him now were acrimonious and, at times, bordered on intense hatred, she couldn't quite let him go. It came as a bitter blow to her that, along with beauty, Stuart's love was something else that she'd never been able to buy.

The thought tormented her. Early in their marriage she had exercised her power over him and Stuart had toed the line just as everybody else in her life did. But, bit by bit, he'd exerted his independence as his own career took off, and she'd lost him. That one failure clouded all her successes. No matter what she achieved, no matter how many people lived in mortal fear of her, Stuart's rejection seemed to mock her. Until he was dead, she would never be able to see herself as truly unassailable. That time was fast approaching, she thought as she sat at her computer and tapped into the Reuters news service. And in the meantime, there were numerous foreign stories that only the sacred Sara Moore would be capable of covering.

Stuart had given Sara a key to his flat as it had become too much of a struggle for him to make it from the bedroom to the front door. She came to see him at least twice a week and there was always a moment, as she turned the lock, when she was filled with apprehension at what she might find inside. Over the previous few months his health had deteriorated rapidly, as if the concealment of his illness from her had been his driving force and, now that she knew, there was nothing to stop him leaving the world behind.

Yet Stuart insisted on staying at his apartment and not at his home with Cynthia. There would have been little care lavished on the dying politician. In any case, they had long led separate lives except in public, and Stuart was seen out very rarely these days. Sara had persuaded him to hire a team of nurses to provide round-the-clock care. The nurses were under strict instructions to call her immediately should an emergency arise. It was now just a matter of time. There had been a scare over Christmas and Stuart had been forced to go into hospital, but he had pulled through; indeed, of late his condition seemed to be much improved.

Today Sara found him asleep, the lunchtime CNN report playing to itself on the TV pushed in front of his bed. The middle-aged, homely nurse who was reading by his bedside looked up and smiled.

'Don't disturb him, Janice,' whispered Sara. 'I'll try to come back later.'

The nurse put down her book. 'He was very insistent that I woke him when you arrived. You know how much he looks forward to your visits.' She stood up and gently shook the politician's shoulder. 'Stuart, Sara's here.'

Stuart half opened his eyes and smiled. 'Sara, my dear, come and sit down.' With some effort he eased himself up on his elbows while Janice propped up the pillows behind him. 'Are those for me?' he asked, noticing the daffodils Sara held in her hand. 'How lovely. Janice, could you find something to put them in?'

The nurse took this as her cue to leave. Stuart liked to spend his time with Sara alone.

'You're watching CNN,' noted Sara, sitting on the bed beside him. 'Isn't that a bit disloyal? Alive has a perfectly good news service. You should try it.'

'And see their viewing figures rise by fifty per cent? I wouldn't give Cynthia the pleasure.'

Stuart's remark was only a slight exaggeration. So far, fewer than 300,000 households had signed up for Alive TV and the company was experiencing financial difficulties. Sara had read in the *Herald*'s competitors that the station was relying too much on advertising revenue, which was put at no more than £500,000 a week, while the weekly £5 million running costs were eating into Cynthia's personal finances.

'Have you heard, she's increased her overdraft by another ten million?' Stuart seemed positively gleeful about his wife's parlous financial state.

'I heard a rumour. There's a real sense of panic at the *Herald*. Paul Robinson, the television editor, resigned on Friday. Cynthia sent word down that he wasn't being favourable enough to Alive's output.'

Stuart picked up the remote control on the bedside cabinet

and changed channels. On Alive 1, *Comet* page 3 girl Mandy Barraclough was presenting *Chart-toppers*.

'And that was Bill . . .' Mandy was struggling to read the autocue. 'Collins!' she said triumphantly. 'And next up, a video from . . . er . . . from . . . from one of your favourites.' Nothing happened. Mandy looked off camera beseechingly. She nodded and confirmed: 'Any second now.'

After watching another thirty seconds of Mandy staring vacantly around her, Stuart switched off in disgust. 'I can't believe Cynthia had the nerve to ask me to put money into that travesty. Things must be pretty tight for her at the moment. I'm sure she's hoping that I'll go under before the station does.'

'Stuart, don't say that!'

'Sara, the fact that I'm dying isn't going to go away if we don't talk about it. Come on, you've dealt with it so well up until now. Before I told you, I was afraid of how you'd react. You'd been through so much – I thought you might want to run away from this one.'

'When you first told me in Stockholm I felt so angry with you. On the night Bette was born, you told me all the hurting would stop. You lied.'

'Death's an inevitability, Sara,' said the politician calmly.

Sara got up and walked over to the window, not wanting to look him in the eye. 'It sounds as if you've given up.'

'That's a very unkind thing to say.'

She turned to face him. Hurting Stuart was the last thing she wanted to do but she was trying to make him fight. 'Why won't you accept any treatment?'

'My dear girl, we've been through this. You know there's no real treatment. And in contrast with so much of my life, I'm trying to manage my death with a little bit of dignity. I'm sixty-six now – at the time I was born that was a fine old age to aspire to. I'm content with that. One can't stop dealing with life because of the prospect of death. I'm glad you feel angry about it. Keep that anger and use it to push you forward.'

'You make it sound so easy. As if it's merely a question of will.'

'But it is. And rarely have I met someone as strong-willed as you. Listen, if this is bothering you we'll talk about something else.'

Sara seized the chance. 'I'm going to Bette's first birthday party this afternoon.'

Stuart's eyes brightened. 'How is your little goddaughter?'

'Gooddaughter,' corrected Sara. 'Remember they had a naming day, not a christening?'

'Hmm,' said Stuart. There were some things he was still very traditional about. 'Anyway, how is she?'

'Fine, by all accounts. I haven't seen very much of Kathy really.'

'Sara, you're spending too much time with the dying and not enough with the living.'

Sara looked down at her hands, guiltily. It was true, but on the few occasions she had seen Kathy in recent months, living had been hardly the word she'd use to describe her friend's existence.

'Say thank you to Auntie Sara,' shouted Kathy, over the noise of eight children fighting for the job of being the balloon-bender's assistant. As Bette gurgled delightedly and toddled unsteadily away with the new bear, Kathy embraced her friend. 'It's been ages.'

'Too long,' said Sara. There had been a tacit acceptance between the two women that their friendship, or at least the time they devoted to it, had been put on hold to allow themselves to fulfil their respective roles as carers. For Sara, though, it was more than time that had been sacrificed. Although it was hard to face up to it, she knew deep down that she had buried herself in taking care of Stuart to avoid dealing with the envy she felt about Kathy's motherhood.

Bette dropped the bear and sat down beneath the table, away from the other children. Kathy sighed and picked her up. 'You're tired, baby, aren't you?'

Like daughter like mother, thought Sara.

Kathy walked with the baby towards the kitchen. 'Come on, let's get the cake and see if we can control this bedlam.'

Sara followed, dodging the marauding children, wondering if her friend minded that there were now several sets of sticky fingerprints on her hand-painted living-room wallpaper. In the calm of the kitchen, she asked, 'Where's Joseph?'

'Working and that's a topic I'd rather not discuss today,' said Kathy, to forestall any inquisition into the state of her marriage.

'Let's talk about Maggie, then. I saw in the *Guardian* that she's been made editor of *Chloe*. I hear she's upping the diet content.' It was a cruel joke, but Sara wanted to get some reaction out of Kathy. Yet worktalk didn't seem to interest Kathy either. Along with her clothes sense and her vitality, somewhere along the line she had lost all her drive and ambition. After only a few months as editor on *Mariella*, she'd relinquished the post and had been given the catch-all title of contributing editor. Sara scoured the magazine every month, but Kathy McCabe's by-line was rarely to be seen.

'OK, let's party,' said Sara with a fake jaunty tone.

Four hours later, exhausted, Sara left her friend. 'Let's keep in closer touch.'

Kathy hugged her by way of reply.

'Felicity! You came at last,' said Stuart, drinking a milky concoction through a straw.

'It's Sara,' said Janice. 'You know who Sara is.'

Sara put down her bag and kissed Stuart on the forehead. 'Of course he does,' she said, hating the way Janice spoke to him as if he were a child.

Sara hadn't seen Stuart for almost a week. Recently the budget for the *Herald*'s sport pages had been enlarged to allow for a series of articles on football in Europe, all of which were to be penned by Sara. The other journalists thought she was on to a good thing, getting all these foreign trips to write about the likes of Juventus and AC Milan, but Sara knew the real reason behind it. Although Dean Gavin wouldn't have said anything, even if he knew, Sara guessed that she was being sent abroad on Cynthia's instruction.

It seemed that there were no lengths to which the proprietor would not go to spoil the happiness of her husband's last few months. Sara knew about the bitter battle that had raged between the couple for years, and despite Stuart's assurances to the contrary, she accepted that sooner or later her job would be its latest casualty. So if Cynthia wanted to spend money on sending Sara away, then so be it.

Coming back from these trips, the apprehension Sara felt on

visiting Stuart increased tenfold. Although she pretended otherwise, his condition was deteriorating at great speed. Today, the biggest shock on her return from Belgium, where she'd spent a week following the fortunes of Royal Antwerp FC, was that Stuart was taking liquid morphine to combat the pain. The drug was affecting his lucidity somewhat, and it broke her heart to see this once eloquent, clear-thinking man catch himself calling her Felicity for the second time.

'What am I talking about?' he spluttered in embarrassment. 'Of course you're not Felicity. You must think I'm an idiot. Sara, welcome back. How was Belgium?'

'As boring as its reputation. Don't ever think of becoming a Euro MP.' She was shocked that in a week his body had sunk further into decline. The weight loss was the most dramatic sign: his cheeks were sunken and the veins in his forehead protruded from under his pale, wafery skin, while his wrists looked as if they would break if held too tight. Sara reached into her bag and produced a book. 'I didn't buy you a Manneken Pis but I did bring you this. It's a preview copy of Alan Clarke's diaries. I think they make even you look reserved.'

Stuart's laugh turned into gasp. 'I don't think I'll get time to finish them.'

'Don't be silly, of course you will.' Her denial of his impending death was for her own benefit rather than his. Not acknowledging it made it less real somehow, and so she continued to make plans for the future with him. 'Did you know that Cynthia has banished me to Ecuador to cover the South American Championships? I needn't go. I don't want to be away so long – it's nearly three weeks.'

'You have to go. Don't give that woman any reason whatsoever to fire you. Hold on. Anyway, you'll enjoy it. Ecuador is a wonderful place.'

'All right, but in the meantime, if you feel well enough, I'd be honoured if you would be my guest at the Football Writers' Association dinner. I might even let you influence my vote.'

'How could I refuse?' he said, managing his old smile and reminding Sara of how much better he had looked only a couple of months before.

* * *

Getting ready for the Football Writers' Association dinner, Sara was buoyed up by optimism. She'd spoken to Stuart earlier in the day and he was determined to come. His nursing team had given their permission, although much to Stuart's chagrin he would have to attend in a wheelchair. Nevertheless, he was in high spirits as the doctors seemed confident that he had entered a period, however brief, of remission.

She had deliberated for ages over what to wear. Tonight she wanted to emphasise that she was most definitely *not* one of the boys. She wanted to stand out to underline the achievement of a woman getting into the association. Rejecting her work suits as too masculine, she finally selected the little black dress she had worn the night she first met Bill. It was still her favourite dress. Putting it on brought back memories of that wonderful New Year's Eve. She smoothed the dress down over her hips and examined herself in the mirror. No wonder Bill fell in love with you, she thought, smiling, glad that the memories it conjured did not bring pain, just gratitude that she had experienced the joy of loving Bill.

Just as she was applying the final touch of lipstick, the phone rang.

'Hello, Sara? It's Janice. I'm afraid Stuart's been taken into hospital.'

Twenty minutes later, Sara hurtled out of a cab and ran up the steps to the hospital still dressed in her evening wear. She stopped for a second to take off her heels and then ran into reception. She was directed to the private room where Stuart had been taken.

'Are you family?' asked the doctor, standing outside Stuart's room.

Sara froze fearing what the doctor was going to say next. 'No. I'm a friend. A good friend.'

'I'm sorry, but I can't let you see him at the moment. He needs to rest.'

Thank God – he was still hanging on. Sara said a silent prayer. 'He did ask that I be contacted. Are you sure that I couldn't see him just for a moment?'

The doctor looked at her watch. 'One minute.'

Inside the room the wasted figure on the bed, hidden beneath a welter of tubes and drips, mouth covered with an oxygen mask and bare, withered arms a mass of bruising, was barely recognisable as Stuart. He looked so ill, so vulnerable, that for a brief second Sara found herself wishing him a speedy death. The reality of dying was so unlike it was in the movies. She remembered crying over *Love Story* with Maggie as a teenager. But in that film Ali McGraw had faded away so photogenically, so tranquilly. The real thing was debasing and frightening.

Sara noticed Janice sitting in a chair by the wall. Her head kept falling to one side as she succumbed to tiredness. Sara shook the nurse's shoulder gently. 'Janice. Janice. It's Sara.'

'Oh, Sara, hi. I must have dozed off.'

'What happened?'

'He seemed right as rain this afternoon. He was talking about the dinner this evening. I was just about to hand over to the night shift when he passed out. It might be bad news, I'm afraid.'

'What?' cried Sara.

'The doctors are concerned. His liver's barely functioning and he has secondaries.'

Sara walked over to the bed and gently brushed her fingers against his. 'Can he hear me?'

There was a flicker of movement in the politician's wrist as he attempted to raise his hand. He was trying to speak, but the oxygen mask made it difficult and the hum of machinery all but drowned him out.

'This isn't it,' he gasped. 'It doesn't feel like the time to go. There's so much still to be said.'

'Shh,' said Sara, 'don't tire yourself. There'll be plenty of time tomorrow to talk.'

Sara sat by his bed all night, willing him to make it through until the morning.

Sara packed away her notebook, relieved that her interview with the Brazilian coach, Alberto Maia, had gone well despite his reservations about a woman football writer. His was an attitude shared by many of the South American footballers she'd interviewed over the previous week or so. Maia, keen to be back with his players, said his goodbyes and Sara decided that in the few hours she had to spare before the evening match she might as well do some sightseeing.

As she walked along the banks of the Tomebamba River, she knew she should be admiring the surrounding mountains, but she was lost in her thoughts. Stuart had pulled through that night, and had since gone home, but the doctors had confirmed that the cancer had spread. The prognosis was not good. Sara called his apartment whenever she could, but sometimes he wasn't even able to speak. She couldn't wait to get her work done and get home so that she could be back by his side. Whatever she tried next time, Cynthia wouldn't be able to make her leave again.

After walking aimlessly for over an hour Sara decided that she needed a drink. But football fever had taken over the city – every bar, every restaurant was jam-packed with fans. The tournament had taken the city unawares and Sara had had to smile when even the manager of AC Milan couldn't get the seat he wanted at a match.

She passed a restaurant called Le Jardin, described in her guidebook as the best in Cuenca. Although she didn't hold out much hope of getting a seat she went inside, glad to be in the shade, if only for a moment. Predictably, the place was crowded and the waiter shook his head regretfully. Just as she was turning to leave, a voice called her name. It was Maia. He beckoned her over to his table. 'Miss Moore, please. There is room here.'

Sara smiled gratefully. 'Thank you,' she said, sitting down next to the Brazilian coach.

'This is Antonio Neves, our best striker,' said Maia, introducing her to the man sitting on her other side.

'Of course. You were great yesterday,' she said, aware of the footballer's nearly black, brooding eyes boring into her.

Neves ignored the compliment.

'So what about the game against Chile?' she asked, wondering if his rudeness was perhaps due to a lack of English.

'I don't want to talk . . .' He didn't finish his sentence. Instead he suddenly jumped out of his seat and walked towards a middle-aged woman who had just entered the restaurant. Although her eyes were

hidden behind dark sunglasses it was clear that she was extraordinar-
ily good-looking. Sara watched as Neves and the woman whispered,
both clearly agitated by the subject of their conversation. Neves
looked across to Maia, pointed to the door and followed the woman
out of the restaurant.

'What a pig,' Sara muttered to herself.

The next day Sara watched the Brazil–Chile game as if in a dream,
only half noticing that Neves wasn't playing. She wrote her notes
on autopilot. All she could think of was getting back to Stuart and
after the game, her head aching, she ran back to the hotel. She was
making her way through the lobby to the lift when she heard her
name being called.

'Senhora Moore, please, here.' The receptionist was waving at her.
'Telephone. Senhora Janice.'

Sara ran towards the desk, her heart thudding in her chest. She
picked up the phone and was just about able to make out Janice's
voice through the hubbub of the reception area. 'Janice? Are you
there?' The line faltered and crackled, the nurse's voice coming over
in waves of meaningless syllables. 'Janice, I can't hear you.' In her
frustration she banged the phone against the reception desk. 'Is he
still alive?'

'He wants . . . come back . . . as poss . . .'

That half-sentence was all Sara needed to hear. 'Tell him I'll be
there within twenty-four hours.'

'I'll be checking out,' she told the receptionist. 'Can you order me
a taxi to the airport?' she called back as she raced towards the lift.

Ten minutes later she was back, handing her credit card to the
receptionist. If I can get on the first flight out I should be—

'I'm sorry, Senhora,' the receptionist's voice interrupted her
thoughts, 'this card no good.'

'Try it again,' snapped Sara, impatience rising in her voice.

The receptionist complied, then shook his head. 'It says cancelled.'

'But it can't be. I work for a British newspaper and this is a
company card. It cannot be cancelled.' As she spoke, it dawned on
her: of course her card had been cancelled. Cynthia fully intended
to leave her stranded there.

The receptionist handed back the card. 'How you pay?'

For a second it was all too much for her and tears threatened. Without the card, she couldn't even pay for the hotel room, let alone book a flight out. She leaned against the desk, dropping her suitcases at her feet. She couldn't let Cynthia beat her – not now. 'Could you get me a London number, please?'

Completely exhausted, Sara stepped out of the cab in front of the hospital, only to be met by a gaggle of journalists including someone from the *Herald*. He shot her a questioning look but she didn't have time to talk to him. Head down, she pushed through the reporters and slipped inside.

The money she'd asked Kathy to wire her had taken some time to arrive, and when it finally did, she'd missed the last flight out of the day. She had then spent an uncomfortable night sitting in the departure lounge, unable to afford a hotel room. At last she made it on to the first flight to London the following morning. She couldn't sleep properly on the plane. Instead she watched its agonisingly slow movement as represented on the map on the video screen in front of her. The first thing she'd done when she'd arrived was to phone the hospital. Mercifully, Stuart was still alive.

Although relieved, she was shocked to find that Stuart was alone. Incredibly, Cynthia couldn't even bring herself to be with him on his deathbed. At first he seemed oblivious to Sara's presence; indeed, the only sign that he was still alive was the faint but ominous beep of the heart monitor next to the bed. For a while she just listened to the sound, holding her breath when it stopped momentarily and willing the machine to beep again.

'Stuart?' she whispered.

The politician's eyelids flickered. 'I told you I'd hang on,' he whispered, a faint smile on his lips.

Sara pulled up a chair next to his bed, the relief that she had made it in time smothering her sadness for the present. She considered telling him why it had taken her so long to get there, but decided there was no point. Precious minutes could be wasted on a subject that wasn't worth discussing.

'This is it, isn't it?' she said instead, finally acknowledging his imminent death. The tears flowed unstemmed down her face.

'You mustn't cry,' he said, forcing his cracked lips to part into a small smile. 'I waited for you. I wanted to thank you for all the joy you brought into my life.'

The dry rattle of his chest told Sara that the effort of forcing out the sentence had exhausted him. She reached for his hand, wary that the lightest touch could cause him pain. Gingerly she bought her hand to rest on his, knowing that she had to make her words count. There was so much she had to tell him; she had to thank him for always being there for her, for always believing in her, but especially for pulling her back from the brink after Bill's death. She needed to tell him just how much his friendship had meant to her.

'I love you, Stuart,' she said, simply.

Stuart swallowed. 'You don't know what it means to me to hear you say that.'

'Oh, Stuart! I don't want you to go. I need you.' She gave in to her grief then, and her whole body rocked with uncontrollable sobs. 'I'm s-sorry.'

'Please . . . please don't cry. I love you too, and I'll . . . always be . . . looking out for you, my darling. There's something . . .' The effort to speak was too much, and each tortured breath threatened to defeat him.

'Stuart, do you need oxygen? Shall I call—'

He raised his emaciated arm in protest. 'No. I want to . . . tell you . . . something. I always wanted a daughter and then . . . I found you . . .'

'You've been like a father to—'

'No. It's more than that . . . you . . .' His eyes closed and he seemed to float away.

Sara gripped his hand, willing him to come back. 'Stuart!' She watched as his lips began to move again, noiselessly forming words. 'Stuart, please!'

At that moment the door flew open and Cynthia Hargreaves swept in. 'How dare you!' she screeched, totally disregarding her husband's condition. 'Get out of here, you little tart. Nurse! Nurse! Call security.'

'Stuart, I'm so sorry,' Sara sobbed, squeezing the dying man's hand.

'Get out! Now!'

'Please, Mrs Hargreaves. Let me stay. He's—'

'I want you out of here *now*!'

Totally shattered, Sara got to her feet.

'Do I need to add that you're fired?' spat the proprietor, holding the door open for her.

Sara was dumbfounded. How could the woman even think about work when her husband was drawing his last breaths? 'You really don't care about anyone other than yourself, do you? You truly are an evil woman.'

Behind the two of them the signal on the heart monitor faded unnoticed into a straight line.

Part II

Chapter Twenty-Three

London, England, 2 July 1993

Gerald Scott paced up and down in front of his desk, wishing that he was anywhere other than here at his office in Lincoln's Inn trying to avoid looking Cynthia Hargreaves in the eye. She had arrived early for the reading of the will and had already worked her way through half a packet of cigarettes. He opened a window, hoping that some fresh air might help his breathing.

'Will you stop pacing about,' said Cynthia, sitting in a fug of smoke.

'I'm not sure, but I think my asthma could be flaring up again,' hinted Gerald.

'Well, I'm sure all that faffing around isn't helping. Now sit!'

The solicitor did as he was told, nervously shuffling the papers on his desk, then opening and closing the drawers for the sake of something to do. 'I'm sure she'll be here in a minute,' he said, fingering a ball of elastic bands sitting in his bottom drawer.

'Gerald! Stop fidgeting!'

Gerald jumped and sat upright in his chair, clasping his hands to prevent them from straying. He looked at Cynthia, totally motionless opposite him. Caught in a patch of sunlight, Gerald rather fancied that the leathery old harridan looked like a lizard basking on a rock. Any second now, he thought, her tongue will dart out and whip in a fly. He shifted slightly when he considered that the fly might be him. 'It was a lovely service, wasn't it? I'm sure Stuart would have approved. The readings were very—'

'What does it matter? The man's dead. Who cares whether he would have approved or not? I could have buried him in an orange crate by the side of the motorway, and I doubt he would say very much about it now.' Cynthia looked at her watch. 'Where is the little tart? I suppose she knows all about what is in that old fool's will?'

'I . . . I don't think so.' Gerald's eye began to twitch involuntarily. It had been bad enough breaking the news about the Herald Group shareholding to Cynthia. She still didn't know about the other half of Stuart's bequest. He couldn't bring himself to contemplate her reaction.

'I'm certainly not asking you to think. But if you must do it, think about contesting the will. I'm sure it's safe to say that my husband wasn't in his right mind.'

Gerald took his glasses off to clean them, giving him the advantage of not being able to see her. 'In my opinion – and I want to stress, this is only my opinion – it would be very difficult to assert that Stuart's will was not admissible to probate on the grounds that the testator, I mean Stuart, was not of sound disposing mind.'

'Oh shut up with your pathetic jargon!' Cynthia pulled back her thin lips in a snarl, making it obvious that Gerald Scott's opinion was an irrelevance.

The intercom buzzed. 'Miss Moore is here to see you, sir.'

'Send her in, Gladys,' said Gerald, hoping that Stuart's taste in women had improved with age. As Sara entered the room Gerald had to admit that it had. Dressed in a sober, slate grey suit, Sara Moore, despite looking strained, was beautiful. Gerald was mesmerised by her green, luminous eyes as she walked gracefully with her head held high towards him and shook his hand.

'Pleased to meet you,' said Gerald, beckoning to a seat.

Cynthia didn't even look up to acknowledge her presence. 'Yes, you're right, Gerald. The funeral was magnificent,' she said viciously. 'Everything was just as Stuart would have wanted.'

Sara took a seat and said nothing. The days since the politician's death had been a nightmare. She had been unable to mourn her beloved friend properly as she had been forced to stay away from the funeral. After the awful scene at his deathbed, she knew that the horrendous woman now sitting next to her would have no scruples about making a scene at his graveside. Once again, she had not had the chance to say goodbye to someone special, and once again she had found herself reading about the funeral of the person closest to her in a newspaper, as if she had not even been a part of his life. She wasn't allowed to grieve, and no one other than Kathy and June knew just how much she was hurting. The headlines expressing a nation's sorrow brought little comfort and the sympathy expressed for the 'grieving' widow made her want to scream at the injustice of it all.

'Miss Moore, I'd like to offer you my condolences on your sad loss. I know Stuart valued your friendship very much.'

Sara took a balled-up handkerchief from her pocket, willing herself not to cry in front of Cynthia. 'Thank you, Mr Scott,' she said quietly. 'His death has left a large void in my life.'

Cynthia glared at her. 'Come on, Gerald, get on with it. Tell Miss Moore how much her body was worth to my demented husband.'

Trying to ignore the older woman's venom, Sara closed her eyes and clutched the arms of her chair. 'Mr Scott, please go on.'

The solicitor produced an inhaler and sprayed two puffs into his mouth. 'We are here today because of a very sad loss, and I know emotions are running high, but let us try to get through this with some dignity,' he said, directing his comment at Cynthia.

Cynthia snorted, a wisp of smoke snaking from her nostrils. 'That's easy for you to say, Gerald. You haven't just been cleaned out by some high-class hooker.'

A single tear rolled down Sara's cheek. She gazed out of the window, hoping that somewhere out there, Stuart had escaped to a better place.

Gerald cleared his throat. 'The last will and testament of Stuart Leonard Fairweather Hargreaves. I Stuart Leonard . . .'

Cynthia banged on the desk. 'Oh, for God's sake, cut the crap and tell the slut how much she opened her legs for.'

Red-faced, Gerald protested, 'There's no need for such language, Mrs Harg—'

'Please continue, Mr Scott,' Sara instructed with as much composure as she could muster. 'Let's get this over with.'

'First, Stuart made Miss Moore one of the executors of his will, in which he bequeathed Miss Moore the monies from the liquidation of his current holding in the Herald Group, which I believe at this moment stands at twenty-two per cent.'

Sara's mouth dropped open. 'But I don't understand—'

'Oh, don't come the innocent,' sneered Cynthia, her grey bob trembling as she tried to control her anger. 'You can leave now. You've had your pay-off.' Cynthia still couldn't believe that, after all, Stuart had had the last laugh. Not only had he left a fortune to his mistress, but in the process he had also put her control of the Herald Group in jeopardy.

Sara rose in a daze but Gerald beckoned her to sit down again. 'I'm afraid I haven't finished yet, Miss Moore, there's something else.'

'Give me that will!' screamed Cynthia, propelling herself at the solicitor.

Gerald jumped up and backed himself against the wall. 'Madam, control yourself!' He flinched, expecting her to take a swipe at him but Cynthia sat down again and tore open the cellophane on another cigarette packet. Loosening his tie, Gerald wished that he'd had the courage to insist that Cynthia had listened to the whole story a week earlier. 'It seems Mr Hargreaves has, um,' he stopped to clear his throat once more, 'left Miss Moore a controlling share – fifty-one per cent, to be precise – in Camden United Football Club.'

The room was silent apart from the ticking of the clock. Several minutes passed before Cynthia spoke. 'A football club? Is this some kind of joke?'

'No joke. The papers I have here show that Stuart, not Peter Barratt, was the owner of the majority shareholding. I'm sure he had his reasons for wishing to remain anonymous but—'

'Why did he leave it to *me*?' Sara's head was spinning.

'Perhaps he thought you could use eleven men.'

Cynthia's remark struck Sara as exactly like something Maggie might say. Suddenly, she saw Cynthia for what she was – a sad, lonely woman. 'You're so wrong about me, Mrs Hargreaves,' she said, softly. 'Your husband was special to me, and I loved him very much. But I loved him like a father, nothing more.'

'There was nothing special about fucking my husband,' spat Cynthia. 'Half the redheads in London have that on their CVs. You were just the tramp lucky enough to hit pay-dirt. Don't kid yourself that there was anything unique about your sordid affair. Only the timing was special.'

Sara couldn't bear to listen to any more. Cynthia's words, Stuart's will, none of it made any sense. She stood up. 'Mrs Hargreaves, I shall be charitable and believe that grief is making you act uncharacteristically.' She looked to Gerald for guidance but the solicitor's head seemed to disappear, tortoise-like, into his shoulders. 'I think it would be best if I left now.'

The solicitor moved from behind his desk to show her out. 'I'll be in touch,' he whispered, surreptitiously giving her his business card.

In a daze, Sara walked to the nearest pub, ordered a double whisky and emptied the glass in one go. 'Another, and change for the cigarette machine,' she said to the barman.

She fiddled with the vending machine, eventually getting it to dispense a packet of cigarettes. As she popped one in her mouth a workman at the bar held out a light, only to have smoke coughed all over him as she tried to inhale.

The workman took a step back. 'Go easy, love. You sound like you've never smoked before.'

'I haven't,' she spluttered, her eyes watering, 'But it's always what people do in films when they've had a shock.'

He smiled. 'Maybe you should have tried a lower-tar brand, love.'

She inhaled again but fared no better, so she gave up, handing the amused man the packet. She drank her next drink more slowly, trying to gather her thoughts. In the last week she had lost her best friend, and her job and now, it seemed, she'd gained half a football team and God knows how much money. It all seemed like a dream. She couldn't understand why Stuart hadn't told her about it. She could have spent more time with him instead of having to worry about Cynthia sacking her. Frustration mixed with the grief she felt for him. Why had there been so many secrets?

How much had she inherited? One million? Five? Ten? Perhaps even twenty times that amount? Whatever the figure, it was more than she'd earn in a lifetime at the *Herald* – or anywhere else. Such vast figures were incomprehensible to her. The only thing she was sure of was that no amount of money would ever compensate for the loss of Stuart. She wanted to cry, but the tears she had blocked in Gerald Scott's office remained locked somewhere inside.

The workman at the bar called over to her. 'You look like you've lost a pound and found a penny, love.'

'I have,' she said blankly. How many millions? It was all too ludicrous. She had to speak to someone, to touch reality again. She had to see Kathy.

The Kathy who opened the door to Sara was a shadow of her former self. Her sallow face was all but hidden from view by her lank, unwashed hair and her clothes were unironed and stained. Sara knew that how Kathy looked on the outside spoke volumes about how she felt inside.

'Hello,' said Kathy flatly. 'I'm so sorry about Stuart.'

'Are you OK?' asked Sara, putting her arm round her friend and leading her into the kitchen. Like Kathy, the room had undergone a metamorphosis. Normally it was warm, welcoming, immaculately clean, but now there were old coffee cups in the sink and last night's supper still sitting in pans on the Aga.

Kathy shrugged as she saw Sara's face. 'I've been caught up with Bette,' she said, defensively.

'Where is she?'

'She's asleep in the nursery. I've only just put her down.'

'And Joseph?' Sara felt that the question had an all-too-familiar ring about it.

'In the States.' Kathy turned on the hot tap and started to take the plates out of the sink.

'Leave it,' said Sara, 'I'll sort it out later.' She looked in the fridge and found a bottle of wine. She poured two glasses and led her friend out into the garden. 'Tell me what's been happening.'

Kathy's face tightened and deep lines appeared around her mouth. 'If I knew the answer to that, I'd be a great deal happier. I don't think Joseph loves me any more. He adores Bette, but I think he also sees her as a trap which forces him to stay with me.'

'What has he said?'

'It's what he doesn't say. When he's here, which isn't often, he's moody and silent and only talks to Bette,' she said bitterly. 'But most of the time he makes sure his few assignments are abroad.'

'Have you asked him directly what's wrong?'

Kathy snorted. 'On numerous occasions. His latest answer is that it's me. That I've changed, I'm not the Kathy he knew,' she said, mimicking Joseph's voice.

Sara studied her friend, finding it hard to contradict Joseph's opinion. Seeing Kathy now it was hard to believe that this dowdy, rattled woman had at one time, and not too long ago, been a go-getting magazine editor. She was even more reticent and down on herself than she had been at college.

Kathy read Sara's thoughts and slammed down her glass.

'I know you're thinking the same, Sara. But it's a chicken-and-egg thing. I have changed, but I think it's Joseph's rejection of me that has changed me. Rejecting me even more isn't going to make me feel any better about myself.'

'I know,' said Sara. 'Do you think there's anyone else?' she asked gently.

'Huh. Anyone else implies the singular. I think there are a lot of anyone elses, but I haven't got any proof and, believe me, I've looked for it – his Amex receipts, his bank statements – you name it, I've read it. I'm sure he wonders why I keep on taking his clothes to the dry-cleaners.'

'When did you last see him?'

'About five days ago, before he swanned off to New York with that stupid bitch Fran Best. She's executive producer on his latest

project. It is about yuppies in peril. Talking of which, I've just been
told by the bank that we're five months behind with the mortgage.
What the hell has he been doing with the money?' she said, angrily.
'I know we're going to lose this house.'

'No you won't,' said Sara, hugging her friend. 'I'll help you
out.'

Kathy smiled. 'I didn't know unemployment benefit was so good
these days.'

'Let's have another drink. There's something I have to tell you.'

The phone rang. 'It might be Joseph,' said Kathy hopefully. She ran
to the answering machine and turned up the volume. Her heart sank
as a woman's voice came tearfully over the line.

'Kathy? Are you there? Is Sara there? Please get her to ring me
if she is. I keep getting phone calls from reporters about her and
Stuart Hargreaves and I don't know what to do. What's happening?
Please tell her to ring me as soon as she can.'

Kathy picked up the phone but was met with only the dialling
tone. 'She's gone,' she said, dejectedly.

In all the turmoil it hadn't occurred to Sara that the press would
bother June. She rang her back immediately. June sounded on
the verge of a nervous breakdown. 'Sara, they haven't stopped
telephoning me all day. I can't cope with much more of it. Why
are they interested in you?'

'Stuart's left me . . . left me a fortune and a . . .' She stopped. It
would be better to fill her mother in on the details another time.

'A fortune! Why? Did he say why he left you that money?'

Sara was shocked by the question. 'Mum, *you* don't think
anything was going on between us, do you?'

'Of course not. It's just . . . I don't know what I'm meant to do.
Should I say anything to the papers? They might go away if I talked
to them.'

'Don't do anything!' she shouted, then in a calmer voice, she
soothed, 'Just ignore them.'

'I think I've put my foot in it,' said June, her voice trembling.

'What do you mean?'

'When the first few rang I assumed it was about work, and I gave them Kathy's number. I'm really sorry.'

It was pointless to shout at her mother. 'Never mind. Look, go out and buy an answerphone tomorrow. I'll give you the money for it when I see you.'

'I don't like to take money from you—'

Sara interrupted her mother, completely exasperated. 'Has it escaped your notice, Mum, that the reason you've got reporters ringing you is because Stuart has left me millions? I can afford thousands of bloody answerphones. Look, I'm really sorry about all this, Mum.'

June burst into tears. 'I wish you were here with me. I can't cope. Sara, please come down, we need to talk.'

'I can't. It'll only make it worse,' explained Sara. If she went down to Backwell, every paper in the country would follow her and set up camp outside the bungalow. 'Do as I tell you and I promise that in a couple of days this will all blow over and then I'll come.'

'Sara, please—'

'Mum, I love you but you have to believe me, this is for the best.' Sara said goodbye, feeling like a complete heel.

As soon as Sara put the phone down it rang again.

'Hello. Can I speak to Sara Moore please?'

'Who is it?'

'Julian Marsh. God, you're difficult to get hold of. Your mother told me where I might find you. Nice lady. '

'What do you want?'

'You won't know me,' he said hurriedly, 'I'm a reporter on the *News*. I'm ringing about Stuart Hargreaves. Is it true that you were lovers and that he's left you a fortune?'

'Go to hell!' she shouted, slamming down the phone.

Kathy came out into the hallway with Bette. 'Problems?'

'Could be. I know a story when I see one, and I've a feeling that this one isn't going to go away.'

'What?'

'That was the *News*, trash and more trash, wanting to know about my "affair" with Stuart. How on earth did they find out about this all so quickly? I'm sure Cynthia wouldn't have announced it.'

They went into the kitchen. While Kathy filled the percolator, Sara sat at the table, gently bouncing the baby on her knee. Bette rewarded her with a smile and her tiny hand wrapped itself around Sara's finger as if to say, 'I trust you.'

'What a gorgeous child you are. Just like your beautiful mum,' she said, finding it hard to get the words out. For so long she hadn't allowed herself to love Bette, seeing it as a betrayal of her own unborn child. It was wrong to have conflated these two separate events and it saddened her to think that she'd missed much of the first year of Bette's life. 'I'm sorry,' she whispered, fighting hard not to cry. 'I'd do anything for you, do you know that?'

Her thoughts turned to Joseph. Where was he? She pictured him swanning about New York with not a care in the world, oblivious to the anguish his wife was going through. It was unforgivable.

The doorbell rang and at the same time the caller rattled the letterbox. The noise alarmed Bette and she began to howl. 'Don't answer that, Kathy,' Sara said, noticing how weary her friend looked. 'Just go to bed and I'll see to Bette.'

The ringing grew more insistent; the rapping on the letterbox continued. Sara knew that whoever it was wasn't going to go away. She opened the door, with Bette on her hip, and at first she thought it must be the Jehovah's Witnesses calling. The first man had the same fervent and determined air, while the one behind him looked as if he would be ready to step in the second the theological debate needed strengthening.

'I'm Julian Marsh,' said the first man.

'I've nothing to say.' Sara tried to shut the door but the journalist was too fast for her and a well-practised foot jammed it open. The other man stepped to one side and lifted his camera, the lens whirring into different positions as it focused on Sara's face. The flash alarmed Bette, and Sara tried to shield the toddler's eyes from the glare. From behind her Kathy appeared. Like a woman possessed, she shoved Julian Marsh off the doorstep.

'Parasites!' she screamed, closing the door.

Shocked at the intrusion, Sara stood motionless as Bette whimpered in her arms. 'What an ugly little man.'

'I certainly think that *Mariella* would recommend a chin implant and some very strong-acting deodorant.'

They both burst out laughing. As if sensing that the crisis had broken, Bette began to calm down as well.

'I don't think that's the last we've heard of them, I'm afraid,' said Sara. She was proved right when, a few seconds later, the phone began to ring again.

Kathy switched on the answerphone. This time it was Dennis Brown, someone Sara had known vaguely at the *Sunday Voice*, asking her 'as a friend' to tell her side of the story. Kathy turned down the volume and said, 'There's no honour among journalists.'

The telephone rang ceaselessly for the rest of the day. Fortunately only Julian Marsh decided to camp outside the door, but even so, both she and Kathy felt under siege, especially when the pizza-delivery boy was hijacked in the garden and given a note from Julian asking more impertinent personal questions.

'I can see the headline now,' said Kathy, peeking through the living-room curtains. '"HEIRESS ORDERS QUATTRO FORMAGGI AND GARLIC BREAD". Honestly, these people are incredible. How did you ever do it?'

Sara put down her pizza, no longer hungry. 'Kathy, if you want me to leave, just say so. I don't want to make you and Bette prisoners in your own home.'

'Don't you dare,' said Kathy, sitting down and putting her hand on Sara's knee. 'It's a bit of excitement. It's the first time I haven't felt sorry for myself in a long while. I'm sure it'll all look better in the morning.'

As soon as Sara woke up the following day she had a feeling of foreboding but it took her a while to remember why. Gingerly opening the curtains, she nearly laughed from the shock. It was as if Julian Marsh and his photographer had been cloned overnight. Now there were ten men and two women standing outside Kathy's gate.

One of the journalists spotted her. 'There she is! Sara, is it true you and Stuart Hargreaves were lovers?'

Flashbulbs went off around the group, and Sara put up two fingers and closed the curtains.

Downstairs, Kathy was already feeding Bette in the kitchen. Sara was both surprised and relieved that her friend was so good-humoured about the whole thing.

'Have you seen them outside?' Kathy laughed. 'They've already waylaid the milkman, but I don't think they'll get much mileage out of the fact that he delivered two pints of semi-skimmed and a carton of yoghurt.'

'How about "MILLIONAIRESS SUFFERS THRUSH"?' suggested Sara. 'I've done worse.' She opened the fridge. 'Is there anything for breakfast?'

'Not unless you want to share Bette's. We've run out of food so it looks like I'm going to have to brave the braying pack.'

'You can't!'

'I know it's a hard job, kid, but someone's got to do it,' replied Kathy, in a B-movie accent. Feeling enlivened for the first time in weeks, she rushed off to get ready and decided to go the whole hog. 'Do you think I look like Jackie O.?' she asked, reappearing in dark sunglasses and scarf.

'Better,' replied Sara, glad to see that her friend had momentarily regained some of her old vitality. She opened the door for Kathy, taking care to stay out of view. In a hail of camera flashes, Kathy sprinted down the path as Sara shouted, 'Go, go, go!'

Sara watched from the window as Kathy nearly amputated Julian Marsh's arm trying to shut the door of her car. But as she drove away all attention turned back to the house. With her friend gone, the humour soon disappeared from the situation. Sara distracted herself by playing peek-a-boo with Bette. When the toddler fell asleep, she set about restoring some order to Kathy's house.

A little later, she noticed that the reporters seemed to be having a picnic brunch and thought ruefully of the many times she had doorstepped people. Perhaps having it done to her was no more than she deserved. If only she had a rational explanation for Stuart's will. She knew that the 'just-good-friends' line sounded pretty flimsy, and that if she said anything remotely like that, the newspapers would make mincemeat of her. She herself would have done exactly the same.

Sara was standing in the hallway erasing the answerphone messages without listening to them when the letterbox opened.

'Come on, Sara, do yourself and your friend a favour. Just tell us the story and we'll go away. All of this fuss can't be good for the baby.'

Sara peered through the letterbox and felt greatly tempted to poke Julian Marsh in one of his beady eyes. 'Go away!'

'Look, if you don't come clean, we'll have to dig deep to dish some dirt. What do you say?' he shouted, his nasal, public-school voice grating on her. 'How long had it been going on?' he persisted through the letterbox. 'Did old Cynthia know? You weren't the first bit on the side he had, you know.'

Enough was enough. Sara went to the kitchen, filled up the washing-up bowl with cold water, returned to the front door, opened it and threw it, the bowl and all, at Marsh. 'As I said before, no comment.'

'I won't forget this in a hurry,' he screamed, the water dripping from his face.

Kathy returned to the farce a couple of hours later bringing supplies and a selection of newspapers. Across the front page of the *Sunday Mirror* was a picture of Sara and Stuart deep in conversation at a charity football match. The camera had lied. They certainly looked more than just good friends. The story underneath was brief, describing Sara as a 'close friend' of Stuart's who had been left a substantial amount of money. At the end of the article there was a terse 'no comment' from Cynthia.

The *Sunday Voice* hadn't led with the story, having unearthed a topless photograph of a very distant member of the royal family. Sara hesitated before turning the page, trying to work out exactly what the poor woman's relationship to the Queen was. As far as she could work out, she was closer in line to the throne herself.

At last she opened the paper and saw her own face looming up from page 3 with the promise of more to come in the centrefold. Again there was that bloody picture of her talking quite innocently to Stuart, with a chronology listing all the events at which they had been seen together, including Stockholm. The *Voice* was careful to avoid libel, and there was no out-and-out accusation of an affair, but the implication was enough. The second part of the story covered the football club. There was a small photograph of an outraged Stephen Powell and some choice quotes which offered his opinion of Stuart Hargreaves and made it clear that his club was not going to accept Sara in through the back door. On the centre pages the headline read: 'FOOTBALL MILLIONAIRESS IN VICE PROBE'. It jolted her until she read a few lines and realised that the paper was making a meal out of its connection with her. There was a rundown of some of her juicier stories, including her very first piece about Mickey Nash.

Sara picked up the *News* next. Here the story had made the front page, and it was by-lined Julian Marsh. He hadn't pulled his punches – the *News* had a far more cavalier attitude towards the risks of being sued than the *Voice*. Rather than offering veiled innuendo, Marsh's piece made full-scale accusations of an affair under the banner headline, 'DEAD MP LEAVES FORTUNE TO YOUNG MISTRESS' followed by 'MOORE, MOORE, MOORE FOR SARA.'

What shocked Sara most were the interviews with people she barely knew and some of the awful photographs they'd dug up, including one of her in a school play with Maggie.

'Well, look at you there,' said Kathy, appearing behind her. 'And if I'm not mistaken, that's Maggie behind you! What on earth is she wearing?'

'A sack. She played a farmer,' said Sara, laughing despite herself. 'Honestly, they're such slime bags. Have you seen this quote from Sean Bottomley?'

'Sean from college whose dad was a dentist? The one who said to you that if you slept with him he could get you some cheap caps?'

'Yep. Listen to this. "We all knew that Sara would make it to the top using whatever assets she had." He was such a geek. And his teeth were terrible.'

Kathy was serious for a moment. 'Do you think Maggie was responsible for any of this?'

'I don't think so. Surely Maggie wouldn't let them print a picture of her looking like that. Besides, I don't think Maggie would be that malicious.'

'You've got to be joking,' said Kathy.

'Look, if Maggie wanted to, she could do a lot more damage than this.' In her heart, Sara still believed that, despite everything that had happened, when it came to the crunch, Maggie would remain loyal.

Chapter Twenty-Four

In his office at the Camden United ground, Stephen Powell picked up the *Sun* and read the headline: 'GIMME MOORE!' Underneath was a story about the owner of Totem and his 'night of love' with Sara Moore, which confirmed Powell's suspicions that she was just some ruthless tart on the make. And it didn't take a genius to work out that Stuart had been priming the bitch all the time. He must have given her that bloody Nash story, thought Stephen. Well, he was going to get even for that one. What else had the bastard told her? he wondered. How much had Hargreaves known? He turned to the sports pages, which were full of the implications of Sara taking over the club. Enraged, he picked up the phone and called Jackie.

'You stupid whore. Why did you sell your shares? Why did you do it?'

It was only nine o'clock in the morning but Jackie sounded four sheets to the wind already. 'Mind your own fucking business.'

'This club *is* my business.'

'Then why didn't you know Stuart Hargreaves owned half of it?'

'Look, you cow, I'm warning you, don't get smart with me. Why did you sell them?'

'I needed the money.'

'What for? Your drinks cabinet?'

As usual Jackie crumbled under Stephen's relentless abuse. 'For the nursing home,' she wailed. 'I couldn't let my mother go into that council home. You didn't see what—'

'Shut it. I don't want to know. You've cost me control of the club all for that crazy old witch. I should have put a pillow over her face when I had the chance.'

'How can you be so cruel?' she cried. 'She's got dementia.'

'Like mother, like daughter,' roared Stephen. 'Can't you see what you've done?'

'Peter told me it would make no difference.'

'Were you sober at the time? I know not a lot goes on in that thick head of yours beyond working out how to get the top off a bottle of gin, but I thought even you would realise the difference between owning forty-nine per cent and fifty-one. I should have divorced you years ago, you useless slob.'

Just as he slammed down the phone, the door opened and Sara strode into the office. Pulling up a chair in front of his desk, she sat down. 'Hello, Stephen,' she said, crossing her legs and folding her arms. It was a gesture of confidence designed to cover up the fact that she was shaking. What was she doing here? The protests of a thousand men filled her head. Women have no place in football.

'I told you on the phone, I've got nothing to say to you. I'm not letting one of that bastard's floozies into my club.' Even if she does look like you, he thought. Not caring whether she noticed or not, he stared at her legs, his close-set eyes drilling into the point where her thighs crossed. For a second Sara reminded him of her. It seemed like a lifetime ago.

'*Our* club, Stephen,' said Sara, standing up and walking over to his desk, 'and if you want to get picky, may I remind you that it's more mine than yours.'

'Linda, you stupid woman,' he shouted to his secretary, 'get security in here.'

A guard appeared almost immediately and put his hand on her shoulder. 'Come on, love, you're not wanted here.'

Sara shrugged off his hand, turned and faced him. 'Unless you leave this office immediately you're fired,' she said icily.

The guard looked at Stephen for directions. 'Mr Powell?'

Reluctantly, Stephen nodded. 'I'll deal with it.'

The set-to disturbed Sara. It was clearly a portent of things to come. For the previous few days she'd been working on autopilot, convinced that if she actually sat down and thought about the problems she was up against, they would seem insurmountable. Taking control of a football club was a leap in the dark. She'd seen the way Powell behaved with Stuart. Had she thought she could just walk into the club and he would happily hand over the reins?

Stephen interrupted her thoughts. 'I'll buy you out,' he bluffed, knowing full well he'd be lucky to afford 1 per cent, let alone the other 50. It had been his dire financial circumstances that had led him to getting into bed with Barratt in the first place. At the time he had been only too happy to ask no questions.

'Stuart left me his share in this club for a reason, and I'm not selling.'

'And that reason is?'

The $64,000 question, thought Sara. She'd racked her brains for the answer. Obviously he wanted to get at Stephen, but why? 'I'm not sure,' she said, feeling stupid.

Stephen sat back with a satisfied smirk. He knew why, but he wasn't going to tell her, and he was going to have the last laugh. This one was as much of a bimbo as all the others Stuart Hargreaves had worked his way through in his time. 'As far as I'm aware, you've got no legal right over this place until probate is granted.'

'Stephen, you'll have to talk to me some time. Surely the sooner the better, because I intend to take a full part in the running of this place.' She tried to say this with as much conviction as she could muster. She knew everything there was to know about the game, but not from the point of view of organising a club. Of course, the option to be a silent partner, as Peter Barratt appeared to be, was open to her, but Stuart would not have bought into the club merely as an investment. Not in secret. Whatever the problem between him and Stephen was, he must have wanted Sara to sort it out from inside the boardroom. 'Now, we can work together, or you can work against me. The choice is yours.'

Stephen was incensed. 'Listen, girly, I've read about you. You've made a lot of enemies along the way. You don't want to make one out of me. Stay out of this club.'

Sara thought he was bluffing. It was an act of bravado from a cornered man. What could he do to her? She owned more of the club than he did. Not wishing to become involved in a pointless slanging match when there were so many more important things to attend to, she opened the door to leave. 'I'll be in touch,' she said, closing it behind her.

Stephen sat down heavily in his seat. He needed time to think. He couldn't afford to buy Sara out, and he needed her money. It might even be useful to have a bit of skirt around the place as a figurehead. Good for publicity. He pictured Sara modelling the Camden strip. Jackie sobered herself up once a year to do it, but these days the airbrushing was costing him more than the revenue from the kit. He would have to convince Hargreaves' tart to be a silent partner.

He picked up the newpaper again, looking at the pictures of Sara with Stuart. The smooth bastard, thought Stephen, he always could get a nice-looking dolly bird. But how much did this one know? Stuart had promised him his comeuppance. Was giving the club to his mistress all that he had in mind? Stephen certainly didn't need this one poking her nose around – she'd come very close to the truth already. Maybe he would get someone to put the frighteners on her to keep her at a distance. To keep her silent.

Angrily he jabbed the button on the intercom. 'Linda, have you got through to Borboleta yet?'

'I'm trying,' replied the secretary. 'I keep getting the Brazilian operator. I think the line might be down.'

'Oh, for fuck's sake,' fumed Stephen. 'Leave it for now. I want you to get hold of Mickey Nash.'

Maggie had been awake all night, seething about Huw's kiss-and-tell story in the *Sun*. Anthony's snoring wasn't helping matters. She nudged him in his big, soft belly and he rolled on to his side, allowing her a few minutes of quiet. She looked at his hairpiece lying on the dressing table and shuddered. Anthony had served his purpose, and soon she was going to have to tell him that it was over. If the letter from *Mariella* came today then she would do it tonight. His wife was away and Anthony had said that he wanted to take Maggie down to Cowes, but the last thing she wanted to do was to spend three days holding down seasickness and fighting off the advances of a sixty-five-year-old. When his wife was in London, Maggie only had to sleep with him on the odd occasion to keep him interested, but three whole days together! You couldn't escape from a yacht and she didn't think her body could stand the bruising.

Anthony's snoring picked up again so she slipped out of bed and went into the living room. She turned on her Excercycle and found that one of the pedals on the machine was coming loose. Anthony had given it to her to celebrate her appointment as editor of *Chloe* and since then she had given it something of a battering. Still, if she got the deputy editor's job at *Mariella* she'd treat herself to a new one. She couldn't wait to leave *Chloe*, the housewives' favourite, to move in more glamorous circles.

Maggie had seen advertisements for job after job on *Mariella*, which had leapfrogged all the competition to become the number one bestselling women's monthly. Now Kathy was out of the way playing happy families, Maggie was sure that, with all her experience on *Chloe*, the job was more or less in the bag.

By the time Anthony emerged from the bedroom, his hairpiece firmly in place, Maggie had already cycled ten miles.

'The paper's here,' he said. 'Gosh, the old tummy's rumbling a bit.'

'I'm not your wife,' snapped Maggie, taking the newspaper out of his hand. 'I'm sure that Marlene has nothing better to do in the morning than cook your breakfast, but I certainly have.'

'Don't be like that, Pussy,' said Anthony. He tried to put his arms round her but Maggie shrugged them off. 'Oh well, I haven't really got the time, anyway. I've rather a busy day today.'

'Yeah, yeah,' said Maggie waving him away.

In the *Mail* she'd noticed a statement from Sara's solicitor, a Gerald Scott, concerning his client's relationship with Stuart

Hargreaves. Naturally, it was all the same crap about the friendship being completely platonic and how Miss Moore was keen for all the fuss to die down so that she could get on with running Camden United as Stuart would have wanted her to. There was so much that Maggie could have told the newspapers about that conniving bitch. But she wanted to wait until she was safely installed at *Mariella* before she drew any attention to herself. If she made herself look like a tabloid bimbo, there was no way in the world that the magazine would take her on.

In the paper, next to Gerald Scott's statement, there was a picture of Sara taken from the *Mariella* swimwear shoot. She's beautiful, thought Maggie, finding it hard to decide whom she hated the most – Sara or herself. No matter how much Sara destroyed other people's lives, she always came up trumps. Why is it always her? Never me, never bloody me, she thought, throwing herself down on to the settee. All that fake sincerity, all that pretence that she wanted to help Maggie. Sara was as ruthless as they came, stepping on anybody to get what she wanted. When she thought of how Sara had criticised her in the past for sleeping with men to get on, it made her blood boil. Sara must have been shagging that dirty old man Stuart Hargreaves even when she was with Bill. Maggie wondered whether Bill had known. Probably not. Butter wouldn't melt and all that. Only she knew the *real* Sara Moore.

'I'm leaving now,' called Anthony from the hallway. 'Don't forget, Pussy, it's anchors away tonight!'

'How could I?' shouted Maggie as the door closed.

'A healthy body is a healthy mind. A healthy body is a healthy mind.' Maggie cycled on, repeating the phrase over and over again to stop herself from thinking about Sara. After another two miles she climbed off the machine and mixed herself a meal replacement drink for breakfast. As she was waiting for the powder to dissolve properly, she heard the postman and raced into the hall to pick up her mail.

Her fingers trembled as she sorted through the post. Circular, circular, bill, circular, the letter from *Mariella*. She tore open the envelope and pulled out the letter. The first word jumped out at her: 'Sorry'.

In a daze, she wandered into her bedroom, reading and rereading the brief rejection. She went directly to her wardrobe, where she took out the cardboard box hidden on the top shelf. As she lifted it down, the bottom split and chocolate bars cascaded all over the floor. Maggie dropped to her knees and, tearing off the wrapping, stuffed first one bar into her mouth, then another, and another.

The bitches, she thought as she gorged on the chocolate. Even when she tried to play fair they wouldn't leave her alone. She knew that Sara was behind all of this, using her influence over that mouse of a friend of hers to make sure that Maggie didn't get the job. Maggie pushed some more chocolate into her mouth, barely chewing it before forcing another chunk after it. Well, that was it. The story of how that self-righteous cow had killed her Yank boyfriend should make very interesting reading.

Just then the phone rang and she jumped guiltily as if she'd been caught in the act. Her mouth was too full for her to speak. Maggie listened to her own voice as the answerphone clicked on after three rings.

'Ms Lawrence, it's Wendy Williams here. Mr Coak—'

'Maggie Lawrence here,' Maggie picked up the phone and cut in once she was able to talk. 'What is it?' she asked the group managing director's secretary.

'Mr Coakley is expecting you for a meeting at ten-thirty. I'm just ringing to check that you'll be there.'

'A meeting?' Maggie wondered why he hadn't said anything. 'Tell him I'll speak to him later. I have things to do this morning.'

'He's not in yet.'

Maggie could hear the smugness in the secretary's voice. As thick as Wendy Williams was, even she had to know what was going on. 'I'm quite well aware of that.'

'He said that it was very important.'

'OK, OK. I'll be there.'

Maggie put down the phone and went into the bathroom. She lifted the toilet seat and stuck her fingers into her mouth. Sara's comeuppance would have to wait a couple more hours.

Maggie arrived at the office at ten. Wendy Williams affected a look of disdain as she glanced first at the clock and then at the editor of *Chloe*.

'Mr Coakley isn't expecting you for another half an hour,' she said, stirring a sweetener into her coffee. 'You'll have to wait.'

'Just tell him I'm here, Wendy, thank you,' said Maggie, stone-faced.

'He won't be able to see you until ten-thirty, as arranged.'

Maggie wanted to kick the bony-arsed secretary all the way back to the typing pool where she belonged. 'You've been sniffing the Tippex again, haven't you, Wendy? It's given you delusions of grandeur. Now tell him I'm here or I'll shut your head in the photocopier.'

Wendy sulkily picked up the phone. 'Mr Coakley, Ms Lawrence is here. I told her she was too early—'

'Oh, for crying out loud,' said Maggie, knocking the phone out of the secretary's hand and barging into the managing director's office. 'What's this cloak-and-dagger stuff all about?'

'Close the door would you, Ms Lawrence?'

Maggie shut the door in Wendy Williams' startled face. 'What's going on? You didn't mention anything about a meeting.'

'Ms Lawrence, would you take a seat. I'm afraid I've got some rather bad news for you.'

'Cut the "Ms Lawrence" schtick, would you, Anthony? It's a bit too formal for somebody who got out of my bed only two hours ago.'

Anthony Coakley stared at her impassively. 'Have you seen *Chloe*'s circulation figures for last month? Down two per cent – despite the free-lipgloss promotion, the new Miriam Stoppard column and the accidents in the home pull-out. Something's going very wrong.'

Maggie lit a cigarette and inhaled deeply. 'You know full well the whole market's down, Anthony. Two per cent isn't significant.'

'It's very significant in the context of your lack of interest. A rumour has been going around that you've been applying for other jobs.'

The old bastard must have been looking at my mail, thought Maggie. 'So?'

'I'm not going to beat about the bush. We need someone committed. Someone with new ideas. Somebody who'll really get behind the magazine.'

Maggie tried to remain calm. She knew *Chloe* was doing no worse than any of the other magazines in the group. 'What are you saying, Anthony?'

'We're going to have to let you go.'

It took a few seconds for the words to register before Maggie threw herself at him, scraping her fingernails across his face. 'You spineless bastard! This is Marlene's doing, isn't it? She's on to you, and she's told you it's me or her. And you knew all about it when you got into my bed, when you gave me all that crap about Cowes. You knew you were going to fire me and you still had to have one last fuck, didn't you?'

'Pussy, don't!' said Anthony, trying to grab her wrists. Maggie kneed him in the groin. 'OK, OK,' he gasped. 'Marlene does know. But what can I do? She wants you out of the office by the end of the week.'

'How could you?' screamed Maggie, knocking the papers on his desk flying. 'How could you?'

'Pussy, you're making a spectacle of yourself,' he said, edging away from her. 'It isn't really all that bad. I'll do all I can to get you another job.'

Maggie ran at him again and grabbed at his head. His hairpiece came away in her hand. 'If getting a job meant spending even one more second on my back under you, I'd rather starve.' With that, Maggie gathered all the dignity she could muster and walked out of his office.

Wendy Williams was outside, beaming, having overheard everything.

'Wendy, love,' said Maggie. 'Feed Pussy while I'm away.'

The secretary screamed as the hairpiece landed in her lap. Maggie's blood was up. Right, now for Sara Moore, she thought.

Chapter Twenty-Five

Sara closed her eyes and tried to shut out the click-clicking of her mother's knitting needles as she started work on yet another jumper. For two weeks now she had been cooped up in the flat with June, surfacing only for the occasional meeting with Gerald Scott, who, having been sacked by an enraged Cynthia, had offered his services to Sara. She had accepted straight away, having appreciated the kindness he'd shown her at the reading of Stuart's will.

As much as she loved her mother, it had been a mistake having June come up to London. Her mother had insisted on it, saying they needed to talk. Yet she had been unusually taciturn. To avoid the continuing onslaught of the press, June had become a virtual recluse. Heaven knows what would happen if a group of reporters chased her up the road.

'All right,' said June, putting down her knitting. 'Let's talk about decorating this flat. It looks like a squat.'

Sara had done little more than unpack at Highgate. Like the Highbury flat before it, the place had never felt like home. Without

Bill, nowhere felt like home. She didn't really care what it looked like, but there were limits. If she let her mother have her way the flat would soon be awash with Toby jugs and shaggy toilet-seat covers.

'Mum, it's fine as it is. Anyway, I won't be here much longer. I've talked to Gerald about buying a house. Perhaps somewhere near the club. He thinks I need to invest some of the money in property.'

'I thought it was all tied up in that football club and the newspaper.'

'Not for long. When I spoke to Gerald this morning, he said that Cynthia has managed to raise the money from the banks to buy me out. I thought about holding on to my shares but I don't think I can take on Stephen Powell *and* Cynthia Hargreaves. I'll sell.'

'I hope this isn't a rude question but how much . . .'

'Millions,' said Sara. She started laughing at the ludicrousness of discussing multi-million-pound deals with her mother.

'Good gracious,' said June, shocked. Then she began to laugh too. 'Mrs O'Neill two doors down from me is putting her bungalow on the market and I was just thinking that perhaps you could move in next door to me. But it's not quite Millionaire's Row, is it?'

'You know, you don't have to stay there, either. I'll buy you a house in London, near me.'

June shook her head. 'I'm happy where I am, love. I don't need a posh house in London. I'd miss my friends.'

'Well, what would you like? I've got all this money. There must be something that would make your life better. A car, a big holiday, more wool?'

'You know, there's only one thing that would make my life better. Having your dad back. I don't want to sound like a spoilsport, but money doesn't buy you happiness.'

'I've learned that the hard way, Mum. But you can do some good with it. I can keep Stuart's memory alive.'

'What for? That man never did anyone any good while he was on this earth,' said June frostily. She picked up her knitting again and cast on a new line.

The subject of Stuart was still a sensitive one. 'Mum, that's so unlike you. I've never heard you talk ill of the dead. What was so wrong with Stuart?'

June refused to look up from her knitting. 'Money can't buy love,' she huffed.

'I started loving Stuart long before he left me all this. He was a wonderful man.'

'He was a . . .' June hesitated, afraid of saying something she would regret. Stuart Hargreaves was dead and buried. She had nothing to fear from him any more. 'I don't want to talk about this.'

In the uncomfortable silence that followed, Sara tried to think of a way of easing the tension. 'Mum, how would you like to go to the theatre?' she asked, sifting through her mail. Since becoming something of a media personality, Sara had been inundated with invitations to film premières and charity banquets. So far all of them had gone in the bin – Sara had no wish to promote herself as the new girl about town – but a night out might at least keep her mother quiet for a few hours.

'Not one of those modern things,' said June. 'You know, where everyone takes their clothes off.'

Sara raised her eyebrows. By 'modern', she guessed that her mother must be referring to *Hair* or *Oh Calcutta!* 'Look, here's an invitation to the first night of *The King and I*. That's not too racy, is it? There'll be lots of stars there.'

'That might be nice,' said June.

Sara turned the invitation over. 'Strange. It doesn't say who it's from.'

Sara went to her wardrobe and looked for something suitable to wear. It had been a long time since she'd been anywhere formal. Most of her evening wear was still folded up in bags. She found a shoulderless green silk dress and put it on, carefully piling her hair on top of her head. Looking in the mirror, she felt that her pale, bare shoulders made her look too vulnerable. She was just about to change when June appeared in a flower-print dress from BHS singing 'Hello Young Lovers, Wherever You Are'.

'That dress certainly brings out the colour of your eyes, dear,' said June kindly.

'You don't look too bad yourself.'

Her mother blushed, smoothing out imaginary creases from the drip-dry material. 'Come on, we don't want to be late. You know I like to buy a box of chocolates and a programme first.'

Even though June had lived in London for many years with Harry, she viewed the West End as only slightly less dangerous than downtown Beirut. Passing even the most innocent-looking tourist, she would eye him suspiciously and tighten her grip on her clutch bag. As they crossed Shaftesbury Avenue, she stood stock-still in the middle of the road, agog at the sight of two innocuous punks. Exasperated, Sara took her firmly by the arm and led her through the throng that had gathered outside the theatre. The two of them made a very odd couple, the elegant Sara towering over her neatly turned-out mother.

When she saw the press cameras Sara's nerve faltered momentarily. Breathing deeply, she controlled her rising nausea – she shouldn't flatter herself that the paparazzi would be giving her attention tonight when there were so many celebrities present. She adopted a straight-ahead stare as she stepped on to the red carpet towards the theatre's entrance.

'Sara, you're looking beautiful tonight,' shouted a cameraman.

'Who's the dress by?' yelled a journalist.

'My mother,' laughed Sara. The question gave her the solution on how to deal with this moment. All she had to do was pretend she was on a catwalk again. Pushing her hips forward, she walked on, the green silk dress rippling against the curves of her body, its hem rising and falling over her long slender thighs. Naturally, the cameras loved it.

'Sara! Look this way, Sara! Long time no see!'

Sara had no need to look around as she recognised the public-school accent immediately.

Unfortunately, her mother stopped. 'Someone's calling you, my love.'

It was too late. Julian Marsh was standing next to her. 'No male escort, Sara?' he said, snidely. 'I take it we are still officially in grieving, so to speak?'

Sara let go of her mother's arm and squared up to him, an action which served only to set off all the cameras around her. Marsh laughed in her face, but before she could respond, she felt a hand on the small of her back.

'Miss Moore. Allow me the pleasure of escorting you and your companion inside.'

Sara looked uncomprehendingly at the man now gently guiding her away from the obnoxious reporter. It took her a few seconds to recognise him. Seeing the look of dismay on her face, the man held out his hand. 'We've never been formally introduced. I'm Christopher Heard, the *Herald*'s diarist.'

'I know who you are,' said Sara, pulling away.

Christopher laughed. 'I'm not doing a story, Sara, I simply thought you needed rescuing.'

Looking at the tuxedoed Heard with his carefully developed debonair leading-man looks, Sara guessed that he did indeed see himself as a knight on a white charger going to the aid of a damsel in distress. 'This is my mother,' she said, in an attempt to distract his penetrating stare.

Totally in keeping with his image, he lifted June's hand to his lips. 'Pleased to meet you.' June was embarrassed, but clearly impressed by his old-fashioned charm. The diarist returned his attention to Sara. 'I know I'm one of them,' he said, nodding to the group of reporters, 'but in this instance I'm off duty, and I'd be honoured if you'd let me protect you from them.'

Sara looked at Julian Marsh smirking outside. She was stuck between the Devil and the deep blue sea. But she wasn't about to succumb to anyone in Cynthia Hargreaves's pocket, no matter how much charm he oozed. 'Thank you, but I'm sure we'll be fine,' she said crisply. 'Come on, Mum. You wanted to buy some chocolates.'

'He looks just like Cary Grant,' whispered June.

They had been in their seats for less than five minutes when Christopher Heard came along and sat down next to Sara.

'What a coincidence,' he said, as Sara became uncomfortably aware of the pressure of his leg against hers. In an overly familiar tone, he asked, 'So, how's it all going?'

'I'm sure you read the papers.'

'Yes. Rather an unfortunate business. But you've been there, you know it's nothing personal.' He smiled. 'And I personally didn't write a word about it.'

'I hardly think you can take credit for that,' said Sara. 'I gather Cynthia had the story killed.'

June interrupted. 'A nice young man on the door gave me this free,' she said, waving her programme with delight. 'The woman who plays Lady Thiang used to be in *Casualty*.'

The lights went down and the overture started, putting a stop to whatever protestations of innocence Christopher had been about to embark upon. Sara watched in a daze as the plot, familiar from having watched the film version many times with her mother, unfolded.

During the interval Christopher offered to take them to the bar to mingle with his famous friends. If he thought he would be able to get to Sara by impressing her mother, he was sadly mistaken. 'You go, Mum,' she said. 'I'd rather not.'

When the bell went for the second half, June returned to her seat flushed with excitement. 'I've just met Elaine Paige!' she confided.

Sara put her head in her hands in despair. The second half seemed to drag on forever and she couldn't wait for the king to drop dead so that she could get her mother out of the theatre and away from the clutches of Christopher Heard.

When the lights came up again, Christopher, perfect gentleman that he was, discreetly produced a pristine handkerchief for June, who had been overcome by the emotional ending.

'Come on, Mum, it's time to go home,' said Sara, brushing away the diarist's hand as he went to take her arm.

Christopher smiled. 'But I promised to introduce your mother to some more people after the show.'

She couldn't spoil June's evening. She had no choice but to let Christopher further ingratiate himself. 'All right,' she relented. 'Five minutes, and then we've really got to be going.'

Sara watched as Christopher led her mother around the foyer introducing her to people. She grudgingly admitted to herself that the diarist was very attractive – attractive, that is, if you went for the type of man who probably spent more time looking in the mirror than looking at anyone else. Everything about him was in impeccable good taste and artfully crafted, right down to his perfectly manicured nails. For a middle-aged man he seemed remarkably well preserved and Sara suspected that he might have had just the teensiest bit of help from the plastic surgeon.

After a decent interval she insisted that she and June were ready to leave. Christopher disappeared and rematerialised almost immediately with their coats. 'I was hoping that you and your mother would be able to join me for dinner,' he said, flashing his perfect bridgework.

'I'm afraid not,' said Sara icily. 'Look, shall we cut the bullshit, Christopher? What do you want?'

June went white with shock; Christopher looked injured. 'I'm sorry, Sara, but you've got it all wrong,' he said. 'If you find my company so abhorrent I shan't press you to join me, but at least allow me to see you safely through the baying pack and into a cab.'

Sara looked at Julian Marsh smirking at her through the glass door and nodded curtly.

'I can't believe I had to rely on Sara to find you. It seems everyone in the world could contact you except your wife,' screamed Kathy at Joseph.

'I gave you a number.'

'You are such a liar, Joseph. And while we're on the subject of lies, why don't you just come clean about your affair?'

'Wha-what do you mean?' stammered Joseph, pulling nervously on his ponytail. 'I haven't been having an affair!'

'Liar,' said Kathy, exhaustion reducing her voice to a flat monotone. 'I tried to use my credit card for a present for Bette but it was refused. Quite expensive, your bit on the side, isn't she?'

'Kathy, don't let's talk about this now. '

'And while we're on the subject of money, what have you been doing with the mortgage payments? We're going to lose all this because of you,' she said, gesturing at the living room.

'And what about you? Why aren't you working?' he asked angrily.

'I have a child to look after, in case it had escaped your notice.' But that wasn't the answer, and Kathy knew it. What had happened to her? She had become just like her mother, downtrodden and beaten. She continued, more quietly, 'I can't go on with this not knowing . . . Joseph, I want you to be honest with me. Just this once. Are you having an affair?'

Joseph walked over to the other side of the room and poured himself a glass of wine. 'Do you want one?'

'Answer me!' replied Kathy, banging her hand on the arm of her chair.

Joseph emptied his glass and said, quietly, 'Yes.'

Despite all the evidence staring her in the face, Kathy had wanted to believe that his answer would be no. She wanted him to tell her that she was being silly, put his arm around her and tell her that everything would be OK between them, that they'd go back to being like a proper family again. Again? They had never been like that. No matter how much she'd wanted it or worked at it, theirs had never been a perfect relationship. When they'd first met, she'd thought it was a meeting of minds. Looking back, it now seemed merely a meeting of designer labels. To an outsider it would have seemed that they had everything, but the glamorous jobs and the beautiful home were just a façade. There was something missing in their relationship, long before Joseph began to abscond.

'Say something. Scream, shout, tell me you hate me, but say something.' Joseph dropped to his knees and clasped her hands. 'Talk to me.'

'Do I know her?' Why am I asking this? she thought. How much pain do I want to put myself through?

'Sort of.'

Kathy knocked his hands away. She ran through a possible list of names in her head but she was unable to believe that there was anyone in her life who could do this to her. 'Sort of? What does that mean?'

'Well, yes you do. It's Fran.'

A beat passed before she realised that he was talking about Fran Best. 'You are joking, aren't you?'

Chapter Twenty-Six

Sara had imagined that house-hunting would be a long drawn-out process, but it just so happened that the first place she saw – a mews house in Primrose Hill – turned out to be ideal. The estate agent, recognising her, had tried to persuade her to look at a mansion in Hampstead, but what did she, a single woman, want with a large house? Anyway, the mews house was ideal. The estate agent went on about the architect-designed conservatory leading out on to the Italianate roof terrace and the terrazzo flooring throughout, but all Sara cared about was that the house was vacant and only a fifteen-minute drive from the Camden United ground in Kentish Town. With her track record, she didn't hold out much hope of this place feeling any more like home than anywhere else she'd lived in London.

Although she was glad that finding a house had been so easy, she now had the problem of what to do with herself until she could legally start work at the club. There was nobody around. Her mother was safely back in Backwell. June knew that her daughter would be better able to deal with being in the media spotlight without having to worry about her.

That morning Sara had woken early and, for a while, entertained the idea of starting her packing. But the move was still a fortnight away and it wouldn't take her more than a day to assemble her belongings. Instead she settled for a long, leisurely breakfast, deciding to use the free time to take stock of the events of the previous few weeks.

Sitting by the window with her third cup of coffee, watching the rush-hour traffic clogging the streets of Highgate, she realised, much to her surprise, that she was feeling very content. Although she missed Stuart terribly, she sensed that his role in her life wasn't over, not by a long shot. First of all, of course, there was the money.

'I'm rich!' she said out loud to the walls. 'Stuart, what have you done to me?' she laughed. It was madness. One day she was worrying about how she would pay her bills, the next she had more money than she would need in a lifetime. 'And I own a football club!' Despite Stephen's hostility, she was thrilled by the idea of installing herself at Camden United. Only the nagging suspicion that the will in some way represented Stuart's unfinished business marred her excitement.

Why had Stuart left her so much? she wondered, refilling her coffee mug. There had to be more to it than simply exacting revenge on Cynthia and Stephen. Yes, they had become very close, especially over the last year, but Stuart didn't owe her anything. Right from the start he had been very enthusiastic about cultivating a relationship with her – a relationship that had never gone beyond the purely platonic. It was almost as if . . .

The doorbell rang. When she answered it, a delivery man from Interflora presented her with two dozen red roses, a knowing smile spread across his pleasant face. She thanked him and tipped him. Pushing the door closed with her leg, she took the card out of the envelope, knowing for certain who the flowers were from.

Sara,
    I know you have been through an awful lot over the past few weeks and are probably feeling very vulnerable and threatened.

Please let me assure you I have no ulterior motive other than wanting to get to know you. I would be delighted if we could meet some time.

Warm wishes,
Christopher Heard

Ever since that night at the theatre the diarist had pestered her with phone calls. She tore up the card but restrained herself from binning the flowers – they were too beautiful.

Ten minutes later the phone rang.

'Sara? It's Christopher.'

'Yes?' She couldn't keep the sharpness out of her voice.

'Did you get the flowers?'

'Yes.' She sniffed one of the roses. 'Thanks,' she added, sullenly.

'Look, I know you find it hard to believe, but I'd like us to be friends. My only motive for pursuing you is that you are a very beautiful and intelligent woman . . .'

'Flattery will get you nowhere.'

'If not a bit prickly.'

Sara couldn't help but laugh. 'So what can I do for you now?'

'I want to take you out for a drink.'

'No. You never give up, do you?'

'I'll ring your mother and tell her you're being nasty to me.'

She laughed again. Looking at it rationally, there was no reason why the *Herald* would want to drag up the story of her friendship with Stuart. But if Christopher was up to something on Cynthia's behalf, wouldn't it be better to try to suss him out? 'If it'll get you off my back, then I'll come. But we're going Dutch.'

Christopher picked her up at seven in his racing-green Morgan and drove her to a small pub by the side of Richmond Park. She had to hand it to him: he was very astute. The pub was about as far away as possible from the superficially glamorous world he normally inhabited and Sara guessed that he'd sensed she wasn't going to be impressed by an extravagant restaurant or a celebrity-strewn party.

Out of his tuxedo he looked very different, but even dressed casually in a pale cream linen suit, which he knew complemented his clean-cut looks, he was the very epitome of what her mother would call 'dapper'. Sara couldn't help but notice his whiter-than-white smile as he flashed it at her constantly. She suspected that he used the same smile to persuade all those unsuspecting debs to reveal trifles about their love lives for his column. It certainly worked – she found herself easing up in his company.

'I'm glad you agreed to see me,' he said, putting a third glass of wine in front of her.

'Why?' Sara sipped from her glass, feeling warm and slightly flushed.

'I told you. I find you very attractive and I want to get to know you better.'

She said nothing. The less she said, the less chance there was of this meeting backfiring on her.

Christopher seemed to understand her need for reticence. 'OK, I'll tell you something about myself. I was born in Simla, a part of India that will be forever England. My family were fierce colonials living out the last days of the Raj. When I was eighteen my parents paid for me to go to the States, where I studied English at Harvard. From there I started work on the *Herald* and worked my way up to the dizzy heights of diarist.' He caught her cynical expression. 'All right then, gossip columnist.'

'What was that?' asked Sara tartly. 'Your entry in *Who's Who*? For someone so keen on delving into other people's lives, you seem remarkably restrained in talking about your own. Where's all the intrigue?' She wanted to let him know that she wasn't about to roll over and succumb to his on-tap charm.

'There's no intrigue, I'm afraid. I was, as you probably know, married for a short while to the Hon. Christina Pride. The marriage worked for my career but we were completely incompatible. Bit of an upstairs-downstairs thing, really.'

'You're hardly downstairs,' responded Sara, noting that his admission had made him quite uncomfortable.

'No, I suppose not,' he said, slightly distantly. His mobile phone rang. 'Excuse me a minute, Sara. Max, hi, what can I do for you?' As he listened the smile returned to his face. 'Does Major know about the affair? . . . This is an exclusive, right? OK. Look, I'm busy now, I'll call you first thing tomorrow. Remember, not a word to anyone else.' He put the phone back into his pocket. 'Sorry about that. Never off duty.'

'I'm sure. Anyway, you were giving me an exclusive on your life.'

'It's no exclusive. Go to any press-cuttings service and you can get the complete story. After Christine, there was a string of beautiful women. Some made it big in showbusiness, the others got their five minutes of fame from embarrassing the royal family. And then,' he paused melodramatically, 'it all grew very, very empty.'

'Ah, peel away that thin veneer of brittle sophistication . . .'

'And underneath beats the heart of a man with a yen for the simple things in life. That was, until I met you.'

Sara chuckled. 'What a complete load of rubbish! You can't help yourself can you, Christopher? Charm just leaks out of you. But you'll have to try a little bit harder than that.'

He tilted his head to one side. 'I love a challenge.'

As if they were playing an emotional chess match, he changed his game plan and began to let slip the odd, juicy titbit about Cynthia Hargreaves. Sara knew that he was trying to draw her into his confidence but she was fascinated all the same.

Christopher bought another drink and sat down, moving his chair slightly closer so that she caught a faint waft of his citrus-scented aftershave. 'You were lucky when she sacked you that she got it over and done with in five minutes,' he said.

'I'd hardly call the way I was sacked lucky,' said Sara, remembering the awful scene at Stuart's deathbed.

'Well, one editor – no names – who worked for her for seven years was summoned to her office at nine in the morning. At four o'clock she finally opened the door and told him in reception, in front of everybody, that his services would no longer be required. Then she shut the door in his face before he had the chance to say anything.'

Sara wasn't sure if he was telling her these things to let her know that he found his employer just as odious as she did, but when he warned her to watch her back where Cynthia was concerned he certainly sounded very genuine. It was a warning she hardly needed anyway.

Another point in Christopher's favour was that he'd asked her very little about herself, accepting her terse answers to the few innocuous questions he did pose about her background as being sufficiently informative. Still, just to make sure, she confined her sparse revelations to matters he would have read about in the papers: the Mickey Nash story, the modelling and the football writing. At no point did she feel that he was trying to prise anything out of her; in fact, he was the perfect companion, and she found that she'd enjoyed herself much more than she'd intended to.

As they walked back to his car, Christopher asked, 'Can we meet again?'

Sara looked dubious. 'I'm not sure it's a good idea.'

'Oh, come on. I'm not looking for a big commitment; you don't even have to like me that much, but I think we could both do with someone to make us laugh once in a while.'

His sudden modesty took Sara by surprise. Perhaps it wouldn't be such a bad idea. Going into battle against Stephen Powell, she could do with as many allies as possible and perhaps Christopher could become one of them. He might be able to help her find out what had caused the bad feeling between the owner and Stuart. And having a contact in Cynthia's camp would do her no harm at all. But she'd have to watch her back. 'We'll see how it goes,' she said.

Cynthia read through the cuttings slowly, savouring this delicious new development. Under the headline, 'BILL NEWMAN IN DEATH CRASH: ENGLISH FIANCEE BEHIND WHEEL' was a picture of the sanctimonious little strumpet who'd managed to dupe Stuart into handing over his entire fortune.

'Sit down, Miss . . .?' She looked up at the woman standing expectantly in front of her desk, who was dressed in a tight-waisted black blazer over a form-fitting short black skirt. The thin platinum blonde permitted herself a small smile and for a fleeting moment, there was something in her eyes which reminded Cynthia of her own younger self. 'What did you say your name was?'

'Lawrence. Maggie Lawrence.' Maggie took a seat and accepted

Cynthia's offer of a cigarette. 'I've contacted the surviving family members and they'd be more than happy to give an interview. Of course, I think this is only the tip of the iceberg as far as Sara Moore is concerned.'

'No doubt. Have you been to any of the other papers with this yet?'

'Of course not, Mrs Hargreaves.' Maggie was too smart not to recognise where the story could do most damage. As soon as the information had been sent through from America, she had arranged this interview with the proprietor of the Herald Group.

Cynthia laced her bony fingers together and rested her elbows on the desk. 'What's your stake in this? How much money do you want?'

Maggie tried to appear as if the thought had never entered her mind. 'Nothing. As I told you, at one point I knew Sara only too well, and when I read about your late husband ... well, I just thought that she shouldn't be allowed to get away with it any more.'

Cynthia saw through her in a second, but she liked the girl's style. 'You mentioned that you thought that this was only the tip of the iceberg. What do you mean?'

Maggie had to bluff now. The *Sun* had already covered the episode with Huw and there was precious little else she could think of. 'The woman will sleep with absolutely anyone to get what she wants. There must be plenty of other men who've had a run-in with her. And forgive me for saying so, but I'm sure they didn't all end up dead.'

Cynthia put her hand to her mouth to stifle a smile. This Miss Lawrence was totally brazen. 'Maggie, my dear. Would you mind awfully if we sat on this story for the time being?'

'But, Mrs Hargreaves!' Maggie protested. She couldn't bear the thought that her one chance to humiliate Sara might be delayed.

Cynthia quelled a flash of anger at having this nobody question her judgement. If the girl did know something else she could prove very useful. 'May I add, Miss Lawrence, that such initiative doesn't go unrewarded here at the Herald Group. I'm sure one of my editors could find a desk for a bright young thing like yourself.'

Maggie regained her poise but inside she was yelling triumphantly. 'Thank you, Mrs Hargreaves. I'll do anything you want me to do.'

'That's good to hear,' said Cynthia leaning closer, 'as there's someone I'd like you to meet. One of my employees is getting very cosy with Miss Moore, and between the two of you, I think we could soon have her sewn up completely.'

Chapter Twenty-Seven

Sara put the dress back on the rail and walked out into the King's Road, unable to stand the obsequious assistant fawning over her any longer. It had been a mistake to come out shopping, but the decorators were getting on her nerves. They were so fussy. She'd wanted the mews house done out in a minimalist style which she'd imagined would be very easy to create. Apparently not. The decorators had spent all morning discussing shades of plasterwork. Wasn't it all browny-pink?

The assistant in the clothes shop was just as annoying. At first she'd been flattered by the profuse compliments but she soon realised that no matter how unsuitable the outfit, the assistant would still tell her that the way her body made ready-to-wear look like couture was amazing. When she'd first gone into the shop a look of recognition had flashed across the assistant's face which probably accounted for the subsequent sycophancy. Perhaps that's what happens when you're rich, she thought. Nobody has to tell you the truth any more.

The next few shops she tried were no better. Sara decided that she would wear something old to the film première to which Christopher was taking her that evening. After all, it seemed ridiculous to go out and spend hundreds of pounds on a dress just to sit in a dark cinema. Christopher seemed to be one of the few people around her not fazed by her newly acquired wealth. She had tried phoning a few of her old friends on the papers but even Dave Teacher had treated her with the kid-glove approach. It was as if she had been afflicted with a terrible illness rather than been left a fortune. People somehow expected her to have changed, but she didn't feel any different. Just alienated.

This alienation wasn't helped by Kathy's odd behaviour. It was obvious that her friend was undergoing some crisis with Joseph, but she refused to talk about it, stonewalling any of Sara's suggestions that they should meet up. And so the big gap left in her life by Stuart's death was gradually being filled by Christopher who was proving to be a surprising source of comfort. He kept their times together light and funny, never pushing her to talk if she didn't want to, and in response to this laid-back approach she found herself opening up to him. Christopher delighted in the tales of her brief modelling career – he knew several of the people she had met on the catwalks – and seemed genuinely impressed by her investigative work. This interest gave her the chance to rehash some of her theories about Mickey Nash. It was one of those topics she still couldn't let go, and a topic with which most people who knew her were bored to death.

For every story she told, Christopher revealed a new detail about himself, and this bolstered her trust. She even admitted that she had taken cocaine in Mickey's Bar to avoid blowing her cover. At first she thought she'd said too much, but Christopher noticed the worried look on her face and told her he'd tried it himself. It was a shared secret. The only thing she couldn't talk about was Bill and the crash; that part of her life was too precious to her and she had no wish to reopen her wounds.

Turning off the King's Road, Sara walked along the street where Kathy lived, hoping that her friend might be at home and perhaps prepared to talk. Only a couple of months had gone by since the press had been camped outside her house, but it seemed like forever. Just as she was about to ring the doorbell, the door flew open and Kathy appeared, Bette asleep in her arms. Her friend's eyes were red-raw. She was wearing a crumpled, dirty tracksuit and it didn't look as if she'd washed her hair for days.

'Kathy, what on earth . . .'

'This is a bad time for me at the moment,' mumbled Kathy flatly. 'You should have phoned. I'm just on my way out.'

She tried to push past but Sara blocked her way. 'Where are you going?'

'What?' Kathy looked confused. Apparently she wasn't sure where she was going. 'For a walk. I need to clear my head.' Their voices awoke Bette, and she began to cry. 'Baby please,' she snapped, 'I can't deal with you as well.'

'Would you like me to babysit?' offered Sara. Kathy wasn't in a fit state to walk around with a small child in her arms. 'I know it's really irritating when people try to interfere, and I know you don't want to talk at the moment, but don't you think it would be better if you left Bette with me?'

Kathy handed over the toddler. 'Thanks, it would help.' She turned to walk away, then stopped for a moment. 'Sara,' she said looking back, 'we will talk. Soon. I promise. When I know what's going on.'

'You know I'm there for you.'

Kathy nodded. 'I'll only be an hour or so.'

Sara watched the disconsolate figure disappear round a corner and then took the child into the house. Almost immediately, Bette went back to sleep. Sara took her up to the nursery, passing on her way a framed photograph taken at Kathy's wedding. In the photo, both Kathy and Joseph looked fit to burst with happiness. But Sara had no doubt that the reason for Kathy's present state had something to do with her husband.

Covering the baby with an eiderdown, she tiptoed out of the room and walked downstairs into the kitchen. Like Kathy, the kitchen was in a mess and she set to work to try to restore order.

An hour passed with no sign of her friend. Sara made herself a cup of coffee and wandered into the living room. She sorted through

the magazines scattered across the floor, picking out the copies of
Mariella and returning them to the shelves lined with all the back
issues Kathy had worked on. Sara leafed through a couple of them,
admiring Kathy's command of fashion. Her style seemed to leap
out of the pages at you. Sara hoped that one day, before too long,
Kathy would find it in herself to go back to work again.

Above the magazine shelves were rows and rows of large
coffee-table books on the history of fashion. Sara pulled out a
retrospective of *Vogue* photography in the sixties to see if she
could find any pictures of Jackie Powell in her prime. There was
nothing under Powell in the index, but then, it was likely that
Jackie would have worked under her maiden name and probably
hadn't been married then anyway. Sara flicked through the pictures,
hoping that she would recognise her face. It didn't take long. Jackie
Ashworth appeared to feature in every other photograph. There she
was at the opening of the Biba shop, cuddling Barbara Hulanicki; in
another shot she was standing in Carnaby Street dressed in a Union
Jack mini-dress.

Sara turned the pages, fascinated and a little saddened at what
time had done to this once stunning woman. There was a full page
of pictures taken at David Bailey's wedding to Catherine Deneuve
in 1965. And there was Jackie again, this time standing with another
woman and two men outside the register office. In the caption
under the picture, the woman next to Jackie, half-hidden under a
wide-brimmed hat and wearing a white dress, was described as 'the
most beautiful model of her generation', known everywhere by the
nickname David Bailey had given her: the Butterfly. The text told
the story of her mysterious disappearance a year later. Apparently,
she was never seen again.

Sara was just about to turn the page when she stopped short. It
can't be, she thought, looking at the picture again. She peered at the
photograph more closely. The man Jackie Ashworth was draped
around was none other than Stuart Hargreaves. And, if she wasn't
mistaken, Stephen Powell was holding on proprietorially to the tiny
waist of the Butterfly.

Maybe it's as simple as that, thought Sara. Perhaps some love
tangle in the heady days of the sixties explained the bad blood

between the two men. Stephen had stolen Jackie from Stuart, and Stuart had never forgiven his one-time friend. It had nothing to do with a business deal at all. But surely Stuart wouldn't have remained so vengeful almost thirty years on? Sara couldn't imagine the kind and gentle man she knew keeping so much hatred in his heart for so long. And, after all, Stuart had already been married to Cynthia at the time. Why should he act so unforgivably over what could have only been a brief affair? Could leaving the football club to Sara really be just one last act of revenge?

No, she thought, it just wasn't in Stuart's nature to be so malicious. He was such a caring person. But then again, look how wrong she'd been about Maggie. Perhaps she had to face the fact that Stuart was just a mean-spirited philanderer who'd never been able to get over a bashing to his macho ego. After all, she knew very little of that side of his life.

'Has she been good?'

Sara looked up from the book to see Kathy standing in the doorway. 'She's fine. She's still asleep upstairs, I didn't hear you come in.' She closed the book. 'Do you want me to make you some coffee?'

Kathy shook her head. 'I think I might lie down myself.'

'Kathy I—'

'Not now, please.'

'I feel I'm letting you down. You shouldn't be going through all this by yourself. Why isn't Joseph—'

'I told you I'll talk when I'm ready. I really appreciate you looking after Bette, but I'd like you to go now.' Kathy walked back into the hall and opened the front door.

Sara followed and tried to cuddle her, but Kathy pulled away. 'Call me,' Sara said, knowing that it was unfair to push her friend at this moment. She understood how Kathy felt. After Bill had died, she hadn't liked it when people had tried to make her talk. 'Any time, day or night. And if you want me to look after Bette, just ask.'

'Thanks again,' said Kathy. 'I know I'm acting like a complete lunatic, but it'll pass – I promise.'

As Sara walked back on to the King's Road, the question-mark over Stuart's motives continued to bug her. She wanted to have all the answers before she started at the club in a few weeks' time. If the sole reason for all the trouble was a fight over a woman, then she couldn't in all conscience defend Stuart's position in using her as a means of revenge. As much as she disliked Stephen, if what she'd guessed was true, then he and Stuart had been just as bad as each other.

One person who might be able to help her was Christopher. Gossip was his business after all, and he'd be sure to know all about an affair between an MP and a famous model, even one that had happened such a long time ago. The mansion block where Christopher lived was only a couple of streets away, and she decided to pay him a visit. She'd never called on him unexpectedly before, but she knew he often worked from home and felt the matter couldn't wait until the evening.

She was suddenly glad to have a purpose again. Wandering around shopping, she decided, was never going to be good for her soul. Unravelling a mystery like this, on the other hand, boosted her adrenaline and took her back to her investigative-reporting days. Slightly out of breath, she ran across Sloane Square, startling pigeons and Sloane Rangers alike, and turned into the square where Christopher lived. When she reached number 12 she was momentarily taken aback by the imposing building before her. Beautifully tiled steps led up to an imposing portico surrounding an enormous glossy black door. Despite his remarks about his ill-fated marriage, she doubted very much whether there was any 'downstairs' element to Christopher's life.

She rang the bell and was surprised when a woman's voice answered over the intercom.

'Is Christopher there?

''Ang on a minute, I'll come down,' said the voice.

A few moments later, an old, shabby-looking woman opened the enormous door, the effort almost bending her double. ''E's out at the moment, do you wanna come in and wait?'

Sara had to stoop to talk to the tiny old lady. 'Oh, don't worry, it wasn't anything that important,' she replied, guessing that the woman was his cleaner, although the poor thing looked too frail even to pick up a broom, let alone use one. 'I'm seeing him tonight, so I can talk to him then.'

'I was just on me way out meself,' said the woman, pulling on a heavy, moth-eaten camel coat. 'So you'll prob'ly see my Chris'pher before I do. Can you tell 'im I was round? I'm Maisie. Tell 'im I've done all 'is sheets.'

Sara was amused at the proprietorial way Maisie had referred to Christopher. Obviously she was a faithful old retainer, and clearly very fond of him. Sara chuckled to herself as she followed Maisie's painstaking progress down the front steps.

The cinema in Leicester Square had been closed for months for a facelift and was reopening with the première of *The Fugitive*. Christopher was attending in his official capacity, and on the way there he had reeled off a long list of people they 'simply had to talk to'. Sara had tried quizzing him on Stuart Hargreaves, but it was clear that his mind was fully occupied by the evening ahead. She resigned herself to the fact that now was not the time to try to talk about it.

They stepped through the security cordon around the cinema and Sara braced herself for the inevitable whoosh of flashing cameras. As soon as they were inside, Christopher was on the job.

'They're losing the battle to keep her out of the public eye,' he said, gazing admiringly at the Princess of Wales. He retrieved a notebook from his pocket and jotted down some notes on Diana's attire – 'Slinky blue evening dress split to thigh/spectacular diamond and sapphire choker.'

Sara could see that Clint Eastwood was charming the pants off the princess and looked on enviously. At sixty-three, the grizzled-looking actor was still incredibly sexy. She turned to remark as much to Christopher, but he had vanished into the star-studded crowd. Her escort reappeared in its centre moments later, nodding enthusiastically at whatever it was that Jerry Hall was saying, and then popped up somewhere else, wearing an expression of concern prompted by something Phil Collins was sharing with him.

It was all rather unreal. Sara decided to relax, leave the egotistical back-patting to the stars, and just enjoy herself.

Christopher rematerialised by her side, beaming. 'Diana is in seventh heaven. She adores all those Dirty Harry films.'

Sara smiled, amused at Christopher's unrestrained enthusiasm for the princess.

'You seem distant tonight,' he commented, waving to Simon and Yasmin le Bon.

She was surprised he had noticed. 'Probate goes through tomorrow. And there are one or two things I wanted to sort out. I was hoping you might be able to help.' Suddenly Sara remembered the old woman. 'I forgot to tell you. I met Maisie today, and she asked me to say that she's done all your sheets. I called round—'

Christopher cut her short, his face blackening. 'What did she tell you?'

Sara thought she noted a hint of panic in his voice. 'I've just told you, she's done all your sheets. Why all the—'

'You had no business coming over to my place uninvited,' he said, rounding on her. 'I want you to tell me everything she said. Now.'

'Who the hell do you think you're talking to?' hissed Sara. The lobby was packed, and she knew that their conversation could be overheard, but she was blazing with anger. 'I know social etiquette is important to you, Christopher, and Nancy Mitford might be spinning in her grave at the thought of someone turning up without first announcing their intention by post, but may I remind you that *you* pursued *my* friendship and it is quite normal for me to call on someone who calls himself a friend.'

Entering into the largest of the cinema's nine auditoria, Christopher recovered his composure. 'Sara, I'm sorry. The way I spoke is unforgivable. Of course, there was nothing wrong with you visiting.'

'Save it,' she snapped, taking her seat as the lights went down.

Afterwards she couldn't remember anything about the film beyond the admittedly spectacular train crash. She was too incensed about the way Christopher had spoken to her to concentrate on it.

As the credits rolled, he sprang up. 'Come on, we need to get to the Savoy for the champagne dinner.' In the lobby he held out her coat for her, all the time looking over her shoulder to see if he'd missed anyone important.

Sara snatched her coat from him. 'I'm not coming, Christopher. I really don't appreciate people trying to make me look small. You invade people's privacy all the time. I can't see why coming over to have a chat with you is such a crime.'

'Sara, please . . .'

Christopher gave chase as she ran down the escalators and out into the square, but he soon lost sight of her in the crowd. He returned to the cinema, perturbed that for a second she had made him lose his cool. Outside there was a long line of black limousines waiting to take the famous filmgoers on to the party. One pulled up alongside him and a smoked-glass window rolled down.

'Get in,' said a voice.

Christopher climbed into the car and found himself sitting opposite his employer. 'Good evening, Mrs Hargreaves. I wasn't expecting you here tonight.' Next to Cynthia sat a thin, blonde woman, clutching a glass of champagne.

'This is Maggie Lawrence,' said Cynthia curtly.

Maggie extended her hand to Christopher. 'Mrs Hargreaves has told me so much about you,' she said.

Sara got out of the cab, still fuming. She paid the driver and searched around in her handbag for her keys, deciding that her friendship with the diarist was over. She didn't need the aggravation. Twice in one day people had criticised her for turning up unexpectedly, but Christopher didn't as yet have anywhere near enough credits in the bank to get away with behaving so rudely.

The streetlight was out and in the dark it was hard to see what she was doing. She reached out her hand and felt for the lock, but the first key she tried was the wrong one. 'Damn!' she cursed. She tried another key. The lock was stiff but finally it turned and she pushed open the door.

It was only a split-second after she heard the sound of heavy breathing that a gloved hand was clamped over her mouth, jerking her head back viciously. Her assailant pushed her into the hallway, his other hand around her waist, pinning her arms to her sides.

'Just do as you're told and you won't get hurt.' The man spoke in a hoarse whisper. He pushed her face against the wall. 'I'm going to remove my hand now, but if you scream, you're dead.'

Sara felt the cold steel of a blade pressed up against her neck and let out a frightened gasp.

'Understand?' he prompted, increasing the pressure of the blade. She nodded furiously, her body completely rigid.

'Now, you wouldn't want me to mess up your pretty face, would you? All I need is your co-operation, and I'll be out of here before you know it.'

'M-my p-purse is in my bag.' She tried to hand it to him but her arm wouldn't move.

'I don't want your *money!*' he growled threateningly in her ear.

'No, not that, she pleaded silently. Please don't let it be that. 'Please . . . please, don't hurt me.'

'Then don't make me,' he teased, his voice laced with menace.

Stay calm, she told herself. Maybe he'll—

'Now listen carefully. I'm just a delivery boy. And this is just a taste of what's to come if you don't do as you're told. An old friend of mine wants me to ask you nicely to stay away from Camden.'

Suddenly she understood. 'You can't just barge in here and threaten me.' Anger was welling up inside her, overtaking her fear. How dare Stephen do this. 'You can tell Stephen Powell—'

He yanked her hair cruelly. 'Shut it. Powell didn't send me. He's your biggest fan. Or at least, your money's. He's what's keeping you alive.'

'Then—'

'I'm working for Mickey. He hasn't forgotten a pretty thing like you,' he said, biting into the side of her neck, his teeth just about holding back from piercing her flesh. Releasing his grip, he whispered, 'It would be a real shame to see you get hurt. So remember, be a silent partner or you'll be made to be one.' With that he was gone.

Terrified, Sara didn't dare move. Even when she heard the screech of tyres she remained perfectly still, noticing for the first time the coolness of the wall against her skin.

As the realisation of the danger she had been in – and of what might have happened – struck, and shock seeped in, she started to shake uncontrollably. Her legs gave way and she collapsed on the floor. Still shrouded in darkness, she cradled her knees to her chest and rocked back and forth. Finally the tears began, at first sliding slowly down her face until, totally overcome by myriad emotions, she completely gave into them and her whole body was racked with sobs.

When the crying subsided she was completely exhausted and could barely muster the energy to get up to switch on the light. But once the hallway was illuminated, she ran round the house in a mad panic, turning on all the lights, the TV and stereo too, then checking and locking all the windows and doors. As she secured the final lock, nausea welled up in her stomach. She only just made it to the bathroom in time. Tears stung her eyes as she heaved violently, her head spinning as she tried to piece it all together. So Nash was connected to Stephen Powell.

When there was nothing left inside her she stood up, her legs still wobbly, and rinsed her mouth, noticing the bite mark on her neck as she looked in the mirror. Thankfully, the knife hadn't cut her. Thankfully? There was nothing to be thankful about.

She tried to think calmly. The anonymous letter sent to her at journalism college had started it all. Had Powell sent it to her? She tried to think it through but it didn't make sense. Why would Stephen ... Steve. Of course. How stupid she had been! Frank, Mickey, Elaine – everyone at the club talked about Steve. It was Powell they were talking about. The match-throwing, the drug deals – Powell was behind everything. Powell couldn't have sent her the letter. Why would he want to alert anyone to what he was doing? No, somebody wanted her to find out what Stephen was up to and nail him. Somebody who knew them both. But until Stuart left her the football club, there was no obvious connection between them. Apart from Stuart himself ...

I've got to think rationally, she told herself, as she pulled herself to her feet and stumbled into the living room. But as she tried to put pieces of the jigsaw together it all came back to the same starting point: the author of the letter. As much as it hurt her to believe it, that person had to have been Stuart Hargreaves.

It made sense, as much as anything made sense at that moment.

Stuart had bought into Camden in 1986, and he'd had to do it secretly because of the hatred which existed between him and Powell. Whatever the nature of the problem between the two men, she had to assume that he intended Sara to sort it out – just as he had intended her to sort out what was happening in Mickey's Bar.

Had she grown to love like a father a man who, for seven years, had been pulling strings to influence the direction of her life? She began to lose the thread of her thoughts again. If Stuart had known all about what Stephen was up to, why hadn't he simply told the police? Maybe he didn't know everything and had used her, an inquisitive young journalist, to do his dirty work for him. After all, he had a great political reputation which would have been tarnished by association with such a sordid story. Perhaps he was more involved than that? What if his hatred of Stephen stemmed from the fact that Powell knew something about him which could ruin him; something which forced him to keep quiet about Stephen's illegal activities?

If that was so, Sara couldn't see how she fitted into the picture. Her head ached as she tried to think back over the years, trawling their conversations to see if she could remember something which might point to Stuart's reason for choosing her. She thought about the graduation ceremony when Stuart had walked into her life. It hadn't been by chance that he was there. By then he had already sent her the letter. But why? Why had he cultivated their friendship so determinedly? He'd even travelled to New York to get hold of her. That couldn't have been a coincidence, either. It was in New York that he had fed her the Leonel Pinto story. He was another criminal figure in Stephen's orbit.

Stuart was a good man, she told herself. It was impossible that she could love someone who was capable of hurting her so much. He couldn't have known what was going on; he couldn't have known that he was guiding her along a path which would lead her into so much danger. Could all of this have started over something as simple as a row about Jackie Ashworth? If that was the case, perhaps Stuart had realised that he'd put Sara in the firing line and his extraordinary bequest was a way of making amends.

But he'd left her the football club too. A football club where the mystery continued. The will was not an end, an attempt to make peace. Stuart wanted her to go on fighting his fight. Why had he chosen her?

Chapter Twenty-Eight

Sara drove into the Camden United car park, still vaguely unsettled by the huge presence next to her. Norman had to be seventeen stone and the passenger seat could barely contain him. His shoulder rubbed up against hers and his knee got in the way of the gearstick. He looked as uncomfortable with the unavoidable physical contact as she was. Although he was not much taller than her, his immense muscular bulk dwarfed her, underlining her svelteness. Together they were Beauty and the Beast. Norman was Sara's bodyguard, and since the night of the attack he had been permanently at her side.

She had thought of handing the matter over to the police, but what could she tell them? That a dead MP believed by all and sundry to have been her lover had, years ago, sent her an anonymous note alerting her to a corrupt deal between the owner of a football club and a small-time Soho criminal with links to an international drugs ring and gambling syndicate? It sounded ludicrous. And where was the evidence? They would have thought she was off her trolley.

It had dawned on Sara that night that somehow it wasn't Stuart, or Stephen, or anybody else who was at the centre of this mystery. She was. Knowing that Stuart had sent her the note didn't solve everything. The key to the puzzle lay in the reason why he had sent it to *her*. The attack told her that she was only one step away from all the answers. Why else were people getting so jumpy? Employing Norman bought her a little time to find out why these people wanted her out of the picture. The second she discovered the truth she'd hand it over to the police and be shot of the whole nightmare.

'Do you want me to come in with you?' asked the bodyguard, adjusting the knot of his tie. For all his fearsome looks, Norman fussed around her like a mother hen.

'I think I'll go alone. But I'd appreciate if you could be nearby.'

'In training they ask you if you'd be prepared to take a bullet for your employer. If you say no you're out. But it isn't just words . . .'

'Thanks, Norman. But it might antagonise Stephen even more.'

'So what?'

'I'm not sure.' She wasn't sure of anything any more. Her whole life had been turned on its head. She'd always prided herself on being in control, but now she was beginning to get a nasty feeling that every development in her life had been carefully manipulated by somebody else. Stuart's intervention had left her in a state of paranoia. For God's sake, she was even starting to suspect her own mother. Carefully avoiding mentioning the attack, she'd phoned June the night before to ask her again why she'd disliked Stuart so much.

'For someone who's only met him once,' Sara had said, 'you've certainly got very strong views on him. It's as if he hurt you personally in some way.'

'His party has,' said June. 'Me and all the other pensioners.'

Sara didn't believe her for a second. June was lying, her faltering voice said it all. 'I remember the way you looked at him at my graduation ceremony. It was as if you'd seen a ghost.'

'I wish he had been a ghost.'

'I've never heard you wish death on anybody—'

June interrupted her. 'Your father had very strong political views.

He couldn't bear the likes of Stuart Hargreaves. Harry was a decent, honest working man . . .' June had dissolved into tears and Sara knew that the conversation wasn't going to go any further. Whatever her mother knew, she was keeping it to herself.

'Well?' asked Norman, brushing imaginary dust off the shoulders of his immaculate black suit.

'What? Oh sorry, I was just wondering why I'm doing this and what I could be getting myself into. Why don't I just turn the car round and drive away from it all?' In the absence of any more suitable candidate, Norman had become her confidant. When she had taken him on, she had filled him in on the events of the past seven years and he had proved a surprising source of comfort and wisdom. 'Why am I still doing Stuart's dirty work?' It pained her to be thinking ill of Stuart. She still desperately wanted to believe that his reasons for involving her in this mess were entirely benevolent, but at the same time she couldn't help being angry at him for putting her in danger.

'You can do. It's easy, just turn round and go. But you'll never find out why he got you to do his dirty work. From the short time I've spent with you, I don't think you're that kind of lady. You're not about to let it rest.'

'No, I'm not,' said Sara with weary resignation, as she opened the car door.

Stephen's secretary, Linda, was in reception picking up the mail. Working for Stephen had obviously affected her nerves as every time Sara saw her the poor woman seemed to be on the verge of an anxiety attack. In her early fifties, with a penchant for tight perms and pastel tracksuits, Linda fluttered around the Camden offices desperately trying to look busy but Sara got the feeling she probably achieved very little.

Seeing Sara, Linda forced a smile which was immediately replaced by a look of open-mouthed horror as Norman appeared in the doorway behind her. 'Miss Moore,' the secretary spluttered. 'Mr Powell says he's much too busy to see you this morning. I could show you round if you like.'

'I'm sorry, Linda. Maybe I'll take you up on that tour later, but there are a couple of things Stephen and I have to get sorted out immediately,' said Sara, marching up the corridor to Powell's office with Norman at her heels.

'But—' The secretary started to protest but a quick glare from Norman silenced her.

'Good morning,' said Sara, walking into Powell's office without knocking. She was glad to see that her arrival startled him. 'I take it you weren't expecting me.'

Stephen flew out from behind the desk. 'Get out.'

Theatrically, Sara clicked her fingers and Norman appeared. 'Is there a problem, Miss Moore?' he asked, eyeing Stephen menacingly.

'Sit down, Stephen,' said Sara, as Norman folded his arms and stood impassively behind her.

Stephen had no option but to comply. 'So this is a woman's touch, eh? Won't the zoo be wondering where he's got to?'

'You're a fine one to talk.' Sara rested her hands on his desk, her face just inches from his. 'You've done yourself no favours.'

'What are you on about?'

'I'm on to you, and everything that's going on here.' She tried to sound confident as she called his bluff but her insides were churning. The reason she was leaning on his desk was to stop herself shaking. 'So much so that someone wants me out of the way.'

'You know I want you out of the way.'

'Yes, but until the other night, what I didn't know was that you were such good friends with Mickey Nash.'

'Name doesn't ring any bells,' he smirked.

'I'm sure you read all about it in the papers. He used to run a club in Soho. A club where Billy Todd got caught taking cocaine. A club where there were a lot of whispers that someone was paying players to throw games. Frank and the boys were very insistent about it.' As she said this, Sara was sure she caught a look of surprise flit briefly across Stephen's face. He obviously hadn't realised how much she'd been able to piece together.

'Game-throwing's a serious business. Have you got any proof?' he asked, his voice betraying nothing.

'You'd be surprised at what I've got.' The knowledge that she'd caught him on the hop emboldened her. 'Powell, you're living on borrowed time in this club. It really was a very silly thing to have done.'

'Don't get too cocky, girly. You might not have a couple of weeks to play with. You do have the habit of running into some naughty characters. Sooner or later one of them is going to do the job properly.'

'Norman, you heard that, didn't you?'

'Certainly did.'

'I don't think he meant it. Women make him a bit nervous, that's all.' Sara couldn't let Stephen see any sign of weakness. Not for a second. Despite what her attacker had said, she didn't doubt that this man would be prepared to have her killed to protect his interests. 'Anyway, enough of the social niceties. I want to get down to business. First things first. Where's the team?'

Stephen fumed impotently. 'You know so much about this place, you find them.'

'Fair enough, but while I'm doing that can you get Linda to sort out an office for me?'

'I don't fucking believe you. You don't get it, do you? You're not wanted here.'

'I get it only too well. If I want to I can take my money out of this place and have it closed down tomorrow.' She turned to leave. 'Norman, make sure he sees to it,' she said, desperate to leave before her knees crumpled. This little scene had taken every ounce of confidence she possessed – and she still had to maintain her composure as she walked back through reception in front of Linda and the rest of the staff.

Linda told her that the players were out on the pitch. As Sara opened the door to the stands, she took several calming gulps of fresh air until she could feel her heartbeat steadying. For a moment she allowed herself to simply stand there and take it all in. She gazed around the stadium, still unable to believe that half of it was hers. Being given a football club was something magical. It was hard to reconcile the feelings that the sight of the stadium instantly conjured up with the nastiness going on behind closed doors. As she walked down the steps of the empty stand she thought about the side of football she loved, the game filled with honour and scented with the warm, innocent memories of her childhood. A game about winning fairly and squarely, not about losing because bastards like Stephen Powell were offering grubby, drug-tainted backhanders.

Her thoughts were interrupted by a dozen different wolf whistles from the team as they passed on a slow lap around the track.

'Concentrate on what you're doing,' came a gruff voice from behind her. 'None of you is that bloody good you can afford to be distracted by a bit of skirt.'

Bristling, Sara turned to see a man in the team's blue and purple tracksuit coming down the steps towards her. He had to be in his mid-fifties, but the speed at which he galloped down showed that he was fitter than most men half his age.

'Can I help you, lass?' he asked. 'Are you one of the catering staff?'

Sara looked at him, trying to gauge if he was genuine or not. Surely he must know who she was? Well, two could play at that game. 'No, I'm not. Who are you?' she asked, though she knew full well. Although she had never been introduced to Reg Bowden, she knew that his dourness was legendary.

The man spluttered with indignation. 'Who the bloody hell am I? I'm the bloody manager, that's who!'

'Your name?'

'Bowden. Not that it's any of your business. Are you one of those jumped-up secretaries?' The Yorkshireman's voice almost strangled itself into a squeak of indignation.

'Try again, Reg.'

As a blush rose from Reg's neck to his receding hairline, Sara knew that he had finally guessed who he was talking to. 'You're Sara whatshername, aren't you?'

'Sara Moore. Pleased to meet you,' she said politely, holding out her hand.

Reg ignored the gesture. 'Now listen here, lass, I know you're in charge, but I've got to say what I feel. I don't hold with it. I've read the newspapers and I'm not impressed. Your morals are your own business, but if you were a daughter of mine, by heck, I'd have summat to say about the way you've been behaving. And if you think that sort of carry-on is the way to run a football club, you're much mistaken. Like I always say, football's no place for—'

Sara cut him off. 'Right, you've made your position clear. I won't interrupt training, but I'd like to see you and the team here at three o'clock.'

'Now listen here—'

'Three o'clock,' insisted Sara, leaving him in no doubt that the conversation was at an end. She'd noticed that the players had stopped running and were doing half-hearted stretching exercises, watching to see if she'd back down to Reg.

As she walked back up the steps, she heard the manager muttering, 'Hard-faced little madam.' Her heart sank. Wasn't it enough that she had Stephen to deal with? Briefly glancing back at the team, she went inside the offices, wondering how long Stuart had expected her to last in such an atmosphere.

The threat of Norman had done the trick, and Linda was waiting to show her to her new office. With the bodyguard a step behind, Linda, clutching an armful of files, led Sara to the back of the building and opened the door of a tiny little room, unfurnished but for a desk and a phone. A buzzing fluorescent strip was a poor substitute for natural light, most of which was blocked out by a fire escape just outside the window.

'You're not accepting this, are you?' asked the bodyguard.

Sara sighed. There was no point in wasting her energies on trivia. Everything was going to be a battle, so she had to decide which things were worth fighting for. For now the office would do. 'It's fine. Norman, why don't you take a lunch break?'

'You sure?'

Sara nodded. 'I think Stephen has got the message for the moment.'

In the cramped confines of the office, Norman had to edge past Linda to get out and as he did so, he accidentally knocked the files from her arms. It was all too much for Linda's nerves and she promptly burst into tears and dropped to her knees. The bodyguard looked at Sara, bemused.

'Leave it,' she told him, and bent down to help Linda pick up the files. 'Are you OK?'

Linda produced a handkerchief from the sleeve of her lemon tracksuit top. 'It's all this bad feeling. I don't know why Stephen can't just accept that you're here.' She blew her nose noisily. 'I think it's nice, you know, having a woman in charge. Makes a change.'

'Things will calm down soon. He'll get used to the idea.'

'Oh . . . blast!' said Linda, picking up the last of the files, her eyes filling up again. 'Blast, blast, blast!'

Sara wondered how anybody working for Stephen could have such a narrow range of profanities. 'What is it?'

Linda opened the file, sniffling. 'I forgot to get Stephen to authorise these. He's going to go mad. He's gone out now, and he said this had to be done this morning. He'll sack me, I know it.'

'If everything's in order perhaps I can sign them. I'm a signatory now, you know.'

'Oh, would you? You'd save my bacon.'

Linda looked so pathetically grateful that Sara sat down and took out her pen. She read through the first of the papers, which concerned salaries.

'Do you want me to go through them all with you?' asked the secretary, reading over her shoulder. 'Or there's Mrs Moynihan from accounts. She's in today.'

Sara flicked through the papers. It all seemed pretty standard stuff. 'It's OK. I'll be seeing all the staff over the next couple of weeks. Mrs Moynihan can fill me in on all the systems then.'

Linda watched anxiously as Sara worked through the papers. 'If ever you don't know where something is, you just ask me, Miss Moore. I do the orders for coffee, tea and biscuits, and if the, er, dispenser in the Ladies' ever runs out, I'm your girl. And if you fancy a chinwag or want to borrow a *Woman's Realm* . . .'

'I'll remember that,' said Sara, looking up from the papers. The poor woman was obviously starved of female company, but she doubted very much that she'd be popping out of her office to see Linda if she 'fancied a chinwag'.

When Sara had finished, the secretary bundled up her files, almost bowing with gratitude. 'It's good to have you here, Miss Moore.'

As Linda opened the door to leave Sara asked her, 'Would it be possible to get this room painted? It's pretty disgusting.'

The secretary was halfway out before she replied. 'I'll see to it right away,' she said, running off along the corridor.

For a while, Sara sat in her office staring at the walls. It was only lunchtime and already she felt exhausted. Being the object of so much hostility was hard work. Anxious to escape the confines of her tiny office, she decided to go for a walk, thinking that a quick gin and tonic might revive her.

The club bar was quiet and dark, and empty – except for a familiar figure propping up the counter. Sara walked towards her.

'Jackie?'

The older woman's eyes glazed over as she studied Sara's face.

'It's Sara Moore, Stuart's friend. Remember, we met—'

'Sit down,' said Jackie, kicking a bar stool. 'You deserve a drink. My old man had a right fit when you arrived this morning.' She cackled. 'Done wonders for his blood pressure.'

Sara laughed. 'What would you like?'

'Whisky and soda, please.'

Sara guessed from the slowness of Jackie's speech that she was probably already on her fifth or sixth drink. As usual, the woman's dyed red hair was backcombed to breaking point, betraying a good inch of black roots. The rhinestones on her hot-pink blouse shimmered over her ample bosom and the zip on her tangerine Capri pants didn't quite do up to the top. Sara couldn't understand how someone who had once looked so lovely and fashionable had developed such bad taste.

Pulling up a stool, Sara hoped this might be an opportunity to unravel part of the mystery. 'I saw some old photographs of you the other day,' she began.

A glimmer of interest showed in Jackie's bloodshot eyes. 'Where was that?'

'In a book. It was all about the sixties. You at Biba, you in Carnaby Street. That kind of thing.'

Jackie smiled and for a second Sara glimpsed a ghost of the model features Jackie Ashworth once possessed. It was as if all the caked-on foundation and bloatedness had simply fallen away. 'I remember,' she said, dreamily. 'Those were the days.' Sara suspected that there were tears in the older woman's eyes. 'We thought we could have everything. It didn't matter what your background was, where you came from. None of it mattered. I thought I could . . .' Her voice drifted away.

Sara wanted to keep her attention. 'There was also a photograph of you and Stuart at David Bailey's wedding to Catherine Deneuve. Stephen was there too, with another woman. You looked beautiful.'

'Thanks. David took a lot of photos of me. Always told me I was going to be the next Shrimp.'

Unsure whether it was better to let her reminisce about the past in the hope of picking up some information or direct her thoughts with a question, Sara plumped for the latter course. 'So you were there with Stuart?'

Jackie stared at her uncomprehendingly.

'Before Stephen, I mean.'

'It would have happened if it hadn't been for the Butterfly,' she drawled. 'There was nothing she had that I didn't. But even after she disappeared it was still her they wrote about.' Unsteadily, Jackie got to her feet, her four-inch stilettos causing her to list precariously to one side. 'I've got to go to the little girls' room. Get them in again, will you?'

Sara ordered another for herself, too, and took the drinks to a table, feeling the beginnings of a headache. Drinking during the day was never a good idea, but she felt she needed it today. Besides, it might make Jackie more willing to talk if she wasn't left to drink alone.

The older woman reappeared and sat down with a lurch, immediately draining half her drink. 'Now, where was I?' she slurred, the sentence coming out as one word.

'David Bailey,' prompted Sara hopefully.

'Oh yes. If only I'd been the Butterfly. I wouldn't be here now.'

'What about Stuart?'

'What about him? He left you this place, didn't he?' She giggled to herself. 'You know, it's my fault you've got a controlling share.'

'How's that?'

'I sold Peter my shares. Oh, everything's my fault to him, anyway. I hope you get rid of the bastard.' Jackie spat out the last word and, without warning, closed her eyes.

'Jackie?' Sara shook her but the only response was a snort. She looked up at the clock on the wall. It was 2.45. She wasn't going to get any more out of Jackie today and besides it was almost time to meet the team. Making sure the woman was comfortable, Sara left her at the table, snoring peacefully away.

Out in the stadium, she had to shield her eyes from the glare of the afternoon sun. She watched unobserved as some of the players ran laps while others played a five-a-side game. Despite everything, she still felt a shiver of excitement as she admired their expertise and skill.

On the sideline, Reg blew a whistle and shouted: 'Relax, lads. We've got a visitor. The lady who's been left half this club thinks she's got summat to contribute. I've been in football nigh on thirty years and I can honestly say that, apart from cleaning the strip, women shouldn't be allowed near the game. But she seems to think different.'

'Building me up to the troops, are we?' said Sara, walking on to the pitch.

'This is no place for a lass, that's all I'm saying. You're a pretty girl, you should be at home looking after a family.'

'I presume you want to keep working here?' Reg went quiet and she continued, addressing the players. 'I've interviewed at least half of you here as a journalist. You know that I know the game inside out, despite what Reg says.' The two drinks she'd had with Jackie had improved her confidence noticeably. 'I'm not here to step on his toes – I'm not the manageress – but as owner of half this club I will have a say in its running. Hiring and firing is my business. And let me just say this: we've lost the last three matches in a row, and a few of you need to buck up your ideas. There's no room for dead wood in Camden any more. Are there any questions?'

The players shuffled their feet, none of them looking Sara in the eye.

'OK, see you again tomorrow.' Sara turned to Reg. 'A word in private, please.'

Reg followed her like a sulky child. 'If I were you,' she said, in the steeliest of tones, 'I'd worry less about me and more about the way we're playing.'

Reg grunted. 'Have you finished?'

'For now.' The manager walked away. 'I'm expecting a win tomorrow night,' Sara shouted after his retreating back. 'Understood?'

The next day, despite the atmosphere behind the scenes, Sara could not help feeling excited as she entered the stadium ten minutes before the match. There was a good-humoured crowd of around 30,000 home supporters, plus 10,000 for Everton. Stephen ignored her when she arrived and refused to move up to give her a seat. So she sat behind him, studying his bald spot. Childishly, he hadn't troubled himself to tell the announcer to mention her arrival to the fans. But all that could wait.

Camden United ran on to the pitch to a rapturous welcome. Sara spotted Ian Sumner with his shaven head. He'd been missing from training the day before and she wondered how his gambling debts were going. Automatically she began to identify every player before the match began, having spent part of the day catching up with the current line-up and familiarising herself with a couple of new faces. But the last player to appear was a mystery. She leaned forward in her seat to get a better view of him. He wasn't in the programme, but there was something very familiar about him.

As Everton ran on to the field, Sara tapped Stephen on the shoulder. 'Who's number nine?'

'Ssh, the game's about to start,' he replied, swiping her hand away.

There was no point in making a scene. As the match got underway, it was clear that the mysterious number 9 was leagues ahead of both his own team and their opponents. Not only was he a marvellous player, he was attractive with it. She admired his swarthy good looks, and even from this distance she could make out the chiselled, refined features beneath his dark, tousled hair. He was unusually tall for a footballer, too, his long, muscular legs tensing as he leaped across the pitch. Where had she seen him before?

It wasn't long before his skill was rewarded with a goal and the announcer answered her question. 'Look at Antonio Neves go! What a manoeuvre! He's scored in his first game for United!'

An ecstatic roar of appreciation from the home crowd drowned out her gasp. The surly Brazilian who had snubbed her in Cuenca! What on earth was he doing in the Camden squad?

Sara was seething. Why had nobody told her about this? In the boardroom at half-time, Stephen was busy talking to the sponsors. It was obviously just a ruse to avoid her. When she tried to interrupt him, he waved her away.

'Later, later,' he said dismissively, returning to his conversation.

Until the game was finished she would find out nothing. Such was her anger that for the second half of the match she couldn't concentrate on the football and drew no pleasure from United's 2–0 win, especially since both goals had been scored by Neves.

Before she could confront Stephen, he had left his seat and was heading down to the pitch. She followed after him and soon they were surrounded by journalists.

'Ladies and gentlemen,' shouted Stephen as Reg joined them, stony-faced. 'How was that for a surprise? It gives me great pleasure to announce that as of today, Brazilian international striker, Antonio Neves, one of São Paulo's best, will be scoring for Camden United. As you can see from today's result, he's worth every penny paid for him. Any questions?'

'The word is you paid two million for Neves,' said Sid Kelly of the *Comet*. 'Do you want to confirm that?'

Stephen smiled. 'It's in that area . . .'

Sara turned on Reg. 'Did you know about this?' she said fiercely, as quietly as she could.

'No, I bloody didn't! I'm just the manager, after all. It was all done in secret.'

Sara whispered under her breath: 'I know I'm no accountant, but I had a brief look at the books today and there's no way we can afford to pay out two million.'

Reg shrugged his shoulders and then pointed towards Kelly, who was asking much the same question.

'From recent reports I gathered the club wasn't doing too well financially. What's changed?'

Stephen smirked. 'We have a new, very generous MD. The bank were quite happy to give us a loan now that we have Miss Sara Moore on board.'

The banks had okayed it? Without her authority? 'Excuse us a moment, gentlemen,' she said, pulling Stephen to one side. 'How the hell could I guarantee two million?'

'I'd set the deal up with Barratt's money,' said Stephen, matter-of-factly. 'Sorry, Hargreaves' money. But since the reins have passed to you, I thought I'd use your money instead. The deal was all there, I just needed a new signature.'

'But I haven't signed any agreement . . .'

'Think about it,' laughed Stephen.

Suddenly Sara realised what had happened. The only things she'd signed so far were the papers Linda had given her the previous day. You fool! she cursed herself, unable to believe she had been so easily tricked into putting up a guarantee for £2 million.

Before she had the chance to collect her thoughts, a camera was poking her in the face.

'Sara, we didn't know you were already at the club. How are you finding it?'

'Give me a chance,' said Sara, dizzy at the turn of events. 'I've only been here two days.' Two days and I've already given away £2 million.

'Was it your decision to sign Neves?'

'Not quite.' She was livid. Stephen was not as stupid as he looked. If she made a fuss now about how he had no right to use her as guarantor or buy players without consulting her, she would look a fool. She would never live it down and the press would have a field day. So much for hiring and firing being her business. 'Let me settle in first, and then I'll tell you all my plans,' she said, giving Stephen a meaningful look.

As soon as the press had gone, she grabbed Stephen by the sleeve. 'What the hell do you think you're doing?'

'Language,' he said mockingly. Then, bending forward, he whispered in her ear. 'Listen, girly, we don't want you in this club. But if I have to suffer you, I'll use you and your dead boyfriend's money. Now, if you don't like it, piss off.' He shrugged her arm away and walked off with Antonio.

Sara could feel the hot tears of anger welling in her eyes.

Reg put his hand on her shoulder. 'He's a bastard, lass, and that's the truth,' he said.

Chapter Twenty-Nine

The babble of English voices all speaking at once made little sense to Antonio, and when Stephen excused himself after a perfunctory chat, he stood quietly in the corner of the room, feeling the resentment from the other players. They were an unprepossessing bunch. Antonio noticed the female owner arriving. They still hadn't been officially introduced. As she walked across the room he couldn't help but admire her pale skin and burning red hair, so different from the women in his country. He made no bones about openly staring at her, and as she came towards him he realised that he'd seen her somewhere else. Where had it been? It was clear that she intended to pass him by without a word, so he moved into her path and stared at her, the blackness of his eyes trying to draw the emeralds from hers.

As she approached Neves, Sara saw him grin, revealing a flawless expanse of white teeth. She knew that it was a smile that had the women of Brazil switching over from their *telenovelas* in droves to catch sight of him whenever São Paulo were on

TV, but she was determined that it would have no effect on her.

Speaking in perfect, but heavily accented English, he said: 'Haven't we met somewhere before?'

'Perhaps,' said Sara, feigning disinterest.

She tried to brush past him and briefly their bodies came into contact, just long enough for him to catch the hint of gardenias in her perfume; just long enough for him to tell that there was no softness to this woman. 'Where?'

'Will you excuse me?' she said coolly. She was psyched up to speak to Stephen and she had no wish to dissipate her fury by reminding the arrogant Brazilian of how he'd once snubbed her.

Stephen was surrounded by his cronies, loudly toasting his latest coup, but as Sara walked towards him, her stride decisive and meaningful, the room fell silent. 'A word, please,' she demanded, her voice clipped.

Stephen made an attempt to ignore her by chatting to the man standing next to him. Then he thought better of it and growled, 'What is it now?'

The whole room was waiting to see what the new owner would say next, but Sara remained unfazed. 'Do you want to do this in front of everyone?'

'Over there,' he said pointing to a quiet corner.

Sara followed him. 'Is this whole bloody thing a feud over Jackie?'

Coming somewhere out of left field, the question confused Stephen. 'Do what?'

'Did Stuart leave me half of Camden because you took Jackie away from him?'

Stephen stroked his bottom lip as if he was seriously considering her question. Then his blubbery face broke into a sneer. 'Do you think your boyfriend left you all this because of that overweight sloshpot?' He punctuated his question with a cruel laugh. 'Do me a favour. Even Hargreaves wasn't that hard up.'

Sara looked across to where Jackie was sitting on the arm of a sofa, wiping her nose with a serviette. She berated herself for opening her big mouth and leaving the poor woman open to yet more ridicule.

Stephen's treatment of his wife was inhuman. 'You are such a bastard. That woman is a hundred times the person you'll ever be.'

'Only in kilos,' said Stephen.

Sara knew that persisting with the subject would only give Stephen more leeway to be vile about his wife, so she changed tack. 'Don't think you've got away with buying Neves, either. I'm on your case, Stephen. You haven't got long here.'

'You're one tough cookie, aren't you?' He moved in close and placed a podgy finger on her chin. 'Now why don't you keep that pretty mouth of yours closed and just let Stephen get on with spending all that lovely money of yours?'

Sara finally knew what it meant to see red. There were literally crimson patches floating in front of her eyes. She knew she was only seconds away from kneeing him in the groin. She had to summon up all of her dignity as she turned to leave, all eyes watching her in silence as she walked through the room.

Antonio stood by the door and held it open for her. Briefly, their eyes met and he could see the anger clouding her beautiful face. Unmistakably, some of that anger was directed at him. Why? And where *was* it he had seen this woman before?

Sara leaned against the corridor wall for a moment to calm her nerves. She'd left Norman at home thinking that she could handle working at the club without him – she felt safe enough there; the bully-boys would only attack when she was alone – but how much more of this abuse could she take? There was no need to put herself though such stress. Briefly she entertained the idea of selling her stake and moving somewhere warm and far away. Like Brazil, she laughed ruefully to herself. She could still see those brooding black eyes boring into her. Another feeling replaced her anger, and she was dismayed to realise that it was intrigue. All the time she had been arguing with Stephen, she had been unable to get Antonio out of her head. Surely she wasn't seriously going to let a little bit of Latin charm blind her to the fact that Antonio was unquestionably in league with Stephen?

She'd followed football long enough to know that this was no ordinary transfer. Was Neves somehow caught up in the gambling syndicate? Or worse still, was he linked to Leonel Pinto? Sara pictured Neves' lean, sinewy frame striding across the football pitch and found it hard to imagine that such a body would have any experience of drugs. She shook her head. This was amazing. Here she was, in the middle of one of the biggest crises in her life, and her brain was turning to mush. It was so long since she'd felt a man's arms around her.

Only the night before she had read through all her cuttings on Mickey's club and the match-fixing article she'd written as a result of her conversation with Billy Todd. Billy had talked about a Brazilian connection. If that macho footballer knew anything . . . She thought of the way he preened in front of her and her fury came flooding back. She marched into reception to find Linda.

'A word, Linda,' she said, spotting the secretary trying to scurry off along the corridor.

Linda stopped dead in her tracks. 'Yes, Miss Moore?'

'I want you to pack up your things immediately and leave.'

'No! Please, Miss Moore, I didn't want to do it,' said the secretary, her bottom lip trembling. 'Stephen told me to get those papers signed without you asking any questions, but he didn't tell me what they was for. If I'd known . . . Oh, Miss Moore, I'm so sorry. I've never done anything dishonest in my life. I'm so sorry.'

Linda looked so downtrodden that Sara relented. The secretary had only been following orders, after all. It would be unfair to sack her because of Stephen. 'OK, Linda, you can stay – for now. But remember, you owe me one.'

'I promise I won't let you down. Honestly, I'm so sorry about what happened. It won't happen again. I—'

'It's all right,' said Sara, wanting to escape her effusiveness. As she watched the secretary walk away she realised that one of the first things she was going to have to sort out was the staff situation. If Linda was representative of Camden's finest, they were in deep shit.

When Kathy called her and said that she was finally ready to talk, Sara was expecting the worst. But the smiling, immaculate woman sitting opposite her now was a million miles away from the Kathy she'd last seen. Under the tight black body and wrapover skirt she was wearing, Kathy had regained most of the weight she'd lost. Her hair, which had disintegrated into rat's tails over the previous year, had now been dyed a vibrant raven and cut in a sleek Louise Brooks bob, the bangs pointing to her eyes, which glowed with a new, positive lustre. There was even a touch of dark red lipstick on her smiling mouth.

'You look absolutely fantastic,' said Sara. 'I take it you and Joseph have sorted everything out. I'm really glad that the two of you—'

Kathy interrupted her. 'Before you go any further, Joseph isn't here. Would you like a drink?'

'I'll get it,' said Sara, going into the kitchen. The house, too, was back to its normal pristine state. She located a bottle of gin and poured two large measures, forgoing the tonic. Whatever the problem was with Joseph, it was better addressed neat.

'Here,' she said, handing a glass to Kathy, who was now curled up in an armchair. 'So where is he?'

Kathy winced as she took a large slug of the gin. 'Shacked up with Fran Best, as far as I know.'

Sara's mouth dropped open. '*Fran Best*? What, that pretentious old cow?'

'Would it be better if he was shacked up with someone nice?'

'What an idiotic thing to have said. Sorry, but I think I'm in shock.'

'Don't be,' said Kathy, a reassuring smile on her face. 'She is a pretentious old cow. Even Joseph can see that. But she's also on a high income and in a position to put a lot of work his way. That sweetens the pot. Money's a big turn-on for Joseph, and I'm afraid I'm not very sexy in that respect any more.'

'What do you mean?'

'I'm completely broke. Of course, Joseph couldn't rely on Fran for hand-outs all the time. That wouldn't look like love, would it? My husband has spent all our savings trying to launch himself in America. Every share, every bond – it's all gone. I was so wrapped up being a housewife and mother that I didn't have a clue what was going on.'

Sara was unnerved by the calmness with which Kathy related this disaster.

'What about the house?'

'The bank has started repossession proceedings. What do you think my chances of getting a council flat are?'

'Kathy! How can you sound so . . . *relieved*?'

'Because I am,' replied Kathy simply.

'But what are you going to do? Could you go back to *Mariella* full-time?'

'Definitely not, I've resigned. There were people there, people I considered to be friends of mine, who knew what Fran was up to. Nobody said a thing. Anyway, it doesn't matter. I'll get a job. I'll sort something out. You see, I'm not frightened by all this.' Kathy came over and sat on the arm of Sara's chair, taking her friend's hand to reassure her. 'The other week, when you looked after Bette, you caught me at my lowest point. From there, there was nowhere to go but up. What's happened has made me take a long, hard look at myself. Do you remember how I always used to say that if there was one thing in life I wanted to achieve, it was to not be like my mother?'

Sara nodded.

'Well, that's exactly how I ended up. A downtrodden nervous wreck.'

'That's not true. You were worn out, that's all,' said Sara. 'I think you're being too hard on yourself.'

'Maybe. Why do you think I fell for Joseph?'

'You shared things. Your taste, it was exactly the same.'

'It wasn't just aesthetics. One of the main reasons was that I thought he was the total opposite of my father. I wanted a man with none of that masculine bullshit, someone who would never oppress me the way my father did my mother. What a joke! At least you knew where my father was coming from. Joseph was the enemy within. He dominated me without me ever knowing how. I think he's what's called passive-aggressive.'

'Always?'

'Probably. Bette's the love of my life, and I would never be without her – I knew that from the second she was born – but I didn't really want to be pregnant. It was what Joseph wanted. It's always been about what Joseph wanted. Now he wants Fran Best, so good luck to him.'

Sara couldn't believe how together Kathy seemed in the light of what she'd been through. She knew that she had to help in some way, and money seemed to be the obvious answer. 'Kathy, don't worry about the house. I'll take care of it.'

'I *was* joking about the council flat—'

'Please. I want to do this for you. I've got more money than I know what to do with, and so far it's given me nothing but headaches.'

'Still not hitting it off with Stephen?'

'Where's that bottle?' sighed Sara, looking around for the gin. 'You're not going to believe any of this.' She related the events of the past few weeks, still not quite able to believe them herself.

Kathy listened intently. When she finished, Sara expected her friend to offer some sympathy. Instead she roared with laughter. 'You've actually got a bodyguard called *Norman*?'

'I don't see what's so funny about that. Kathy, I think you're losing it a bit. Your husband's run off with another woman and I'm running a football club with a man who's put a price on my head.' Suddenly she began to laugh too. 'And I've got a bodyguard called Norman.'

'And you've just spent two million pounds on a Latin beefcake,' shrieked Kathy.

Sara sobered up. 'There's nothing even remotely amusing about Antonio Neves. That arrogant jumped-up . . . God, he really thinks he's something special.'

Kathy raised a newly plucked eyebrow. 'It's sounds as if you think he's something special too.'

'What? The man's a pig. Honestly, I look at that face of his and I want to—'

'Sara, it's all too clear what you want to do, but I thought you were seeing Christopher Heard.'

'Not any more. Apparently there was a breach of etiquette. Anyway, he wasn't really my type and I never completely trusted him. And for the last time, I'm not interested in Neves.'

Kathy raised the bottle of gin to the light to see if there was anything left in it. 'That's the last of the gin. I suppose it's Tennent's Extra for me from now on.'

'I'll pay for the house.'

'I won't let you do that. I've got to sort out my life for myself.'

Sara thought for a moment. 'What about working for me?'

'What could I do at a football club? Be a masseuse?'

'You've got brilliant organisational skills and I could really do with an ally at the club. Perhaps you could do the fund-raising. Please. This is the first time I've laughed in weeks.'

Kathy considered her options. 'Buy me a bottle of Gordon's, and you're on.'

Chapter Thirty

After spending a wonderful weekend with Kathy and Bette, Sara walked into her office on Monday morning with a surge of optimism. The decorators had finished and they'd even managed to fix a brass plaque on her door which read: 'Managing Director'. True, it was a minor victory in the great scheme of things, but she felt she had made her first imprint on the club. The thought that Kathy would soon be working alongside her further lightened her mood. Her friend had agreed to start as soon as she found a suitable nanny for Bette. In the meantime, Sara had to begin unravelling the tangled mess that was Camden United on her own. Her first priority was to look into Antonio's transfer, but barely had she read the first couple of lines of his contract when the player himself sauntered into her office.

Sara glared at him. His cocky insouciance irritated the hell out her. 'I was just analysing your contract, Senhor Neves.'

'Antonio, please.' The look that greeted him wiped the smile off his face before it had even properly formed on his lips. This woman was so stern, so cold, but so very beautiful too. He prided himself on being able to tell what was on a person's mind by reading their eyes, but Sara's unfocused stare blocked his attempt. 'Whatever,' he said, sitting down opposite her.

'What can I do for you, Senhor Neves?'

'I knew I had seen you before. It came to me after the meeting. I saw you at Le Jardin. In Cuenca.' How could he forget that terrible day, with all the panic that had led to him being in this very room now?

Sara was at once both delighted that she had left an impression in Cuenca and infuriated that he had remembered but didn't feel the need to apologise for ignoring her in the restaurant. 'Maybe,' she said, determined not to admit that she could remember him, too. 'I was there covering the football. I really am very busy at the moment. Was there anything else?'

Antonio wanted to apologise for snubbing her, but it didn't sound as if she even remembered the incident. 'You seem very angry with me,' he said with genuine concern in his voice.

'Not *with* you. Personally I have no feelings towards you at all,' she said, noticing that she could smell the odour of fresh sweat. Antonio was wearing his football strip and had obviously come straight from training. It was a very intimate scent. 'But professionally it's a different matter.'

'I don't understand.'

Normally, if Sara wanted to get a psychological advantage over somebody, she would stare them straight in the eye until his gaze wilted. But it was impossible with this man. No matter how hard she tried, he returned the look fiercely until eventually she found herself dropping her head and staring at his legs. As Antonio stood before her, she saw the way his powerful thigh muscles flexed, the dark hairs on his legs glistening with moisture, his tanned skin contrasting with the whiteness of his shorts. How long had it been since a man had touched her?

'Miss Moore,' Antonio said softly. 'Is there something wrong?'

She felt a surge of embarrassment, sure that he had watched her looking at him. 'What's wrong,' she said sharply, 'is that without my knowledge I was used as guarantor for two million pounds to enable your transfer. This club can't afford that kind of money, Stephen knows that. So why did he buy you?'

He shook his head and strands of his wet, black hair fell across his forehead. For a second he looked vulnerable and boyish. 'I can't help you. Before I came here I had never met Mr Powell.'

Sara snorted. 'I don't believe you. There's something very wrong about this deal.'

'Why do you say that?'

'Because that's the way Stephen Powell works.' Then she thought about the Brazilian connection with the drugs ring and the game-fixing. 'What about drugs?'

'What!'

'Or did you throw games in Brazil?' continued Sara, trying to ignore the anger in his eyes.

The muscles in his clenched jaw twitched. 'I have *never*,' he managed, fighting to keep his voice under control, 'thrown a game in my life.'

'Then why are you here?' she asked, glad to see that he was as uncomfortable as she was.

'I didn't want to come to this country but it was not in my control. I was sold' – he ran his fingers through his jet-black hair, struggling to find the right words in English – 'like a slave.'

'Oh, I don't think so,' she said, getting up and opening the door to indicate that their talk was over. 'Three thousand a week and a fifty grand sign-on? That's not a bad sweetener, is it – for a slave, I mean?' Suddenly she felt his hand on her elbow and he pulled her close to him, his face only inches from hers. 'What do you think—'

But Antonio cut her short. 'Just because you cannot see my chains, it does not mean that they are not there,' he whispered, his voice hoarse with the effort of keeping his temper under control.

'Get your hand off me,' she said, though she made no attempt to remove herself from his grasp. She didn't want him to let go, only to increase the pressure of his hold; his touch made her feel alive again.

For what seemed like forever, they stood there, frozen in what was not quite an embrace although there was no mistaking the sensual current between them. Sara's chest rose and fell. She strove

324 K a r r e n   B r a d y

to keep her breathing from betraying her as Antonio's face moved closer, his mouth slightly open. Despite her anger, despite how being this near to another man felt so disloyal to the memory of Bill, she closed her eyes expectantly only to feel Antonio let her go. When she opened them she found that he had gone.

Sara was furious at herself for letting her defences down so easily. And for what? Nothing had happened just then, she had just allowed a painful memory to resurface and confuse her. That had to be it. How dare he speak to her like that! How dare he touch her! She dialled security's number to have the volatile Brazilian escorted from the building, then put the phone down before anyone could answer. That would be the way Stephen would deal with it, using strong-arm tactics instead of intelligence. If she wanted to be rid of Antonio Neves for good, she needed to understand how he'd arrived there in the first place.

She guessed that the transfer was the latest in a long line of dodgy transactions. Putting Antonio's contract to one side, she called Linda and arranged for all the necessary documents pertaining to the club's finances to be delivered to her office as soon as possible. Then she sat back in her chair and replayed the conversation with the Brazilian in her head. Like a slave – how ridiculous. Such a typically Latin overstatement, obviously designed to have her swooning at his fiery passion. Well, it hadn't worked.

At twelve o'clock nothing had arrived from Linda and Sara took an early lunch, hoping that Stephen wouldn't be in the club restaurant. She knew that he was in the building but for the moment he seemed to be keeping out of her way.

The restaurant was nearly empty, and when the meal she'd ordered finally arrived she could understand why. Looking down at the ration-book salad and pink potted meat it occurred to her that if this was what the catering staff considered fit for management, then the food being served on the terraces had to be a disgrace. Barely had she eaten the first mouthful when a middle-aged blonde in a fur coat sitting at another table waved to her. Sara vaguely recognised her, having seen her in the directors' box on occasion, but she didn't know her name. Out of politeness she waved back, but the woman obviously took this as an invitation because she was standing up and heading Sara's way.

'The shit they serve in here,' she said picking her teeth. 'You're Sara, aren't you?'

'Yes, who are—'

'Patti.' On the hand she held out to Sara two of the false nails were missing.

'Would you like to sit down?' asked Sara, hoping the answer would be no.

Patti's words came out like machine-gun fire. 'Love-to-but-I-can't-stop. I've got a hair appointment at two. I just wanted to say congratulations, I really envy you, you jammy cow. I tell you, if some old git wanted to offer me millions for the privilege, I'd be on my back before you could shout penalty. I know people call you a bimbo, but what I say is the bimbos are the ones who do it for free. You're a woman after my own heart, you are, and I reckon we're going to get along famously.' With great deliberation she stared at the Rolex on her wrist. 'Shit! I'm going to be late. Mind you, I don't know why I bother. They don't look at the grill when they're lighting the oven, do they?'

Patti let out a raucous shriek and left, leaving Sara open-mouthed and devoid of any appetite she might have mustered for the appalling meal.

A waitress walked over and stared at her untouched plate. 'Anything wrong?'

Sara said nothing, not wanting to take out the anger she felt towards Patti on the unsuspecting waitress. Instead, she went to look for Linda, and found the secretary with her feet up on her desk struggling with the *Chloe* crossword.

'Peg-bag!' said Linda triumphantly, oblivious to Sara's presence.

Sara counted to three before she spoke. 'Linda, have you sorted out those files yet?'

The secretary threw down the magazine guiltily. 'I'll see to it right away.'

'Don't bother, I'll do it myself.'

'Well if you're sure ...' Linda returned her energies to her puzzle.

'One across,' said Sara pointing to the crossword. 'F-I-R-E-D.'

'No, I'm sure it's apron. You see, two down is peg-bag and . . .' She looked up at Sara. 'But, Miss—'

'You had your chance. You're sacked.' Before Linda had the chance to pull any of her histrionics, Sara had walked away.

By the end of the afternoon, Sara's newly yellow-painted office was strewn with unpaid invoices, staff files and an auditor's report the size of a telephone directory. It was from this report that she learned to her dismay that Camden was over £2 million in debt – and that was without the cost of Antonio. As each document uncovered another disaster, Sara began to indulge in her dream of running away from it all.

The nervous hush which greeted Sara the following morning told her that Linda had put the word around that Camden's new MD was up to something. Only Louise the receptionist was her normal talkative self.

'Good morning, Miss Moore,' she said, handing Sara her mail.

'Call me Sara.'

'Sara, you don't mind if I get someone to relieve me for ten minutes, do you? I must see Mrs Moynihan in accounts, and if I don't go now I'll be at the end of the queue.'

'Queue for what?' asked Sara, sensing the first challenge of the day. She'd taken some of the accounts to study in bed the night before and had noticed that Neil Albert, a player who had left the club six months ago, was still being paid his win–draw bonus. Mrs Moynihan's name was on the ledger.

'Wages queries. Mine were down again last week. I know she sorts it out eventually, but my bank's complaining that I'm overdrawn.'

'Leave the desk. I'm coming with you,' said Sara, already marching along the corridor to the accounts department.

'See, I told you,' whispered Louise, catching her up as she discovered the queue outside Mrs Moynihan's office. Three players and two typists were standing there, wage slips in hand, looking furious. As Sara swept past them and into the office, thunder-faced, they cheered.

'I'm sorry, I'm not seeing anyone for another twenty minutes,' said Mrs Moynihan from behind a pile of paperwork. 'Could you wait outside with the others?'

The man occupying the other desk looked up and smirked. 'Surely yours can't be wrong, Miss Moore. You've only been here a week.'

Hearing the name, Mrs Moynihan, a dowdier version of Linda, looked up and froze. 'Miss Moore, how lovely to finally meet you.'

'I wish I could say the same.' Sara pulled up a chair in front of the book-keeper's desk. 'Mrs Moynihan, tell me something. When was Neil Albert transferred?'

'Let me think,' she replied, scratching her head with the end of her pen. 'Adrian, when was it?'

'A good six months ago, Beryl,' he replied.

'That's right. I remember now – it was the same time I was having my patio relaid.'

'Six months, right? So tell me, Beryl, why are you still paying him his win–draw bonus?'

Adrian began to laugh.

'I'm sorry, Mr, er?'

'Fellows. Adrian Fellows, Camden's accountant.'

'Mr Fellows, you'll forgive me if I don't find this in the least bit amusing.' Adrian gave her a suit-yourself shrug and carried on working. Sara looked Beryl in the eye, knowing what she was going to have to say and hoping that the woman wasn't a crier. 'It won't do, will it?'

'I'll inform the bank today,' said Beryl, contrite.

'I'm sorry, but that isn't good enough.'

Beryl threw down her pen. 'I'm fed up with the complaints. Every Tuesday morning it's the same thing. She's fifty pounds down here, he's not got his bonus there. Nobody's perfect, you know.'

Sara shook her head in amazement. 'You're a book-keeper. When it comes to numbers, it's your job to be perfect.'

'Mr Powell has always been very satisfied with my work, and if you have any problems with it I suggest you take it up with him.'

Sara lost her cool, angered at the woman's outraged indignation. 'I don't have to take anything up with anybody. I own this place, Mrs

Moynihan, and you're fired. Adrian, would you see to the people outside?'

Beryl stood there open-mouthed. Finally, she began to cry. 'Fifteen years I've given this club.'

'And God only knows how much money you've lost us in that time,' said Sara, walking out of the office.

Outside, a familiar figure in a fur coat had joined the queue. 'Hiya, Sara,' cooed Patti. 'That old bag's not trying to stitch you up as well, is she?' She beckoned Sara over. Her missing fingernails had been replaced with a new set of talons. 'Now I know you and Stevie don't see eye to eye, but what I thought is we could all go out for a meal one night – you know, get to know each other properly. You seeing anyone at the moment? I'm sure Stevie could bring a friend, make it a foursome, eh?' The office door opened and Patti pushed in front of the queue. 'Catch you later.'

Louise, who was still waiting patiently to be seen, rolled her eyes and muttered something under her breath.

'Who is that woman?' asked Sara.

'Patricia Matlock,' said the receptionist. 'She's Mr Powell's . . . she um, does the publicity, I think.'

It was obvious that the receptionist didn't want to be seen speaking out of turn, but there was no doubting who, or rather what, Patti Matlock was. Sara couldn't believe that Stephen had the nerve to put his mistress on the payroll. Poor Jackie. How did she put up with it? For a moment, Sara thought about ignoring the problem, but then she remembered their conversation in the restaurant and before she knew it she was back in the accounts office.

'You've upset her,' said Patti, pointing to Beryl, who was emptying her desk, crying hysterically. 'Oi, Beryl, get Adrian to sort out your severance pay, love. That way you'll be sure that it's right.' She looked at Sara. 'You just can't get the staff, can you?'

'Obviously not when we have to employ the likes of you. I'm afraid your "services" are no longer required here, either, Miss Mattress.'

Patti squared up to Sara, hands on hips. 'What did you just say?'

'You heard me, you're fired.'

'You bloody cow!' screamed Patti. 'You can't do that!'

'Watch me,' said Sara, striding out of the door for the second time.

As she reached her own office, the phone began to ring. Quick work, thought Sara, knowing who it would be.

'What the bloody hell are you playing at?'

Sara held the phone slightly away from her ear. 'Stephen, if you want that woman around, then you pay for her yourself. As the majority shareholder my decision stands.' She slammed down the phone. If she was going to be investing money in the club she was going to call the shots. Sod everyone else. Her hands trembling, she opened the next file, wondering what new horrors lay in store.

The next day, Wednesday, became known as the Day of the Long Knives at the club. It began with the sacking of the programme manager, Sean Lee, and his assistant on the grounds of incompetence. Overnight, Sara had read through the figures and as far as she could work out, the unit cost of the programme was around a pound. Added on to that was the cost of two salaries plus a company car. The programmes only sold at £1. A quick call to a printer revealed that United had been paying way over the odds for paper, and although Sara didn't actually have any proof, she guessed that Lee was taking a cut from the artificially inflated costs.

Having sorted out that particular problem, she turned her attention to the matter of catering. The dreadful standard of the food wasn't the half of it: food and drink sales hadn't shown a profit at the club in years. When she looked at the staff list to see who was in charge of that little mess, she found out that the catering manager, Dennis Flynn, was also listed as the chief scout. He was not on the payroll for either job, but he was invoicing the club for £2,000 a month. A quick chat with Louise established that Flynn was another of Stephen's friends and his primary duty as 'chief scout' was driving Stephen to away matches.

'Louise, could you track him down and send him in to see me?' asked Sara wearily. While she waited for Flynn to turn up, she ran through the stock figures again. There was no way that all the supplies they ordered were being sold: the figures just didn't add up. Flynn had to be siphoning off the stock.

There was a tentative knock on her door. The expression on Dennis Flynn's face showed that he wasn't expecting a pay rise. 'I was told you wanted to see me.'

'Every month you invoice this club for two thousand pounds for your services. Can you run through exactly what they are? Aside from robbing us blind?'

Flynn smiled. 'I'm not answerable to you. Stephen employed me – take the matter up with him.'

Yesterday, when she'd fired Beryl Moynihan, she'd felt some guilt when the woman burst into tears, but Flynn's arrogant self-assurance was a challenge. 'You're sacked, Flynn. You're not stealing from my pocket.'

'I don't think so,' he laughed. 'Stephen and I have a special relationship.'

'Did you see that plaque on the door as you came in? What did it say? This is my club now, and as of now I no longer require your services. And before long the whole of the catering staff will be following you out of that door.'

'And come Saturday you'll have forty thousand people wanting a bite to eat. Can you make that many sandwiches?'

'I won't need to,' said Sara, thinking on her feet. She hadn't really considered what they would do, but as she didn't know the first thing about catering, it seemed sensible to hand it over to somebody who did. Nobody could do a worse job than Flynn, at any rate. 'I'm franchising the catering.'

'Is that so?' declared Flynn smugly. 'Listen, missy, we'll see what Stephen has to say about that.'

As soon as Flynn had gone Sara phoned Stephen. If she could get away with sacking Powell's mistress, then the scout didn't stand a chance. 'Dennis Flynn's on his way to see you. It seems he doesn't believe I've got the authority to sack him. Put him right, will you?' Without waiting for an answer she put down the phone and called Louise into her office. She dictated a letter of redundancy to be given to the forty or so catering staff.

'Anything else?' asked Louise nervously, when they'd finished.

'There certainly is,' replied Sara. 'This afternoon I want all the remaining staff, and the team, in the boardroom for a three o'clock meeting.'

Louise left looking as if she'd had the fear of God put into her. Poor girl. She hadn't done anything wrong – or at least, if she had, Sara had yet to discover it. But Sara was reaching the stage where nothing would surprise her. Sitting there alone, doubts started to creep into Sara's mind about what she was doing. Was it right to deny so many people of their livelihoods? If I don't do it, she told herself, these people are going to eat their way through all of my money in less than two years. This was a business, not a charity for the friends of Stephen Powell.

She realised that she was throwing herself into the business side of things to avoid the exhausting conundrum of why she was actually there in the first place. Initially she had believed that she was on a crusade on Stuart's behalf to finish his unfinished business. But since the attack, which brought with it the realisation that Stuart had been less than honest, things had changed. Now the unfinished business was her own.

At three o'clock Sara entered the crowded boardroom where the sense of outrage mixed with fear was palpable. Every pair of eyes in the room was on her as she pulled a chair out from under the table and climbed on to it. For a while she said nothing, searching the sea of upturned faces in vain for an encouraging smile. She almost wished she'd brought Norman in with her, more for moral support than anything else. Now that she'd made her show of strength he kept a low profile, but the knowledge that he was never far away was reassuring.

There was Adrian Fellows, suppressing an amused grin. Stephen sat nearby, totally impassive. At the back, against the wall, was Antonio, taller than all the other players around him and infinitely better looking. He was wearing jeans and a white T-shirt which showed off his muscular forearms, and for a brief second she thought that she'd never seen a man look so good. Then she remembered him touching her – no, grabbing her – and she looked away, her eyes alighting on the more comfortable sight of Louise. Clearing her throat, she began, concentrating her attention on the receptionist.

'Thank you all for coming,' she said, then raised her voice a touch, reminding herself to speak slowly. 'I'm sure you've all heard what's been going on over the last few days. First, I'd like to assure you that there will be no more sackings or redundancies – for the time being, at least. But there will be changes. The office staff has already seen the first of those changes, and now I'd like to address the team. I've been looking at your expenses, and to be honest, I'm amazed. When I saw your drinks bills it made me wonder how some of you manage to play.' An anonymous hiss could be heard. Sara ignored it.

'It's got to stop,' she went on. 'You'll pay your own expenses from now on. This club has over two million pounds' worth of debt, and I won't authorise another expenses form until we're back in the black, which I hope, with your help, will be in the not-too-distant future. I don't want the players to think I've singled them out: this goes for the office staff as well. I really believe that Camden can be a great and profitable team again, but each and every one of you has to get behind me. This club cannot carry anyone any more. There have been too many people taking too much out and putting too little back.' She looked at Stephen pointedly.

'This is going to change. Everybody in this room, including me, has something to prove. We must prove that we are a worthy part of the Camden machine. Any one of you out there who doesn't believe that can have a letter of resignation on my desk by tomorrow morning. For the moment, that's all I want to say. Thank you for your time.'

She climbed down off her chair to the sound of a single pair of hands slow-clapping her.

'Stirring stuff,' said Stephen, following her out of the room.

'I meant what I said,' snapped Sara. 'You can work with me or get out.'

'But what if no one wants to work with you?'

'That,' she said with more certainty than she felt, 'is not going to happen.'

Chapter Thirty-One

It was crunch time. Sara stood in front of her office door on Thursday morning picturing a pile of resignation letters waiting for her on her desk.

'Kathy, you look,' she said, pushing her friend inside.

'There's nothing here,' replied Kathy, sitting down. 'See? I told you. Can I use your phone? I want to check that the nanny's OK.'

'She'll be fine. You only left her an hour ago.'

'I'll feel better if I do.'

While Kathy made her call, Sara unpacked a new coffee machine and went off to fill a jug with water. On her return she found Kathy nervously checking her make-up in a compact mirror.

'Everything all right at home?'

'Yes. Do I look OK?'

Sara nodded, appreciating that her friend's nervousness always took the form of concern about her appearance. 'You look great.'

'How about the outfit?' She was wearing a severe navy-blue suit, its A-line skirt cut just on the knee.

'Very headmistressy. It'll scare the hell out of Stephen. Speaking of him, I think it's time you two met. We'll have coffee later. The sooner you know what you're up against, the better.'

As they made their way to the other side of the building, Kathy asked, 'Doesn't all this conflict bother you?'

'It did,' whispered Sara. 'Right up until yesterday afternoon at the meeting. But as I was speaking it suddenly occurred to me that I was actually having the time of my life.'

Kathy shook her head. 'I'll never understand you.'

Sara smiled. 'On the contrary, you understand me completely. That's why I want you here. Here, this is Stephen's office. Prepare yourself – it smells a bit in there.'

'What of?'

'Corruption,' said Sara, dramatically. 'And tobacco and BO.' She knocked on Stephen's door and entered. 'Stephen, this is Kathy. She's here to work on the fund-raising. I don't want her hindered by you in any way.' Sara sensed her friend flinching at her aggressive manner but she had no intention of wasting polite words on a man who wished her dead.

'The new chief scout, eh?'

Sara understood the dig. 'Actually, Kathy's going to be working on a commission basis. Expect to be seeing a lot of her from now on.' She gave him an infuriating smile. 'Starting tonight, on the coach.'

'You've got more front than Selfridges. And after what you told the team yesterday.'

'No one's complained. They had their chance. Do you want me to save you a seat?'

'Fuck off.'

'Charming,' said Kathy outside, wondering why she hadn't stuck with fashion. 'I see what you mean about him.'

'That was one of his good moods,' laughed Sara. 'He didn't try to hit me once. Come on, let's find Jackie. I know you've been dying to meet her.' One of the carrots she'd dangled in front of Kathy was the chance to meet one of the legends of sixties fashion, even one who'd fallen so far from her pedestal.

In the bar, Jackie was bent over the jukebox, her gold leggings stretching obscenely across her spreading backside. She waved at

Sara and Kathy. 'I wouldn't let them take this one off,' she said, as Dionne Warwick belted out 'Walk On By'. 'It reminds me of better days.'

Sara smiled. 'Jackie, meet my friend Kathy.'

'I can't believe I'm finally meeting you,' said Kathy. 'You were a big heroine of mine.'

Jackie's delight at being recognised soon faded to a frown. 'I'm amazed you can tell it's me,' she said, indicating her puffy face.

'Oh, but I've seen so many photos of you. You certainly gave the Shrimp a run for her money,' gabbled Kathy.

'Next to the Butterfly I was just a moth.' It sounded like a well-rehearsed line, a sympathy-getter, and Jackie apologised. 'There I go again, maudlin and miserable. Let's have a drink.'

'It's a bit early,' said Sara.

'It was a bit too early to have to read this over breakfast,' said Jackie, rummaging in her handbag and producing a crumpled copy of the *Herald*. 'Have you seen this? Page thirteen.'

'I haven't read any of the papers yet,' said Sara, looking at the headline: 'A JOY FOREVER?' The article was about fading beauty and was aptly illustrated by two pictures of Jackie. The first showed her at a Melbourne racetrack with the Shrimp in the sixties, shocking racegoers with the amount of knee they were displaying; the second featured Jackie unconscious at a recent Camden United Christmas party, her bosom dangerously close to escaping from her boob tube. The piece was pure malice. Only Brigitte Bardot fared worse than Jackie, and only then because she was better known.

Sara scanned the article and read out a quote from an unnamed source claiming that Jackie had been forced to sell her shares in Camden United to help pay off her drinking debts. 'That's such a lie,' she said. 'Jackie told me why she sold her shares,' she murmured to Kathy.

'Stephen gave them that quote,' said Jackie. 'I'm sure of it.'

Sara handed Kathy the paper. 'Here, look at this.'

'Oh my God,' said Kathy. 'I don't believe it. Did you read the by-line?'

'It's the women's page, so it must be Elizabeth Legge. That's her style.'

Kathy thrust the article under Sara's nose. 'Read it.'

'I don't believe it,' said Sara. The author of the piece was Maggie Lawrence.

'Do you know this bitch?' asked Jackie, her voice breaking with emotion.

'Unfortunately, yes,' replied Sara, shaken. So Maggie was working for Cynthia, was she? And if Jackie was right, she had spoken to Stephen, too. She was a time-bomb waiting to go off. 'Jackie, I'm sorry. I think this article was written to get at me.'

'She didn't say that you looked like a pig in a wig, did she?'

'She can talk,' seethed Kathy. 'I'm going to call the *Herald* and have it out with her.'

'Don't you dare,' said Sara. 'Promise me. Jackie, I will have that drink.'

Jackie reached into her handbag again and produced a bottle of gin. 'Here,' she said. 'The stuff they serve in here is watered down.'

The article cast a depression over their chat. Sara did not want to admit to her fears. She was certain that Maggie had intended the article for her eyes. It was a warning shot.

Kathy broke the silence. 'Jackie, we're going on the coach to Slough tonight. Come with us.'

Jackie shook her head. 'I'm not up to Stephen.'

'Come on,' pleaded Kathy. 'I hate football and I want someone to talk to. Please. There are loads of things I want to ask you about *Granny Takes a Trip*.'

'Oh, all right then,' said Jackie, secretly delighted that someone would be interested in her reminiscences for once.

Stephen's eyes nearly popped out of his head when he saw his wife swaying between Kathy and Sara, making for the coach parked outside the ground with its engine running.

'Bloody hell,' he said, 'it's the fucking Andrews Sisters.'

The team groaned collectively as they saw the women climbing on board.

'No swearing in front of the ladies,' shouted Benny Wright.

'Bollocks!' shouted someone from the back, who sounded suspiciously like Ian Sumner.

As Sara moved along the coach the team's hopeless midfielder, Dick Davenport, leered at her. 'When your top button's undone I can see all your wares.'

There were muted adolescent giggles as Sara leaned over his seat. 'Really? Well, when I sell you to Crewe, you won't be able to see anything from there, will you?'

'At least Crewe pay your expenses,' shouted the voice at the back.

Sara could see that the whole of the team were waiting to see how she'd respond. She marched to the back of the coach and said, 'Sumner, when I was going through your expenses one name cropped up again and again. Manor Park Massage. It was always the same price, too – thirty pounds for "therapy". Would you mind explaining to me and the rest of the team what exactly that therapy was?'

A cheer went up along the coach.

'Sumner, you dirty sod!'

'Thirty pounds? You cheap bastard.'

'Manor Park Massage? You get it twice there for that price.'

'All right, boys,' shouted Sara. 'Cut the noise. Relegation will hurt your pockets far more than having your expenses cut.' She sat down next to Kathy.

'I don't know how you do it,' said her friend, full of admiration.

'Don't speak too soon. I can see myself falling flat on my face very easily.'

For most of the journey the team were quiet, playing cards and reading newspapers. After a while Reg stood up to give them a pep talk.

'Now listen here, lads,' said the manager, 'this is an important one. I want you to watch the video of the competition, get a feel for Redwood's defence. If we lose this one, it's relegation for sure.'

As the video started Jackie rooted around in her handbag and found the half-empty bottle of gin. 'Want some?' she said, pushing it towards Sara.

'No thanks.' Sara wanted to stay alert. Stephen was up to something. He was talking on his mobile phone and every few seconds he would turn and stare at her. She was going to have to keep an eye on him. Jackie went back to reading the *Herald* article. She was drinking the gin straight from the bottle as if it were Perrier, and as they drove into the Redwood ground, it was obvious that Sara and Kathy were going to have to carry her off the coach. Allowing everyone else to file past first, they heaved her into a standing position.

'Leave me alone,' she slurred.

'She isn't staying on here, love,' shouted the driver from the front.

'It's OK, she's coming.' Sara wished she had stopped Kathy from pressing Jackie to join them. This was her first away match and here she was having to deal with an inebriated and increasingly belligerent woman. Stephen would be having a field day. They hoisted her up and along the aisle as best they could, her feet dragging on the floor. The steps down from the vehicle proved difficult. Jackie suddenly lurched forward, knocking both Sara and Kathy off balance, and the three of them fell out of the coach and on to the pavement.

'Shit,' screamed Kathy as her knee twisted to the side.

'Fuck,' yelled Sara, her head coming into contact with the kerb.

'Balls,' bellowed Jackie as her gin bottle crashed into the gutter.

Suddenly there were flashbulbs going off, accompanied by a roar of laughter. Sara propped Jackie up on the kerb and checked that she was all in one piece. Glancing around, she saw Julian Marsh. Typical. But how had he known that she was going to be there? It didn't take her long to come to the conclusion that Stephen was at the bottom of this.

'Sara, is this a good example of how you're going to beat the boys at their own game?'

Sara tried to stand up as elegantly as was possible in the circumstances, painfully aware of the gaping holes in her tights and her ripped blouse. 'Marsh, if you don't get out of my face immediately—'

Without warning, Jackie ran at the reporter with the broken bottle in her hand. 'You bastards! The lot of you! Call me a pig in a wig, would you?'

'Jackie! No!' Kathy grabbed hold of the woman and eased the glass out of her hand. 'They're not worth it.'

'Come on,' said Sara, staring at Marsh. 'Let's get her inside.'

Sara missed the first half trying to sober up Jackie with cup after cup of black coffee. At half-time, she left Kathy in charge and went off to the Redwood boardroom to confront Stephen.

As she entered the room, twenty or so portly men stopped talking and stared at her.

'You can't come in here, miss,' said the steward.

'I beg your pardon?'

'Directors' wives to the left. No ladies are allowed in here.'

'I'm no lady. I'm the MD of Camden United.'

The man shifted from foot to foot, unsure what he should do. 'You'll have to wait here while I go and find out.'

Finally, Henry Benson, the chairman of Redwood, came over to her. 'We'll make an exception for you, Miss Moore. You must feel very honoured and humbled to be here.'

Sara was speechless. She looked around the room, which was hardly bigger than a broom cupboard and about as expensively appointed. Its drabness served only to highlight the chairman's excruciating dress sense. With his fur coat, trilby and fat cigar, he looked like the offspring of a bizarre union between the Crazy Gang and the Marx brothers. Taking Sara's silence as appreciation, he continued, 'We don't usually allow women in the boardroom. We're here to work. Even my wife's not allowed in.'

'Too bloody right,' shouted someone.

'You're pathetic, the lot of you. You can stuff your little boys' room.' She turned to leave but Stephen grabbed hold of her arm. 'I heard you had a bit of an accident. You shouldn't drink before a game.'

Sara turned on him. 'I don't. You called Marsh, didn't you?'

Stephen laughed. 'Certainly did.'

I don't care about me, but how could you have humiliated your own wife like that? Didn't you see how upset she was about the *Herald* story?'

Before he could reply, Henry Benson appeared by his side. 'Come on, Stephen, the second half's about to start.'

Sara followed them back to the directors' box and soon gathered from the buzz of conversation that Antonio had been causing a sensation, scoring two goals in the first twenty minutes. Red-wood's defences had clearly been thrown by the new star of the Camden squad.

Five minutes into the half, Kathy and Jackie joined her, Stephen's wife more in body than in spirit. They watched Antonio as he expertly swerved around the defence.

'So that's him,' whispered Kathy. 'He's gorgeous.'

'Not two million pounds' worth of gorgeous.'

'I would say that was cheap.' As Kathy spoke, Antonio scored his third goal and the Camden United supporters were beside themselves. 'Nice bum, too.'

After the next kick-off Antonio once again tore up the pitch, one man against eleven, impervious to Ian Sumner's screams to pass the ball. The Brazilian was lining himself up for a fourth goal when one of Redwood's full-backs aimed a blatant kick at his shins. Antonio fell to the ground, rolling over and over. The referee blew his whistle and on came two medics with a stretcher.

'Not another drama queen,' said Kathy.

Sara was on her feet, craning her neck to see what was happening. 'I think he might really be hurt. God, I think they're bringing on a stretcher. I hope it's just a precaution.'

'Is that a note of concern I hear?'

'Two million pounds' worth.'

With Antonio off the pitch, Redwood came back with a venge-ance, closing the gap to 3–2 and in the final minutes narrowly missing a goal which would have equalised the score.

Leaving the box, Stephen ignored his now sleeping wife and Sara realised that she was expected to play nursemaid again. 'Kathy, do you think you could get Jackie back on the coach? I'm sorry to lumber you with her, but I've got to talk to Reg about Antonio.'

'She'll be no problem,' replied Kathy. 'She's passed the point where she can do any more harm.'

Sara tapped uncertainly on the changing-room door. Judging by the din coming from inside, she wouldn't have made herself heard with a battering-ram. Oh well, she said to herself, here goes. As she opened the door a dozen naked men ran for cover.

'It's all right,' she shouted. 'I've seen it all before.'

'Not one like this,' said Dick Davenport, whipping off his towel.

'You're right,' she said squinting. 'Not without a microscope, anyway.'

'Good on you, girl,' shouted someone from the showers.

She found Reg sitting by the lockers. 'You must be pleased,' she said.

The manager didn't look it. 'It wasn't much of a team effort, was it? I know these foreigners laugh at our four–four–two formations, but Christ, he's in our country now.'

Sara automatically opened her mouth to defend Antonio and then thought better of it. It wasn't she who had bought him. And Reg had every right to be as angry as she was about not having been consulted in his signing. 'Where is he?'

'At the hospital. You should go and see if he's all right.'

'Me?'

'It's your bloody team. I thought you wanted more involvement?'

'You're right,' said Sara, chastened. 'I'll go straight away.'

She ran back to the coach to find Jackie asleep on Kathy's shoulder. 'Do you mind if I don't come back with you?' she asked. 'Reg thinks I should go to the hospital to see Antonio.'

'A chance, I think, for Nurse Moore to practise her bedside manner,' smiled Kathy.

Sara was exasperated by her friend's innuendo. 'I'm telling you, I would never dream of going out with a footballer. They're only interested in three things – drinking, clothes and the size of their penises. Can you take Jackie back to your place? I can't stand the idea of Stephen humiliating her any more tonight.'

Sara got off the coach. Actually, she had not seen Antonio drink. Evidently he cared about his clothes, because he always looked fantastic. As for number three . . .

Chapter Thirty-Two

Sara had expected to find the Brazilian striker having his leg strapped up in the casualty department. She was alarmed to learn that he'd taken a nasty knock on the head and was being kept in for observation. Antonio was asleep when Sara entered his hospital room. She was annoyed with herself that she was disappointed. Still, it gave her the chance to study his face unobserved without his dark, haunting eyes tearing into hers. His hair was so black in contrast to the starched, white pillow and she found herself longing to run her fingers through it. Resisting the temptation, she eyed his full lips, two shades darker than his olive skin, and smiled, thinking how kissable they were. His bare, tanned chest gently rose with each breath he took, the dark hairs around his navel beginning a trail which disappeared tantalisingly beneath the sheets. The urge to touch him was almost overwhelming. Antonio stirred and the moment was broken. She reminded herself that this man was probably a friend of Stephen's and consequently out of bounds.

Opening his eyes, the footballer gave a brief nod, a greeting that was neither warm nor welcoming.

'Reg thought I'd better come and see how you were,' she said, brisk and businesslike.

Antonio turned his face away from her. 'You need not have bothered. I'm fine.'

'It's not for your benefit,' snapped Sara, striding over to the bed. 'You're an investment. I need to know if I can expect a return.'

'It's always money with you. Such a beautiful woman and yet your attitude is very . . . very ugly.'

His criticism simultaneously enraged and excited her. Sara didn't want him to think her so mercenary, but at the same time she wanted him to know that she was in control. 'Obviously I'm concerned about your wellbeing too, but it's hard to overlook the fact I have two million pounds riding on it.'

In obvious pain, Antonio sat up, the sheet dropping down just past his naked hips, his swarthy face clouded with anger. 'So you only care if it doesn't cost too much?'

His chest tensed when he spoke. His temper only increased his desirability. 'It isn't like that at all,' she said. 'Look, let's call a truce. Tell me what the doctors said.'

'They suspect a ligament problem,' he replied, trying to gauge her reaction. Satisfied that she seemed sincere, he continued, smiling for the first time. 'They might have to operate.'

'Is there anything you need?'

'I'm so hungry. The food here is disgusting. You haven't got any chocolate, have you?'

She shook her head and returned the smile, imagining herself sliding a piece of chocolate between his lips. 'You're wrong to think that I only care about money. That isn't what motivates me at all. There are other more important reasons for doing the things I do. There's a lot you don't know about how I came to own this club.'

'Then tell me. Or perhaps you don't trust me?'

'I don't – I mean I can't. Antonio, I need to know the truth. Are you in league with Stephen?'

The silence seemed to last forever. They were both caught in the deadlock of mutual suspicion. It was Antonio who broke first. 'Sit down,' he said, tapping the bed beside him. Sara did so, slightly embarrassed by the proximity of their bodies. Antonio cleared his throat. 'Let me tell you something. When I was young I lived with my mother in one of the many *favelas* around Rio.'

'What's a *favela*?'

'A . . . what is it?'

Sara was endeared by the way Antonio ran his fingers through his hair as he struggled to find the right word in English. She'd seen him do it before, that time in her office when he had told her that he was a slave. That day it hadn't been quite so lovable. Then again, maybe it had.

'A shanty town!' he exclaimed triumphantly. 'Anyway, my father didn't stick around long after my mother gave birth to me. We were better off without him, even though my mother had to . . . sell her body . . . to keep food on the table. She couldn't give me much, but she wanted the best for me. Football was my obsession and she encouraged my dreams. I spent most of my childhood imagining that one day I would play for Brazil. All I wanted to do was to earn enough money to give her a proper home. That woman deserved the earth.' He stopped. 'Maybe you don't need to know this.'

'Please, go on.' There was such tenderness in the way he spoke. Sara shifted on the bed and for the briefest of moments, her hand brushed against his.

'One day I came home from the park to find bulldozers on our doorstep. It seems that our home was . . . an eyesore . . . an affront to the good people of Rio. In a second everything we owned was gone, and we were forced on to the street. My mother tried to make the best of it. Always she made the best of it, even when we slept in doorways. She said, "You have to make the dream stronger; you have to believe that there is a better life waiting for you."' Antonio's voice broke slightly. 'She had . . . tuberculosis. All that was waiting for her was death. There was no funeral – there was no money for one. I was sixteen and penniless.'

Sara wasn't sure what to say. 'Sorry' was inappropriate – Antonio was not asking for her pity. Instead she reached out and gently placed her hand on his, this small intimacy sending a jolt of electricity through her body. She sensed that the barrier between them was crumbling. 'So what happened then?' she asked, her voice lowered to a whisper to match Antonio's.

'I survived by selling things – peanuts, telephone tokens – and shoe-shining. And when there was no work I begged or picked pockets. I had the fastest hand in Rio,' he said, holding up a credit card which seconds earlier had been in Sara's pocket. He handed it back and let out a low generous laugh. 'Then one day a miracle happened. I was playing football with my friends when a scout from São Paulo saw me and signed me up on the spot. Before I knew it I had been picked as a reserve for the World Cup team. But as you know, Brazil went out in the second round.' He shrugged. 'Maybe God thought that one miracle was enough.'

'There's still a big leap from São Paulo to Camden—'

She was interrupted by the arrival of a nurse. 'Visiting hours are over, I'm afraid. Mr Neves needs his rest.'

'Of course.' Sara had had no idea she'd been there for so long. She stood up, but Antonio kept hold of her hand. 'Shall I come back tomorrow? If you're still here, that is.'

'I would like that. Let's just keep our fingers crossed for that two million pounds, eh?' He gave her that smile again and her stomach somersaulted.

When Sara entered her office the next morning the first thing she saw was the *News* spread out on her desk, open at the second page, which featured several photographs taken during the fracas with Julian Marsh the night before. The picture of her rolling about on the pavement with Kathy and Jackie was particularly damning. Before she could read the accompanying piece Stephen put his head round her door.

'You're one classy bird,' he said, a smirk spreading across his face. 'I should think the FA'll be on to you. You know how hot they are on violence.'

Sara chose her words carefully. 'As hot as they are on match-fixing, I imagine.'

'Look, you little bitch,' hissed Stephen, 'you haven't got the missing link to protect you today.'

Sara smiled calmly. 'Norman is only a phone call away. As are the police. Now, will you piss off? I've got work to do.'

'Watch your back, Sara,' he shouted from the corridor. 'I'm warning you.'

For all her bravado, Sara was shaken. Stephen was not above using physical intimidation. The threat from Mickey's thug proved that. At least she could feel secure in her home now under Norman's watchful eye. The quicker she got to the bottom of what was going on at the club, the safer she would feel. She picked up the *News*, reading the strapline. 'WHAT HAVE A RICH BITCH, A WASHED-UP FASHION EDITOR AND AN ALCOHOLIC FORMER MODEL GOT IN COMMON? THAT'S WHAT STEPHEN POWELL, CHAIRMAN OF CAMDEN UNITED WOULD LIKE TO KNOW.'

Sara glanced at the story underneath in which she was portrayed as a bimbo, Kathy as the aforementioned washed-up magazine editor and Jackie – poor Jackie – as a permanently soused hag. Further on in the piece Christopher Heard's name cropped up. She was incensed to read that apparently he had dumped her. For God's sake, they'd only gone out with each other half a dozen times!

Kathy came into the office. 'I see you've been brought the good news already.'

'Hold on a sec.,' said Sara holding up her hand without raising her eyes from the paper, where she was reading, with total disbelief, that Christopher was now dating the hot new editor of the *Herald*'s women's page. 'Did you see this?' she said, her voice hoarse with outrage.

'The pictures were enough. I don't think I'll ever get to be editor of *Vogue* now.'

'According to this drivel I've been dumped by Christopher in favour of Maggie Lawrence.'

Kathy's mouth dropped open. 'Right that's it, I've had enough. Give me that phone.'

'I don't want you to talk to her. Just leave it.'

'For how long? Until she's written a front-page story about how you killed Bill?'

'She wouldn't do that to me.'

Kathy just couldn't believe that Sara still had such a blind spot where Maggie was concerned, even now. 'Let's quickly recap what she's done to you so far, shall we?'

'Drop it, Kathy!' Sara knew in her heart that Maggie would write about Bill at the drop of a hat. Or at a phone call from Kathy. As long as they didn't retaliate, perhaps she'd be satisfied with what she'd achieved so far. 'I'm sorry. I didn't mean to shout.'

Kathy smiled. 'Forget about it. Anyway, how did it go with Senhor Neves?'

'It was OK,' said Sara, blushing. 'He talked a lot about his childhood. I think he was going for the sympathy vote.'

'Did he get it?'

Sara laughed. 'Maybe. I thought I'd go back and see him again this afternoon. What are your plans?'

'Well, I need to get things going properly here, and if I have any spare time, I'd like to spend it with Jackie. I think we should try to persuade her to go into rehab.'

'It's a good idea, but I doubt you'll get much joy. If I were married to Stephen I'd be on a gin drip.'

'I know it won't be easy, but if she were sober, she might think about divorcing him. And look what getting rid of a husband did for me.'

'This?' replied Sara, holding up the *News*.

Back at the hospital, Sara found Antonio up and dressed, sitting on his bed reading a report of the previous night's match.

'How are you feeling?' she asked, sitting on the bedside chair.

The footballer smiled. 'OK,' he said. 'They say everything is fine. A false alarm.'

'I'll tell the bank,' she said drily, and then, more softly, added, 'I'm glad.'

'I'm going home tonight, and I should be able to play again in a week or two – if you haven't already booked my ticket back to Brazil.'

'If you couldn't play I would have made you buy your own ticket.' She smiled to let him know that she wasn't serious. 'Antonio, last night . . .'

'Yes?'

'Well, you didn't explain how you came to England.'

'I'm not quite sure I can.'

Sara rose from her chair. 'I want to trust you, but if you can't give me a straight answer, then—'

Antonio placed his hand on her arm. 'Please, sit down. It's just that things aren't as simple as you think.'

'Try me.'

He shifted his position on the bed. 'When I became famous in Brazil, I decided to use that fame to do something for the children still out in the streets and *favelas*. You've heard of the death squads, no?'

'I've read about them.'

'They kindly clear the "rubbish" from our streets. Last year alone there were nearly five hundred children murdered. Some of the killing is so that the property developers can move in and take over the land.' Antonio became animated with indignation, his voice echoing around the room. 'One child was found dead on the beach with a sign around his neck saying: "I killed you because you have no future."'

Sara shook her head slowly, horrified.

'So I started a campaign to heighten public awareness of what was happening. I wanted to create safe places for them to go. As you can imagine, that made me very unpopular in certain circles. A lot of powerful people would rather I didn't say the things I say. You do remember that day in Cuenca, don't you?'

Sara blushed. 'Yes, I do.'

'Well, that day I'd been warned if I didn't shut up I would be made to. In my country, that's no idle threat. My friend the Contessa, the woman you saw me with, came to Ecuador especially to warn me not to return to Brazil. She works with the children, too, but *nobody* would ever threaten the Contessa. The woman is a living saint. Me – I'm just a footballer.'

Sara was beginning to think Antonio was considerably more than that. 'So did you go back to Brazil?'

'I had to. I didn't know what else to do, where to go. I suppose I could have gone anywhere in the world, but I had my reasons for wanting to stay in Brazil. Someone very important to me.'

Sara's heart lurched. She hadn't been expecting this.

'His name's Oscar.' Sara's look of surprise made Antonio laugh. 'He's five years old and he lives on the streets of Rio. But he represents hope. He is a brilliant little football player, and, with the right help, he could be the next Pele. He is a beautiful, happy child, and he has become a very important part of my life. Do you understand that feeling?'

'Yes, yes I understand.'

'I wanted to take care of him. But these children do not trust adults any more. After so much abuse, it is only to be expected. I wanted to prove I was different, but I never got the chance.'

Antonio exhaled, his chest falling and rising under his snowy-white shirt as he unburdened his heart. As she watched, unable to take her eyes off him, Sara realised that she herself was barely breathing at all. Her face felt flushed. Surely he could see it?

'Now he will think I have deserted him,' Antonio continued. 'Men broke into my home. Luckily, I wasn't there. But then I knew it was no longer safe for me to stay in Brazil. An agent organised it for Camden United to buy me, and here I am.'

'What happened to Oscar?' she asked, chilled by the thought of a death squad hunting down a five-year-old child. Antonio seemed so suffused with grief about the boy that she wanted to kiss him, to reassure him.

She stood up, restless.

'I don't know. I tried to find him before I left but I couldn't. My friend Flavio is still looking for him. He's a journalist – he's got lots of contacts. But I don't know what will happen if he doesn't find him.' His voice was choked with emotion. 'Could you pass me some water?'

As Sara stretched for the jug, her breast brushed against his chest and instinctively she pulled away, spilling the water. Antonio reached out and caressed her hair, enjoying the silky touch over his hand. Sara moved closer, shivering as his fingers moved up to her neck, and in response she hunched her shoulder, trapping his hand against the hotness of her cheek. The pressure of his touch grew stronger and gently he pulled her head down towards him until their mouths met. His lips, firm but yielding to the softness of her own, felt just as she had imagined they would feel. She could admit it to herself now: from the first moment she had seen him run on to the Camden pitch, she had been deeply under his spell.

'You're beautiful,' he whispered as his kisses moved down to her neck. Sara grabbed a handful of his hair and pulled his head up again, unable to stand having his lips away from hers. She kissed him long and hard, holding him close, feeling his powerful muscles flexing as he responded to her embrace, allowing the delicious, musky aroma of his body to invade her nostrils, both delighted and frightened that for the first time since Bill's death she truly desired a man.

Kathy paced up and down Sara's office waiting for Jackie. In front of her were several books containing photographs of Jackie in her prime. Jackie was rarely pictured without the Butterfly at her side. It was such a sad story. In 1966 her disappearance had elicited a storm of media interest, not unlike that surrounding Lord Lucan. And, like him, the Butterfly had never been found. Kathy tried to put herself in Jackie's shoes. How would she feel if Sara were to disappear? She readily acknowledged how much of her strength she drew from Sara. If she were not there, Kathy could easily see herself falling into a bad relationship for comfort; maybe even going back to Joseph. Perhaps the Butterfly's disappearance had been the start of Jackie's problems. Whatever it was, she had to try to persuade Jackie that life didn't have to be this bad.

'Hi.' Jackie walked into the office, swaying slightly on her five-inch heels, her knotted top showing a white tyre of flesh hanging over her ski pants. 'If you're about to show me the *News*, don't. Stephen has kindly cut out the article for me.'

'Well, I did want to talk about that,' said Kathy, nervously pacing up and down. 'I hope you don't mind me saying this, but I really think you've got to do something about your drink problem.'

'I do mind,' snapped Jackie. 'I know I haven't got much self-respect left, but I sure as hell don't have to listen to a virtual stranger putting me right.'

Kathy walked over to where Jackie was standing and said gently, 'No, you don't, but I've been where you are now.'

'You drank?'

'It wasn't so much that, but, like you, I almost let a man destroy me.' Emboldened by Jackie's silence, Kathy told her about Joseph's affair. 'So now I'm here. It's not quite what I had mapped out, but I'm getting back my self-respect.'

Jackie softened. 'Thanks. It was nice of you to be so honest. But it's not the same thing. You're young, you have your whole life ahead of you. I'm finished. Even if I sobered up, what would I do? Where would I go if I left Stephen?'

'Let's take one step at a time. Sober, things might not look so bleak. You'll never know what opportunities are around unless you're fit to recognise them. Why not try a clinic? *Mariella*, the magazine I used to work for, once did a piece on one of them. Some are just like health spas. Think about it.' To underline her point, she opened one of the books. 'Look at you here. You're amazing. And the Butterfly, she was something, wasn't she? You must have been devastated when she disappeared.'

Jackie looked at the picture and closed the book. 'So you're handling the fund-raising?'

Kathy got the message. 'I'm not really sure what I'm doing, to tell you the truth.'

'Oh, it's easy. Listen . . .'

For the next hour they discussed the various ways in which the club could raise money. Despite having drunk her way through her time at the club, Jackie knew everything there was to know about the workings of Camden United. 'I think women should be encouraged to come to the game,' she said. 'Perhaps we should reduce the prices for them. It works in nightclubs.'

'Great. What about kids?'

'Again, reduce the price and you could have a special club for them. Other teams do it.' Jackie was warming to her theme. It wasn't often she was able to give advice. 'They could meet the players. And why not section off part of the ground into a family zone?'

'You're brilliant at this,' said Kathy, genuinely impressed. 'Why haven't you been doing the fund-raising?'

Jackie snorted. 'Stephen doesn't want his stupid tart of a wife on the payroll. His stupid tart of a mistress was a different matter, of course. I hate that man so much.' She paused. 'Fuck it. Where's that clinic?'

'The one we covered for *Mariella* was in Kensington. But I'm sure there are loads of places.'

'No, Kensington sounds fine. How much do you think it costs?'

'It was about a thousand a week.'

'Christ, I haven't got that kind of money.' Jackie's face fell, and her voice retreated into defeat. 'It's hopeless.'

'But what about the money from your shares in Camden?'

'After I sorted my mother out, Stephen took the rest. He said if he left it with me I'd piss it all up the wall.' She laughed ruefully. 'He was probably right.'

Kathy could have kicked herself for being so thoughtless. It had never occurred to her that Jackie wouldn't have any money. 'There are plenty of other places that are cheaper.'

'Let's forget about it, eh?' said Jackie.

Just then Sara walked into the room. 'Sorry, did I interrupt something?' she asked, turning to leave.

'Come back. We were just talking about Jackie booking into a clinic,' said Kathy, noticing that Sara seemed to be in a total daze. 'She says that Stephen wouldn't pay for one.'

'I don't think a clinic could cure Stephen of what he's suffering from,' said Sara, absentmindedly. She ran her fingers across her cheek where Antonio had touched her, trying to recall every moment of their first kiss.

Kathy stared at her friend. What planet was she on?

'Jackie, not Stephen. You'd give her the money, wouldn't you?'

'Sure,' said Sara, her green eyes unfocused.

'No, sorry. I couldn't accept,' replied Jackie. 'I'm not a charity case.'

Kathy quickly interjected: 'Jackie's been a great help in ideas for fund-raising, Sara. Perhaps you should take her on. And,' she said, turning to Jackie, 'the cost of the clinic could be an advance on your salary.'

'That sounds perfect to me,' said Sara. 'You know, you can go along for ages sleepwalking. You talk, you eat, you work, but you're asleep all the same. And then somebody comes along and wakes you up.' She clicked her fingers for emphasis. 'Just like that.'

Jackie hadn't a clue what Sara was talking about, but she was alert enough to recognise that she was being offered a lifeline. She had to take it. 'Sara, I will accept your offer, but I'll work for the money.'

'I'm glad,' said Sara, smiling dreamily.

'If it's OK with you, I wouldn't mind sorting it out straight away.' Jackie got up to leave. At the door, she paused. 'Thank you so very much – both of you.'

As the office door closed behind Jackie, Kathy turned to her friend. 'What on earth's got into you?'

'He kissed me,' sighed Sara, 'and then—'

'Yes?' said Kathy excitedly.

'And then . . . I kissed him back.'

'I take it you no longer believe that there was anything funny about his transfer?'

Sara's shoulders drooped. 'Kathy, I think you've just rained on my parade.'

Chapter Thirty-Three

The Variety Club dinner was being held at the Dorchester. When Sara arrived at the entrance she was immediately surrounded by paparazzi. After the *News* debacle, it seemed wise to be amenable to their requests and pose for a couple of shots.

'Not got a date tonight, Sara?' asked one photographer.

'Sadly, no.' Antonio was still taking it easy to be on the safe side, and after that beautiful afternoon at the hospital, she had decided that she needed some time to sort out her feelings – and to uncover the real reason for his transfer. It would be so awful if it turned out that he'd been lying to her.

'Shame,' said the photographer and his shutter clicked again. 'Beautiful, just beautiful.'

'Thank you.' Although it was a chilly October evening, she was wearing a shoulderless black dress cut very low at the back. Her breasts were held in by little more than a prayer and the full skirt of the gown was slashed almost to the hip. Kathy had said that the dress reminded her of Anita Ekberg's in *La Dolce Vita*. There would be precious little of the sweet life tonight: Stephen was going to the dinner, too.

'One more, Sara.'

She ran a hand through her hair and swept it back off her face, knowing just how to play up to the camera. Once a model, always a model.

'Thanks, boys,' she said as she walked into the hotel. She was bloody freezing.

Inside a steward showed her to a table where Stephen was already seated. If he was surprised to see her, he didn't show it. Instead he ignored her, which suited her just fine. Unfortunately, the man sitting next to her didn't do likewise.

'Hello,' he said, holding out a hand heavy with sovereign rings. 'I'm Nick Grant, chairman of Highgate FC. You must be Stephen's girlfriend.'

'Certainly not.'

'What about it?' shouted Stephen. 'Jackie's out tonight.'

She introduced herself to Grant coldly, paying no attention to Stephen. Mercifully, Stephen turned his attention to a man with flamboyantly blow-dried hair who was wearing a loud Prince of Wales-check suit.

'Yeah, sure, he's here now,' said the man, speaking into his mobile phone. 'Stephen, mate, a word in your ear.'

Stephen nodded and moved away from the table. Sara cocked an ear in his direction, straining to hear the conversation. She heard mention of Sweden and four hundred thousand, but Stephen, catching sight of her, led the man away, leaving her to fend off Nick Grant's suggestive remarks.

After knocking his hand off her knee for the umpteenth time, she asked, 'Who was that man Stephen was talking to?'

Grant looked vacant.

'The one with the elaborate hair and mobile phone?'

'Oh, that's Johnny Taylor. Agent extraordinaire. Done a few deals with him myself.'

'Really, what type?'

'Well,' whispered Grant, the best part of two bottles of champagne loosening his tongue, 'if you want to make a little extra money.'

Sara was intrigued. In the hope of learning something useful, she didn't immediately slap his hand away when he put it back on her knee. 'Go on.'

'Johnny Taylor's the man.' Grant tapped the side of his nose. 'Not strictly on the level, mind, if you know what I mean. He can be a bit of a shyster, you've got to handle him right.'

Sara stood up. 'Would you excuse me for a moment?' She wanted to meet Taylor. Perhaps he could enlighten her about Antonio's transfer and perhaps, more importantly, he might provide a clue to what Stephen was up to. Standing on tiptoe, she peered over the heads of the crowd, looking for the agent, hoping that he was no longer with Stephen. Finally she spotted him jammed up against the bar, a bottle of champagne on ice beside him on the counter. She cut through the crowd and squeezed in beside him.

'Johnny,' she said, squeezing in beside him. 'I'm Sara Moore. From Camden. I thought it was time we met.'

'Too right it is,' replied the agent, clearly unable to believe his luck.

Trying to dodge the elbow of the woman next to her, Sara said, 'Can we go somewhere quieter?'

Taylor picked up the ice bucket and led her to an adjoining room dotted with low-slung sofas. All were occupied but Taylor went over to one and told the occupants to make themselves scarce. Sitting down, he patted the seat next to him and said, 'Now, this is much cosier.'

'It certainly is,' she said, forcing a smile. 'Now, Johnny, I'm sure you've read the papers. You know I'm the one calling the shots at Camden now.'

'I heard you're sinking a lot of money into the place. Want some?' said the agent, proffering the champagne.

'Come on, Johnny, let's talk business,' laughed Sara flirtatiously. 'Who are you representing at the moment?'

'Right, then. I've got Andrew Mackie on my books, the Scottish international. I can get him for a good price.'

'Mr Taylor, have I got "idiot" tattooed across my forehead? He's a has-been and you know it. You'd be lucky to get Boreham Rovers to take him.'

'OK, OK,' he said, curling a lock of her hair around his finger. 'I was just checking you out, to see if you knew what you were talking about.'

'Well, Johnny, take it as read that I know what's what. To tell you the truth, I'm more interested in foreign players. They can make you a lot more money, don't you think?' she said, winking.

Taylor tried to look as if he had no idea what she was talking about. 'I haven't any on my books at the moment,' he stonewalled.

'What about in the future?' asked Sara, pouring Taylor another glass of champagne.

'Maybe,' he replied carefully, keeping the tone of his voice neutral.

Sara decided it would be a good idea to change the subject. 'My new fund-raiser's just negotiating a great deal with Casserly Cars for Camden's shirts,' she said conversationally.

'Really?' Taylor looked surprised. 'I thought Stephen sorted out all that himself. He's never given anyone else a look-in. Always said he could do it better.'

'Obviously he can't. What you seem to keep forgetting, Johnny, is that I'm in charge of the club now. In every sense.'

Johnny's face was like an open book. She could see him working out the various possibilities that Sara's control of the club might offer if he kept in with her. 'Allow me to get another bottle of champagne,' she said, to give herself time to think.

As she waited at the bar, Sara wondered what to do next. Really, the man was quite revolting. But if he thought he could make money out of United through her, he'd have to show his hand. She'd have to convince him she'd taken quite a shine to him if she was going to get this sort of information out of him on their first meeting. But she couldn't afford to play a waiting game. If she didn't get Stephen soon, he was going to get her. It was survival of the fittest, and if that meant using every dirty trick in the book, then so be it. She puffed up her cleavage and returned to the sofa. 'Here we are,' she said, pushing Taylor along slightly so that she didn't have to sit on his lap. 'What shall we drink to? I know – to our future relationship. I think you could be good news for United. Cheers.'

Taylor was pretty drunk, and it was all the encouragement he needed. For the next half-hour she heard about almost every deal he had ever done. She kept on making all the right noises, and topping up his glass. He was too full of himself to notice that she hadn't touched a drop herself. When his words started to slur, Sara decided it was time to return to the matter in hand.

'You've made some great deals, Johnny. Pity you weren't involved in the Neves transfer.' Please don't let Antonio be involved, she thought.

'What? Oh yeah, Stephen wanted to go that one alone.'

'Must have cost you.'

'Why don't we talk about this at your place?'

'So you'd like to get into bed with United in more ways than one?' she teased with a girlish giggle. God, this was disgusting. 'Come on, Johnny, I'm enjoying myself. I'd like another drink.'

Taylor picked up the champagne and emptied the last half-inch into her glass.

'There you go.'

'Thanks.' Sara tried to sound as seductive as possible without making herself sick. 'I don't think it's fair that Stephen is keeping all the good ones to himself. And I like you, Johnny. I'm sure I could put some business your way, if you get my drift.'

'That sounds good but, hey, I don't want to step on Stephen's toes. You know what an SOB he can be,' said Taylor, leaning so close to her that she could almost taste his hairspray.

'He need never know. I'm not going to tell him.' Sara arched her back to pull away from his probing fingers. 'What kind of return was he looking at?'

'The last transfer I was involved in was a couple of years back. A German player, Hans Müller. We knew that his club were willing to sell him for seven hundred and fifty grand. So Stephen gets me to offer a million on condition he gets two hundred grand as a bung and the German manager gets fifty K for his trouble. And, of course, there was a small percentage off both of them for me for arranging the deal,' he said, smirking.

'But it would have been Stephen's money.'

'At that time he was relying heavily on his partner's money – whatshisname, Peter Barratt. Stephen persuaded him that the club needed Müller and Barratt put up the readies. Or perhaps your MP friend did.' He leered unpleasantly.

'Did Barratt ... never mind,' she said, deciding that she didn't have the time now to unravel this extra twist in the equation. 'If I did a similar deal with you, how would I hide the payment?'

'That's easy. Open a foreign bank account. I prefer Swiss myself. That's something we should discuss somewhere more private ...'

'I haven't finished my drink,' said Sara, taking the tiniest sip. Time was running out now. 'So how much do you think he got for Antonio?'

Taylor looked at her suspiciously. 'Why do you want to know that?'

'Hans Müller was a couple of years ago. The payback must have gone up since then.'

'I don't know. It wasn't a simple transfer, payback or not. It was all done hush-hush. He probably made half a million.'

'Half a million,' repeated Sara, whistling.

Just then her saviour arrived in a most unlikely form. 'Would you like to dance?' asked Stephen, his face clouded with fury. He grabbed Sara by the arm and pulled her to her feet. 'Allow me.'

'I'm sorry, Johnny,' she said. 'Another time, perhaps.'

Johnny said nothing. Sara could see that the agent thought he had put his foot in it by encroaching on another man's territory. Never had she been happier to see Stephen Powell. She allowed him to escort her on to the dancefloor.

'What were you talking about?' he growled.

'None of your business,' Sara replied, yanking her arm away. 'And the only time you'll ever get me to dance will be on your grave.' She walked off, barely able to contain her delight. So Stephen was taking backhanders. Now that she knew this, she was certain she'd be able to prove it from the books. At last she was getting somewhere. If only she knew how Antonio fitted into the picture.

The next morning, Sara was back at Camden, steeling herself for another day of abuse. Stopping in reception, she told Louise to send Reg in to see her. In her office there was a note from Kathy to say that she was seeing a local brewer about possible sponsorship.

Sara knew she should be pleased with her progress but as soon as she sat down she began to worry that she was starting to behave just like Stephen. She only hoped the end was going to justify the means. There was a problem, too, with the loyalty of the staff she hadn't sacked. Stephen had given them an easy time over the years and she couldn't tell whether their allegiance still lay with him. The players posed another hurdle. And then there was Reg.

'Speak of the Devil,' she said as the manager put his head round the door. 'Come in, Reg. How are you?'

The manager sat down. 'Fine. Neves came back this morning.'

'Good.' The news quickened her pulse.

'He's out training now. It was a bad business, that signing.'

'Do you know if Johnny Taylor was involved in it?'

'That crook? It wouldn't surprise me, but I must admit I never heard his name mentioned. Why?'

'Stephen was talking to him at the dinner last night. I'm sure they were plotting some deal. I spoke to Taylor afterwards and the drink had loosened his tongue a bit.' She didn't want to say too much, still uncertain about where the manager's sympathies lay.

'You're probably right, but I can't help you, I'm afraid. Now what did you want me for?'

'Are you willing to work with me, Reg?'

'If you'd asked me that straight out a few weeks ago, lass, I would have said no, in no uncertain terms. But I would have been wrong. You're probably the best thing that's happened to this club.'

This was a major breakthrough. Sara felt her spirits lift. 'Thank you, Reg. That means a lot to me.'

Reg seemed embarrassed. He produced a dog-eared notebook. 'I've got one or two ideas myself.'

'Just hear me out and then we'll talk about them. First of all, I've been on to some builders for an estimate for replacing the old gym. Secondly, I know the players think I was unfair to stop their perks, but by way of compensation, from now on I want the team staying in the best hotels and travelling on the most comfortable coach.'

Reg looked impressed.

'Now on to more delicate matters. I think we need a new coach. Jock Wilson has had his day. And we need some new players. Neves has shown, if nothing else, what a decent player can do for the team. Unfortunately, this will mean getting rid of some of the others. I want Dick Davenport put up for sale for starters. I've looked at his form since last season and it's appalling. And,' she continued, in full stride, 'I want Les Sutton to be warned. How many times does he have to be fined for not showing up before he gets the message? Turn up every time or don't bother coming at all. Now, what did you want to say?'

'You took the words right out of my mouth, lass. But you know you're not going to be very popular. Jock's quite well liked by the lads.'

'I'm getting used to that. What is it parents always say? "It's for their own good, and they'll thank me for it in the end."'

'I'll get working on some names for you.'

'Great. I'll see you tomorrow.'

'Christ, you don't hang around,' he said with admiration. Sara was taken aback when he rose and shook her hand. 'You and me'll make a great team.'

As he left, Kathy arrived looking flushed with excitement. 'I've done it! Five hundred grand for five years. R&R Breweries are going to sponsor a stand with their name on it. And,' she paused dramatically, 'I've clinched the deal with Casserly for the shirts. Stephen had one of his buddies in the furniture business sponsoring them for forty thousand a year. Casserly Cars are willing to stump up two hundred thousand.'

Sara hugged her friend. 'I knew you'd come up trumps.'

Kathy undid her briefcase and began taking out her papers. 'There are certain conditions Casserly want you to agree to—'

'Kathy, could we do this later?' asked Sara, standing up. 'There's someone I need to see.'

Sara went to look for Antonio. She had to be sure that he had no involvement in any crooked transaction. She desperately needed to be able to trust him.

The team were out on the pitch, but the Brazilian wasn't with them. Reg had not wanted him to overdo it on his first day back and had sent him off to get changed. Walking back through the tunnel, Sara entered the labyrinth of underground passages that led to the team's locker room. The smell of male sweat seemed to have permeated the whitewashed bricks, reinforcing their proclamation that this was boys-only territory. The only thing missing was the usual din of the players' voices. Usually when you entered this grotto you were quickly immersed in an atmosphere akin to that of a primary school class full of hyperactive children, but with the players still on the pitch it was silent. The corridor was chilly from the wind whistling down from the stadium and she shivered as she called Antonio's name through the changing-room door.

'Hello, anyone here?' she called into the white-tiled room.

There was no reply, only the sound of the shower. She walked into the showers and stopped dead in her tracks. Antonio was standing there, his back to her, lathering shampoo into his hair. The muscles on his back flexed as he massaged his head. Sara stood there, transfixed by the suds snaking their way down his naked body.

'Oh, I'm sorry.'

Antonio spun round and brushed the soap from his eyes. 'Sara?' He made no attempt to cover his body.

'I didn't realise anyone was here,' she lied, trying to keep her eyes above waist-level. 'I wanted to speak to you about . . . your transfer.' She looked at the ceiling in embarrassment. 'But it can wait.'

'I was just thinking about you,' he said, walking towards her. As he moved his whole body became a mass of constantly shifting sinewy muscle. He didn't look vulnerable in his nakedness as most people do. He moved with the confidence of a panther.

'I know Stephen took money—'

'I was imagining making love to you,' said Antonio, keeping his gaze steady.

'I think I'd better go. We'll talk about this some other time.'

'It was beautiful.'

'Antonio . . .'

Suddenly, without warning, he took her hand in his and pulled her sharply against him. She held his stare until he lowered his face, his lips meeting hers.

'Antonio, this is wrong,' she said, pulling away, the spray from the shower soaking her blouse. Her desire for this man crowded out all other thoughts and she needed space to think.

'How can it be wrong?' he whispered, drawing her into his arms again. Never had he felt like this about a woman before. It wasn't only her beauty that enthralled him; it was her strength, too, although he could sense the underlying fragility. He wanted to hold her, protect her, make everything in her world safe. 'I love you.'

'How can you say that? You hardly know me,' she said, wanting him to say it again in spite of herself. 'It takes years to grow to love somebody.'

'With some people, an hour can be a lifetime.'

'That's—' But Antonio's lips silenced her and for a moment she was lost in the feverous passion of his embrace. 'Stop!' she gasped, her hands pushing against his chest, aware of the hardness of his pectorals flexing under his taut, damp skin.

His fingers dug into her shoulders. 'Look me in the eye and tell me you don't feel the same.'

'I . . . I . . .' How could she answer when the proximity of his body destroyed all rational thought? Her need to have him take her, possess her, was stronger than anything she'd ever known before, but was that love?

'Tell me!' he demanded, his voice thick with violent desire.

'Yes! Yes! Yes!' she cried, surrendering to her destiny. 'I love you.' There were no more words to say. Frenziedly Antonio tore at the buttons on her blouse, desperate to feel her naked body pressed against his while Sara, kicking off her shoes, tugged at the zip on her skirt. Then Antonio forced the skirt down over her long legs and fell to his knees, his mouth tracing kisses across the flatness of her stomach. He reached up and eased her knickers slowly over her hips, down over her thighs, to join the rest of her clothes on the floor.

Antonio leaned back on his haunches, his eyes greedily taking in every curve, every contour of her ravishing, naked body. 'You are exquisite,' he said, rising to his feet and lifting her in his powerful arms. Then he carried her under the warm spray

of the shower, wrapping her legs around his waist. 'So beautiful.'

Sara caught her breath as her back met the coldness of the tiled
wall. 'I want you. Now. Deep inside me,' she pleaded.

Antonio shifted his position slightly and obeyed.

Chapter Thirty-Four

Sara bounced into the office with a breezy hello to Louise. The receptionist didn't respond in her usual friendly manner. 'What's wrong?' Sara asked.

'Nothing,' replied Louise, but the worried look on her face said otherwise.

'Come on, I know something's up. Has somebody upset you?'

The girl appeared to be on the brink of tears. 'It's not about me. I suppose I might just as well show you because you'll find out soon enough.' She held out a copy of the *Comet*.

There was a picture of Bill, taken a few weeks before he died, under the heading 'SOCCER MILLIONAIRESS IN DEATH DRIVE.' There was a photograph of her, too – one which must have been taken in the previous few days because it showed her getting into the Porsche Carrera to which she had just treated herself. The caption described her as a lady who had always enjoyed fast cars.

The piece, attributed to 'a *Comet* reporter', was very careful to stay on the right side of the libel laws, but there was no getting away from the implication that Sara had caused the death of Bill Newman. The paper had even interviewed his sisters, and they hadn't minced their words. Obviously the *Comet* had paid for a reporter to go to America and visit them. A little further down there was a mention of Mary, who was quoted as saying that the day Bill died was the saddest day of her life. They'd left out anything she might have had to say about Sara, and this omission made the article all the more damning. Seeing the photograph of Bill was actually worse than reading the spiteful newsprint. The vision of him staring up at her from the page brought it all rushing back, making Sara feel like she'd been kicked in the stomach.

'I shouldn't have shown it to you. I'm ever so sorry, Sara.'

Sara tried to smile. 'I would have found out sooner or later, as you said, and I'd rather have been told by someone who cares.'

Louise visibly relaxed. 'I don't believe a word of it.'

'Let's not talk about it. Are there any messages for me?'

'Only one from Johnny Taylor. In fact, he's rung several times this morning. He was very insistent that you get back to him. He became quite abusive on the third call.'

'If you can take his abuse, can you just tell him I'm out for the rest of the day and you have no idea where I am?' Clearly Taylor had finally sobered up and realised just how much he had let slip.

Sara read the rest of the article on the way to her office. So Maggie had finally done it. Sara had no doubt that she was involved in this: the copy bore all the hallmarks of her venom. The details of Sara's modelling stint in New York were conveyed in such a tawdry fashion that you'd have been forgiven for thinking she'd been a stripper. And then the Mickey Nash story reared its head yet again, embroidered with the suggestion that she had gone further than was journalistically necessary in her investigations. She read on, enraged, as the filthy rag revealed and revelled in her supposed coke parties with the club owner. It had to be Maggie.

Seething, Sara walked into her office and picked up the phone. 'Maggie Lawrence,' she barked at the *Herald*'s receptionist. She was put on hold. The bland muzak infuriated her even more.

'Maggie Lawrence, women's page.'

'How could you?'

There was a pause on the line and then a laugh. 'Hi, Sara. I was wondering how long you could stand it before you rang me.' Maggie was trying to brazen it out but all the same there was a tremor in her voice.

'How could you?' Sara pleaded, the tears sounding in her voice.

Maggie's voice became harsh. 'It's just typical of you to blame me, isn't it? Can't you think of anyone else who might know those things about you? Or do you think you're so adorable that no man could do the dirty on you?'

It was Sara's turn to pause.

'Who did you tell every sordid little secret about Mickey's Bar? And brag about your poxy modelling career? You didn't really think Christopher was interested in you, did you? It was just a job. He was carrying out Cynthia's orders. But you must have had a good idea that he was checking you out. Do you really think you met by accident? Who do you think sent you those theatre tickets? You're always so bloody sure of yourself. Not everyone falls under your spell, Sara.'

'Christopher didn't know about the crash.'

'He did as soon as somebody pointed him in the right direction. Then it was straight over to New York to interview the sisters.'

'But you know none of it's true.'

Maggie was on a roll. 'It must be, I read it in the papers. This has been a long time coming, but finally your vanity has got the better of you. At last your shit stinks, like everyone else's. Oh, and this isn't the end of it, not by a long chalk. You just wouldn't believe the biggie we've got coming next. Not in your wildest dreams.'

'What the hell did I ever do to you to deserve this?' she cried. But Maggie had put down the phone.

Sara rested her head in her hands and sobbed, unaware that someone had walked into the room.

'Sara, what is it?'

It was Antonio. 'I'm fine. Please go away.'

He walked round to her side of the desk and gently placed an arm around her shoulder. 'Please tell me what's wrong.'

She pointed to the newspaper. 'I don't know how much more I can take . . .' Even in her despair the feel of his arm gave her goose-bumps. She wanted so much to lie back against his powerful body, to be taken care of. Suddenly she felt so tired, it was all too much. She let her body relax against his and felt him respond by holding her a little tighter. But the picture in the paper of Bill stared up at her, and it suddenly felt very wrong for another man to be consoling her.

'I'm sorry, Antonio,' she said, pulling away and rising to her feet. 'This isn't right. I've got to go.'

'Sara, wait!' Antonio called after her, but Sara didn't look back.

She gunned the Porsche through Camden, only half aware of the crowds milling across the street from one shop to another. This was madness. Did she want to run someone over and provide the perfect follow-up story for the *Comet*? She pulled over to collect herself, ignoring the drunken tramp leering in through the window and waving a can of Tennent's at her. It was just before eleven. Kathy wouldn't be back at the office for a while: she was out seeing several companies who'd shown an interest in sponsoring individual matches.

In angry frustration, Sara banged her hands on the steering wheel. She'd been so guarded around Christopher. How could he have twisted what she'd told him about the cocaine? With Maggie behind him, that's how. He had written the story, even if it had carried Maggie's stamp. Maggie would have had no hesitation in taking the full credit if she'd worked on it alone.

She wanted revenge. For several minutes she fantasised about smashing up Christopher's Morgan, but smashing up his face would be much more satisfying. She would have to confront him. She beeped her horn impatiently at the tramp and edged the car back into the traffic. Soon shabby north London gave way to the shops of the West End, which, in turn, were replaced by the imposing terraces of SW1.

Half aware that she'd gone through a red light, she turned the corner into Eton Square, her tyres squealing. Jumping out of the car, she ran up the front steps of the apartments and rang Christopher's bell. There was no response. She kept her finger on the bell, venting her frustration, until finally someone heaved open the massive black door. It was Maisie.

'Chris'phers out,' she said, registering the anxiety on Sara's face. 'Are you awright?'

Without replying, Sara pushed past Maisie, ran up the stairs and into the flat, shutting the door behind her in the hope that it might keep the old woman at bay for a while.

She found Christopher's office at the end of an L-shaped corridor. She turned on an anglepoise lamp to illuminate the gloom, revealing a room as immaculate as the man who worked there. There was nothing on the desk except for his laptop and a fax machine. Next to it was a filing cabinet with each drawer neatly labelled alphabetically. Inside the one marked K to R was a series of blue folders. Sara flicked through, recognising many of the names of the great and the good. Lawson, Linley – she moved to the middle of the drawer – Minnelli. No, further on. Moore. Pulling the file out she saw that it was devoted to Roger Moore. She replaced it and took out the next one. Sitting down at the desk, she tipped out the contents. Most of the cuttings were from articles with which she was already all too familiar.

Among them was a piece of pink paper. Unfolding it, she found that it was a birth certificate for someone called Justine Butterworth. The mother's name was given as Felicity Butterworth; the father's was unknown. At first she thought it had been put in the wrong file – unusual for someone as meticulous as Christopher. The name struck a chord somewhere, but Sara couldn't remember where she'd heard it before. It was only when she noticed that Justine's date of birth was the same as hers that her heart started to thump.

The second official paper compounded her anxiety. It began: 'In the matter of Justine Butterworth an infant. Whereas an application has been made by Harry Moore ...' An adoption certificate.

Sara felt dizzy. She grabbed the desk for support. None of this made any sense. Felicity Butterworth – where had she heard that name? She scrabbled through the papers and found an envelope with a Brazilian postmark. The letter was addressed to Stuart Hargreaves. Trembling, she took out the letter inside, half knowing already

what she was going to find. As she'd suspected, the letter was from
Felicity. It was dated 2 November 1981.

Dear Stuart,
I know this letter will come as a great shock, but I can't hold
this in my heart any longer. This is no way to prepare you
gently for what I have to tell you and therefore I must come
out with it straight.

Today is our daughter's fifteenth birthday. Yes, I gave birth
to a baby girl and you are the father. I named her Justine after
my mother, and from the moment I saw her I loved her with
all of my heart. Yet I gave her away, and there has not been
one day in those fifteen years when I have not been filled with
remorse for what I had to do.

Why didn't I tell you about it? There were so many things I
didn't tell you. Those were very black days for me, but to tell
you about them now would only seem like making excuses.

Stuart, I loved you and never wanted to do anything that
would hurt you. I gave away our child, and for fifteen years I
have kept it a bitter secret in the misguided belief that I should
not allow this one mistake to come between you and your duty
to your country. But I was wrong, terribly wrong.

I cannot bear this burden all by myself any longer. For the
past fifteen years I have lived in Brazil, devoting myself to the
comfort of the poor and the dispossessed to try to make up for
what I did. But it isn't enough. You must use everything within
your power to find Justine and make amends. But should you
find her, you must never tell her who you are. How can you
possibly profess paternal love for a child you have never
known? How can you explain to her that her mother loved
her with every last breath and yet so cruelly gave her away?

I make no apologies for this letter. I have borne this secret
alone for long enough. My shame is your shame, and until
you do something neither of us will know any contentment.
I wish I could find some of the loving words which came to
us so easily back then.

Felicity.

Numb, she flicked through the other papers – Stuart's will, a memo from Cynthia Hargreaves to Christopher, telling him to send her theatre tickets – until she found the final confirmation that this nightmare was indeed real. She hiccuped a dry sob, cupping her mouth with her hand as though she could physically keep her emotions back, and read the details on a photocopy of her own birth certificate, drawing comfort from seeing the names of her mother and father typed out in apparently incontrovertible proof of her parentage. But the date was wrong. The date her birth was registered matched that on the adoption slip. It wasn't her birthday. Her mum and dad weren't her parents. Her mother and father were Felicity Butterworth and Stuart Hargreaves.

Sara didn't even hear the key in the lock. It was only when she heard Christopher's voice that she realised that she was about to be caught in the act. She didn't give a damn. How could she, in the aftermath of such an earth-shattering discovery? Her whole life, her childhood, her identity – everything – had been turned on its head.

'Mother, I can't believe you let her in,' Christopher's voice seemed to come from a long, long way away.

'And 'ow was I meant to stop 'er?' It was Maisie's voice. Surely Christopher had called her Mother? She rose from the chair and, taking the pieces of paper with her, walked slowly into the hallway. She coughed.

Christopher whirled round and stood stock-still, his mouth gaping open. 'What the hell do you think you're doing?'

'I might well ask you the same question,' she hissed, thrusting the papers into his face. 'What's this all about?'

'What's wrong, son?' asked Maisie, on the verge of tears.

'Keep out of this, Mum.'

'Your cleaner is your *mother*?' asked Sara, for one second forgetting why she was there.

'No. Yes. Never mind. What are you doing here?'

'Isn't it obvious? How else was I going to find out that Stuart was my father? From the front page of the *Comet*?'

'No. Cynthia's blocked the story. She doesn't want people to know about Stuart's illegitimate child. It would reflect badly on her.'

Sara couldn't believe she was having this conversation. 'Where the hell did you get all this from?'

'Cynthia found the papers when she went through Stuart's effects. She gave it to me as background material,' he said matter-of-factly.

'How do you live with yourself?' whispered Sara. It didn't seem to occur to him what information like this could do to someone.

For the first time since she had confronted him, Christopher showed some emotion. 'It wasn't money, if that's what you think. I'm not that cheap.'

'No?'

'Cynthia always likes to have something over her employees – a little bit of extra insurance. It keeps them loyal.'

'So what tawdry little affair is she holding over you?'

Christopher let out a bitter laugh. 'I wish it were that simple. With me, Cynthia has a whole file on my illustrious background. Or rather lack of it.' He held his hand out to Maisie.

'Go on,' said Sara.

'All that stuff I told you before about India was crap. I was born in the East End to Maisie and Albert Worgan. I was named John. I desperately wanted to get away from my background so I recreated myself. I became Christopher Heard. Cynthia found out about it when she rang and spoke to Maisie here one day. My mother didn't know that she and Dad were a dirty secret. That, of course, is why I was so thrown when you said you'd met her. Anyway, Cynthia knew that she could easily ruin my cred. as a gossip columnist if the story got out.'

'God, what a terrible secret.' Sara's voice was heavy with sarcasm. Poor old Maisie – what had she done to deserve a son like this?

Maisie's vain offspring at least had the grace to look slightly ashamed. 'I know it doesn't make it right, but that's why I did what Cynthia wanted. I know you won't believe me when I say I did really like you.'

'You're damned right, I don't,' spat Sara furiously. 'I want to know what else you've got on me. Who's my mother?'

'You've seen the name.'

'So?'

'And you don't know who she is?' he asked in amazement.

'If I did I wouldn't be standing here talking to you,' she snapped.

'She's the Butterfly.'

'Felicity Butterworth is the Butterfly?' repeated Sara, thinking of all the pictures she'd seen of the model. 'And she's my *mother*?'

'She disappeared in 1966, just before you were born.'

'Where is she now?'

'I assume you've seen that letter. Somewhere in Brazil, probably. There was no address on it.'

The doorbell rang. 'Excuse me,' said Christopher as he pressed the intercom to admit the caller. He was too distracted to worry about Maisie or ask who was there but the voice calling from the top of the stairs was all too familiar.

'Hiya, it's only me.' Maggie Lawrence appeared in the hallway, dressed from head to toe in red, her face turning the same shade at the sight of Sara. 'What the fuck is she doing here?'

'Leave it, Maggie, Sara was just going.'

'No, I'm not leaving it,' screamed Maggie. 'She's here to get you back. She just can't stand losing you to me.'

'I don't believe you,' said Sara, quietly. 'You're completely insane.'

'Don't you dare talk to me about insane! I know you, remember? I took you into my home after you killed Bill and you were a fucking zombie. I looked after you, and how did you repay me?'

'You're not going to bring up that slug Huw again – not after all the disgusting things you've done to me.'

'Sniffing around him like some sex-crazed bitch on heat.'

Sara looked at Christopher, pleading with him. 'Shut her up. Shut her up now.'

'I'm not finished yet.' Maggie was screeching at the top of her voice, jabbing a finger into Sara's chest. 'You know, there's a poetic justice to all this. I take it you now know a little bit more about your family tree. Darling June and dear, dead Harry lied to you. Nobody cared enough about your feelings to tell you the truth. Well, I'll tell you. Your real mother was some slag knocked up by a man who'd poked every tart in London. A quick fuck up an alleyway, more than likely. They were no strangers to it. But to top it all, that slag of a mother chucked you away with the rest of the rubbish when the knitting needle failed.' Maggie was purple with rage. 'Just like you made me throw away my baby. Now you know how it feels.'

Sara lost it completely. With all the force she could muster, she dealt Maggie an almighty whack across the face. Then, her heart breaking, she left, clutching the damning papers to her chest.

Chapter Thirty-Five

Sara sat in her car, staring into space, oblivious to the rain splashing against the windscreen, her knuckles white from gripping the steering wheel. She felt as if she were in free fall. She was the little girl whose daddy had spun her round, promising he'd hold on to her and never let her go. But it was just another lie: he let her go and she was hurtling through space. Harry wasn't her father, Stuart was. And he'd lied too. 'My name is Justine Butterworth,' she said out loud, over and over again, as if the repetition would somehow make it real. Everything she had ever believed in had been taken away. Why had nobody ever said anything? There had been so many times when she'd asked June outright why she was so antagonistic towards Stuart, and June had looked her in the face and simply lied. That was it. She had to go and see her to demand some explanations.

Sara drove in a trance, hardly noticing that she had reached the M4. Out on the open road she forced the accelerator to the floor and was soon reaching speeds of 120 mph, not caring if there were

police patrol cars around. Her mind was blank; she no longer knew
who she was. The only certainty was that she wasn't the person she
had thought she was yesterday. It was like waking up with amnesia.
She needed a whole new past to be written out for her.

In just over an hour Sara reached the outskirts of Bristol and
was forced to lower her speed to 60 mph as she dodged the
city's traffic. Soon she had crossed the city and was on the dual
carriageway approaching Backwell. Finally, she reached June's
village, turning into the road lined with identical pastel-coloured
bungalows.

Sara stopped in front of her mother's neat rose garden and
switched off the engine. The bungalow, once so reassuringly
familiar, now seemed alien, a place groaning with deceit. For a
moment, she thought that she might just drive away again but
before she had a chance to make up her mind the door of the
bungalow opened and the porch light came on.

'Sara, is that you?' called June from the hallway.

Sara was shaking. All the confrontations she'd had in the past
paled into insignificance compared with this one. She'd rather face
a million Mickey Nashes than the deceptively benign old lady
standing in her slippers at the end of the path.

June came down to the gate and a delighted smile spread across
her face. 'Sara, my love, what are you doing here?' she asked as her
daughter climbed out of the Porsche. 'My, what a lovely car! Why
didn't you ring? I would have made you a birthday cake.' She held
out her arms for a hug but Sara pushed past her and walked into
the house.

'Sara?' called June, running after her. 'What on earth is the
matter?'

'Why didn't you tell me?' Sara reared up to her full height, for
once not trying to minimise her stature in the cramped living room.
'You lied to me, *June*.'

It was the first time her daughter had ever used her Christian
name and it sounded so strange on her lips. Immediately, June
knew what Sara was so upset about and she began to panic. 'What
have I done?'

Sara pulled out the papers she had taken from Christopher and searched through them until she found what she was looking for. 'I assume this is familiar,' she said, thrusting her birth certificate into June's hand.

'Of course. It's your birth certificate,' she replied, her voice a whisper.

'Yes?' said Sara, impatiently.

June started to cry. The harshness of Sara's voice frightened her. This was the moment she'd dreaded for twenty-seven years. 'Sara, please.'

'Look at the date, Mother. It's six months after I was born.' A thought suddenly occurred to her. 'So that's why you insisted on getting my passport for me when I was going to New York? You never wanted me to see this. Did you think I could live my whole life without seeing my birth certificate?'

June dropped on to the sofa and began to sob. 'Sara, please believe me, it was for the best.'

'For the *best*?' screamed Sara. 'The newspapers were investigating me. How long do you think it would have been before this was on the front page? How can you say it was for the best?'

'Your dad and I thought—'

'Who do you mean? Stuart or Harry?' asked Sara, a sob catching in her throat.

'Harry, of course. He was your father and I'm your mother, whatever that certificate says.' June's voice rose. 'I may not have given birth to you, Sara, but I am your mother.'

Sara looked away, trying to shut out June's distress. She needed to go on, to get to the bottom of things, and if she didn't get her answers now, she knew she'd never have the courage to upset her like this again. 'Were you and Stuart in this together?'

'He . . . he contacted me when you were a teenager. I don't know how he found me. I begged him not to tell you. I thought we should let sleeping dogs lie. I couldn't see how it would benefit you to know. It was too late in the day.'

'Did you know he was helping me all along? Right from the beginning of my career.'

'Yes,' replied June, flatly. 'But I didn't want him to.'

'He sent me a letter anonymously. You read about that club in the papers. I was nearly killed doing his dirty work ...' She sobbed. 'I hate him, and I hate you for not telling me the truth.'

June's face had drained of all colour. 'Oh, Sara, please forgive me. Stuart was wrong, and I'd be the last person to defend him, but I do believe he was only trying to help you along.'

'No, he wasn't,' she replied bitterly, 'he was just getting me to finish some unfinished business.' She didn't go on to say that, despite everything, she was still doing his dirty work. It would merely cloud the matter in hand.

June tried to put her hand on Sara's arm but her daughter shrugged it off. 'How often did you speak to him? When did it start?' In her head another piece of the jigsaw fell into place. 'My school fees. I suppose he paid for those?'

June looked down at the floor.

'And what about the medical bills? Tell me,' pleaded Sara, the foundations on which she'd built her life beginning to disintegrate. 'God, how could I have been naïve enough to think Dad would've had an insurance policy that paid out fifty-five thousand pounds?' How many more lies was she going to unearth?

'Stuart insisted. I was no match for him, Sara. You know what he was like.'

Sara shook her head in disbelief, and a strand of hair fell into her eyes. Pushing it away impatiently she said, 'And even while I was getting all that stick from the newspapers about having an affair with him you still decided to keep quiet?'

'I wanted to tell you. I came up to London to tell you after he died, but it just never seemed to be the right moment. And I didn't know whether it would do more harm than good.'

'The damage your lies have caused is irreparable.' Sara knew she was being cruel, but her own hurt was too great to leave any room for generosity.

'Don't say that, please, Sara. Nothing's changed. I'm still the person who brought you up, who loved you as my own. No, more than my own. You were so special to us. We *chose* you.' June stood up and opened the sideboard drawer. Pulling out a tattered, yellowing sheet of paper she said, 'Look, Harry, cut this out when we first had you. It says everything we felt.'

There was a poem printed on the paper. As Sara read it, her eyes brimmed with new tears.

> Lord, let the wind be beautiful with song,
> The stars unusually gold and bright.
> The child we have wanted for so long
> Is sleeping here beneath our roof tonight.
> In some-day moments, Lord, when we explain
> To ~~him~~ her that (s)he is not our flesh and blood,
> O may our love be as a gentle rain
> Upon a greening meadow or a wood.
> May our togetherness be as a tower,
> Our faith more strong than any steel or stone,
> And please, Lord, never let there be an hour
> When (s)he will feel that (s)he is not our own.

The poem as printed used the masculine pronoun, but Harry had carefully added an 's' in front of all the 'he's in black ink. Sara began to cry openly. 'But you didn't explain, did you?'

June went to embrace her, 'Sara, please—'

'I'm sorry, I just can't handle this at the moment. I've got to go.' Sara moved away and took a deep breath, trying to control her sobbing. 'Just tell me one thing. Do you know where my real mother is?'

'I'm here,' cried June. '*I'm* your mother.'

'Well, where is Felicity Butterworth?'

'I don't know. I honestly don't.'

'OK. I'm leaving now, I'll—'

June grabbed Sara's hand. 'Please don't go. You can't leave me like this. It's late. You're in too much of a state to drive. Stay with me tonight. We'll talk about it in the morning. We'll sort it out, make everything all right.'

'I can't. I've nothing to say. Mum . . .' she left the word hanging in the air for a moment before continuing, 'I need time to think.

We're both too emotional at the moment.' At the front door she tried to give the poem back to June. 'Here.'

June brushed it away. 'Keep it. It'll remind you of just how much we loved you.'

Sara folded the yellowing piece of paper, put it in her pocket, and walked out to her car.

Kathy stood outside Stephen's office, trying to summon up the courage to go in. She could hear him on the telephone and, as usual, he didn't sound in the best of moods.

'Listen,' he shouted, 'I thought we had a deal with that defender? The way he performed, you'd think he was trying out for England. What the fuck was he playing at? I lost a hundred grand. He's got to be sorted. Hang on a minute, Frank, someone's listening. Who's out there?'

Kathy jumped. She thought about walking away, but her concern for Sara was greater than Stephen's wrath. Sara had been missing for two days now. Norman was still at Primrose Hill and he was beside himself. After all, he was supposed to be protecting her. She wouldn't have gone away without leaving a message. Something terrible must have happened. 'It's just me, Mr Powell, Kathy Clarke,' she said, walking into his office.

'Are you eavesdropping?'

Kathy hesitated, overwhelmed by the smell of stale body odour that permeated Stephen's paper-strewn office. 'No, of course not. I wanted to wait until you finished your conversation. I just—'

'If you've come to talk to me about Jackie . . .' He stopped talking, realising that he still had the telephone in his hand. 'Sorry, Frank, I've got to go. I'll give you a bell later – and I'd feel a lot happier if you could come up with some sort of explanation by then.' He threw the receiver on to its cradle. 'So what do you want? Out with it. I haven't got all day.'

'I just wondered if you knew where Sara was. We had a meeting arranged yesterday but she didn't turn up, and she's not in today. I tried phoning her—'

Stephen interrupted her. 'Are you accusing me of something?'

Kathy hadn't seriously considered that Stephen could be behind

Sara's disappearance, but the memory of the threats he'd already made against Sara created a new sense of panic. Why did Sara not make better use of Norman's services? If Kathy had somebody like Stephen on her case, she would want round-the-clock protection. 'Well, it wouldn't be the first time, would it?'

'Perhaps she's had a car crash,' he said with a menacing sneer. 'I read in the papers that she's a bit naughty behind the wheel. I don't know and I don't give a shit. But while we're on the subject of missing persons, have you seen old lard-arse this morning?'

Kathy couldn't bear the way he spoke about Jackie. She gave him a look full of loathing. 'You're disgusting.'

Stephen put on a whiny voice. 'Oh, no, I've really been put in my place now, haven't I?' He stood up and roared, 'Go on, fuck off out of here, you whingeing tart!'

Kathy stalked out of the office. The sooner Jackie was rid of him – the sooner they were all rid of him, for that matter – the better. She headed back to the bar, where she'd left Jackie sipping on an orange juice. Kathy hoped that would be all she was sipping when she returned. Today was the big day. Stephen's wife was due at the Four Seasons Clinic in a couple of hours, and the first rule was that all clients should arrive sober.

'Did you find her?' asked Jackie. Her voice had a new crispness without the influence of alcohol.

Kathy shook her head. 'As you can imagine, Stephen wasn't very helpful. He was in a very bad mood but he cheered up at the thought that Sara might have had a car crash.'

'You would have heard something,' consoled Jackie. 'Bad news travels fast. The police or the hospital, someone would have been in touch. She'll turn up. People don't go missing like that for long.' She went quiet, thinking about Felicity. 'You didn't say anything to Stephen about me, did you?'

'Of course not. But we'd better get going, he was asking where you were. Have you got everything with you?' Kathy cast an eye over the four suitcases lined up by the bar.

'Just about,' she replied, smiling.

'Let's go, then. I've told the cab to wait around the corner, just in case. I only hope we can carry all this.' Kathy picked up two of the suitcases. 'God, Jackie, what are you taking?'

'Only the essentials.'

Kathy dragged the cases along the floor wondering whether her arms would stay in their sockets. If her plan worked out, Jackie wouldn't be needing any of the stuff she'd packed for much longer. As soon as Jackie sorted out her drinking, Kathy would sort out her wardrobe, hair and make-up for her. She glanced across at Jackie affectionately. The candy-floss ginger hair, the Dusty Springfield eyes, the cheap dresses and precipitous heels. All that was going to change.

They finally made it to the taxi, where the driver watched impassively as they struggled to get the suitcases in.

'Thanks,' said Kathy.

'Where is it you want?' he asked, ignoring her sarcastic tone.

'Four Seasons. It's just off Kensington High Street.'

'Never heard of it. What is it, a hotel?'

Kathy looked behind her, half expecting Stephen to come running round the corner any second. 'Kind of. Can we just go, please?'

The driver tutted but drove off. Both Jackie and Kathy breathed a sigh of relief. They'd escaped without Stephen seeing them.

'That was the easy bit,' said Kathy.

'I know. What if I can't do it? What if I have to go back to Stephen?'

Kathy took Jackie's hand in hers. 'I know you can do it. And once you're back, we can all work together. From what Sara has said, Stephen isn't going to be around much longer.'

'I wish I could believe that, but he always comes up trumps. We'll be the ones out on our ears.' She was very worried that her husband had already seen off Sara, but she didn't want to upset Kathy.

'It's going to be fine,' said Kathy, wishing she believed that herself.

Kathy told the driver where to turn off along Kensington High Street and as he parked outside the clinic, Jackie looked out the window apprehensively.

'Come on.' Kathy jumped out of the cab, and once again without any assistance from the driver, wrestled with the suitcases.

'That'll be nine-fifty,' said the driver watching her lift the bags on to the kerb.

Kathy sorted out all the change in her purse and counted out the exact fare. 'Oh, and here's a tip. The next time you see a woman struggling like that, get off your fat arse and help her.'

'That's not like you,' said Jackie, as the cabbie drove off in a huff.

'I think it's being around Stephen. It starts to rub off.'

'I know you're really worried about Sara. But she'll be all right. She's smart, and she knows what she's doing.'

Kathy smiled, wanting Jackie to be right. If she didn't calm down a bit the clinic would assume she was the client rather than Jackie.

As soon as they entered the clinic's revolving door, the roar of the London traffic faded to a subdued hum. All was calm inside, from the muted green, plant-bedecked colour scheme to the relaxed-looking white-suited staff. At the beechwood reception desk, Jackie spoke in a whisper. 'My name's Jackie Powell.' She nearly added: 'And I'm an alcoholic,' the way they did in the films.

'Ah, yes Mrs Powell. You're in room 402.' The receptionist waved at a man standing by the lift. 'Tony, can you show our new guest to her room? Mrs Powell, the doctor will be round to see you after you've settled in.'

'Do you want me to come with you?' asked Kathy.

'You've done more than enough. I'll be all right now. Go on, I bet Sara's trying to get in touch with you.'

'Are you sure?'

'Yes. Go on, before I lose my nerve.'

The two women hugged and Kathy said, 'I'll come and see you on Sunday. Good luck.'

Antonio walked into Stephen's smoke-filled office, worried that Stephen had some bad news about Sara. Nobody seemed to know where she was.

'You asked to see me,' said the Brazilian.

'I just wanted a quiet chat while madam's not around.'

'Do you know where Senhora Moore is?'

'What's it to you?' asked Stephen, suspiciously.

Antonio paced round the room, wishing he could open the window and let in some fresh air. 'I ... she wanted to see me about the transfer. I thought—'

'Now, you listen to me,' said Stephen, standing up behind his desk. He walked over to the footballer. 'Your transfer is between me and your agent. It's none of that bitch's business. And while we're at it, your agent led me to believe you'd behave.'

'I don't understand.'

'There's nothing for you to understand. You just do as you're told.'

Antonio stood still, every muscle flexing as Stephen came closer to him. 'What do you mean?'

'I want you to drop a game.'

'How could you benefit from Camden losing?'

'That's not for you to worry about.'

'But—'

'You'd be well paid.'

'I don't want—'

'You owe me one. After all, you would be dead now if I hadn't dragged you away from Brazil.' Stephen clicked his fingers. 'I could send you back there just like that.'

Chapter Thirty-Six

Sara had checked into a hotel in the centre of Bristol and for two days she hadn't left her room. Her intention had been to go to a travel agent and book a flight, anywhere, and leave the whole sorry mess behind her. But when it came to the crunch, she couldn't just up and go like that. For one thing, Kathy would be worried out of her mind. Even if she called her to let her know, it wouldn't solve the bigger problem. It was impossible to leave so much unfinished business. She realised that wherever she went in the world, questions about her identity would remain hanging over her head. It wasn't something from which you could run away. Not until everything had been sorted out – the club, Stephen, her mother June, her mother Felicity, everything – could she escape. She couldn't even begin to deal with her feelings for Antonio. Yes, she had said she loved him. But she knew now that love was no guarantee against betrayal.

Leaving the hotel, Sara drove back up the M4, not much more slowly than she'd driven down it a couple of days earlier. Yet her anger had now given way to remorse. She shouldn't have left June in that state. But she didn't know what else she could say: the sense of betrayal was too strong to allow Sara to forgive her there and then. She didn't know where to go next, either. She would have liked to have talked to Kathy, but she had no wish to return to the club. What she wanted to do, more than anything else, was to find her real mother. The only clue she had to her whereabouts was the letter from Brazil. It was funny how that country kept recurring in her life.

As she edged her way on to the A40 she thought about Stuart and their conversations over the years. She remembered the time he had told her that he was a weak man who had sacrificed much for his career. Had that included Felicity? Had he known Felicity was pregnant? Had he wanted her to have an abortion? Was that what he had meant? She wanted to hate him, but in spite of everything, she couldn't. If he had not wanted her as a child, he had certainly tried to make it up to her. But what about her mother? Why hadn't Felicity kept her? Why had she given baby Justine away like so much jumble? Sara felt that familiar ache in her stomach as she thought about the children she'd never be able to have. What would make a woman want to give up her child? She didn't know where to turn. The one person who held all the answers was dead.

But his wife was still alive. Sara pulled over by a phone box on the corner of the street. Christopher Heard owed her a huge favour.

'Darlings, I can't take your call at—'

It was his answering machine. She cut off the call and dialled the number of the *Herald*. To her surprise she was put through straight away.

'Christopher, it's Sara.'

'Sara! I just want to say—'

'Don't bother with the small talk. I need to get in and see Cynthia and I need your help to do it.'

'But—'

'Shut up, I'm thinking. Is she having any meetings – with anyone she doesn't know, I mean?'

'I'd have to check with her secretary, but I do happen to know that she's scheduled to see a group of bankers this afternoon. I don't see how that helps.'

Sara thought quickly, remembering that at the *Herald* the names of any visitors for Cynthia were put on a separate list at reception. 'All you've got to do is put a name on the list downstairs. Tell reception the bank's just rung through on the wrong line to say they're sending someone else.'

'I'll get the sack.'

'If you don't do it immediately I'll call the *Mail*. I'm sure Nigel Dempster would be very interested in Maisie.'

'OK, OK. What shall I call you?'

'Miss Smith will do. I'm on my way now.'

Cynthia smiled at the group of men around the table, but inside she was cursing Stuart for creating a situation in which she, Cynthia Hargreaves, had to go cap in hand to the money men. 'I'm sure you'll see from our projections that we are expecting to get enough revenue to cover the running costs for the next quarter.'

'But they're just projections,' said Samuel Belfield. 'There's no hard evidence that Alive TV is going to reach its audience target, is there, Mrs Hargreaves? And there's no mention of BSkyB here. Can you compete with them?'

'Of course,' she snapped. Then, remembering who she was talking to, she adopted a more reasoned manner. 'Mr Belfield, isn't it? I think with our mix of programmes we can compete with BSkyB on every level.' She clicked her fingers at the *Herald*'s company secretary. 'John, show Mr Belfield BSkyB's market share and the forecast for ours.'

John jumped up from his seat and did as he was told, passing copies to each of the bankers.

'I see here you're planning a channel of classic films,' said another. 'I assume "classic" means films which have been shown several times on TV before?'

The other bankers laughed.

'You think the idiots that buy these dishes care if they've seen it all before?' Cynthia saw John shaking his head worriedly and calmed herself. 'Of course, we've signed up several of the Hollywood majors to supply new product.'

Mr Belfield coughed. 'At an extortionate price, I would say.'

'It's my mon—' Cynthia didn't finish her sentence. It wasn't her money now. She hoped Stuart was burning in hell.

'Mrs Hargreaves, if we lend you the fifteen million you're asking for, over what timescale are the repayments going to be made?' asked Mr Belfield, looking down at the folder of documents in front of him. 'I can't see any mention of that.'

'I knew that any timescale I put in would be whittled down by you fellows – and ladies,' she remembered to add, just in time, for the benefit of the two female bankers. 'So I thought we would thrash it out here,' Cynthia finished with a false laugh. Until all this had happened, she'd never had to ask anyone for a penny in her life. It was so humiliating. Just then the door to the conference room opened. 'What the hell are you doing here?' snarled Cynthia.

Sara pointed a finger at her. 'I want a word with you.'

'How did you get in? John, I want this woman arrested.'

'Stay where you are, John,' warned Sara.

The company secretary remained motionless.

'John!' screeched Cynthia.

There were uncomfortable murmurs and coughs from the bankers as the beautiful but dishevelled and obviously unhinged woman advanced on the *Herald*'s proprietor.

'Cynthia, if you don't want me to embarrass you, you'll step outside now and give me a minute of your time.' Sara was surprised to hear her own voice sounding so calm.

'One minute, that's it. Excuse me.'

'In the meantime if we could just turn to page four to run through the ideas for the pay-per-view sports channel,' said John to distract the bankers' attention.

'I can't believe you have the audacity to show your face here,' hissed Cynthia as she closed the door.

'Believe me, Cynthia, I'd rather be anywhere else but I need to find Felicity Butterworth. My mother.'

If Cynthia was surprised that Sara had this information she didn't let on. Instead, she laughed in Sara's face. 'I have no idea where that slut is. And even if I did know, why would I help you? I wouldn't even be having that dismal little meeting in there if it wasn't for you. Now get out, before I have you carried out.'

Sara ignored her. 'Why did Stuart—'

'Haven't I made myself clear? I've nothing to say to you,' said Cynthia. 'Except perhaps one thing. How did it feel to find out you had been lusting after your own father?' Satisfied by the look of horror on Sara's face, Cynthia went back into the conference room. 'John, tell Christopher Heard to come to my office at six sharp. Now, gentlemen, ladies, where were we?'

Opening the door to her mews house, Sara felt like crying. Norman wasn't there. He was probably trying to find her. The emptiness of the place was palpable, echoing and intensifying her loneliness. She wouldn't have Norman forever, anyway. Perhaps she should get a cat, something that would at least be pleased to see her at the end of each day. In the darkness, she could see the flashing red light of her answerphone. She switched it on, glad to hear a human voice. Most of the messages were from Kathy, the note of panic in her voice increasing with each call.

Sara picked up the cordless phone and dialled Kathy's number as she rummaged in the fridge for something edible. Everything smelled bad, so she settled for a bottle of wine. Cradling the receiver between ear and shoulder, she struggled to open the bottle. The cork popped out just as Kathy answered.

'Kathy, it's Sara.'

'Where have you been?' asked Kathy. 'I've been at my wits' end.'

'I'm sorry . . . it's . . . it's . . .' She broke down.

'Sara, what's wrong? What's happened?' Kathy pleaded, panic in her voice. 'Not Nash? I warned Stephen—'

'No, no, it's nothing like that. It's about Stuart,' she managed. 'You're not going to believe this,' she said, drinking straight from the bottle. 'Stuart was my father.'

'What?'

Even saying the words felt strange. 'June and Harry aren't my real parents. They adopted me. Stuart was my father and Felicity Butterworth was my mother.'

'The Butterfly is your *mother*?' squeaked Kathy.

'Yes.' Sara began to cry gently. 'Kathy, I just don't know what to think. As soon as I found out I went down and saw my mother, June, that is – God, this is all so confusing – and I had it out with her. After that I booked into a hotel and just hid.'

'Sara, I'm on my way over now.'

'No, please. I want to be on my own. I'm still really angry. I don't want to use you as a punchbag.'

'I'm your friend. That's what I'm there for.'

'I know, and thank you. But I'm still trying to get my head round it.'

'How did you find all this out?'

'That's the worst part of it. What am I saying? It's all the worst part. Christopher Heard was investigating me – with a little help from Maggie.'

'Christ, that woman is one evil—'

'Forget it. She's no worse than anybody else in this. At least she's not afraid to come out and say what's on her mind. Which is more than June has ever been able to do.'

'Nobody could possibly love you more than June.'

'I don't want to hear that. I don't want to be told how a bunch of liars loved me. Stuart controlled my life for years, and he's still doing it from the grave,' said Sara, her voice raised with indignation and hurt.

'Please, Sara, let me come over.'

'No. I'm going to go now. Could you do me a favour and bring some pictures of the Butterfly into work tomorrow?'

'Are you sure you're up to going in?'

'What else is there aside from work? I'm really angry that Stuart left me such a mess to sort out. I can't walk away from it, though, and he knew I wouldn't be able to.'

'If you want to call at any time in the night, you know you can.'

'I know. I'll see you tomorrow,' said Sara, hanging up.

She poured herself a large glass of wine and went upstairs to her bedroom, where she spread out all the documents she had taken from Christopher. She reread the letter from Felicity to Stuart, hoping to discover something about her mother's personality. Perhaps she should just leave it. Her mother obviously hadn't wanted her. But how could she leave it? She needed to find out about her beginnings. She had to discover why she'd been rejected. The letter said so little. She put it back in its envelope with the Brazilian postmark. Was there a chance her mother could still be there now?

The doorbell rang. Damn, thought Sara. It had to be Kathy. Obviously her friend hadn't believed her when she'd said she wanted to be alone. She walked wearily down the stairs and opened the door. 'Kathy . . .'

But it wasn't Kathy.

'Sara! Where have you been?' asked Antonio frantically.

'What are you doing here?'

'I . . . Kathy asked me to come.'

'What?'

'She was worried and thought maybe I could help. Can I come in? It's a bit cold,' he said, shivering as he smiled.

'Antonio, this really isn't a good time.' Sara tried to close the door but the Brazilian stopped the door with his hand.

'Sara, please,' he said, pushing his way into the hall. 'I want to know what's wrong.' He followed her through to the chicly spartan living room. 'Why are you hiding from me?'

'You think this is about you? God, you flatter yourself.'

'I thought it was about *us*.'

'There is no us.' She began to cry.

'Don't say that,' said Antonio passionately. For the previous few days he had thought of little else but the two of them. 'I thought I meant as much to you as you mean to me.'

Sara collapsed on to a deep, low-backed smoke-blue sofa, the events of those few days weighing heavily upon her. The only truly decent, honest person she'd ever loved had been Bill, and he had been taken away from her. How could she open her heart to Antonio, a man shrouded in so much uncertainty? How big a fool could she be? Her tears came thick and fast; her chest hurt. When Antonio sat beside her, taking her in his arms, it felt so right that she knew, for just that moment, she could be the biggest fool in the world.

'It hurts me so much to see you like this,' he said, kissing away the tears from her eyes. 'I feel your pain like it is my own.' He smoothed back her hair from her face and pressed his lips gently against her temple. 'What's wrong?' he whispered.

Her story came out in pieces. The confusion on Antonio's face echoed her own. Every now and then, when the anguish became too much, she would stop and he would squeeze her tighter, urging her on. Yes, she was spinning, but this man was promising that he wouldn't let her fall. Words tumbled out of her, one minute angry, the next hurt, but even in her blackest rage, Antonio held on, saying nothing, just letting her feel with every bone in her body that he was there for her.

Finally, Sara felt as though she were no longer talking about herself. Repeating the story over and over did nothing to make it any more real. As her diatribe ended, Antonio's kisses took on a new urgency, and though her body ached to respond to him, to be healed by his love, she found herself pushing him away.

'How can I do this?' she asked, wrapping her arms tightly around herself. 'I've just told you how the people I loved most in the world schemed and lied to me, and here I am opening myself up for you to do it to me again. Your transfer—'

'Sara, how many times do we have to go through this?'

'Then make me believe you. Tell me you had nothing to do with it.'

'Stephen arranged the transfer with an agent. I was running for my life – there was no time for me to be involved. Sara, I love you and I could never betray you.'

Sara looked at him and saw the one rock-steady point in the shifting sands of her life. He was the only thing she had to hold on to. If she didn't trust him, she would go mad. She had to surrender to the love she felt for him. 'I believe you,' she said, welcoming him into her arms again.

Chapter Thirty-Seven

When Sara arrived at the club late the following morning, Kathy had already been at work for two hours, finalising the details of the Casserly Cars sponsorship deal. Kathy seemed worried that she'd made a mistake in confiding in Antonio, but Sara reassured her that it was the best thing that could have happened.

'It's so strange,' said Sara, glancing at the Casserly file, relieved that at least Kathy was keeping things ticking over at Camden. 'I feel so down and so up at the same time. I'd hate to think I was one of those women who don't care that their lives are terrible as long as they've got a man.'

Kathy laughed. 'You're not like that at all. You've fallen in love, and if that helps to ease the pain for the moment, what's so wrong with that?'

'I just don't want it to get in the way. I've got so much to sort out.'

'Oh, that reminds me,' said Kathy, pulling three photographic books out of her bag. 'You said last night you wanted to look at these. I've put post-its on the relevant pages.'

Sara opened the book on *Vogue* in the sixties she'd seen in Kathy's house. She hadn't paid much attention to the shots of Felicity Butterworth then – she'd been looking for pictures of Jackie – and she couldn't remember what Felicity looked like. The first was in black and white, and with the sixties penchant for whiting out everything, it was hard to make out Felicity's – her mother's – features. But the next photograph was in colour and the image was clearer. Sara couldn't believe she had flicked past this without noticing the startling similarity to herself. It was eerie, like looking in a mirror. Felicity had the same red curls and translucent green eyes, features Sara had always believed she'd inherited from Harry.

'She was beautiful,' said Kathy.

The use of the past tense shook Sara. With all the emotional turmoil of the past few days, it hadn't even occurred to her that Felicity might not be alive 'What if she's dead?' she asked.

'I'm sure she's not. Surely there would have been some press coverage.'

'No one's seen her for nearly thirty years. Why would there be?'

'Perhaps Jackie knows what happened to her.' Kathy hit her head with the palm of her hand. 'What an idiot I am. Why didn't I think of her in the first place? I'm going to see her tomorrow. Why don't you come with me?'

'Do you think she can be trusted not to tell Stephen?'

'Absolutely. She wouldn't give that man—' She stopped. Sara was immersed once again in the pictures of her mother. Kathy had read the books. There was scant biographical detail about the Butterfly but she knew that every word and illustration would be precious to Sara. 'I've got to get on,' she said, slipping out of the office.

Impatiently, Sara turned to the next picture, the one taken at David Bailey's wedding. Stephen was standing with his arm around Felicity and Jackie was huddled next to Stuart. It was hard to see the resemblance in this photograph as most of Felicity's face was hidden by a wide-brimmed hat.

Sara wondered if the affair between her parents had begun at the time this picture was taken. This is my family, Sara told herself; this is my mum and this is my dad. The gulf between this picture and the family snapshots of Harry and June taken with Harry's old Brownie couldn't have been greater. Stuart and Felicity had their photographs in *Vogue*; Harry and June had theirs in a shoebox in the sideboard.

Turning to another of the books, Sara found some beachwear shots which, if she squinted, could have come from the *Mariella* Coney Island shoot. She ran her fingertip over Felicity's features, so reminiscent of her own. She stared at the Butterfly trying to categorise what she felt. Intense curiosity, certainly; anger, too, she decided. It was unfair that so much of her fury had been directed solely at June. There were four people party to this deception, and possibly only two of them were dead.

As usual, the Four Seasons clinic was a haven of calm. Sara and Kathy both stood in reception listening to the muted strains of Satie wafting from the concealed speakers. 'I think I could do with a few weeks in here,' said Kathy.

Sara smiled nervously, dying to speak to Jackie.

'Kathy, Sara, over here,' sang out a confident voice.

Both women turned to see Jackie appearing from one of the consultation rooms, looking happier than they'd ever seen her before. Four days at the clinic, and already she was beginning to lose some of the puffiness around her face. She'd lost a few pounds, too, but that was nothing compared to the psychological weight she was shedding. With the help of the clinic's intensive therapy sessions, she was working through why she felt the need to be in an abusive relationship and without alcohol to blur her mind, she was rapidly coming to the conclusion that she didn't need to be in one at all.

'You look fantastic,' said Kathy, full of admiration for what Jackie had achieved. 'When you were drinking your eyes had that hooded look all the time. But I can see real vitality in them now. I mean it. You're doing something to be really proud of.'

'Yes, you look great,' added Sara, inspired by the older woman's decision to confront all her demons.

'I've had a little help,' replied Jackie, looking across at the staff milling around. 'I've got to admit that I'm starting to feel like a new woman. It's just a shame I've got this old woman's body.'

'I knew you were going to say that so I've booked us into Mischa's for a complete make-over this morning.'

'It's early days, Kathy,' said Jackie, frightened by Kathy's confidence in her. 'I'm not out of the woods yet. What's the point of a make-over when I could be back on the bottle next week?'

'It's not going to happen. Look, I'm celebrating. The bank has finally given me back my credit card and I want to indulge myself. The clinic has okayed it.'

'I need to speak to you,' said Sara, unable to hide the urgency in her voice.

'What's wrong? Is it Stephen?'

'Indirectly.'

'God, that man,' seethed Jackie. 'Let me get my coat.'

Mischa's was a new beauty salon in Knightsbridge catering to the professional woman. In the large grey-painted reception area, alongside the luxurious cream leather sofas, there were telephones, fax machines, even a computer for those women who felt too guilty to surrender themselves totally to the expert pampering of the Paris-trained staff.

'How am I going to afford this?' whispered Jackie as they were shown into one of the treatment rooms.

'Don't worry about it,' said Sara, as she loosened her towel and climbed on to a massage table. 'You can bill Stephen.'

'What?'

'I'm joking. It's my treat. There's a lot I want to ask you about Felicity Butterworth.'

'Oh? Why is that?'

Sara took a deep breath. 'Because I have just discovered that she's my mother. And Stuart Hargreaves was my father.' As she spoke she saw first the shock and then the sadness in Jackie's face as the woman took in the fact that she was looking at the child of her long-lost friend.

'I should have guessed,' she said finally. 'I knew there was something familiar about you, but I was always too sloshed to work out what it was. Looking at you now, it's as if she were here again. What did the drink do to my mind? My life has been—'

'That's all in the past,' interrupted Kathy, not wanting Jackie to falter. 'It's all over with.'

'The past is never over with,' said Jackie. 'Look how Sara is still having to deal with it. These things creep up on you. How can you ever escape from them?'

'Jackie, we can talk about this at another time,' said Sara. Perhaps in her own haste to find out about Felicity she was putting an unfair burden on Jackie at such a delicate stage of her recovery.

'I don't mind. Talking about it is the only way we're going to get through. Ask me anything you want.'

'Do you know where she is?'

Jackie shook her head. 'I never heard anything of her after she disappeared.'

Sara wasn't surprised by this. 'What do you know about her and Stuart?'

'Felicity used to be Stephen's fiancée, and—'

Three masseuses appeared. On tenterhooks, Sara waited for them to prepare their treatments and very soon the air was filled with the smell of ylang-ylang mixed with frankincense as the three women's bodies were covered with aromatherapy oils. For a while the attentive hands of the masseuse soothed away her concerns, but gradually the unpleasant idea that she shared the same blood as a woman once attracted to Stephen Powell undid all the magic being performed on her back.

'You were saying,' said Sara, feeling that perhaps she didn't want to hear what was coming next.

'They were together for quite a while and—'

Sara sat up. 'Oh, my God!' she exclaimed with a suddenness which startled the masseuse and made her drop a bottle of oil, 'Stephen couldn't be my father, could he?'

Jackie laughed. 'Stephen fires blanks.'

Her massage finished, Kathy swung her legs off the table. 'He's infertile?'

'You'd have more chance getting pregnant by a warm bus seat,' said Jackie as they wandered into the next treatment room.

'Thank God for small mercies,' breathed Sara.

'Seaweed or mud?' asked one of the assistants.

'Seaweed, please,' said Kathy, lying on a bed.

Jackie eyed the tub of green, foul-smelling gunk suspiciously. 'I think I'll stick with the mud.'

'Me too,' said Sara, wondering whether much of this beauty treatment wasn't wasted on her. How could she relax?

The three of them lay on adjoining beds as their bodies were painted brown or green, making it impossible to have a serious conversation. Once they were almost totally covered, the assistants wrapped them in tinfoil and left them for forty-five minutes.

Sara broached the subject again. 'If Stephen was going out with Felicity, how did Stuart fit into the picture?'

'They were having an affair, and at the same time I was having an affair with Stephen.'

'You didn't have an affair with Stuart as well, did you?' asked Sara incredulously.

'Of course not,' replied Jackie, indignantly. 'The sixties weren't quite that swinging. I did love Stephen then, you know. It wasn't something cheap. At least, not to begin with.'

'I'm sorry,' said Sara. Once again she cursed herself for pushing Jackie too hard. In her burning need to know everything she was riding roughshod over the ex-model's feelings. Jackie wasn't responsible for any of this. She continued more gently: 'Did Stephen know about Felicity's pregnancy?'

'No. He would have told me. He talked about her constantly.' Jackie was fighting to keep her emotions in check.

'I'm getting very hot under all this,' said Kathy, wanting to break the mood. She looked at Sara, and then at Jackie, her heart going out to both of them.

But Jackie was not deterred. 'Stephen was obsessed with Felicity,' she went on. 'I always felt like the consolation prize. You know, he's going to go ballistic when he finds out you're her daughter.'

'You won't tell him, will you?'

'Of course not. I don't care if I never speak to that man again.'

'Good for you,' said Kathy.

'Why do you think she disappeared?' asked Sara, beginning to feel uncomfortably hot under the foil. 'Do you think it was just the pregnancy?'

'Um . . . well . . . possibly,' replied Jackie, shifting uneasily. 'No, there was more to it than that, I'm certain. There was talk of . . . I think Felicity had become dependent on drugs. God, this is hard to talk about.'

This news came as yet another blow to Sara. Her mother a drug addict? She thought of June's cosy simplicity and wished with all her heart that she had been born of her body.

'It was just a rumour—'

Jackie was interrupted by the return of one of the assistants. 'I think you ladies are done now,' she said, looking at her watch. 'Now, you could just shower off the beauty packs or you could try the hydro treatment.'

'Would you leave us for a few minutes?' asked Sara agitatedly. 'I don't think I'm properly poached yet.'

Kathy waited until the assistant had gone. 'Sara, I really think you should drop this. For now at least.'

'Let her go on,' insisted Jackie.

'Did Stephen have anything to do with Felicity's drug problem?'

'I don't know. I've never seen him take anything.'

'He just sells it,' said Sara bitterly. She wondered if Stuart had known about Felicity's addiction. Perhaps he blamed Stephen, she thought, remembering Stuart's vehement anti-drugs stance.

'I know he's a bad penny but surely—'

'A bad penny? You don't know the half of it.' She filled Jackie in on the salient points of the Mickey Nash–Ronnie Firetto–Leonel Pinto fiasco, her voice rising as she listed each corrupt detail.

Jackie's face crumpled. 'I never knew any of this, I swear.'

Kathy peeled off her foil and stood up, seaweed dripping off her body. 'Stop it, Sara. What do you think you're achieving from all this? Why are you trying to hurt Jackie?'

Sara was in full flight now. 'And the list goes on. There's game-throwing, a little set-up he has with someone called Frank, you name it.'

The assistant returned. 'Ladies, can we please go to the shower room now? We have another appointment waiting.'

Kathy hurriedly got up and left the room. As Sara unpeeled her tinfoil shroud, she said to Jackie, 'I'm sorry. I really am.'

Jackie touched her shoulder. 'It's OK. I thought I was the only one hurt by that bastard. But you're stronger than me. You'll beat him. Felicity would have been so proud of the way you turned out.'

Sara was deeply touched by Jackie's magnanimity. 'I shouldn't have gone on like that. I don't know what I was thinking of.'

'Forget about it,' smiled Jackie. 'Stephen gets to you like that.'

In the next room, the assistant, smiling through gritted teeth, asked, 'Hydro or shower?'

'We'll have the hydro,' said Kathy. Two minutes later she was bitterly regretting it. The treatment consisted of standing naked at the end of a tiled room with something akin to a water cannon trained on you. They all screamed as the powerful jet of icy water first hit, though all welcomed the respite from the painful conversation.

As the jet was turned off, Kathy said through chattering teeth. 'Frank!' She'd suddenly remembered the conversation she'd overheard outside Stephen's office the day before. 'Stephen was on the phone yesterday to someone called Frank.'

'Do you think it was *the* Frank?'

'Put it this way, he was moaning about losing a hundred thousand because a player was playing too well. I didn't hear him say which player, though.'

'I'll ask for an itemised bill,' said Sara, wrapping herself in a towel. 'There's a fifty per cent chance it was Stephen who made the call. What time was it?'

'About ten o'clock. Are you going to ring him? How will you recognise his voice?'

Sara thought back to the night in Mickey's Bar when Frank had given her money. To keep you honest, he'd said. 'I'll know.'

Shivering, they dressed and allowed themselves to be herded into the hairdressing salon. Sara refused to let them touch her hair and sat to one side watching Kathy and Jackie, seated in hi-tech chairs in front of a powerfully lit mirror, allowing the hairstylists to give them the once-over. The prognosis for Jackie's over-dyed, over-permed locks wasn't hopeful.

'What have you been using on this?' asked her stylist icily as he rubbed a clump of dry, split ends between his fingers.

'The colour's called Ginger Peachy,' said Jackie, defensively.

'It's got to go,' declared the stylist.

Jackie looked at Kathy for support. 'What do you think?'

'I think red's completely wrong for your colouring,' said Kathy truthfully.

'But Stephen . . .' Jackie stopped and stared at her reflection. 'I was just about to say Stephen liked it that way. Do you know why? Because it made me look more like Felicity. Even after she'd gone I still had to compete with her. Stephen punished me for not being Felicity. I loved her too, you know, but I've had to pay for her disappearance for nearly thirty years. It wasn't fair. I didn't deserve to be treated like that. And all those terrible things he did, is still doing!' Tears began to roll down her pink, scrubbed cheeks. 'Have you got a tissue?' she asked the stylist.

He handed her a tissue. 'You can have that colour if you want,' he said guiltily.

Jackie blew her nose. 'Get rid of it. I want it back to brown.' For Jackie this was a symbolic gesture. With the changing of her hair colour she was saying a final goodbye to the control Stephen had exerted over her. 'I'm divorcing him.'

Kathy looked at her. 'Make that a double divorce.'

'You're divorcing Joseph?' asked Sara, jumping up from her seat. 'Are you sure?' Kathy had been very quiet about the state of play in her marriage.

'Of course she is,' said Jackie. 'Do you want to be coming to the Four Seasons in ten years' time to visit her?'

Antonio fed Sara some melon, licking the juice that dribbled down her chin.

'I've had two hours' sleep,' she yawned. 'This is going to kill me.'

'But what a way to go,' he smiled, kissing her stomach. His mouth moved over the dip of her navel, his tongue flicking into the tiny well. Sara wallowed in delicious anticipation as his kisses then traced a line down between her thighs. When Antonio's lips brushed against her sex and lingered there, his tongue delving deep into her, she sighed, arching her back as she ran her hand through his thick black hair.

'Don't stop,' she begged, her body trembling at his touch. By now Antonio knew her body like his own, and his tongue moved faster, deeper, responding to the urgency of her needs. The sensation spread from between her thighs, taking control of her whole body. 'Please. Oh, my God. Yes!' she cried out, writhing in ecstasy.

Sara lay back, spent, but Antonio lifted his head, giving her a lop-sided smile. 'I haven't finished yet,' he said, pulling himself up until they were face to face. He pinned down her arms and she groaned, feeling the reassuring weight of his body on hers as he entered her. At first, he moved slowly, but soon his passion took over. Her fingernails dug into his back as he thrust deeper and deeper into her, bringing her once more to the brink. Both were lost in the moment as their bodies became one and their mutual desire forced them over the edge.

Sara relaxed, smiling at Antonio. 'How am I ever going to get any work done?' she asked, ruffling his hair.

'If I could, I'd never let you leave this bed,' he said, playfully biting her nipple.

'I know,' she said. Over the past week she had spent little time at the club, retreating into her relationship with Antonio, needing this time to restore her equilibrium to face the hurdles ahead. She had finally released Norman from his contract. The episode of her 'disappearance' to Bristol had dented his professional pride. It was hardly fair to expect him to protect her when she left him at home most of the time. Besides, she had Antonio to look after her now, and with him at her side she believed she could handle anything else that life might throw at her – even Stephen. Antonio was right: an hour could be a lifetime.

Antonio sat up, pushing his hair out of his eyes. 'I have to ring Flavio,' he said, looking at his watch. 'But from his silence I guess he has not found Oscar yet.'

Sara touched him gently on the shoulder. 'He will.'

'It will be so perfect. The three of us together – and then some little brothers and sisters.'

Sara's stomach lurched. In all the hours she had spent talking to Antonio about her life she had omitted one glaring detail. She had told herself it was too soon; deep down, she knew that she was avoiding the subject for fear of Antonio rejecting her.

'I've got something to tell you,' she said, nervously. 'In fact, I've been meaning to tell you for a few days, but it never seemed to be the right time. No, that's not true. The truth is I'm scared to tell you, but I can't go on keeping it a secret.'

His blackish-brown eyes took on their familiar haunted look. 'What do you mean?' he asked, his voice fearful.

'I didn't try to trick you; after all, we hardly know each other . . .'

He grabbed her hands. 'Sara, what is it? Tell me.'

'The car crash in New York. It left me with serious injuries.'

Antonio's eyes widened in horror. 'What happened to you?'

'I can never have children.' She kept her eyes fixed on his face to catch his immediate reaction. Even if he tried to cover it up afterwards, denied his true feelings, that first look would tell her all she needed to know.

'Oh, Sara, Sara,' he said, drawing her towards him, nothing but his love for her showing in his eyes. 'That is so sad. You have known too much pain.'

'If you don't want to—'

Antonio silenced her by squeezing her tightly. 'I love you. There is no more to be said than that.'

'You want a family,' cried Sara, her tears falling on to his chest.

'I want you, above everything. It's true I want a family. And when I find Oscar I will have one.' Antonio rocked her in his arms. 'Everything will be all right. You'll see.'

Though his body brought comfort his words brought on a new wave of tears. Sara rested her head against his damp chest, sobbing as she thought about how much of their happiness was riding on that little boy. What if Antonio didn't find him? What then? Could just the two of them still be a family? The telephone rang and she covered her ears. 'Go away,' she cried.

Antonio reached over and before Sara could stop him, he answered it.

'Where's that cow of a wife of mine?'

'Stephen? Is that you?'

Sara snatched the phone out of his hand and slammed it down, but it was too late. Stephen had heard Antonio's voice.

Chapter Thirty-Eight

Sara returned to the office the following day, still troubled by Stephen's phone call. She wanted him to know as little about her personal life as possible – there was no point in handing him ammunition to use against her. She pictured news of the romance appearing in the *News*. It would be just like Stephen to give them the story, knowing that she would then have to fend off another horde of reporters. It would suit his purposes to keep her sidetracked for a few days.

Just then the phone rang.

'Hello, Sara Moore.'

'Is that really you?' came a familiar New Jersey twang.

'Jay!'

'The one and only. How you doing?'

'Well, I'm a multi-millionairess with my own football club, although you must know at least some of this as you've managed to track me down,' she laughed and for the next ten minutes she filled him on the missing years, Jay punctuating her story with a series of astonished whistles.

'Looks like you've landed on your feet,' he said. 'I'm glad things are going well for you – you deserve it. Listen, I had to call as I've got some news I thought you'd want to hear straight away. It's about Bill – or rather the crash. The lorry driver finally admitted that he was responsible for the crash and Bill's death. He'd been drinking and veered on to your side of the road. It wasn't your fault, Sara.' There was a long pause while he waited for her response. 'Sara, are you there?'

'Yes. I think I'm in shock. Why admit it now, after all this time?'

'Apparently, he's found God and he wanted to cleanse his soul.'

'Look, Jay, thanks for ringing. I need time to digest this. I'll call you next week, OK?'

'No problem. You take care now.'

It wasn't my fault. Oh, Bill— But before she could dwell on the news further, Sara's thoughts were interrupted by a now familiar voice.

'Louise said you wanted to see me urgently,' Reg said from the doorway.

'Come in and shut the door.'

'What's up?' he said, throwing himself into the seat in front of her desk.

'Well, it's – um – a rather delicate matter.'

'Are they up to their usual tricks? I've told the team time and again, if one more girl comes here saying they were all in a bedroom with her I'll swing—'

'No, nothing like that,' said Sara hastily. 'It's to do with Stephen. Look, there's no easy way to ask this and if I could do it myself I would but . . .'

'Come on, lass, out with it.'

'I know it's a lot to ask, but I need you to look through Stephen's office for evidence of offshore companies.'

'Offshore?'

'Addresses like the Channel Islands, or Liechtenstein, or maybe the Dutch Antilles – let's say any foreign address. Plus any documents that show where he has his bank accounts. In fact, anything that looks like it might be for his eyes only.'

Reg whistled, 'Not a tall order, then.'

'Look, you don't have to do it, really. I'll understand. I'd do it myself, but I can't get anywhere near his office.'

Reg thought for a while. 'Will this help you get rid of him?'

'I sincerely hope so.'

'Then I'll do it.'

Antonio tightened his bootlaces and threw on his football shirt. The team were already making their way out on to the pitch but as he went to leave the changing room, a hand grabbed his shoulder.

'Not so fast, mate. I want a word with you,' said Stephen, his fingers tightening on the footballer's shoulder blade.

'Let go,' said Antonio, shrugging off the man as if he were no more than an insect.

Anger clouded Stephen's face, but he knew that physically he was no match for the Brazilian. Not that there was any need for strong-arm tactics with him. 'You know that little chat we had before? Well, today's the day. You don't score and create a few penalties, you hear?'

'No way.'

Stephen smirked at him. 'OK, I'll put it another way. If you do score the bitch gets hurt, and I mean really—'

Antonio lunged at Stephen and grabbed him by his shirt collar, forcing him on to the tips of his toes. Their faces were almost nose to nose. 'If anything happens to Sara, I swear I will kill you with my own bare hands.'

'Nothing'll happen,' said Stephen, sweat breaking out on his forehead, 'if you just do as you're told.'

Antonio tightened his grip, causing Stephen to choke. 'I'm warning you.'

'It's not just me you're up against,' Stephen said, laughing with contempt. 'And if you touch me now, she'll definitely be hurt. Now get your fucking dago hands off me.'

Antonio swallowed his anger and released him.

'That's better,' said Stephen, dusting himself down. 'And it would be a good idea if you warned her to stop sticking her nose in where it's not wanted. Or someone might cut it off.' Antonio pulled back his fist but Stephen ducked out of the way and ran down the corridor, coughing. 'Don't even think about going to the police – I've got that one covered,' he spluttered over his shoulder.

Antonio smashed his fist on the metal locker. What could he do? He knew from Sara how dangerous this man was. Stephen wouldn't think twice about hurting her, or rather, getting one of his thugs to do it. An image of Sara lying beaten and bloody flashed through his mind. He couldn't bear it if she was hurt and he was responsible.

'Antonio, get out here now,' shouted Reg.

He looked briefly in the mirror and saw that his face had been drained of all colour. There was nothing he could do now.

'Antonio!'

Sara walked into the ground, greeting everyone in sight. The programme-sellers beamed back, pleased to be noticed by the management for once. There were thousands of fans milling around and her name ricocheted across the car park.

'Good on yer, Sara!'

'Thanks for Neves.'

'You've saved us,' said one little boy dramatically.

She smiled, amused at the irony of being praised for something Stephen had done.

The next thing she knew, she was surrounded by a horde of adolescent boys dressed in the team's colours begging her to autograph their shirts.

'Give us a kiss,' giggled one.

Sara blew him one, provoking every male within a radius of fifty yards to demand the same.

'Thanks for your support, lads, but I've got to go.'

Minutes later she walked out on to the pitch, breathing in the fresh wintry air and savouring the sight and sounds of the packed stadium.

'They all fancy you, lass,' shouted Reg, beginning his famous nervous walk around the pitch before the game started.

Sara laughed. 'How do you think we'll do?' she asked.

'Hard to say. Although since you've been in charge, the boys seem to have perked up quite a lot. And Neves is on excellent form.'

'Good.' Sara lowered her voice. 'How's the other business going?'

'I haven't been able to get into his office on me own, but I'll do it, I promise,' said Reg, looking up at the directors' box, where Stephen had just arrived with his numerous hangers-on.

'I'd better go up,' she said as Reg sat down in the dugout. 'Good luck.'

Sara took her seat in the directors' box, studiously ignoring Stephen. As she watched Antonio trot out on to the pitch, sending the crowd wild, she felt a surge of pride. She searched out his face for his usual pre-match smile, but it wasn't there. Granted this was a big game, but never had she seen Antonio looking so preoccupied.

The match started and Sara became aware that she was grinding her teeth as Cantona swerved with the ball all the way down the pitch. Camden's defence were reacting as if they'd just got out of bed and Reg was apoplectic. In the dugout he was shouting, screaming and waving his arms about.

Ross Heywood, Camden's goalkeeper, was yelling a stream of abuse at the defenders when, suddenly, Les Sutton woke up and blocked Cantona. Stealing the ball from the Frenchman, he crossed it to Sumner, who passed it on down the field to Antonio. The star striker ran with the ball down the left side past Man United's Keane. Ploughing on, his dazzling footwork soon left Ince and Bruce for dust.

Sara jumped up and down with excitement. 'Come on, Antonio!' she screamed. Stephen threw her a scathing look.

The Brazilian passed the ball back to Les Sutton, who took a shot. Schmeichel, the goalkeeper, managed to punch it over the bar. Benny Wright took the corner, and Antonio stopped the ball with his chest, deftly snaked in and out of Pallister, then Bruce again, kicking the ball with a sure-footed force. But the ball went ten yards wide of the post.

'No!' screamed Sara.

The Manchester United support was ecstatic and they began to taunt Antonio with chants of 'Loser' and 'Go home.' Then to Sara's surprise, she heard her own name reverberating around the stadium as a few of the undesirables among the away fans childishly began to chant, 'Moore's a whore.' Sara smiled gamely, in no doubt that Stephen would have liked to have joined in.

After a pep talk from Reg at half-time, Camden played an even more exciting game – and as a team, for once. Heywood was on top form, at one stage almost doing a back flip to stop a penalty. The only weak link in the chain was Antonio who, unbelievably, missed two more goals.

In the last five minutes Antonio tackled Cantona, his feet bringing the Frenchman to his knees. The referee blew his whistle and pointed to the spot where Cantona was writhing on the ground.

The Camden supporters were in uproar, as were half the team, who surrounded the referee and argued against the penalty. Antonio looked crestfallen as he helped Cantona up. The referee shooed the players away and waited for Hughes to take the penalty. Sara held her head in her hands, lifting them only when the roar confirmed her fears. He'd scored, making it a one-nil win for the away team.

After the match, as Sara attempted to get to the dressing rooms, she was accosted by the press. She remembered how, as a reporter, she had waited in the tunnel for the players. Now she knew just how intimidating it felt to be surrounded by journalists and photographers jostling for space and thrusting microphones and cameras in your face. She could barely make out one reporter's question from another.

'Miss Moore, what are your future plans for the team?'

'—transfers like Neves?'

'Do you intend to spend—'

'—you and Stephen Powell—'

'—wrong with Neves today?'

'Enough,' shouted Sara above the din. 'One question at a time.'

'What's wrong with Neves? You must be very disappointed.'

Sara couldn't see where the question came from. 'Of course it was a disappointing result, but as you all know, even the best have their off days.'

'Is it true that you have taken over from Reg Bowden in deciding who's signed? Are you the manageress?' the reporter finished aggressively.

Sara looked around for Reg, but he had disappeared. 'No, I'm not, and I don't believe you got that information from Reg.' She paused, waiting for a response. None was forthcoming. 'I think that there are certain people in this business who are terrified of a woman's involvement – unless, of course, she's serving tea or selling the story of her night of love with Gazza to you lot.'

'Do you think all this lovemaking is good for you?' asked Sara, breathlessly, lying back on the bed. If Antonio asked her the same question the answer would definitely be yes. She could feel herself growing stronger through his love and her life was beginning to seem manageable again. 'I mean, you did miss several chances on Saturday,' she said, wagging her finger at him. 'I think I should get a reduction on you. Reg is having to rest you for the next game.'

'We all have our off days,' said Antonio, his smile fading. 'Nobody's perfect.' He had had to tell the manager he thought he'd come back too soon after his injury, but the problem wasn't going to go away. What was he going to do the following week? And the week after that?

Sara propped herself up on her pillow. 'I know. I was only joking. Is anything wrong?'

'No,' he said unconvincingly, climbing out of bed. How could he tell her and still keep her safe from harm? One of the things he loved most about her was her fighting spirit. She wouldn't back away from Stephen, and then what would happen? Suddenly he saw her again, lying unconscious, bleeding. He had to protect her.

'Has Stephen said something to you about the match?'

'Why do you say that? He has nothing to say to me. The man is nothing.'

Sara was surprised by his vehemence. 'Why do you say that?'

'I . . . I don't like the way he's treated you.' Antonio pulled on a pair of grey sweatpants, unable to look her in the eye. She would be able to tell he was lying. 'I wish I could take you away from all this.'

'Calm down, Antonio. It'll be all right.' She loved his protectiveness, but she didn't want him to worry so much. Stephen seemed to have backed off for a few days and she sensed she had him running scared. She patted the duvet. 'Come back to bed.'

Antonio was torn. He looked at her smiling at him, inviting him back into her bed, and he wanted so much to feel her body next to his. But there could be no lies in that bed. He would be forced to tell her the truth. 'I think I'll go for a run,' he said, walking out of the bedroom.

On Saturday morning, two hours before kick-off, Reg burst through the door of Sara's office. 'I've got 'em,' he said, breathlessly.

'How much is there?' she asked, rising from her chair.

Reg held out a sheaf of papers. 'I hope they're the right ones, lass.'

'We'll have to look later. We'd better copy them now.'

Sara peered round her office door to make sure that no one was in the corridor and beckoned to Reg. 'Come on.'

Sara shuffled the papers, trying to tidy them as much as possible before pushing them into the photocopier's feeder. The first dozen went through but then the machine jammed. Sara opened the top of the copier. All the originals were crumpled. The smell of scorched paper seemed to draw attention to her clandestine activity and beads of perspiration began to form above her lip. Tugging the papers free, she smoothed out the creases and tried again. This time they all went through and soon she had a neat stack of copied documents. She hurriedly shoved them into an envelope and gave the originals back to Reg.

'Do you think you'll be able to get them back now?'

'I hope so,' said Reg, 'but you'd better keep watch.'

Sara stood at the end of the corridor, her heart thumping as she listened for any sound that might signal Stephen's impending arrival. To her horror she heard his tuneless whistling somewhere in the distance.

'Shit,' she said, under her breath. 'I don't believe it.' She had to act quickly. Running back along the corridor in the direction of the whistling, she turned a corner and bumped into Stephen's podgy frame.

'Watch where you're going!'

'Sorry, Stephen. Actually, you're just the person I'm looking for,' said Sara. She'd hardly said a word to him for weeks, but now she was going to have to try to engage him in conversation.

He looked at her suspiciously. 'Why?'

'Um, I just wondered . . .' She clutched the incriminating envelope to her chest.

'Come on, out with it. I haven't got all day.'

'I wondered if you thought we should get rid of Dick Davenport.'

Stephen looked surprised. 'What are you asking me for? You've been making unilateral decisions since the day you got here. Get out of my bloody way.' He tried to push her aside but Sara stood her ground, trying to gauge how long Reg would need.

'Look, we have to work together. Can't we at least be civil to each other?' she asked.

Stephen cleared his throat and then spat in her face. 'What do you think?' he laughed.

Sara didn't even flinch. Calmly, staying rooted to the spot, she wiped her cheek and said, 'I guess this means we won't be spending Christmas together.'

'Get out of my way.'

Sara breathed a sigh of relief as she heard the squeak of the manager's trainers approaching along the corridor. Reg walked casually past, nodding to them briskly. If she'd had to hold out any longer it would have come to blows.

Back in her office she locked the door, closed the blinds and tipped out the contents of the envelope on to her desk. There were some computer printouts of accounts along with bank statements and various letters. She picked up one of these, headed Red Admiral Entertainment. The address given was a PO box number in St Peter Port, Guernsey. The letter concerned leases Stephen owned on buildings at several addresses and it was signed by a Robin Ripley. It came as no surprise to find that one of the properties mentioned was none other than Mickey's Bar, although it appeared that its name had now been changed to Cherie's.

The Red Admiral, it suddenly struck her, was a butterfly. Was this a coincidence, or a sign of Stephen's continuing obsession with her mother? Did he still feel the same way about her, thirty years on? Not wanting to think about her mother's association with this man, she turned to the computer printouts, which dealt with a company called Borboleta. The name had a familiar ring, although she was sure it had nothing to do with Nash. She said it aloud in the hope that this would jog her memory. Nothing.

She moved on excitedly, but the next file contained details of gate receipts which was not something she'd asked for. Reg must have picked it up by mistake. Then a slip of paper caught her eye. It was a copy of a tax return informing the Inland Revenue of the gate receipts. Not all of the document was legible as a Post-it note had still been attached to it as it was photocopied. Squinting, Sara tried to decipher Adrian Fellows' handwriting on the note. SP, 6/11/93 Gates – 35,204. IR – 33,704. AF.

'Damn him,' said Sara out loud. She looked at the tax form again. Sure enough, the attendance for that week was given as 33,704. Stephen was obviously keeping some turnstiles to himself. The money from 1,500 tickets was bypassing the taxman and going straight into his pocket.

As Sara picked up the next file, she heard footsteps in the corridor and that unmistakable flat whistle. The temptation to rush out and confront Stephen with what she'd found was strong but she let it pass. First she had to get an idea of just how far the corruption went. Revenge, she reminded herself, was a dish best eaten cold. She could wait a few days.

The next file she read dealt with players bought and sold over the previous five years. By each name was the price paid or received. Skimming the list, she noticed nothing untoward until, threequarters of the way through, she reached the name Johann Hoffman. Hoffman had been bought from Dusseldorf for £1.4 million (using 'Peter Barratt's' money). This was unbelievable. Hoffman hadn't even reached the first team. It bore all the hallmarks of a Johnny Taylor deal, decided Sara, wondering how much of the transfer fee Stephen had 'earned'.

Frustratingly, nowhere in any of the papers was there any mention of Frank. Sara still had nothing more to go on on the gambling front than hearsay. But there probably wouldn't be any documentary evidence of that. Everything was done under the table. There were no official figures to manipulate. The receipts from the club shop were another matter, however.

According to the figures in the file, the shop's manager, Fred Samson, had supposedly ordered £400,000 worth of goods, yet there were sales of only £200,000 instead of what should have been in the region of £800,000. Sara had been in the shop earlier in the week. It was practically empty of stock. She decided that a quick call to the suppliers to check that the goods had actually been delivered wouldn't go amiss, but when she saw the name of the company she realised that there wouldn't be much point. The suppliers were called Chrysalis Clothing. This constant homage to Felicity was very creepy and it gave Sara the unpleasant feeling that perhaps her mother might have been involved in some way. Perhaps she should just let things rest as far as her mother was concerned. Hadn't she found enough horrors in her past already? A drug-addict con-woman and a philandering MP – what great stock she came from.

Sara glanced at the clock and put down the shop file. The match was about to start.

As she climbed the stairs to the directors' box, Sara was smiling from ear to ear. At last she had what she wanted: soon Powell would be out of the way and she could set about turning Camden into a legitimate enterprise. And perhaps Antonio would soon hear news of Oscar. Things were looking good. She wanted to rush up and kiss Stephen for being so stupid. But the sight which met her at the top of the stairs wiped the smile clean off her face. Unbelievably, on Stephen's arm, was none other than Maggie Lawrence.

'Sara,' she purred, 'how nice to see you.'

It seemed as if everyone in the directors' box was holding their breath waiting for Sara's response, but there was nothing she could think of to say.

'Cat got your tongue?' asked Stephen, squeezing Maggie's waist.

At least Maggie had the grace to seem embarrassed, thought Sara, noticing how uncomfortable she looked as Stephen touched her. She stared at her one-time friend, shaking her head in disbelief. The last time she'd seen Maggie had been that awful day at Christopher's, but then Sara had been in such a distraught state that she hadn't really taken in the further deterioration in Maggie's appearance. The chic slicked-back hairstyle and the slinky black catsuit initially made a dramatic impression, but on closer inspection Maggie looked dreadful. She was painfully thin, her body no more than a collection of jarring angles, and all the make-up in the world (and she certainly seemed to be wearing most of it) couldn't hide the way the vicious circle of starving, bingeing and vomiting had aged her. Despite all the cruel, unforgivable things she'd done, the strongest emotion Maggie aroused in Sara at that moment was pity. This twitchy, bird-like woman to whom she had once been so close had to be seriously mentally ill.

'I didn't know you were a football fan,' said Sara, finally.

This was the lead Maggie was waiting for. The part where she really socked it to Sara. 'I'm not here for the football, I'm here for Stephen.'

'What?'

Stephen elucidated by groping Maggie's bottom. 'I've traded Jackie in for a younger model. What do you reckon?'

It was too sad. How bitter and twisted Maggie had become. Sara thought of how Jackie had endured Stephen's mental torture for nearly thirty years. She couldn't wish the same on anyone, not even Maggie. 'Maggie, please don't do it,' she said, quietly, 'not even to get at me. It's not worth it. Dating Stephen Powell? Even you can't hate yourself that much.'

Maggie was confused. She'd expected Sara to scream and shout, even throw another punch, but she was spoiling things with her pity. As Sara walked past her without another word, Maggie looked at Stephen. Why the hell was she doing this to herself?

Chapter Thirty-Nine

Sara spent every spare hour of the next few days studying the documents stolen from Stephen, eager to unravel the threads of his crooked business deals as quickly as possible. She was worried that Maggie's arrival on the scene might herald the start of a new offensive. For every new company she came across, however insignificant, she ordered the relevant fiches from Companies House. The updated Red Admiral fiche held little new information but she made a note of Robin Ripley's directorship of another company, called Winluck. However, she had nothing to link the name to Stephen, and so far she had drawn a blank regarding Borboleta, too.

This evening she was going over the photocopies of the Borboleta computer printouts and she had spread them out across her bed. Now that Antonio was living at Primrose Hill, the bedroom had become the focal point of the house. They worked, ate, slept and, above all, made love there.

Down one side of the printout was a column of figures which she assumed represented sums of money. Opposite each figure was a name. After puzzling over it for some minutes, Sara realised that all the names represented different companies. Many appeared to be foreign.

Antonio came up behind her and began to kiss her hair but she gently pushed him away. 'Not now, I still haven't made head nor tail of this.'

'I'm worried about you,' he said, stroking the nape of her neck.

'Mmm, that's nice,' she said, responding to his fingers, rolling her head from side to side. 'Why?'

'Your determination to ruin Powell. Why not leave it? You run the club anyway.' It was the closest he'd dared push the subject so far.

Sara hunched her neck. She looked up at him suspiciously. 'A few days ago you said you hated the man. Why do you want me to leave him alone all of a sudden?'

Antonio went over to the window and stared out at the night sky. He didn't know which was worse: telling Sara everything and leaving her at risk, or continuing with the lie, knowing that this would give her just cause to doubt him. He knew how hard it had been for Sara to trust him after she'd been let down by so many people but he just couldn't tell her the truth. Stephen would kill her. This he was sure of. 'All those things you told me about him. What if he tries to hurt you again?' He turned to face her. 'I couldn't stand to lose you, Sara. My life, it would mean . . .'

Sara relaxed and her suspicions evaporated instantly. She could see that she had hurt him, and she vowed that this would be the last time she let any doubt about him cloud her mind. 'You're not going to lose me, you big fool. Now come here and give me a kiss.'

Antonio returned to the bed. As he went to remove the paperwork, he noticed the printout. '*Meu deus!*'

'What is it?' asked Sara, kneeling up and looking over his shoulder.

'This name, Borboleta,' he said, 'it's a Brazilian property company. These people are responsible for many of the slum clearances. They have their own death squads. There have been so many campaigns against them including mine. But why is it here?'

'Borboleta?' Sara repeated the name. 'Does it mean something?' she asked, knowing the answer already.

'It's Portuguese. For butterfly.'

Sara shivered with excitement. 'Do you understand what this means?' she asked, hugging him. The mystery around Antonio's transfer had finally been solved. How could she have ever thought him anything less than totally honest? 'I always said your transfer wasn't right.'

'For the last time—'

'No, listen to me,' she said, shaking him. 'Borboleta is another one of Stephen's companies . . .' She hesitated, an unpleasant thought flashing through her mind. It was a Brazilian company. What if Felicity were in some way involved with it? No, that's stupid, she told herself. The Butterfly had flown away from Stephen a long time ago. How could she be running one of his companies? 'Stephen made money from your deal, I'm positive about that, but there's something else here. Don't you think it's highly suspicious that his company is one of those you've campaigned against?'

A blush of anger flashed across Antonio's face. 'That bastard! I'm going to see him now.'

Alarmed, Sara gripped him tightly. 'Antonio, you can't. I mean it. He'll wonder where you got the information from.' If she was right and Antonio's enemies had arranged the transfer, his life was as much at risk here in London as it had been in Brazil. But that wouldn't put him off. She had to persuade him that she was at risk to stop him.

'I won't tell him,' he said, pulling away.

Sara jumped off the bed and followed him into the hallway. 'Please!'

'I've got to do this,' Antonio said through clenched teeth. He balled his fists. 'That man has brought misery to thousands of people.'

He ran down the stairs. Sara gave chase, propelling herself after him. As he went to open the door, she threw herself against it to bar his way. 'You've got to calm down,' she said.

'You have no idea how much harm Borboleta has caused.'

'So now you want to let Stephen hurt you, too?' she shouted, the panic rising in her voice. She put her hand to her mouth. 'Oh my God! Now I remember where I've seen that name before. Jay and I did a story on Leonel Pinto at the *Globe*—'

'Pinto! What's that bastard got to do with it?'

'One of the things we were investigating was money-laundering through a property company. Borboleta was mentioned, but nothing was ever proved. And guess who gave me the story – Stuart!' Was there any part of her life in which he hadn't interfered? she wondered. 'I knew Stephen had to be buying his supplies from Pinto, but I didn't know the connection went further than that.'

Antonio put his hand on the latch. 'Sara, would you move out of my way?'

'You're not going to see him. Please,' she begged. 'Not tonight. Just stay here with me. I'm frightened. We can sort it out tomorrow, but tonight . . .'

Antonio relented. 'OK,' he said, taking her hand, 'I'll stay.'

When Sara awoke the next morning she was alone. In a state of pure panic, she drove to work, fearing the worst, and by the time she pulled into the Camden car park, she had decided to call the police. The envelope containing Stephen's documents lay on the passenger seat. She cursed her stupidity. Why hadn't she handed them over to the police as soon as she'd found them? Had her vanity in wanting to wrap up the whole case by herself put Antonio in danger?

Just as she got out of her car, she spotted Stephen going into the building. She ran after him, finally catching up with him as he walked into his office.

'Where is he?' she gasped, her breath coming in short, anxious stabs.

Stephen sat down behind his desk. 'I take it you're talking about your fancy man?'

'Where is he?'

'With another bird if he's got any sense.'

'I know he came to see you this morning.'

Stephen picked up his newspaper and shrugged his shoulders. 'Maybe he did, and maybe he didn't.'

Sara tore the newspaper from his hands. 'I know . . .' She stopped.

What was the point? Throwing the envelope on the desk, she said, 'Take a look at those.'

Disinterestedly Stephen took a few of the pages from the envelope. 'Well, well, well. Congratulations, Miss Marple, you've solved the case.'

She leaned over the desk. 'And don't think about destroying them – I've made copies, of course.'

Stephen looked unimpressed. 'So what? What are you going to do about it?'

'Go to the police. It's the end, Stephen.'

Stephen burst out laughing. 'I don't think so. When you go to the police you'll have to report your Latin lover at the same time.'

Sara suddenly felt icy cold. 'What are you saying?'

'You don't think he just happened to be off form on Saturday, do you? He's like me, knows a good deal when he sees one.'

Sara didn't believe a word of it. 'Antonio threw that game? Do you seriously expect me—'

Stephen opened his drawer and threw a chequebook at her. 'I should know, I've been paying the money into his bank account.'

Sara looked at the cheque stubs. According to the most recent, a cheque for £200,000 had been paid to Antonio. The account holder on the chequebook was Winluck. 'So what? You can write anything on a stub.'

'You're right. But what about this?' Stephen produced Antonio's bank book. 'Only Neves could have opened an account in his name. He's a well-known face. Enough people must have seen him do it. If you want more proof, I've got it.'

Sara's head began to swim. She knew Stephen was a liar, but the bank book stared up at her disconcertingly from the desk. She'd promised herself that she would never doubt Antonio again, but what was she to make of the strange way he'd behaved over the Man United game? There was no good reason for him to have been off form that day – up to then he'd been playing better than ever. And why had he wanted her to leave Stephen alone? Was it for her own safety, or was it because he knew Stephen would tell her this?

'You're lying. Antonio would never do that . . .' She floundered. How could she argue Antonio's innocence on the basis that he'd told her he loved her? She'd had her suspicions, but she'd been so desperate to trust in that love that she'd allowed them to be allayed. So what if he did love her? June loved her, too; so had Stuart. It didn't stop either of them from telling her lies.

Stephen was triumphant. 'You thought you were so clever investigating Mickey, Ronnie, then me. You always knew there was a Brazilian connection, didn't you?'

'That was Pinto,' she insisted.

'And Neves, too.'

'No!' Antonio had been so angry about the Borboleta connection. But maybe it wasn't anger; maybe it was fear. Perhaps she'd come too close to the truth. When all was said and done, she barely knew Antonio. In a moment of desperation she'd clung on to him for the sake of her sanity. He was her rock, but it was she who had cast him in that mould. And now the rock was fast disappearing in a sandstorm of uncertainty. She was spinning again.

'You let your fanny rule your head,' sneered Stephen. 'Just like any other woman. Go to the police, if you like, but I'm taking Neves down with me.'

Sara ran back to her office, her head bowed, tormented by the image of the bank book. Antonio was waiting there for her. He must have known what was going on in Stephen's office. What a complete fool she had been, yet again.

'Get out,' she said, her voice devoid of all feeling. 'Get out of this office and get out of my life.'

'Sara, listen to me.' He tried to take her hand, but Sara slapped it away. 'It's not what you think.'

'Did you throw the game?' she asked mechanically. In the short time she'd known him, Antonio had demanded every kind of emotional response from her. Now there was nothing left.

Antonio's chest heaved. 'Yes,' he said quietly.

'Get out.'

'It was a set-up,' he said, his dark, sad eyes beginning to moisten. 'I did it because Stephen said he would harm you. I didn't take the money, believe me.'

'I don't know what to believe any more,' said Sara, her head in her hands. 'You promised not to lie to me. But Stephen has a bank book with your name on it. He said he could prove you opened the account. He said you were connected with Pinto, with the gambling syndicate.'

'And you take his word over mine? I've never lied to you.'

'You have lied. I asked you about the match and you told me there was nothing wrong. Everyone has their off days, you said.'

'I thought he would kill you!'

'This,' said Sara, fighting to keep his tear-filled eyes from breaking her resolve, 'is killing me! I opened up to you. Despite everything that had happened to me, I was ready to be hoodwinked one more time. Well, congratulations. You've made me the biggest fool in the world.'

'Sara, I love you,' he said, trying to draw her towards him. His words couldn't penetrate the shield she'd put up again, but if he could just hold her he could make her believe him with his body.

'Don't touch me!' she hissed, tapping a last reserve of anger. How dare he think he could make it all right like that? 'I think you should go. Now.'

'But, Sara—'

'Go! Leave the country. Go back to Brazil.' She couldn't turn Antonio over to the police, but while he remained in England, Stephen would have something to hold over her. She leaned against the window sill, watching the first splattering of rain darkening the metal of the fire escape. 'I'm releasing you from your contract. As of this moment you no longer play for Camden.'

'It's Antonio again,' said Kathy, holding her hand over the phone.

'Tell him I'm not here.'

'He's calling from the airport.'

What a surprise, thought Sara. After the confrontation, she had stayed away from the club and had refused to take any of his calls. He had passed on messages through Kathy, vowing that he'd stay in England and fight to get Sara back. What a joke! Barely two weeks later he was at the airport. How very convenient it was for him that Brazil had no extradition treaty with Britain. 'I don't care.'

Kathy listened to Antonio, concern spreading across her face.

'Sara, you've got to talk to him. He says they've found a body of a young boy and it could be Oscar.'

Sara jumped up, took the receiver from Kathy's hand and replaced it in its cradle. 'Why should Oscar be any more real than all the other stories he told me?' she said, walking into the conservatory.

Despite the cold outside, the conservatory was incredibly hot and the glass walls dripped with condensation. Sara plumped a paisley patterned cushion on a wicker sofa and sat down, tucking her legs underneath her, shutting out all thoughts of the little boy. What she'd just said was disgusting, but she had to protect herself. She couldn't allow herself to believe that anything about Antonio was genuine, even Oscar. As hard as she tried to shut it out, the image of a five-year-old lying dead in the street kept flashing through her mind. Once again she felt bereft, a pain which was almost intolerable.

'I couldn't find any egg-nog,' said Kathy, appearing with a tray of mince pies a few minutes later. 'Not that I'd drink it if I had. Will gin do? It's not very seasonal.' She put the tray down on a low wooden table and pulled up a wicker armchair, aware that she was gabbling. 'I love this conservatory – it's so tropical.'

Sara glared at her. 'Like Brazil, you mean?'

'I wish you'd speak to him before he goes. It would make you feel so much better.'

'I don't care if I never speak to him again.'

'You don't mean that,' said Kathy, noticing several empty wine bottles tucked between the sofa and the wall. She took a bite from a mince pie, the hot filling scalding her tongue.

'Kathy, did you just come over here to give me a hard time?'

'I came over to inject a little festive cheer into your life,' she said pointing to the mince pies. 'I baked them myself.'

'Shirley Conran, eat your heart out.' Sara poured herself a large gin and raised her glass. 'Merry Christmas.'

'It won't be for June,' said Kathy, throwing a screwed-up card on to the coffee table. 'That was in the bin.'

'Do you normally go through people's rubbish?' asked Sara, snatching the card and tearing it up.

'Jesus, I was just scraping a baking tray! Did you read it before you threw it away?'

'No.'

'Don't you *care* how she's feeling? She's on anti-depressants, you know.'

'Did she write that in her Christmas card? That's cheery. And they were bearing gifts of gold, frankincense and Valium.'

Kathy shook her head. 'I've never noticed it before, Sara, but you're a very mean drunk. Of course she didn't write it, she told me herself.'

'You've been speaking to June?'

'Yes, I've been speaking to your mother. You may not care about her, but she's worried sick about you, and so am I.'

Sara fingered a mince pie but left it on the tray. Was she doomed never to spend Christmas like normal people? For several years the memory of Bill had haunted the holiday and now Antonio was joining the queue. 'You shouldn't worry. I'm fine.'

'No, you're not,' said Kathy. 'I know you. When things are bad you throw yourself into your work, just as you've been doing for the last few months. But when things are really awful you start to retreat. Like you did after Bill. Like you're doing now. Sara, why aren't you coming into the office?'

'It's Christmas. Everybody takes time off at Christmas.'

This petulance was something Kathy hadn't seen before. It was so unlike Sara. 'I wish Stephen thought the same way. Sara, I need you back at Camden. You're so close to catching him.'

'Give me a couple of days, eh?' She would hand the papers over to the police in her own good time. All the urgency was gone now. The moment Antonio stepped on that plane, she'd lost anyway.

'Maggie's in the office all the time, you know. We had words this morning.' Kathy was hoping that this news might goad Sara into action. 'She said that once again you'd managed to get me completely under your thumb.'

'That's probably true,' said Sara, flatly. 'What did you say?'

'I told her that the last time I cared about what she thought was probably also the last time she'd had a decent meal and a menstrual cycle.'

'And you say I'm mean?'

'I think it was called for.' Kathy looked at her friend, casting around desperately for something that would lift Sara out of the blues. 'You're still coming to me on Christmas Day, aren't you?'

'Actually, I was planning to spend it here.'

'You can't,' Kathy protested. 'Jackie'll be there, and it would be awful if you weren't too.'

'I need to be on my own.'

'Please.'

'I really should be on my own. You're not the person I should be taking this out on.'

'Yes I am,' replied Kathy, putting her arm round her.

Sara flinched. 'There are a couple of presents for you and Bette in the living room. They're not much, but I haven't felt like going shopping. We'll talk soon.'

On leaving the clinic, Jackie had temporarily moved in with Kathy and though Christmas was approaching and both their lives had taken a turn for the better, a gloom hung over the house.

'We've got to get some more evidence, nail him once and for all,' said Kathy. She was worried by Sara's apparent inability to do anything just then, but she couldn't let Stephen win, for Jackie's sake as much as Sara's.

'I remember catching him in the loft once at home,' said Jackie. 'When I asked him what he was doing, he told me to mind my own business. I thought he probably had a dirty-magazine collection up there, but it could be something else.'

'We could go and look. Have you still got keys?'

'I don't think it's such a good idea,' said Jackie. 'What if he's there with that new bit of his, that Maggie?'

'He isn't,' said Kathy, pulling on her coat. 'Louise told me he was taking Maggie Christmas shopping.'

Kathy ordered a cab and an hour later they were standing in front of Stephen's house in Epping, with the taxi waiting for them just along the road.

'I'm scared,' said Jackie, biting her nails.

'So am I,' said Kathy, gripping her hand. 'But just think how good we'll feel if we sort out this mess for Sara. She'll be back any day now.' Kathy almost laughed, thinking how like Sara she sounded.

This would be exactly what her friend would have done if she'd been on form.

'I think I'm going to be sick. Just seeing this house brings all the unhappy memories rushing back. I need a drink. A real drink.'

Kathy pushed Jackie up the drive. 'No, you don't. It might be the same house but you're a different person. Come on, let's get it over and done with.' She wouldn't have said no to a whisky herself.

Jackie's hand shook as she fumbled with the key. Part of her was hoping that he'd changed the locks, but the thought of helping Sara spurred her on. She owed her this favour. If it hadn't been for Sara and Kathy, she'd probably be lying in a heap somewhere in this house clutching a bottle and waiting for Stephen to come home and abuse her. The door opened and she peered gingerly inside. 'Hello?'

The house appeared to be empty. The two women went inside, psyched up to take flight at the slightest noise.

'He's not here,' said Kathy, loudly for reassurance.

Jackie walked briskly through the house to make sure, even looking behind the doors and curtains. 'Let's find what we've come for and get out quick.'

Upstairs, she used a rod to pull down the loft flap. As it opened, a set of steps was released. 'There's a light up here somewhere,' Jackie muttered, climbing the stairs, her hand searching around in the dark. 'Ah, here it is.'

'Do you want me to come up?'

'There's not much room,' said Jackie, her voice muffled. 'You stay on guard.'

Kathy giggled nervously. She felt just like a heroine from the comic books she had read as a child. She could hear Jackie grunting as she shifted boxes, then the sound of the boxes falling over. 'Have you found anything?'

'Give me a chance! It looks like everything Stephen has ever owned is up here. Damn!'

'What's wrong?'

'I hit my head on a bloody golf club. Hang on a minute, I think I've found something.'

'What is it?'

Jackie's dusty face appeared in the hatch. 'I was right about those magazines. Disgusting old pig.'

'Get a move on, Jackie.'

There was more rummaging and scraping, then Jackie reappeared, waving some papers. 'If I'm not mistaken, these look like company documents but they're not for Camden. This one says Red Admiral . . .'

'Chestnuts roasting on an open fire . . .' The velvety voice of Nat King Cole coming from the stereo conjured up a rose-tinted picture of the kind of Christmas Maggie had never known. She sank into the fuchsia Dralon settee and accepted Stephen's offer of a drink, wondering how much alcohol it was going to take to make the evening even halfway bearable. From the Queen Anne television unit to the 'antique' globe cocktail cabinet, the tacky Epping house was an exact reproduction of her parents' home a few miles up the road in Dagenham. As they'd driven up the gravel drive past the stone lions sitting sentinel at the gateway and parked by the neo-Georgian porch, Maggie had wanted to run.

Stephen handed her a tumblerful of whisky. 'Make yourself comfortable and I'll let you open your Christmas present,' he laughed, grabbing his crotch.

Maggie's nose twitched as she caught a whiff of Stephen's rancid body odour and she downed the drink in one, eager for it to take effect as quickly as possible. 'Do you mind if I have another one?'

Stephen brought her the bottle and sat down next to her, putting his arm around her shoulder. 'Show us your tits,' he leered.

'Let me have that drink first,' she stalled.

Stephen handed her the bottle and lunged at her breast, causing her to drop the whisky on the burgundy shag-pile carpet. Its contents leaked out and she attempted to right the bottle but Stephen pushed her back on the settee. As his hands began pawing at her body, Maggie replayed in her head the conversation she'd had with Cynthia at Canary Wharf earlier in the day.

'My dear,' Cynthia had said, her voice laced with menace, 'from what I gather you have absolutely no compunction about using your body for professional purposes.'

'I'm not sleeping with Stephen Powell, and that's final,' said Maggie.

Cynthia read from a blue file marked with Maggie's name. 'Oh dear, the *Bournemouth Clarion*. That was a rather inglorious start, wasn't it? And dear Anthony Coakley – you certainly don't discriminate on age. Something of an equal opportunities slut, aren't you?'

Any day now the banks were going to foreclose on the satellite loan, a situation which was driving Cynthia into a state of near hysteria. She had focused all her rage on Sara, whom she still regarded as the root of all her problems. Maggie had had just about enough. 'Listen, you—'

Cynthia picked up the file and slapped it across Maggie's face. 'Be quiet. If you want to keep your job and the contents of this file a secret, then you'll do as you're told. Be very nice to Stephen and find out what that bitch is up to.'

Shaken, Maggie left the proprietor's office, went to the canteen, bought five chocolate bars and binged for the first time in six months.

And so here she was, allowing Stephen to tug at the waistband of her knickers as he sank his teeth into her left nipple.

'Stephen, we've got to talk,' she said, gasping at the pain.

He looked up at her, a string of saliva running from his lips to her breast. 'Hang on a minute, love, I need a piss.'

Stephen climbed off her and she gratefully eased herself into an upright position. When he'd gone she looked in her handbag and found first the bottle of Amitriptyline – although it would take more than an anti-depressant pill to get rid of her malaise – and then her sleeping tablets. Usually she took them only in the small hours, when her constant insomnia exhausted her. Now she took them simply to dull her senses.

'I'm in the bedroom,' shouted Stephen.

Her feet leaden, she put down her bag and mounted the stairs. Had the thought of what lay in store for her not been so horrific, Maggie would have laughed at the sight which greeted her in the bedroom. Stephen, pasty-faced and naked, was spread-eagled on top of – she might have guessed – a circular waterbed.

'Get your drawers off and get over here,' he ordered.

'I've got something to tell you.'

'Oh fuck, you're not on the rag, are you?'

'It's about Sara. Stuart Hargreaves was her real father – and her mother is Felicity Butterworth.' She could have pussy-footed around, broken the news gently, but what for? She despised him. 'I thought you should know.'

Stephen didn't reply. Instead he curled up in a foetal position, looking like some obscenely overgrown baby.

'Did you even know she was pregnant?' asked Maggie sluggishly. The sleeping pills were beginning to do the trick.

His voice was almost inaudible. 'No. But I could have forgiven her. She was the only woman I've ever loved and that bastard ruined her.'

'I think I should leave,' said Maggie, not wanting to wait around for him to start crying. She'd delivered the bad news and that was enough. Why should she have to deal with the fallout as well?

'Stay with me,' pleaded Stephen.

He sounded pitiful and his vulnerability disgusted her even more than his oafishness. 'You need some time on your own to sort this out.'

Stephen jumped up and grabbed her. 'Please.'

'Stephen, I . . .' She could barely keep her eyes open as he pulled her on to the waterbed. She didn't protest until she felt her underwear being pulled over her knees. 'No, I don't want to.'

Stephen took no notice. Yanking her thighs apart, he thrust into her. 'Fucking bitches, you're all fucking bitches,' he said, his obese belly pounding against her stomach.

Neither awake nor asleep, Maggie lay there in a kind of limbo, only vaguely aware of the discomfort of his dead weight on top of her body.

'Dirty, disgusting whores,' roared Stephen, pulling her hair.

Maggie's frail body rocked in time with the waterbed. Never once in her life had she known what it was like to have a man make love to her. She'd let her body be used time after time, but what would doing this with someone who loved her feel like? What would it feel like to have someone really love her? But who could? She was worthless, totally worthless. Stephen was, too, but somehow, here, now, on this bed, what they were doing debased them both even further. They were ideally suited, she realised, slipping gratefully into unconsciousness.

'Filthy slags,' Stephen continued, oblivious to the fact that she was dead to the world.

Chapter Forty

Kathy took a thick file from her big leather handbag. 'I think there's enough here to prove Stephen's involvement,' she said with some pride. 'Look.' She pointed to the first letter in the file. 'Here's a letter about Winluck dated March 1991, showing the names of the accounts it paid money into. See, there's Sam Margetts.'

'And Antonio, too, no doubt,' said Sara, drily. 'I'm not interested. I already know enough about Winluck to tell the police. When I'm ready.'

'Sara, you've got to fight this thing,' said Kathy, wondering if her friend had moved from the conservatory sofa at all since her last visit. She was still wearing the same clothes, but thankfully the number of bottles at her feet hadn't increased.

'Shouldn't you be stuffing a turkey or something?'

Kathy ignored the remark and took out another letter. 'We found this from Frank Doherty. Yes, it's that Frank,' she said, seeing a glimmer of interest in Sara's eyes. Sara had checked but Frank's number hadn't come up on Camden's telephone bill. Kathy continued excitedly: 'But it's more than that. This letter links the gambling syndicate with Borboleta. From what I can work out, they were using money from the drug-dealing, laundered through Borboleta, to pay off the players. The Brazilian connection.'

'Don't forget Antonio,' said Sara, but she could feel herself beginning to buckle under the force of Kathy's enthusiasm. 'What else have you got?'

Kathy produced some documents proving Stephen's ownership of Red Admiral and Chrysalis Clothing, plus a letter referring to his share dividends in Borboleta. 'And this, I believe,' said Kathy, pulling out her pièce de resistance, 'is a bank-deposit book for Credit Suisse!'

Sara took the bank book and flicked through the pages until she came to September's dealings. Days before Antonio's transfer, a deposit of £500,000 had been made. Damn him, she thought. Damn him to hell. And Stephen, too. They'd made a total fool of her and how had she responded? By sitting around like a vegetable. Maybe she couldn't win now, but she could certainly make sure that they lost.

'Kathy, I want you to do me a big favour,' she said, standing up. 'The files I photocopied are in my office. Could you collect them and take them to the police, along with these?'

'At last!' exclaimed Kathy. 'Hold on a minute, where are you going?'

'To see Stephen,' replied Sara. 'I want to see his face when I tell him what I've done.'

'What are you doing here?' asked Maggie, opening Stephen's front door. She wiped her face, hoping that Sara hadn't noticed the tears.

'I want to see Stephen.' Sara walked into the hallway, barely acknowledging the emaciated woman rattling around in what was obviously one of Jackie's old negligées. How could she have slept with him?

Maggie looked down at herself and covered her body with her arms; she felt so ashamed. 'Sara, I . . .'

'Leave it, Maggie,' snapped Sara. 'We have nothing to say to each other.' She stood at the bottom of the stairs, leaning on the banister.

'Stephen!' she called, looking at her watch, hoping that Kathy would be on her way to the police station by now.

'Get the fuck out of my house,' yelled Stephen, flying down the stairs in a red terry dressing gown which barely met across his middle. 'Maggie, what the fuck do you think you're playing at letting that slag in here?'

'The slag won't be staying long,' replied Sara, cringing as she looked around at the multitude of clashing colours in the hallway. 'I've just come to tell you—'

'I know you're Stuart's bastard.'

Sara looked at Maggie. So that had been her big plan. Well, it had fallen flat. Surely the little bit of sadistic pleasure to be gained from telling Stephen in no way merited having to sleep with him. 'I wouldn't have to be a genius to work out who told you that.'

'That upper-class shit ruined my life,' raged Stephen. 'Felicity was mine, and he took her. He ruined everything. And now,' he shouted, walking away from Sara down the hallway, 'I'm going to ruin your life, too.'

'It's an empty threat,' said Sara, following him into the lounge. He couldn't destroy her life any more than he'd already done. 'I've got all the evidence I need to go to the police now. You can say what you like about Antonio, I don't care.'

But Stephen had one last card up his sleeve. 'You should care. You sent the poor sucker packing, and guess what? He was innocent all along.'

Sara felt as if she'd been kicked in the stomach. 'What do you mean?'

Stephen began to laugh. 'You stupid bitch. We set him up. Frank did a really good job opening the account. Got some dago who looked the spit of your boyfriend to sign up and everything.'

Sara had to hold down the nausea welling in her throat. Her mouth tasted of bile and she was beginning to feel unsteady on her feet. What had she done?

'I thought that would shut you up,' he said, pouring himself a whisky, even though it was only ten o'clock in the morning. 'But this is the best bit. You're going to love this. I took out a little bit of insurance, just in case your feelings about lover boy started to waver.

I don't think you're going to go to the police at all.' Sara watched as Stephen picked up the phone and dialled an international number, praying that what she feared most of all was not true.

'What's going on? What have you done?' Sara pleaded desperately, the panic rising as Stephen remained silent, waiting for his call to be answered.

'Is he awake? ... Good, get him to the phone ... Well, take the fucking gag off, you moron!' Stephen laughed as he handed the phone to Sara. 'Honestly, how can he talk with a gag on?'

Sara could hardly speak, fighting as she was to keep the nausea down. 'Antonio?'

'Sara, I'm so sorry ...'

The pick-up on the international line faded away. 'Antonio, where are you? Talk to me!'

'... don't have to give in. Not for me ...' His voice, weak and strained, faded again.

'Antonio!'

Stephen snatched the phone away from her and cut it off. 'That's enough. Now, if you want him kept alive, give me back the papers and get the fuck out of Camden.'

Sara was stunned into silence, fearful that any second now she would just faint.

'Stephen, please,' interrupted Maggie.

He whirled around to face her. 'What do you want?'

'Hasn't this ...' Maggie didn't know what to say. It had all gone too far. She didn't want this. What if they killed him? It was way beyond her. Sure, she had wanted to get her revenge on Sara, but she'd already done that – in spades – and wrecked her own life in the process. And now that she had used up all her adrenaline and with it all her venom, there was no hate left. She looked from Sara to Stephen, seeing all too clearly the downward trajectory of her life. The way Stephen had abused her body the night before underlined the indisputable fact that she had finally reached rock-bottom. No one had ever needed her or even liked her, apart from Sara – and look how she'd repaid her. Sara was the only friend she'd ever had, the only person who'd ever shown her love. All the things she had blamed on Sara were her own fault. And now, to cap it all, she was party to a kidnapping. Would murder be next? 'I think—'

'I don't care what you think, you stupid skinny tart. Now fuck off back into bed. It's the only place you're any use,' he snarled, raising his hand. 'This is between her and me.'

Maggie quietly did as she was told, too defeated and ashamed to do what she wanted to do, which was to reach out to Sara and beg her forgiveness.

Sara had watched the exchange between Maggie and Stephen as if in a trance. This couldn't be happening. Was it already too late? Was Kathy at this very moment handing over the files to the police? She had to stall for time: she couldn't let Stephen know she didn't have the papers. 'I'll get them. Give me a few hours and I'll sort everything out.'

'You know, I almost feel sorry for Antonio. He thought he had escaped the people trying to kill him, but they just sent him here, where I could keep closer tabs on him,' said Stephen, enjoying every minute of Sara's distress. 'Pinto needed Antonio out of the way because of all that damn campaigning. The mistake he made was not killing him straight away. Soft-hearted bastard. He felt there'd be too much of a national outcry. Still, I made a bit of money in the transfer, so I wasn't complaining. Until now.'

Sara bit her lip, willing herself not to cry. Her stubbornness was going to get Antonio killed. She had to stop Kathy. 'Stephen, I'll give you the papers – and all the copies.'

Sara turned and ran out of the house. As she hit the fresh air, the nausea overtook her and she retched violently, her empty stomach providing no physical release. Her eyes filled with tears, she ran blindly along the street looking for a phone box. When she finally found one, it was occupied. She banged on the door, begging the man inside to let her use the phone.

When she eventually dialled Kathy's office number there was no answer. She tried reception.

'Louise, is Kathy still in the building?'

'She's just left. A cab's waiting for her.'

'Stop her!' screamed Sara hysterically.

Several agonising minutes passed before Louise returned. 'Sara?'

It was too late – Kathy had gone and Antonio was as good as dead.

'Sara, I've got Kathy for you.'

Oh, thank you, God. 'Kathy!'

'I was just on my way.'

'Forget about it. Photocopy everything and then bike it over to Stephen's, as quickly as possible. They've got Antonio, and if I don't . . .' Sara began to sob. '. . . and even if I do it might be too late. Oh, what have I done?'

'Sara, slow down. I can't understand what you're talking about.'

'Stephen and Pinto . . . Antonio was innocent.'

'Oh, God.'

Sara tried to calm herself. She had to think straight. 'You have to give Stephen two copies of everything. He knows I've copied the documents once already. Oh, this isn't going to work!'

'Sara, we have to try.' Kathy was trying to sound businesslike but her voice was choked with fear.

'Kathy, just do this for me and hold on to a copy for dear life until you hear from me again.'

'Where are you going? Can't you come back to the office now?'

'I can't,' sobbed Sara, 'I've got a plane to catch.'

Chapter Forty-One

'What has this to do with Sara?' cried Antonio, the ropes cutting into his wrists as he struggled to work himself free. One or two shards of dull light poked through the cracks in the door; otherwise the room was in permanent darkness. Drops of sweat snaked their way down his forehead, stinging his eyes; his mouth was parched, his lips cracked. Never had he been as afraid as this. Hearing Sara's voice had been wonderful and terrible at the same time. Where was she? She'd sounded far away, but on the mobile phone it was difficult to tell. If they were in contact with her, the chances were that they had her captive, too. 'Is this about money? If you leave her alone, I will give you everything I have.'

'*Silencio!*' said the man who had been guarding him for the four or five days he had been in captivity. Sleeping and waking at odd hours, never knowing if it was night or day, Antonio was beginning to lose track of the time. This man seemed to be here during the day – another guard did the night duty – so it must be daytime. But what day was it?

'You've got to tell me! She has nothing to do with all this.'

It took the guard only two or three steps across the small, stifling, windowless shack to reach Antonio, and without a second thought he hit the captive across the face with the back of his hand. 'I said, shut up.'

'You damn coward!' shouted Antonio, tasting the blood from his cut lip. He tried desperately to stand, but, his hands and feet bound tightly, he succeeded only in falling over, scraping his face against the rough concrete of the floor.

The guard let out a cackle, pushing Antonio away with his foot. Just as he was about to strike Antonio again the door of the hut opened. As a second man entered, Antonio was momentarily blinded by daylight. Then the door closed. The voice was familiar. This second man was the one who seemed to be in charge. He'd been there on one other occasion. When had that been? Was it two days ago? Maybe three. It was so hard to know anything except that he was still in Rio. Between the time the gunmen had bundled him into the boot of a car and his arrival at this shack, no more than thirty minutes had elapsed.

The men whispered to each other and Antonio strained to hear what they were saying. He heard Sara's name. 'Tell me what you want with her,' he called out in the darkness.

The man in charge spoke. 'Your fate, Senhor Neves, is in the hands of this woman. You have to pray that she loves you very much.'

It wasn't easy getting on a flight over the Christmas holiday and after spending the best part of a day waiting around, Sara had reached the point where she was considering hiring a private jet to get her to Rio when a last-minute cancellation liberated a seat. The ten-hour flight felt like an eternity. It brought back memories of the agonising trip back from Ecuador while Stuart lay dying. If only she'd known then what she knew now. Sara's mind raced with thoughts about what lay ahead. She castigated herself for not having believed Antonio, for banishing him from her life. There was no guarantee that he would be safe in spite of her bargain with Stephen. If something happened to him because of her actions, how would she ever get over it? As the plane began its descent towards Rio

International Airport, Sara found it hard to shake off the fear that she might be too late.

Once off the plane and through customs, Sara zigzagged through the crowds of slow-moving people as she ran through the packed airport, dirty and sweaty despite the heavy air conditioning. Locating the tourist office, she waited impatiently in the queue behind a noisy, mixed crowd of backpackers, well-heeled businessmen and American tourists. Having left London in such a hurry she hadn't even had time to pack a case, let alone arrange for a place to stay.

'*Bom dia*, Senhora, how can I help you?'

'I need a hotel room.'

'In what price range? *Caro?*' asked the assistant, looking her up and down.

'Pardon?'

'Expensive?'

'Whatever.'

'May I recommend the Copacabana Palace on Avenida Atlantica? It is very popular with royalty. Lots of pop stars from your country stay there too. It is—'

'Fine, can you book it?' interrupted Sara. She gave him her details.

'How long for?' he asked, as he picked up the telephone.

'I don't know,' replied Sara. 'Where can I change money?'

'Travellers' cheques?'

'Cash.' She hadn't had time to do any more than raid a hole in the wall at the airport. Thank goodness for credit cards.

The man pointed out a bureau de change, where Sara exchanged every last note she could find, stuffing the money haphazardly into her bag.

On a nearby news-stand she spotted Antonio's face immediately, staring out at her from the front page of the *Jornal do Brasil*. Buying a copy she rushed back to the tourist office, ignoring the strange look the assistant gave her when she asked him to translate the news item.

'Is he alive?' she asked, her heart pounding.

'Let's hope that he is. They still don't know where he is.'

'Do they say who's behind it?'

The man read through the story. 'There is conjecture that it is to do with his campaigning on behalf—'

Sara didn't need to hear any more. There was obviously no mention of Pinto, Borboleta or Powell. She was the only one who knew who was behind Antonio's kidnapping and why. She snatched the paper back and stared fruitlessly at the jumble of foreign words. Then she had a stroke of luck: the author of the report was Flavio Cardoso, Antonio's friend. She would go to her hotel and try to contact him immediately via the paper. She hadn't known he was a journalist. Perhaps he wasn't – perhaps he'd just contributed this piece as a friend of Antonio's. In any event, the paper would know where she could find him.

Hurrying from the air-conditioned confines of the airport, Sara caught her breath as the searing heat assaulted her senses. 'Taxi,' she shouted to a group of men standing by some rusting, dented cars. One of them jumped into the driver's seat of his pride and joy and pulled up in front of her. She threw the solitary bag she'd brought with her into the back and leaped in.

The driver pushed the accelerator to the floor as if he sensed the urgency of her mission. Or perhaps he always drove like that. The scenery flew past as if in a speeded-up film and for the first time since her arrival, Sara took in the fact that she was now 5,000 miles away from home. Visiting South America as a football reporter had been completely different. Then she had stayed in the same hotel as the other journalists, eaten with them, drunk with them, watched football with them. In that hermetically sealed world she could have been anywhere. Now she was on her own. As they shot past one ramshackle hillside shanty town after another, Sara shivered despite the heat. Antonio could be anywhere. How long would it take to search through even one of those towns? Was Antonio being kept prisoner in one of them? Perhaps she was driving past him right now. Tears welled up as she thought of what he might be going through. What if they killed him? Her fingernails dug into the palm of her hand as she clenched her fists, willing him to still be alive.

Every so often the *favelas* would disappear from view as they passed through a tunnel bored through the hillside and the smell of car fumes would replace that of the stagnant harbour. As they emerged from one such tunnel, the statue of Christ the Redeemer came into view, staring down, arms outstretched, from the purplish sun-dappled summit of Hunchback Mountain and, for a brief second, Sara was lost in the sight.

'It's beautiful, no?' asked the driver.

'Yes,' said Sara, distractedly wishing there was the time to properly appreciate such splendour.

As the taxi's wheels squealed through the skyscraper-filled centre of Rio, the speedometer nudging 100 kph, Sara held on to the door handle for dear life and closed her eyes, opening them only when the driver announced that they had arrived at the Copacabana Palace, a multi-tiered, creamy yellow building which looked like a huge wedding cake. Shakily, she climbed out of the taxi, handed the driver enough notes to make him smile and entered the building.

'*Como vai*, Senhora Moore?' asked the receptionist.

Sara nodded.

'We have a lovely room for you, overlooking the ocean. How long will you be staying?'

'I don't know. Maybe a week.'

'That is OK. How will you be paying?'

Sara searched through her bag of cash, finally unearthed her new platinum AMEX and gave it to the receptionist. 'Can you telephone this newspaper, please,' she asked, pointing to the *Jornal do Brasil*, 'and put the call through to my room?'

'Of course.' The woman clicked her fingers at a young uniformed boy waiting by the desk. 'I will return your card later,' she said as the bellboy picked up Sara's bag.

In her suite the boy showed her the bedroom, the sitting room, the bathroom, the bar and the view, then hovered expectantly by the door. Sara dipped into her money bag and produced a 50,000 cruzeiro note which convinced the bellboy of the existence of Santa Claus. Waiting for the phone to ring, she unpacked her few belongings and then paced the room, feeling that she was wasting precious time. If she couldn't get hold of Flavio, what should she do? On the flight over, her guilt and fear had wiped out all practical considerations, but now here she was in a strange country trying to find someone even the local police couldn't trace.

The hopelessness of the situation began to sink in. She paced from room to room, trying to dispel her panic. Finally the phone rang.

'*Jornal do Brasil.*'

'Flavio Cardoso, *por favor.*'

Muzak drifted down the phone by way of reply. Sara felt the faintest stirrings of hope. At least they hadn't denied all knowledge of Flavio, so obviously he worked there.

'*Bom dia.* Flavio Cardoso.'

'*Você fala Inglès?*'

'Yes. Who is this?'

'My name is Sara Moore—'

'Antonio's girlfriend! Where are you?'

'Have you any news? Have they found him?' she asked. *Please don't let him say that he's dead.*

'I'm afraid not. Senhora Moore, *where are you?*'

Sara heaved a sigh of relief. 'I'm staying at the Copacabana Palace.'

'You are here? Do not move – I'll be there in under an hour.'

Putting down the phone, Sara wondered what Antonio had told Flavio. Did the journalist know that she had believed the lies about his friend? That she was partly responsible for his predicament? She looked out of the window, barely seeing the seascape in front of her; all she could see was Antonio. She pictured him making love to her, and the memory was as vivid as if he were there in the hotel room by her side. She remembered every contour of his body, every little blemish and scar on his skin; she even imagined she could smell him, that musky, rich, manly scent that perfumed her bed and filled her with desire. Stop it, she told herself. Antonio wasn't there, and that kind of thought would break her if she wasn't careful. She had to be strong.

For a while she just walked around in circles. What was taking Cardoso so long? She couldn't bear being left alone with her thoughts. Antonio, gagged, maybe hurt, maybe with a gun held to his head, all because of her. And what about Oscar? Was it his body Antonio had flown home to identify? How could she have been so callous as to doubt the boy's existence? A family, Antonio had called the three of them. Thinking of families led her to the Butterfly. Life certainly played some funny tricks on you. Before the kidnapping, Sara had planned to come to Brazil on a very different mission: to find her mother. That no longer mattered. What was the past but just so many unpleasant shadows? She had to look to the future now – a future she fervently wanted to believe would include Antonio.

Another twenty minutes passed before at last the phone rang again and the receptionist informed her that a visitor was on his way up to see her.

'Flavio?' she inquired anxiously, opening the door seconds later. The man standing in front of her was dark-skinned like Antonio but of a much stockier build, his brown hair shaved in a utilitarian crew cut.

'Yes. Hello,' he said, slightly out of breath, taking both her hands in his. Flavio followed Sara into the room and took the seat she offered him, loosening his tie and smoothing down his crumpled beige suit. 'I—'

Sara spoke over him. 'Do you – sorry, you go first.'

'I am sorry I cannot bring you any good news. We have been searching since he was taken. And the police ... well,' he said, throwing up his hands. 'Nothing. It is like he never existed.'

'Please God let him be all right,' cried Sara.

Flavio jumped up from the seat and put his arm around her shoulders. 'I'm sure he will be. This won't sound very pleasant, but I think his body would have been found by now if anything had happened.'

'Yes ... yes, you're right,' said Sara, clinging on to that crumb of comfort as if her own life depended on it.

'How did you find out what had happened?' he asked, stepping away from her.

His olive-green eyes were searching her face. 'It's a long story,' she said wearily, sitting on the bed. Filled with remorse, she told Flavio what had taken place at Stephen's house, the once strange-sounding names of Pinto and Borboleta now rolling off her tongue with ease, so big a part of her life had they become. Flavio listened intently, allowing the occasional guttural expression of disgust to punctuate her monologue. 'I haven't given the file to the British police, but that's no guarantee that they won't hurt him – or kill him,' she concluded. 'What have they got to lose?'

'*Meu deus*,' said Flavio finally. 'I might have guessed that a piece of scum like Pinto was behind this.' He took her hand again to reassure her. 'But at least now we have some leads.'

'Shouldn't we tell the police?'

Flavio snorted. '*Merda*, no. They're probably in on it. In Rio, who knows who's the good cop? I will go on looking myself. I have many friends in the *favelas* who know of Pinto. Perhaps someone has heard something.'

'What about Oscar? Antonio said he was coming back to Brazil to identify a body.' Sara couldn't bear to admit that she hadn't spoken to Antonio directly, let alone add that she hadn't believed it was true.

Flavio gave her a gap-toothed smile. 'It wasn't him. And, better than that, he is safe. A lot of money had to change hands, but we eventually discovered him living on a garbage site, half starved. But he is safe now. Sadly, Antonio was abducted before we found the boy. That good news would have helped him through this ordeal.'

'Is Oscar staying with you?'

'Oh no. I'm not a suitable candidate – a bachelor with no home-making skills who works very long hours,' he said, allowing himself a small, hiccupy laugh. 'He is with a friend of Antonio's, the Contessa Maria Santos, who runs the charity Viva As Crianças. The poor woman is beside herself: she blames herself for Antonio's disappearance. She was in the States when he returned to Rio.'

'Antonio spoke of her,' said Sara, remembering the fleeting glance she'd had of the woman in Cuenca. 'Can I see Oscar?' she asked, feeling that if she could do nothing more in the search for Antonio for the present, at least she could care for the child he loved so much.

Flavio seemed surprised by her request. 'Yes. By all means. When?'

'As soon as possible.'

Flavio could see the wisdom of giving Sara something to occupy her mind while he worked on the new leads she had given him. 'I could take you there now,' he said.

*   *   *

They drove to the Contessa's house as the scarlet sun sank into the sea. On the way, it became clear from Flavio's answers to a few discreet questions that Antonio had never mentioned her betrayal of him to Flavio.

'He just wanted to find Oscar and return to England for you,' said the journalist. 'I have never seen Antonio so passionate about someone. I hope you will invite me to the wedding.'

'Of course,' Sara smiled, wanting to share his optimism. But even if Antonio got out of this alive, would he ever be able to forgive her?

'Ah, here we are,' said Flavio, turning off the coastal road and driving up a winding cliffside path at the end of which stood a nineteenth-century white-stoned mansion, set in a floodlit tropical garden.

As Sara got out the car she could hear the restful sound of the ocean crashing on the shoreline below her. 'It's beautiful,' she murmured.

'Come, come,' urged Flavio, the palm of his hand on her back. Ringing the bell, he waited impatiently, rocking on the balls of his feet. The door was opened by a maid and after a quick conversation which Sara didn't understand they were ushered into what seemed to be a ballroom. A thousand lights were reflected in the vast antique mirrors on the walls from the massive chandelier above, and at one end of the room gold brocade portieres were drawn back to reveal French windows thrown open to the gardens and the ocean below. Sara could smell the salt in the air, mixed with the scent of the orchids growing in abundance outside. She wondered what Oscar made of all this opulence after the sights and smells of the garbage tip.

'Flavio!'

Sara turned to see the Contessa walking towards them across the polished wooden floor of the ballroom, her head held high, the picture of elegance in a full-length emerald silk dress. Much of her face was obscured by dark glasses as it had been that day in Cuenca. Sara wondered for a moment whether the Contessa was perhaps blind.

'Maria, this is Sara Moore, Antonio's girlfriend. She has brought us news of the kidnappers.'

The Contessa snatched the glasses from her face. 'Sara Moore?'

'Yes. I'm very pleased to meet you,' said Sara, looking into the Contessa's green eyes. 'I just wish . . .' she faltered. The Contessa's face had suddenly drained of all colour.

'Oh, merciful God!' whispered the Contessa. She wobbled slightly and then fell to the ground in a dead faint, the skirt of her dress spread out around her like a water lily.

'Maria!' Flavio tore off his jacket and placed it carefully under the Contessa's head.

'I don't understand,' said Sara, kneeling by the Contessa and holding her limp hand. Her own heart was thumping strangely, just as it had when . . . The green eyes! Sara felt the ground spin away from her and she clutched at Flavio's shirtsleeve. 'It's her!' she cried. 'It's her—'

'Who?' asked Flavio, panicked by this extraordinary turn of events.

Sara couldn't speak. She was mouthing words but nothing was coming out. Flavio led her to a chair. He was completely bewildered and didn't know whose needs he should attend to first.

'Sara, speak to me. What is going on?' he said, shaking her shoulders.

Wide-eyed, Sara stared at the woman lying prostrate on the floor, 'The Contessa,' she gasped. 'She is my mother.' The green eyes. She had known from the moment the Contessa had removed her glasses, though it had taken a couple of seconds to sink in. Sara hadn't merely been looking at a woman she'd seen once before – she had been looking at an older version of herself. She had glimpsed the future and her mother had stared back into the past.

Chapter Forty-Two

When the Contessa came round a few minutes later, Sara was kneeling by her side and holding her hand.

'Mother . . .' whispered Sara tentatively. The Contessa began to weep inconsolably. 'It's OK, it'll be all right,' she said over and over again, calming the woman until eventually her weeping slowed.

Flavio helped the Contessa up and guided her into a small, unlit anteroom. Sara followed, lost in a sensation that was becoming all too familiar: one of being in a dream. Flavio threw open the carved wooden shutters on the windows, bathing the room in moonlight, then helped the older woman on to an opulent chaise-longue. He indicated that Sara should sit opposite, which she did, her whole body by now riven with shock. Flavio turned on the lights and the Contessa screamed 'No!'

The journalist realised his mistake and flicked the switch. 'I'm so sorry!'

'My eyes,' said the older woman, 'are very sensitive to the light. Too many years in the sun!'

'Shall I leave?' asked Flavio nervously.

'I think it would be for the best,' said the Contessa, her trembling hands fumbling with a cigarette lighter. 'But if you want Flavio here . . . ?'

Sara shook her head.

'I need to make a few phone calls about Antonio,' said the journalist, grateful for the chance to escape.

'I don't know what to say to you,' said the Contessa when he had gone. 'This has been such an awful shock. There must be so much you want to know.'

But where to begin? thought Sara. She looked at her mother, now wreathed in moonlit smoke, and asked, bluntly, anger fermenting in her voice, her most important question. 'Why did you give me up?'

For a moment the Contessa did not respond and the only sound came from the crickets singing in the garden. 'You must understand,' she said finally. 'Things were very different in England in 1966.'

'How could a mother do that to her child?' As Sara said the word 'mother' she had trouble relating it to the woman opposite. She felt as much of an orphan as Oscar.

'Oh, Sara, there were many reasons. I was with someone else, not your father—'

'Stephen Powell.'

The Contessa looked startled. 'How do you know all this? Did Stuart tell you?'

'Indirectly,' said Sara bitterly. 'You do know that the mess you two caused between you has resulted in Antonio being kidnapped?'

'How can that be?' exclaimed the Contessa.

'The sins of the father. When Stuart died he left me a fortune. And half of a football club—'

'Camden,' sighed the older woman.

'Stuart used me to get back at Stephen. Every move I made in my life was orchestrated by him. He sent me notes, fed me stories, pretended that we had happened on a friendship just by chance. But he had tracked me down ruthlessly and then used me to fight his battles. And it was all because of you!'

'I never knew any of this, I swear to you. I sent Stuart a letter about you expecting that to be the end of the story but Stuart tracked me down using contacts in the Foreign Office and told me that he had found you. He told me your name and said you were happy. I didn't want to know any more. It hurt too much. I had no idea he had meddled with your life in this way. We never spoke again.'

The Contessa began to cry, and Sara gave full vent to her anguish. 'You think us meeting like this is the most wonderful coincidence, but it isn't. It was inevitable that I would end up here. I didn't want to find you; I didn't want you to be part of my life, but then, I've never had any say in the direction my life has taken, have I? One of the only things I ever did independently was to fall in love with Antonio.' She stopped to suppress a sob. 'Because of you, Stuart had me investigate Stephen, and as a result Antonio is God knows where. You knew he was at Camden. Why didn't you warn him about Stephen?'

'I didn't know until a long while after he'd left. I spend much of my time abroad raising money for the charity. It was dangerous here for Antonio, and when I found out where he was, despite what I do know of Stephen, I thought he'd still be safer in England. Stephen had no idea of my identity and I truly didn't know he was involved with such people. You have to believe me.'

Sara was not to be consoled. 'I'm getting pretty tired of people telling me I have to believe them. My whole life has been built on lies. Why should I believe you now?'

There was a knock on the door and Flavio entered, looking from Sara to the Contessa, embarrassed to have intruded on a scene of such distress. 'Um, sorry to interrupt, but I have to go and talk to some people about Antonio. I must act quickly.'

'I'm coming with you,' said Sara.

'I'm afraid you can't,' said Flavio, looking to the Contessa for support.

'Sara, it is much too dangerous,' said the older woman.

'I want to,' said Sara, feeling that looking for Antonio might put her back in touch with reality. 'Sitting around here—'

'Please, Sara,' implored the journalist. 'I will come straight back. Where I am going is no place for a woman. And it seems you have much to sort out here. This is quite the most incredible thing I have ever witnessed . . .'

Sara looked at her mother. The tears were flowing unstemmed down the Contessa's face. It seemed that she had no choice but to continue with this agonising conversation. Flavio departed, leaving them once again in silence, each woman racked by her emotions, torn by the need to say everything and nothing at all.

It was the Contessa who spoke first. 'The sixth of November 1966, the day of your birth, the day I gave you away, was both the happiest and saddest of my life,' she began. 'But I felt at the time I had no choice.'

'Did you tell Stuart you were pregnant at the time?' interjected Sara.

'No. He had just been made an MP. It would have ruined his career – and his marriage.'

'But you must have known how desperately unhappy he was with Cynthia.'

'Unhappiness is not a reason to evade duty. Your father was an honourable man. I didn't want to be the cause of his downfall. This wasn't so long after the Profumo affair. Scandals couldn't just be shrugged off back then. And there would have been a scandal if Stephen had found out that I was pregnant. And so I disappeared.'

'That still doesn't explain why you gave me away,' cried Sara, the pain of rejection stabbing at her like a knife. For the first time in weeks she thought about June. This is how she must have felt when I walked out of that door, Sara realised with anguish.

'There was . . . oh, there is so much I have to tell you,' said the Contessa. 'But I am so tired, so confused.'

'I came here to see Oscar,' said Sara. She felt totally shattered herself and wanted some respite from the subject.

'And so you will. In the morning. I'll have someone show you to a room. You will stay? Please.'

Sara didn't want anything from this woman, but she was too tired to argue. 'I'll stay.'

The following morning Sara descended the dramatically sweeping staircase at the centre of the house, feeling as awful as she had done the night before. Her tears had kept her awake and from somewhere above her, she had heard the Contessa weeping, too. As she wandered through the house she found the older woman sitting in a drawing room, dressed in an expensive but understated grey suit, her dark glasses once again in place. Sara guessed that underneath them the Contessa's eyes were as red as her own.

'Such a terrible night,' said the Contessa, awkwardly. 'Would you like some breakfast?'

'I couldn't eat a thing,' said Sara flatly.

'Neither could I. Sara—' She was interrupted by the arrival of a small boy, who came running into the room and tried to hide behind the Contessa's legs. 'Oscar!'

Sara crouched down so that she and the child were roughly the same height. He looked younger than his five years. *'Tudo bem?'* she asked, holding out her hand. Oscar peeped out from behind the Contessa and placed his hand in hers. Feeling the individual bones, Sara was shocked to realise that he was malnourished. She had believed that in the previous twelve hours she had shed every last tear in her body, but now a fresh wave threatened to spill over. This was the child Antonio had said would one day be her son.

Oscar quickly withdrew his hand and clung on to the Contessa as if she would disappear if he let go for too long. 'Antonio?' he said, looking up at the older woman.

The Contessa shook her head sadly. *'Não.'* She turned to Sara. 'I haven't told him what has happened, but I'm sure he senses something.'

A maid appeared with Flavio in her wake.

'Flavio! Flavio!' shouted Oscar, bounding over to the journalist.

Sara jumped up. 'Any news?'

'I'm afraid not. Those who may know something are keeping silent. I'm afraid my threats cannot match Pinto's. I came to tell you that I'm going to Vigario Geral. There's a man there who – well, he's my only lead.'

Seeing the despondent look on Flavio's face, Oscar ran from the room.

'He knows,' sighed the Contessa.

'Flavio, this time I'm coming with you,' said Sara, the tone of her voice making it clear that she wasn't prepared to take no for an answer. She had to escape from her mother for a while, and she sensed that the Contessa needed some space too. And they both needed time to think.

Vigario Geral was a sprawling *favela* eighteen miles outside of Rio. As they got out of the car, Sara was horrified by the poverty which surrounded her. It looked as if one gust of wind would destroy the whole ramshackle place, and she suspected that the occupants of Vigario Geral often hoped it would. Thousands of people lived there in the makeshift shacks cobbled together from corrugated iron, cardboard and wood which lined the narrow unpaved alleyways running with raw sewage. There seemed to be little electricity, even less fresh water and barely any sign of hope.

Sara had walked scarcely two feet before she tripped and, looking down, saw a dead rat riddled with flies, which were eating away at its insides.

'Be careful,' said Flavio, kicking it away.

'It's so awful,' said Sara, hugging herself. The dust and dirt caught in her throat. 'How do people survive this?'

'The human spirit is an amazing thing.'

Soon they were surrounded by raggedy barefoot children, the sound of their voices reverberating along the alleyways. They pulled at Sara's skirt, their hands outstretched. '*Grana, grana,*' they shouted.

'They want money,' said Flavio, trying to shoo them away.

Sara searched in her bag and threw a handful of notes into the crowd. Immediately the children began to fight over it, scrabbling on the ground to see who could pick up the most, screaming and punching each other. Sara had never felt so bad about acting on a charitable impulse.

'It's just down here,' said Flavio, holding on to her elbow as she stumbled over the rubbish.

They came to a hut no different from the hundreds of others. When Flavio hammered on the rickety door the whole place shook.

'Cesar! Cesar!' Flavio banged on the door again. This time it was opened by a man who could have been about thirty – his bloodshot eyes and three days' growth of beard made it hard to tell. He was clearly agitated to see Flavio on his doorstep. They spoke rapidly to each other and Sara made out the names Antonio and Pinto amid the babble.

The man threw up his arms. *'Não. Não. Sai fora!'*

Flavio lunged at Cesar and grabbed him by his ripped and grubby vest, addressing him in a low and threatening voice.

'OK, OK,' said Cesar, holding up his hands in surrender. 'Acari.'

'Obrigado,' said Flavio, sarcastically thanking the man and letting go of his vest.

'Come, Sara. He says Antonio might be in Acari.'

Flavio drove off like a man possessed. Sara said nothing, the *favela* having profoundly shocked her. She hoped that Acari would be better, but when they arrived she saw that it was almost identical to Vigario Geral. The only difference was that the alleyways were strangely empty. As they walked along in the unnatural silence of the shanty town, their clothes sticking to their bodies with sweat, Sara moved closer to Flavio, growing more uneasy with each step they took.

Suddenly, there was the crackle of gunfire. Flavio grabbed Sara and dived to the ground.

'What's happening?' cried Sara, her face pushed against the dirt.

'Sshh.'

'Do you think it's Antonio?'

'No.'

Just then five hooded gunmen burst out of a shack, a wailing woman chasing after them.

'The bastards,' spat Flavio.

'Who are they?' whispered Sara, her heart pounding.

'It's the police.'

'The police?'

'They have their own death squads to help keep the numbers down. What's a few more dead children?'

'I can't believe it,' said Sara, distraught. How had Oscar managed to stay alive for so long?

'Believe it,' Flavio said grimly. 'We have to get away from here quickly.' He helped her to her feet. 'Keep low!'

Bent double, Sara ran as fast as she could, her feet sliding in the mud. How could people do this to each other? How could human life be worth so little? The only crime of these people was that they were poor. There had to be many thousands of Oscars who never escaped. Her whole body was tensed in anticipation of the next gunshot, but they made it back to the car hearing no more than the same woman's shrieks of despair.

'I'm taking you back to Maria's,' said Flavio, gunning the car.

Sara was too shaken to argue.

The Contessa ran up to greet Sara as she got out the car. '*Meu deus*, what has happened?'

Sara looked at her mother and burst into tears. 'It was terrible – masked gunmen and, and a poor woman. They're animals!'

'Come into the house,' said the Contessa, giving Flavio a wave as he got back into the car. 'You shouldn't have gone. This kind of thing goes on day after day. What if you had been caught in the crossfire? To lose you now . . .'

'But we still don't know where Antonio is. If these men can kill little children so easily why wouldn't they just shoot him?'

The Contessa held her daughter close and took her into the drawing room. 'He is too important. Sadly, the children are not.'

Sara sat down on a carved mahogany stool while the Contessa poured a good measure of whisky into a crystal goblet. She sipped the drink, feeling it burn the back of her throat, welcoming its calming properties.

Her mother stood behind her and stroked her hair, now matted with dust. 'I can't believe how much you look like me,' she murmured.

'There's a lot we haven't said yet,' said Sara, feeling slightly discomfited by the woman's touch.

The Contessa began to pace around the room, wringing her hands. 'I know you think very little of me now, and I'm sure after I tell you the rest you will despise me, but there is nothing to be done. I must tell you the truth.' Her voice changed, becoming much harder, and the words came tumbling out.

'Stephen introduced me to heroin, and I got hooked,' she said without preamble. 'That was how he planned to keep me. I couldn't leave him, because he gave me what I needed, what I craved. It was only when I became pregnant with you that I knew I had to find the strength to quit. For the nine months of the pregnancy I stayed clean, although every day was a battle. I was so frightened of lapsing once you were born that I just couldn't risk keeping you. I wanted you to be safe and happy. And you were happy, weren't you? Your parents were good people?'

'The best,' said Sara, quietly.

'So you see, I was a mess.'

Sara could find no words of comfort to offer her mother. 'Did Stuart know you were on heroin?'

'No. I managed to keep it hidden. He only found out when he tracked me down a couple of years after I'd written to him. He, like you, needed to know why I had gone against the maternal instinct.'

A few more pieces began to fall into place in the jigsaw of Sara's life. No wonder Stuart had hated Stephen so much. She remembered how he had talked in New York of the innocents who suffered at the hands of drug-dealers. Stephen's continued involvement in the traffic of narcotics must have been an ongoing reminder of what had happened to Felicity. 'Why did you change your name?'

'That's another long story. After your birth I came to Brazil. I'd been here many times with Stephen on business, and I knew that I had good friends here who would give me shelter. I left England with only the clothes I stood up in, feeling very sorry for myself.'

The Contessa drank some whisky and resumed her confession. 'Then, for three years, the Butterfly flitted from party to party, living off a succession of rich men, feeling nothing but self-pity.'

Sara was surprised by this switch to the third person. She guessed it was her mother's way of distancing herself from and showing contempt for the person she'd become. 'What changed you?'

'I remember the moment so clearly. It was a hot day and I was driving home from some ridiculous luncheon. I stopped at some traffic lights, cursing them for holding me up in the heat. Beggar children were running up to the car trying to sell me matches and sweets. I shouted at them to leave me alone. I was repulsed by their poverty. Most of them moved on to try their luck elsewhere, but one remained: a little girl, holding a box of matches in her dirty little hand and staring at me with such need. She could have been no more than three years old.'

'The same age as I would have been then,' said Sara, realising the significance of this fact.

'I bought the matches, hoping to salve my conscience, and drove away, wanting to put the incident out of my mind. There were thousands of children just like her. What could I do about it? But that little girl came back to me in my dreams, only now she was you. The thought that a box of matches could be all that stood between you and hunger was too hard to bear. And so I began visiting the *favelas* in between the cocktail parties and the fashion shows, taking food, giving out money. I thought it was my penance for giving you up, my repayment to God.'

The Contessa looked upwards. 'Then I met Mauricio, my late husband, and it felt as if I had been reborn, been given a second chance. So when I married the Conte I changed my name. I was no longer a butterfly. Felicity Butterworth died a long time ago. I am Maria Santos, just as you are Sara Moore, not Justine Butterworth.'

Sara knew that it had been hard for her mother to say that. It was an admission that Justine Butterworth no longer existed, had never existed beyond those first few hours, and an indication that the Contessa claimed no maternal right over the child she'd had adopted. Sara thought of June, her mum, the woman who had brought her up. She needed to speak to her soon. 'And is Maria Santos happier than Felicity Butterworth?'

'Infinitely,' said the Contessa, smiling. 'I truly believe that everything that happened to bring me to Rio happened for a purpose. The work I do for Viva As Crianças isn't about buying a place in heaven, it's the reason for my existence on earth.' She lit a cigarette, waving her tortoiseshell holder about in the air. 'But I'm rambling here. Maybe I'm just trying to impress you with all my good works to make you hate me less.'

'I don't hate you,' said Sara quickly. 'I . . .' She didn't know what she felt, other than that the Contessa's story had touched her very deeply.

'Oscar is in need of a bath. He's been digging up the rosebushes again,' said the Contessa, abruptly ending her confession. 'Perhaps you would like to take him?'

'I'd love to,' said Sara, standing and following the older woman into the hallway.

'Oscar!' called the Contessa. The little boy came running in from the garden, skidding to a halt on the tiled floor.

'Antonio would be so happy to know that he was safe with you,' said Sara, her voice breaking with emotion.

'I know,' said Maria, soothingly. 'And he will, very soon.'

'I hope you're right,' replied Sara, looking at the little boy. She held out her hand. 'Come with me, Oscar.'

The little boy held back at first, then, visibly debating whether or not he could trust Sara and deciding that he could, he put his little hand in hers.

Sara took him to the bathroom and ran him a bath. Shyly, he refused to allow her in there with him. He left a pile of clothes outside the door with her. As time began to pass, Sara became worried. What was he doing in there? She knocked on the door but there was no answer.

'Oscar? Oscar?' She rapped on the door frantically. What if he had drowned? Obliged to ignore his wishes, she opened the door, scared of what she might find.

Inside the little boy was very much alive. Naked and wet, he was bent over the bath, manically scrubbing the inside of the tub with a towel. He looked at Sara guiltily and she could see the tears in his eyes.

'What's wrong?' she asked.

Whether or not he understood the question, he pointed to the bath. '*Sujo*,' he said, rubbing at the ring of dirt around the tub.

Sara thought she was going to start crying with him. All the pain he had suffered, and here he was worried silly about a dirty bath. 'It's OK,' she said, gently wrapping him in another towel.

Oscar allowed her to hug him as she dried him, his tears slowly abating. She picked him up and carried him to his bedroom, where she lay down on the bed next to him and held him until he fell asleep.

'Book,' said Sara, pointing to a row of books.

'*Livro*,' came Oscar's reply.

For the past two days, while Flavio had searched fruitlessly for Antonio, Sara had tried to make herself useful by looking after Oscar, taking personal pride in his improving health. He had gained several pounds and a healthy colour was slowly growing in his cheeks. Today they were beginning to teach each other their respective languages. Sara was impressed by Oscar's brightness and depressed at her own lack of linguistic aptitude. The time spent with the child passed quickly but there wasn't a minute of the day when she wasn't thinking of Antonio. Earlier she had rung Kathy, but there was no news that end, either.

'Garden!' shouted Oscar, bouncing on a chair.

'OK,' said Sara, knowing that he wanted to go off and play.

The boy ran out into the garden and Sara joined the Contessa, who was humming quietly to herself as she arranged a huge bouquet of flowers in the drawing room. There was such a meditative calm around her, and after two days of intense, tearful conversation it was nice to share the quiet moment. Sara felt they had reached an equilibrium. In time, she hoped that her former feelings for Stuart would be restored as well. The Contessa was angry with him for meddling so much, but she went to great pains to assure Sara that, fundamentally, he had been a good man.

'We'll find him, you know,' she said, startling Sara for the umpteenth time with her similar looks. 'You mustn't worry.' The arrangement finished, she wrapped the cut-off stems in paper. 'I loved your father like you love Antonio,' she said, more to herself than Sara. 'Thank God I got a second chance with Mauricio.'

Sara knew that Antonio was her second chance, too. Stuart had been right: she had found love again. She didn't want to think about the possibility of having to find it for a third time.

'And then there will be grandchildren. Lots of them, I am sure of it.'

'Why did you never have children with the Conte?' asked Sara, to deflect this dangerous line of conversation.

'The children in the *favelas* are all my children. No, that's a silly grandiose answer.'

'The papers call you *A Mamaẽ*.'

'And you believe everything you read in the papers?' laughed Maria wrily. 'I think the real reason I never had any more children was that I had such a strong picture of you in my mind. How could they live up to a fantasy? And here you are, and you're more than I ever dreamed of.'

Sara's blushes were spared by the ringing of the phone. Every time it rang, or somebody came to the door, she held her breath, steeling herself for the worst, and she sensed that the Contessa was doing the same.

'Hello? Yes, of course, who is it?' Maria held out the phone for Sara. 'It's someone called Maggie.'

Chapter Forty-Three

Maggie stopped talking for a moment, thinking she could hear Stephen's car at the bottom of the drive. When the car – someone else's – passed the house, she spoke again. 'Sara, I know you probably just want to hang up and I don't blame you. But don't, please, I have something to tell you.'

'How did you get this number?'

'I persuaded Kathy to let me have it.'

'What do you want to tell me?'

'I'm so sorry,' sobbed Maggie. 'I don't know how I ended up like this, but it wasn't your fault.' It had started with her parents, but she had never taken responsibility for her own life. Like them, she was a manipulative bully. Well, for the first time ever she would take responsibility. She would put things right. 'But that's not why I'm ringing. I know no amount of apologising can put right what I've done. It's about Antonio. Have you found him yet?'

'No. Why, do you know where he is?'

'I've stayed with Stephen to find out – I couldn't have lived with myself if I didn't. I can't live with myself anyway. Cynthia fired me but then ... she ... the bitch is going down the tube ...' she rambled.

'Do you know where Antonio is?'

Maggie could hear the sharpness in Sara's voice. 'I heard Stephen talking about a place. It was called Arc ... Ac—'

'Acari?'

'That's it.'

'Where in Acari?'

'I don't know. I think there was mention of someone called Correa, Roberto Correa?'

'Thank you, Maggie. You don't know how much this means to me. I'll call you as soon as I find Antonio. Perhaps it will be possible for us to put all this behind us.'

'I'd like that,' said Maggie. 'I'm so sorry – for everything.'

She put down the phone and opened a bottle of Stephen's whisky. Then she took out her sleeping tablets and anti-depressants. Opening both bottles, she tipped out as many as the palm of her hand would take and thrust them into her mouth, quickly taking a swig of the whisky to wash them down. Gagging, she drank some more alcohol, feeling the tablets sticking in the back of her throat and then slowly dissolving. She waited a few minutes for the nausea to die down, and then repeated the procedure twice more until both the pills and the alcohol were all gone.

Flavio was waiting for Sara in the shade outside the *Jornal do Brasil* offices. The Contessa had been horrified when she had mentioned the name Correa, begging Sara to stay in the house, and she knew if she mentioned it to Flavio he'd definitely take off without her. Her hunch proved right.

'Sara, you can't come,' said the journalist, taking in the news. 'The man is a hired killer who works for the highest bidder. He'd kill you as soon as look at you.'

'This isn't up for discussion, Flavio. I feel responsible for what happened. I have to be there.'

'We can't do this without guns.' He allowed the words time to sink in, hoping to dissuade her. 'People are going to get hurt.'

The thought terrified her but she refused to budge. 'I'm coming.'

Flavio shrugged his shoulders. 'Get in the car, then.'

They drove through the city, too weighed down by the fear of the threat they faced to make conversation. Instead, Flavio made several calls on his mobile phone and then parked outside a run down apartment block. 'Wait here,' he said, getting out.

Sara sat in the car on her own for twenty minutes, convinced that everybody who passed could read her mind and tell what she was up to. This wasn't like hitting Mickey Nash or being hit by Ronnie Firetto. If Flavio was procuring a gun, it was because he intended to kill someone with it. Part of her wanted to get out of the car and run. She had never felt as frightened as this before in her life.

Flavio came out of the apartment block with a telltale bulge under his jacket. Surely everybody in the street could see what he was trying to hide? She looked about her nervously but nobody seemed to be taking any notice. The journalist opened the door and threw the gun, wrapped in a cloth, beneath the back seat. Even just being in the car with it made Sara feel nauseous.

'Where are we going?' she asked, her voice reduced almost to a squeak.

Flavio started the engine, a look of focused concentration on his face. 'To meet a few friends, and then to Correa's house in Acari. It isn't far from where we were the other day.'

By the time they arrived at the restaurant on the outskirts of Rio the sun was beginning to set and the oncoming night added another layer to Sara's disquiet. Acari was dark enough in the day; how were you supposed to run from gunmen in the dark?

Flavio sounded his horn and four men dressed in camouflage trousers and green flak jackets emerged from the restaurant and piled into the back of the car. All were armed and Sara felt she was losing touch with reality again. She thought of all her confrontations with Stephen. When she had screamed at him across the desk, she had sometimes been worried that he might hit her, but never had she seriously feared for her life. Only when the intruder at her house in Primrose Hill had attacked her had she been really scared, and even then it had all been over so quickly. It was nothing like this.

She gathered from the hushed gravity of the conversation that the men were discussing their plan of action.

'Sara, are you sure you don't want to get out here?' asked Flavio. All traces of the avuncular if easily embarrassed journalist she had met a few days ago had vanished without trace. 'There are taxis over there. One of them would take you back into town.'

Her need to be there for Antonio was stronger than her fear. 'No,' she said resolutely.

Flavio looked to the four men for support but they shrugged, obviously indifferent as to whether she came along or not. 'OK,' he said impatiently, 'but you stay in the car when we get there.'

Sara nodded and for the rest of the journey closed her eyes, trying to summon sleep to shut out all thoughts of what might be about to happen. But not surprisingly when the car stopped half an hour later, she hadn't slept a wink.

The five men got out and dropped to the ground.

'Be careful!' hissed Sara as Flavio closed the door and slipped a balaclava over his head. The others did the same and in the almost complete blackness of the night, Sara was only vaguely aware of the shadows moving away from the car.

Then, much to her own surprise, she climbed out of the car herself and followed in the general direction they had taken. She would be there for Antonio. And, yes, if it came to it, she was prepared to die for him. Stumbling along an alleyway in the dark, feeling the walls of the shacks to find her way, she had to grit her teeth to keep them from chattering. As something ran across her foot, she had to stifle a scream. It was a cat, she told herself. A small, skinny cat.

The alleyway turned a corner and Sara reached out into the darkness, fearing that her hands would come into contact with someone's face. Her hands recoiled at the thought. Pull yourself together, she told herself, there's no one there. Who else would be stupid enough to be walking along in the dark like this? Emboldened, she took a large stride and went flying over a bundle of rags, hitting her head against the corrugated-iron wall of a shack. A hollow boom sounded along the alleyway and she stayed on the ground. She was just as likely to be shot by Flavio's men as by anyone else.

Underneath her the bag of clothes began to squirm. It was a man lying there. This time Sara had to put her hand over her mouth to prevent the scream from coming out. The man was unconscious and smelled of drink, and so Sara rolled over his body and lay by his side, deciding that it would be better if she went back to the car. This was just too dangerous.

She got to her feet and dusted herself off, not wanting to think about what she might have been lying on in the foetid alleyway. Turning to retrace her steps, she found to her horror that she could no longer see the car. Just then a gun went off. Where had it come from? Blindly, Sara ran forward, and immediately bumped into a wall. Another gunshot. Was it behind or in front of her? She was now breathing so heavily she was sure the noise would give her away.

She heard a man shouting. Flavio? No, the voice was thicker than his. Somewhere nearby a fight broke out, but still she couldn't tell if she was walking towards it or away from it. She began to panic and broke into a run. When she reached the end of the alleyway she turned, running straight into the barrel of a gun.

'Sara!' hissed Flavio. 'You stupid . . . ! I nearly killed you!'

'Where's Antonio?' she sobbed, as Flavio put his arm around her waist and led her through the night.

'In there,' whispered Flavio, pushing her into a nearby hut.

Inside, two of the four gunmen, holding flashlights, were untying Antonio's hands and helping him to his feet while the other two tied up and gagged one of his captors.

'Antonio!' she cried, falling on him. 'Thank God!'

'Sara, what are you doing here?' he said, holding her away from him, his voice cracked and barely there. The flashlight momentarily lit up Sara's face. 'You're bleeding.'

Sara touched her forehead and felt the stickiness of her blood. 'It's just a scratch. Are you all right?'

'I am now,' he said, taking her in his arms. 'I can't believe this. Am I hallucinating?'

'No, I'm here,' she said, kissing his dry, blistered lips.

Flavio came back into the room. 'I've lost Correa. Come on, we need to get out before he comes back with reinforcements.'

'Can you ever forgive me?' asked Sara, looking deep into Antonio's dark brown eyes. She lifted her hand and traced his split lip with her fingers, hardly daring to believe he was here by her side.

'Of course I do,' he whispered, the hospital bed creaking as he drew her towards him. His face was bruised and one rib had been broken from the last beating he had taken. He winced as he hugged Sara close to him in an embrace that said it all. 'I love you.'

'I thought I might never hear you say those words again . . .'

'Pull the curtain,' he said, his voice filled with pent-up longing. He desperately wanted and needed Sara more than any other woman he had ever known.

Sara felt his lips brushing against her cheek as his hard body pressed against hers. She took a deep breath, finding immense comfort in his familiar smell. Her lips searched out his and as they kissed, she was overwhelmed by the power of their mutual love. Antonio drew her closer and slowly unhooked the buttons on her dress. 'All those days I kept myself occupied by thinking of this moment.'

Sara undid his white hospital gown, eager to feel his nakedness.

A cough came from the other side of the curtain.

'*Merda!*' cursed Antonio.

Sara quickly did up her dress and peeped out around the curtain. It was a nurse, who seemed more flustered by the footballer's fame than by the fact that she had just interrupted him in a passionate clinch. Antonio spoke to her briefly. 'She just wants to check my rib and then I can leave if I want to,' he explained to Sara. He grimaced as the nurse examined the bruising on his chest. 'Ahh!'

'Are you really OK to leave so soon?' Sara asked, her voice full of concern.

'I'll be fine. Don't worry. What did Kathy say about Stephen?'

'He's been arrested. There are so many charges against him that she's lost count of them. It's a pity the same doesn't go for Pinto.'

'I don't know. With the Contessa on the case, he probably

doesn't stand much of a chance,' he said laughing. 'How was Kathy?'

'She and Jackie are fine . . .' She paused. 'There was some awful news, though. You know I told you that Maggie was the person responsible for us being able to find you?'

'Yes. I must thank her.'

'That won't be possible,' said Sara, her voice breaking. 'She's dead. She took an overdose right after she'd spoken to me.' Unable to hold back the tears any longer, she started to cry. 'Now I'm never going to be able to sort things out with her . . .'

Antonio held out his hand to her, but before he could speak the Contessa popped her head around the curtain, followed by Oscar. Ignoring the nurse, Oscar jumped on the bed and threw himself on to Antonio, oblivious to the pain he was causing as he hugged him.

Noticing Sara's tears but choosing not to comment, the Contessa looked at the scene on the bed and smiled. 'I'm sorry, Antonio, I did tell him to be careful but he couldn't wait to see you.'

'Don't worry,' he laughed. His gaze met Sara's and she smiled back, her eyes still wet from the tears she'd shed for her friend. Her grief for Maggie would have to be suppressed for another day.

'I can't believe you're going tomorrow,' said the Contessa. 'We've had so little time together. There's so much more to be said.'

'This isn't the end,' promised Sara. 'You'll come to England. And we'll be back.'

'Did you speak to June?' asked the Contessa.

Sara nodded. 'I spoke to Mum this morning, and I'm going to see her as soon as I get back.'

Oscar squealed as Antonio tickled him mercilessly. 'He says he wants to know if he has to go to school in England.'

'Most definitely,' laughed Sara.

Epilogue

England, June 1994

'Wake up sleepyhead,' shouted Sara, pulling the duvet off Antonio.

He groaned, blindly searching for the cover. 'No more, enough!'

'One more time,' she teased him.

He opened his eyes. 'You're insatiable.'

'Oh well, if you're not up to making love on your honeymoon . . .'

They had been married a couple of weeks and a weekend away in the Lake District was all their busy schedule had allowed.

'Sara, we only stopped half an hour ago.'

'OK, I'll just read the papers then.'

Antonio made a playful grab at her as she jumped off the bed and ran to the door of their hotel room. Outside was the pile of newspapers and magazines they had ordered.

'You look at *Hello!*,' she said, handing the magazine to Antonio. 'I'm sure the reporter was in love with you.'

The first paper Sara studied was the *Herald*. Its front page announced that it had been bought by a consortium. On page 2 there was a picture of herself, the caption describing her as one of the major new shareholders of the Herald Group. She turned quickly to the hatches, matches and dispatches. Half a page had been devoted to the memorial service for Stuart three days earlier. It had been a wonderful service. Sara had spoken about her friendship with Stuart and how proud she was that he had been her father. Cynthia was not present – no one had seen or heard of her since the sell-off of the Herald Group, though a vicious rumour had it she could still be seen late at night haunting her office on the fifteenth floor at Canary Wharf.

Sara had also inserted a small memorial announcement for Bill. She would never forget him, but she knew that he would have been delighted to see her so happy now.

'Hey, look at this,' she said, picking another paper. For once the *News* had some good tidings. 'Stephen's trial date has been set, and it says here he's having to sell his part of the club to pay for his defence. Thank God Jackie got her divorce settlement in first.'

'Sara.'

'They've thrown the book at him – match-fixing, fraud, drugs – and this piece says he's lucky there's no extradition treaty with Brazil as the authorities there would like to talk to him about drug-smuggling and—'

'Sara.'

'Sorry, what?'

'Would you mind if I bought Stephen's remaining quarter?'

'I'm sure Jackie would be delighted to have you on board. I don't know about the major shareholder, though. I hear she's a bit of a bitch.'

'No, she's a pussycat,' said Antonio kissing her neck. 'And anyway, I'm sleeping with her. I think I can keep her sweet.'

'I'm sure you can,' said Sara, kissing him back.

'Look at how beautiful you are,' he said, showing her the *Hello* spread on their wedding.

Sara blushed, but she had to agree that her happiness had manifested itself physically. She positively glowed. 'Don't you think the Contessa and Jackie look great? The book is going to be such a success. With their stories in Kathy's words, how can it fail? And look at June: she's so proud, and she adores you and Oscar. Speaking of whom . . .'

Antonio looked at the alarm clock and groaned. 'Oh no, have you seen the time?'

She laughed. 'One, two, three—'

The door burst open and Oscar leaped on to the bed. 'Arsenal! Arsenal!' he chanted.

'You little traitor!' shouted Antonio, as Oscar attacked him with a rolled-up newspaper. 'Sara, whose idea was it to bring our son on our honeymoon?'

Sara looked at them both and smiled.

THE BROKEN MAN

Also by Josephine Cox

QUEENIE'S STORY
Her Father's Sins
Let Loose the Tigers

THE EMMA GRADY TRILOGY
Outcast
Alley Urchin
Vagabonds

Angels Cry Sometimes
Take This Woman
Whistledown Woman
Don't Cry Alone
Jessica's Girl
Nobody's Darling
Born to Serve
More than Riches
A Little Badness
Living a Lie
The Devil You Know
A Time for Us
Cradle of Thorns
Miss You Forever
Love Me or Leave Me
Tomorrow the World
The Gilded Cage
Somewhere, Someday
Rainbow Days
Looking Back
Let It Shine
The Woman Who Left
Jinnie
Bad Boy Jack
The Beachcomber
Lovers and Liars
Live the Dream
The Journey
Journey's End
The Loner
Songbird
Born Bad
Divorced and Deadly
Blood Brothers
Midnight
Three Letters